# Shadow of the Elders
## Will Elm

Book Cover by Particular

Maps by Lilly Lockwood

First edition 2025

# CONTENTS

To all those who believe.

# CONTENT WARNING

This novel is a work of fantasy fiction and contains scenes that certain readers may find difficult or upsetting to read. These scenes include violence, death, battles, assassination attempts, mutilation, imprisonment, manipulation, and physical and emotional abuse. There are also representations of depression, anxiety, panic, discrimination, and the use of in-world derogatory language.

As an author I tried to ensure these depictions are meaningful, realistic, appropriate, and necessary to the story. Descriptions are rarely graphic or gratuitous. However, if you find such topics unpleasant, you may wish to read with caution or not at all. But know this, the story is not about these traumas; rather it is about what comes after.

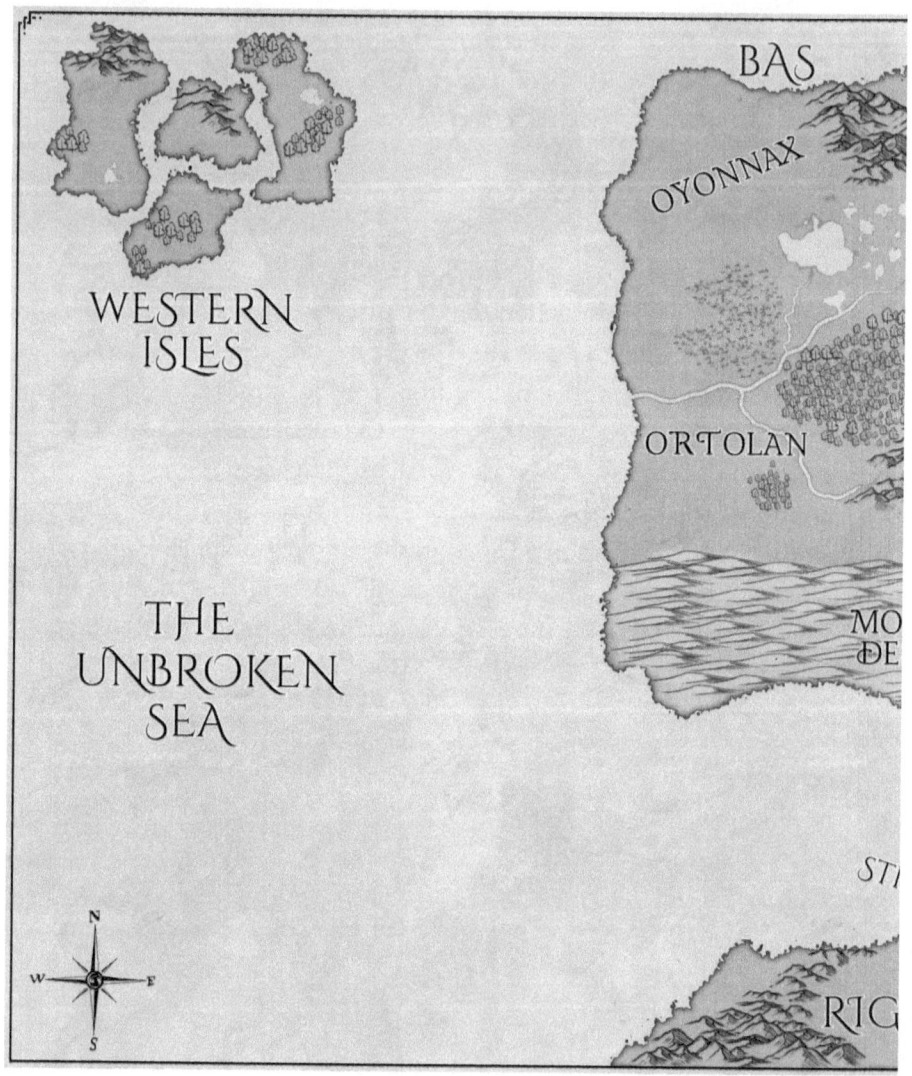

# PROLOGUE

*You are the land, and it is you.*
*Whatever you take from it, you will return to it.*
*It is wondrous. It is life.*
*But thorns still draw blood.*

—Balafre Proverb

IStor Lysant stood at the window and raged. How could she have been so forsaken? She was a daughter of Sah, Lord of the Istori. All land was her dominion. But as she stared out from the watchtower, she saw only destruction. No moons, no stars; the only light came from flames that engulfed her world.

"No prophecies will be made tonight," her Seal-Bearer said. He was a tall man with a short, trimmed beard, wearing red robes adorned with three interlocking circles on his chest.

"Unacceptable!" Lysant turned from the window. "Sah speaks and we must listen. Now more than ever."

Her Seal-Bearer bowed his head in respect. "Divine One, there is nothing I can do. The clouds obscure our vision. The smoke—"

"Yes, I know of the smoke! I see the fires. Do you think I am unaware?"

"Of course, Divine One. My apologies." The Seal-Bearer kept his head bowed.

"I do not want your apologies!" Lysant slammed her fist against the stone wall behind her. "I want Sah's words. If you cannot produce them, then perhaps someone else can."

"I do not understand."

Lysant rose and walked to the Seal-Bearer. She grabbed the collar of his robe and shook him until he met her gaze. "Find me an Ascetic."

1

"Divine One, you do not mean—"

She shook him again. "You would dare question me? Now go before I throw you to the fires." She released the man, who promptly bowed, turned, and exited the great hall.

Lysant paced in front of the window and waited for his return.

The Ascetics would know some way for her to hear the calls of Sah. They had to. Their fanaticism was useless otherwise. Still, she could hear the words of her Seal-Bearer from some deep recess of her mind, "Careful, Divine One. There are worse fates than burnt fields."

Nonsense. Her fists tightened around her staff. There was only one fate for her. Glory.

By the time her Seal-Bearer returned with an Ascetic, the fires from outside had nearly reached the Temple in which they stood. Smoke wafted through the window. The night air was scorching.

The two men stood in front of Lysant, waiting for permission to speak. She nodded at them.

"Thank you for calling upon me, Divine One. How may I serve you?" the Ascetic said.

"My Seal-Bearer has informed me there will be no readings tonight. The stars cannot be seen. What say you?"

"Yes, Divine One. The message Sah writes in the stars cannot be observed. But there are other ways to hear Sah. We—"

"You do not believe him." Her Seal-Bearer gestured at the Ascetic with annoyance. "He is—"

"Silence!" She glared at her Seal-Bearer. Then she faced the Ascetic and said, "Continue."

The Ascetic bowed. "We have cultivated a new plant that should bring you visions from Sah themself. You no longer need the stars to hear their voice. Instead, it will be within you."

"Interesting. And you have confirmed this?" Lysant said.

"Not yet, Divine One. It has been a difficult planting season. But I am confident." The Ascetic put his hand on a small pouch that hung around his waist and smiled.

"You see, it is a trick." Her Seal-Bearer stuck his finger in the Ascetic's face. "They do not embrace Sah, they reject them. They seek to poison you, or worse."

Lysant straightened and walked towards her Seal-Bearer. "I have heard your thoughts and, on a better day, I may have heeded your advice. But you offer no alternative to me." She placed a hand on his shoulder. "My glory will not wait."

"Divine One..." The Seal-Bearer's voice faded as he stared at the ground.

Lysant turned and walked away from him. She beckoned for the Ascetic to follow. "Will it work?"

"I believe so, Divine One. If it were sown and tended to—"

"You mistake me," Lysant said. "You see the state of the land. There is no time. Give me the seed. I will take it tonight."

"Divine One?" The Ascetic shook his head. "It has never been consumed as a seed. I am unsure of its effects in that state."

"Do not do this..." The Seal-Bearer continued to stare at the ground while his hand moved to the hilt of the dagger that hung from his waist. "Do not make me..."

Lysant extended a hand to the Ascetic. "The seed."

"Y-Yes, Divine One." The Ascetic reached into her bag and pulled it out. "Here."

Lysant gazed at it as though it was something foreign. And as a seed, it was. Too big and heavy and thorny, she wondered how they would ever plant them in the ground. The thought vanished, replaced by a sharp pain in her back.

Before the Ascetic could place the seed in Lysant's hand, her Seal-Bearer drove his dagger into the Istor's back. He removed it and stabbed her again. A tear fell from his cheek.

Lysant turned towards her Seal-Bearer with her eyes wide and mouth hung open. She stumbled forward and then fell onto the floor of her great hall.

"What have you done?" The Ascetic kneeled beside the fallen Istor.

"You! It was you!" The Seal-Bearer's face contorted by fury. "I could not let you taint her return to the earth. Now she will find a home there. You won't be so lucky."

The Seal-Bearer stepped forward and grabbed the Ascetic. He pierced the man's white robes with his dagger over and over until blood pooled at his feet. Then the Seal-Bearer stepped back and watched the Ascetic fall to the ground, just as Lysant had.

Before the life drained from the Ascetic's body, he reached out to Lysant with the hand that held the seed. He placed it in the woman's wound and said, "For Istor." Then he collapsed onto Lysant's back.

Lysant coughed. Her breathing became uneven. She struggled to find the glory that was promised to her.

But then a pulsing sound echoed in her ears. A brightness shone from all directions that warmed her like the sun at its zenith. When she opened her eyes, a dark void no bigger than a pebble formed in front of her.

Above the pulsing sound, an unfamiliar voice said, "Welcome."

"Sah?" Lysant said.

"No. But you enter nonetheless."

Somewhere, deep under the ash-laden fields that surrounded the temple, roots took hold and grew deeper. It would be some time before a tree emerged, but the first branch had already arrived.

# PART I

# CHAPTER 1

UNDER THE MOONLIGHT, SAVIQUE raced through the fields. His bare feet felt the cool, damp dirt that nurtured the wheat and barley and onions growing there. It was the richest soil in all Bas. At least that was what he had been told, and it was what drew wanderers from all corners of the world to work there. It was also what gave Foreman Crevir all his power.

But on this night, it was just the ground. And Savique did not linger on it, nor on the bountiful yield of the estate. No, he rushed to his destination to ensure Crevir and his guards did not see him and mistake him for a thief or a Noye.

Even in the dark, he could see the outline of the camp on the horizon. The hundreds of small, nearly identical huts made from mud, sticks, and clay stuck out against a backdrop of trees and open sky. It helped that the fires from supper still flickered weakly in the camp's center.

Moments later, he arrived among the huts safely and stopped to catch his breath. Once it steadied, he walked into the camp. It did not take him long to find for what he searched. When he arrived at a hut marked by a yellow flower, he slipped inside.

"Savique, where have you been?" a small woman with a weathered face said.

"You know I do not approve of this," he said. "You are lucky I came at all."

"What else are we to do?" An old man with a long beard, specked with gray, rose from his seat. "Crevir cuts our shares—twice already this season and we have not begun planting. The worst awaits us if we do not act now."

"Yes, the Foreman takes too much already."

Savique said nothing. He knew they were right, it was the reason he came, but the plan made him anxious. He remembered the sight of the first man who he saw caught stealing. All that blood. It sent a shiver down his spine.

"Besides, Savique, you worry too much," the small woman said. "Crevir won't even check the eastern storehouse until after the next harvest."

"That is what the sowers say," Savique said. "But they don't know what that man has in his mind."

"I trust the sowers more than you, outsider." A voice from across the hut shouted. A young man, short but thick—his thighs were as wide as Savique's head—pointed at him.

"Easy now, Mascheix," the woman said.

"No. He's been here what, two or three harvests. And he wants to question the sowers?" Mascheix pounded the table where he sat, sending droplets of wine from his mug into the air. "Men and women who grew up on this land. Some of the most trustworthy people I know! Who is he—"

"Enough of this squabbling!" The old man slapped his leg. It made a dull slapping noise, but it was loud enough to quiet the hut.

He glanced at Savique, then at Mascheix, then back at Savique. "Did you come here to stop us?"

Savique shook his head. "No." It was unconvincing.

He was a strong worker and had been successful in gaining Crevir's trust over the years. And he lived a respectable life because of it. Yes, the Foreman had cut their rations again, but he had enough to eat. He ran his hand through his hair and thought of his wife.

"No." This time Savique said it as though he meant it. "I am here to help."

"Good to have you." The small woman clapped him on the back. "We couldn't have done it without you."

Platitude or truth, he did not know. Regardless, he smiled. "No, you could not have done it without my chisel."

"We needed a hammer too," she said, grabbing and shaking his arm.

"We can find a hammer anywhere," the younger man said. "Probably a chisel, too. We didn't—"

"Stop that." The old man pointed at the younger one. "He is a part of the group now. We are happy to have him, no matter what convincing it took." The old man grinned at Savique.

Savique met the old man's stare, crossed his arms, and shrugged. He thought about telling him the truth, but decided against it. There was no use in upsetting the man now that he had agreed. Still, he was not there for any of them, nor was it the old man's persuasions that brought him out on that night. It was wife's.

She had lost weight and complained of stomach pain. Savique would have thought it a passing illness if not for the child she carried in her belly. His child. So, he shared his rations with her and found extra helpings of water and tea to soothe her stomach. It revived her for a few days, but he was still wary.

And then it happened again. She withered until she looked like a branch with a burl. And though he continued to give her as much food and water as he could, there was not enough for her to gain weight. She may not have worsened, but she did not improve.

His mind changed then. He needed more for his family to grow and be healthy. And that was why he went to the hut that night; to ensure that they would all survive.

***

THE LOCK FELL TO the ground. It landed with a dull thud. Savique only had to tap the hammer a few times against his chisel to break the bronze contraption in two and send it falling to the dirt in front of the storehouse door.

A rush of excitement flowed through him. Gone was the anxiety and worry that had consumed him earlier. Now, his heart beat quickly and his breath shortened with anticipation of what lay behind the unlocked door.

"It's open," Savique whispered over his shoulder.

Hushed cheers and muffled exclamations followed.

"I told you he would make good on his word. He knows rocks," the small woman said to the younger man behind her.

"Yes, but metal is not a rock."

"Close enough. Besides, he—"

"Shh!" The old man interrupted their bickering. "Both of you quiet down. You'll get us heard and found out. You want that?" After a moment of silence, he continued, "The hardest part is just beginning. So everyone, stay silent."

Savique nodded to the old man, who nodded back at him and then gestured at the door. Savique put his hand against the wood, then paused.

He could still leave, run from the storehouse, and not look back until he was home. Even if guards saw him, he could outrun them. But once he walked past those doors, he would be cornered. And a thief. If anyone saw him then, he would be a chicken in the coop when the butchers came.

The old man did not wait for Savique. He shoved Savique to the side with one hand while his other pushed open the door. Savique's eyes bulged as he peered into the storehouse. Not from joy or excitement, but from shock.

He expected to see wooden barrels of food and drink stacked as high as huts and as deep as the fields. Instead, he saw a few meager piles of leather bags, a dozen clay pots, and only four wooden barrels. It was more than the thieves could carry with them, but it was nowhere near what should have been there.

Savique scratched his chin. Perhaps the yield was in another storehouse or on its way to the Vizier. But no explanation made sense. The harvest season had ended only a week ago. Even accounting for what the Vizier took, the stores should have been full. There should have been enough to feed the entirety of Bas.

If the estate was truly low on crops, it meant something terrible for everyone there. Everyone on the continent too.

"Savique, enough daydreaming of your next meal." The small woman took his bag and held it in front of his face. "Start filling your sack."

He did exactly that. And though the thieves were amateurs and made more of a mess than they intended, they filled their bags full without interruption and exited without being seen. Before they left the storehouse, the old man closed the door and hung a broken lock through its handle. It was their only attempt to cover their tracks.

The heavy bags made Savique's back ache as they walked back to the camp. It did not help that he and the rest of the thieves had to move low to the ground to hide themselves from any guards on duty. Walking upright with the bags was onerous, squatting and crawling with them was torturous. And it required more than a few breaks.

But they had stopped only a moment ago when Savique heard Mascheix's voice. "Stop," he whispered and held out his hand.

"Again?" Savique asked. "Who is slowing—"

"Guard outpost up ahead. Looks like it's full—Shh."

Savique's heart pounded. If the outpost was full, then they should go back and around, avoid this route even if it meant a longer trip. He couldn't say this, couldn't say anything for fear a guard might look and listen for someone. For them.

He felt a tap on his shoulder and looked up with eyes full of fear, as though he expected the great beast Bierru to snatch the head off his body. But it was only Mascheix gesturing for him to turn around and go back the way they came. Someone had thought of the very plan he had, and relief washed over him.

But as he turned and walked a back along the same route he had come, he forgot about the ditch he had just stepped over. His foot landed awkwardly, and though he was still squatting close to the ground, he fell over and released a short, unintentional burst from his mouth. "Mmph!"

Someone shouted, "Who's there?"

The words brought a crushing weight onto Savique's chest. He couldn't breathe. The voice was not one he recognized—and his fellow thieves would never shout—which meant it could only be one thing. A guard.

"I asked, is anyone there?" The guard held a lantern towards the field, producing a faint light in front of his face. To Savique, it was no brighter than a firefly.

"It was probably just a deer or fox running through the fields looking for a snack." Another voice chimed in.

"No, I heard something. It sounded like a voice."

"I think it sounded more like a bird."

"Maybe it was Favon here to steal your newborn."

"If it was someone, it was probably just Marre from the third. You know he likes to wander during the night sometimes. Leave him be. If he hasn't said anything, he'll be gone in a moment."

While the guards continued their discussion, Savique righted himself and began slowly crawling his way back towards the others. His breathing returned and his panic faded as he realized the guards did not see him. If they had, they would not have called out questions and shined a light. They would have been beside him before he knew it.

He met up with the others beside the storehouse and, at a safe enough distance, they turned and made a loop around the fields. They shuffled past an empty outpost and then another with a single guard who appeared to be paying more attention to the stars than the fields.

And with that, they returned to the camp. Exhausted but excited, the group found their way into the hut, still displaying a yellow flower, and broke out into celebration.

"I can't believe it worked!" the small woman said to Savique.

He smiled, unsure of how to interpret the words, and asked, "What?"

She patted him on the back. "I was sure someone was going to see us or—"

"Then why did you..."

"Because I had to," she said, staring into Savique's eyes. "We have to. You understand that now, right? I know you didn't get it then, but now—I mean, you saw the reserves. Where has our harvest gone?"

"I..." Savique shook his head. "I don't know."

"I do. Crevir has it." She pointed at Savique to reinforce her point. "He'll take what he wants, give the Vizier what is due—more to gain favor—and then we get the rest. We do the work and we get whatever is left over. That's why we had to take it. It's the only way to get what is ours."

"That's right," Mascheix added. "This will feed so many in the camp, for weeks, maybe even last until the growing season, no matter what that bastard does." The young man spit on the ground. "May his body turn to salt."

"Yes, it was an important thing we did tonight, Mascheix," the old man said. "But it will not be the last time we are called upon to be brave. Even you, Savique. Not only a cutter after all, huh?"

Laughter erupted from the group. Savique smiled dismissively, unimpressed by the joke.

After the laughter died down, the old man continued, "For now, everything we took will remain here in my pots. We will distribute things in the morning. Head back to your huts." He glanced at each of them. "And thank you."

The group nodded to the old man and at each other. They shared a few more pleasantries and then Savique turned to leave. Before he did, a hand clasped on his shoulder. It was Mascheix.

"I was wrong to question you. You did well tonight. It would not have been a success without you." Mascheix patted Savique on the chest. Savique returned the gesture of respect.

"Thank you." Savique said. "You as well."

He exited the hut without another word. Once clear of the place, he threw his head to the sky, exhaled, and basked in the glowing moons. It had all been a success. Then why, he wondered, were the stars running across the sky portending misfortune.

# CHAPTER 2

A BEAR STOOD ON its hind legs and roared. It bared its teeth and shook spit from its jowls as it loomed over Vaten, who cowered on the ground. The young man, just past his nineteenth name day, had no way to fend off an attack from the beast whose black fur seemed to blot out the sun.

"Help! Ajeau? There's a bear!" Vaten yelled.

The bear lowered and closed its mouth, but it was not pacified. The beast pawed at the ground as though it were digging for some prize buried deep below. But for the bear, the prize was right in front of it.

"Ajeau? He's going to charge!" Vaten yelled again and pressed himself into the tree behind him, hoping he could dart to either side once the creature rushed him. He hoped he would be quick enough.

A snarl and a low growl followed. The bear stopped pawing at the ground. It was ready to attack, and no longer needed to signal its aggression. It had already given its prey its final warning.

In a frenzied outburst, Vaten grabbed a stick near him and hurled it at the beast. It had no effect. The bear did not appear to feel it hit him.

"Ajeau!" Vaten screamed. "Hurry!"

Then Vaten saw something out of the corner of his eye. From his right side, a rock flew past him and connected with the bear's snout. It drove the beast's head down and toward the side for a moment.

The bear twitched from the assault, then turned and looked in the direction from where the rock came. As it did, another rock struck its face. The beast roared and shook its head.

Another rock glanced off the bear's arm. The beast took exception to it and rose onto its hind legs once more. It stretched its arms wide as though it were ready to swat down the next rock that came its way. But it didn't and the next rock hit its gut.

While the bear focused on the rocks and the person who threw them, Vaten searched near the tree for something he could use to drive the bear away. Anything sharp or hard. But all he could find were brittle sticks. One, though, had been broken just right, so its end was a sharp point.

Before the bear lowered and took off toward the rock-thrower, Vaten rushed at it and drove the stick into the leg of the unsuspecting creature. It screamed loudly, then whimpered, as Vaten ran back behind the tree.

When the whimpering eventually stopped, Vaten peaked around the tree to see if the bear had left. It had not. Instead, the beast hobbled towards him. He sank to the ground and hoped for rescue. Finally, he saw Ajeau approach from the far side of the tree.

The young woman crept towards the unsuspecting bear with a large stone in her hands. Before the beast reached the tree, and Vaten, she swung it into the bear's face with such force that it seemed to turn the beast's shoulders with its head.

Blood flew from its muzzle as it let out another loud scream. This time, however, when it whimpered, it did so as it retreated from the pair. A few moments later, neither Vaten nor Ajeau could hear its steps. It was gone.

Ajeau dropped the rock and asked, "What were you doing?"

"Just searching for seeds and nuts," Vaten said. "You know, something to eat."

"You didn't notice the—the bear?"

He shook his head. "I didn't see it until it cornered me."

"You dolt." Ajeau gave him a soft push. "It was probably looking for food too and you got between it and its snack—"

"I think you mean I was the snack." Vaten chuckled.

Ajeau's eyes rolled into her head. "Good one. But I'm serious. You were lucky."

"I know. But it's what you would have done."

Ajeau paused, considering the statement. Then she said, "Maybe. But still, I would've had something to defend myself with. Odd though, I didn't think bears were alive anymore. Certainly not big ones like that. Must be one of the last."

"If it was, I got a good shot in on the last bear alive with that stick."

Ajeau smiled. "Yeah, you did. And I nearly took its head off with a rock."

Vaten laughed. "If only you had! We might be eating meat tonight for the first time in—since when, that fish Denavir?"

"Yeah, maybe. I don't even remember the taste of it. But come on, let's sit and eat whatever food you could scavenge. Half of it is mine, remember."

"How do you figure?" Vaten shrugged with a grin on his face. "I found it. It's mine, simple as that."

"I just saved you from a bear! And don't forget I gave you the last of the sweet root."

Vaten laughed. The sweet root, despite its name, was sour and bitter, and Ajeau gave away the rest to him only because it made her sick to keep eating. "I guess I can't argue with that," he said. He had every intention of sharing his find with Ajeau anyway—he always did—but he enjoyed testing her patience as much as she enjoyed testing his.

The friends finished their brief meal, then continued their trek through the dead forest. What had once been a place full of green was now gray and brown. Trees stretched to the sun devoid of their leaves, which now lay curled, cracked, and decomposed below them. The empty, twisted branches snaking high through the canopy reached out as if they were arms grasping for water. Water that never came.

The endless expanse of trees, so full of life the first people of Bas named it using their word for spirit, was lifeless. The drought had not spared even the Tentir. Every trunk Vaten and Ajeau passed was a ghost.

But neither thought of this. They thought only of survival, of finding their next meal or their next sip of water. They would even accept a path out of the vast wasteland surrounding them. Too long had they wandered the earth, lost, far from any familiar sight.

When they walked through the Tentir Forest, they did not think of the stories their kin had told about the place. About its great and wondrous land. They thought only about leaving it.

*\*\**

THE SUN OVERHEAD BEAT down on Ajeau and Vaten as they moved through the forest. When they could, they kept to the shade around the trees and shrubs, but it never cooled the air as much as they wanted. So they took frequent breaks and waited for the sun to set and night to chill the earth.

But before the sun fell below the horizon, Vaten noticed a glade in the forest with what looked like a stack of wood in the middle of it.

"What do you think about that?" Vaten said and pointed towards the clearing.

"Is that some kindling? But it looks...organized. Strange." Ajeau shook her head. Then she smiled and walked towards it. "Let's check it out."

"Wait." Vaten grabbed her shoulder as she went by. "We don't know whose camp that is or if that timber belongs to someone. What if whoever left it didn't want anyone coming by?"

"It's probably just a traveler who didn't want to carry it. Besides, it looks overgrown." She patted Vaten's hand. "Whoever left it hasn't been here in a while. I don't think anyone has."

"Maybe no one's touched it because no one was stupid enough to wander into some camp in the middle of the forest."

"Oh, don't be so afraid. I don't see any bears." Ajeau flashed Vaten a quick smile. Then said, "Or traps."

"That's exactly my point. We wouldn't see them if they were well-disguised."

Ajeau sighed and shrugged. "Well, you can sweep the ground with some branches if you want, but I'm going. You never know, there might be some dried meat. Or wine."

"That was cruel and you know it," Vaten said. The words only brought up memories of celebrations, dancing, and joy. On some nights, Crevir's Estate had been so full of joy they could not hear the barks of the jackals nearby. It had been a long time since then.

As Ajeau walked towards the clearing, Vaten sighed but resigned himself to following her. He knew better, but her impetuousness and bravery were infectious. And, as usual, she was right. At least about the traps.

The camp was in the middle of a flat piece of land bordered by hills and, at the back, a rock face that curved in a semi-circle. The natural features of the area made it a well-protected spot. Not enough to fend off an army, but enough to pick off the occasional raider.

It was clear from the overgrowth, no one had used the land in some time. Vines grew on the rocks. Bushes, devoid of leaves, dotted the landscape. Even the piles of wood had dead foliage within it.

Vaten stared at one stack, confused. The design was bizarre and too specific to be used only for storage. It was as if the wood was a sculpture. Not of a person or a beast or a plant. Then what, he wondered. It reminded him of those seeds that would stick in his foot or the head of a mace.

But even that was not precise. This was more angular, sharper. It resembled a sphere, but instead of smooth rounded curves, the ball consisted of sharp cone-like protrusions. And the whole design sank into the ground at a single point, the middle of three interlocking rings.

Vaten ran his hand over the wood and felt its notches and splinters. As his fingers moved along, they removed a layer of dirt and debris from the logs. And that was when he noticed the timber, all of it, was decorated with carvings unlike anything he had seen before.

"What is this?" Vaten said. "It doesn't look Bassian."

Ajeau walked toward him, peering at the wood as she moved. "No," she said. "I'm not sure what it is."

"Do you think they belong to Lord Balay? I have heard—"

"Don't even start with it," Ajeau said, holding up her hand. "Balay is dead, and he is not haunting the Tentir."

"But..." Vaten glanced around the campsite nervously. "You know what they say, the Lord has power, even after his death."

Ajeau scoffed. "Come on. That is a story for kids. You can't possibly believe it."

"I don't know, he—"

"What else do you believe in?" Ajeau said. "The demon bird of Intheos? Villea, the baby snatcher? What about the spirits who enter our world through—"

"I get it," Vaten said, annoyed. "It is too incredible to believe. You're right."

Ajeau laughed, then shook him playfully. "Besides, you know as well as I, the only ones with power now are the Viziers. But I don't imagine a Vizier would create this. It's not for food."

Ajeau may have been right, but it did not comfort him. What they stood in front of felt ominous, like it was important to someone. And he wanted to know who.

"Then who would create it?" Vaten asked.

Ajeau shook her head. "I don't know."

After a moment of silence, Vaten said, "Maybe it's some kind of V'eauvian meeting place or waypoint in the forest."

"I don't know." Ajeau paused as she inspected the object. "I don't think it's V'eauvian, at least not any I can remember. Maybe it was the Noye. They've been known to mark—"

"Noye?" Vaten's head spun to Ajeau. He glared at her, then slammed his fist against the wood. "Eau damn it! You know how I feel about them," he shouted.

Ajeau put her hands up. "I know, but…Tille used to say they left messages in the trees."

Vaten's head dropped. He barely heard a word Ajeau said. Instead, he stared at a broken leaf on the ground and let images of the Noye run through his mind.

Men and women on horseback as tall as the grain towers on the estate, laying waste to fields and villages and people who stood in their way. He may never have met one, but he had heard the stories and their deeds. And like monsters, his imagination filled in the rest.

He swore to find them and make them rue what they had done. Those were the thoughts that drove him in his early days. But that was long ago, before he left the estate. That's where he thought he left them. He was wrong.

Ajeau gave him a moment, then walked over to him, jabbed at his shoulder, and said, "You alright?" He didn't move. "Come on. We'll find your dad someday. We have plenty of time."

"Yeah…yeah." Vaten said, defeated.

"Let's drink a little water and rest a bit. You'll feel better. Nothing here anyway, just these stupid—" Ajeau pushed at one of the objects with her foot. It rocked and then settled back into place. She did it again, pushed with all her strength. The object tilted, teetered on its single leg, then fell back into place once more. She never heard the soft crunch when it did.

***

Darkness enveloped the Tentir Forest. Vaten and Ajeau warmed themselves by the fire and listened to the silence. No beast, nor even fly or frog, announced themselves on that night. All was still. Even the wind seemed extinct.

Though they needed the rest, remaining in the camp at night was perilous. All sorts of fiends preyed on those who gave in to comfort over prudence, and the light from the fire could be seen for miles around. No matter how isolated they felt, safety always took priority.

"We should move on now," Vaten said. "We've been here long enough."

"I know, I know. Just let me rest a small time more." Ajeau lay on the ground, stretching her fingers and toes in a caricature of relaxation.

"No. Come on." Vaten kicked a few leaves in her direction. "Get up already. If you fall asleep, you're impossible to wake up. And when you do wake, you're always so upset with me."

"I like sleeping," Ajeau said with her eyes closed. "And hate interruptions."

Vaten sighed softly through his nose. He was tired too, and the prospect of sleep enticed him. He began to convince himself the clearing would be safe for the night. No one had disturbed this site in ages. What were the chances someone came tonight?

He lay down and closed his eyes.

Before he fell asleep, Ajeau stood up, put out the fire, and in the growing darkness said, "Let's go. You're right, it's not safe to stay here overnight."

They returned to their journey northward, following the green star. It was a strange feeling to both know the direction they moved and be lost at the same time. Yet, that is exactly how they felt.

North was not only the shortest way to exit the forest but it would also take them near Nouv'eau, the seat of the Lord, the largest city in Bas, and the site of Ajeau's birth. She did not know anyone in the city, and never remembered being there, but she thought they might find assistance among its crowds. The V'eauvians were her people, after all.

Vaten hadn't objected to the plan. They had no other direction, and it seemed plausible someone in Nouv'eau could help him find his father. The city was rumored to be large enough to hold the entire population of Bas. If that was true, then perhaps his father would be there waiting for him. Still, they had to make it out of the forest first.

Vaten and Ajeau said little to each other as they continued their march in the darkness. There was not much to say, and walking in silence was safer, anyway. Talking only increased the chances someone found them.

With the moons still high in the sky, Ajeau spied something on their path that concerned her.

"Vaten. Look." She pointed at a light, distant and faint.

Vaten squinted and leaned forward. "Is that a light?"

"Yeah, hard to see, but it's there."

"Shit." Vaten sighed. He was exhausted.

"Stay here," Ajeau said. "I'm going to see if I can find out what it is."

"Don't be stupid. You'll get yourself killed."

"I won't get too close," she said with the same dismissive smile she wore every time she heard his objections. "But we need to see if we can keep moving in this direction. Who knows, maybe they'll be fellow travelers and want to share the spoils of their latest hunt." She laughed.

Vaten closed his eyes and shook his head.

Ajeau stopped laughing. "Shit! It's moving. Quickly, I think. And it's coming towards us. Let's find a place to hide." She grabbed his arm and pulled him along. They walked carefully, making as little sound as they could, always keeping the light on their left side.

Vaten breathed heavily. It was not the walk but his fear. Anyone who moved with a lantern in the night did not mind being seen or approached. They were secure in their passage, confident they could fend off any attackers. What made them so confident, he did not know. And he did not want to find out.

"Stay near the trees. We'll blend in," Ajeau whispered.

Vaten nodded. "Right. And remember if we get separated, make the call at high sun. We'll reunite where we can."

"Agreed." Ajeau crouched and stepped forward slowly.

A quiet whine and then a dull thud. She looked up to see an arrow stuck in a tree not more than two paces in front of her. She glanced at Vaten and opened her mouth. But she didn't need to say a word. Both took off in a mad dash away from the direction the arrow came.

Running in the dark was difficult. Vaten stumbled on rocks and roots. He ran into and off trees. It was slow, clumsy, and all the while, he heard arrows punctuating the air around him.

Archers? Vaten could hardly believe it. Even the richest traders wouldn't have been stupid enough to waste arrows on them. Not soldiers either. None of the options that flew through his head made sense. And it drew his attention away from the ground in front of him.

A log, from a long dead tree, covered in leaves, laid on the forest floor. It had not known many feet when it was alive, nor dead as a log. But it met Vaten's right foot. And he fell hard to the ground, exclaiming in pain and cursing the log's existence.

Vaten grabbed his leg and moaned. Then he heard leaves crunch in the unmistakable pattern of footfalls. "Ajeau, can you help me? My leg is wrecked."

There was no response.

"Ajeau? Did you hear me?" he said in a panicked whisper.

Again, there was no response.

The leaves crunched closer. The footfalls slowly making their way to him. He stood and tried to hobble away. A hand grasped his arm. He froze.

"What you doing out here, boy?" a deep voice, with a strange accent, asked. Panic flashed through him as he realized the person was not Ajeau.

The man was still talking, still asking questions. "This a trap? Where's the other one I saw? You trying to—"

Vaten ignored the man. With his free arm, he made a fist and began driving it upward toward the man's face. But he saw it coming, moved faster than Vaten thought possible, and grabbed the arm before Vaten even made it past his waist.

"What you trying to do?" He chuckled and strengthened his grip on Vaten, lifting him off the ground.

Vaten struggled, flailed, and tried a few futile kicks. He grunted and then a frightened "No" slipped from his mouth. He looked for an escape. In the darkness, he found none.

The large man wrenched Vaten's arms behind him. The pain grew until Vaten thought he would lose consciousness. He didn't. He was forced to live his nightmare, caught in the clutches of some unknown person who would take him off to be sold, or worse. His journey, possibly his life, was over.

A smaller man appeared next to the large man. He had a bow in his arms, arrow notched, and moved gracefully, seemingly without disturbing the ground. He whispered something in the ear of the large man and retreated. Vaten heard the sounds, but did not understand them. They were in a language he did not know.

The larger man turned and, still holding the restrained Vaten, followed the small man. Both men looked around as they walked. Vaten knew what they were doing; they were looking for Ajeau. It gave him some small bit of hope; they hadn't found her. At least not yet.

A short time later, the two men and Vaten arrived at a caravan. The large man tossed Vaten to the ground as if he were the bones from a finished meal and spoke to the others there.

From his position, Vaten could not see the entire camp, but he saw several carts stacked with wooden boxes and counted nearly twenty people, all of whom held weapons. He saw sickles, daggers, staves, and bows covered in blue paint.

Yet they had no banners, flags, or sigils with them. Not that he would've recognized them, but their absence entirely was conspicuous. They flew no colors. If they were traders or merchants, they didn't have the backing of the Lord or a Vizier.

The large man finished his conversation and returned to Vaten. "You come with me now, boy," he said in his unnatural speech.

He lifted Vaten to his feet and walked him to a cart hitched to a pair of horses. When they arrived, Vaten's face fell. He saw four others, disheveled and gaunt, bound to a brass ring on the wooden floor of the wagon. The realization struck him; he was a prisoner now. For a moment, he could not breathe. Then, in a sudden spasm, he turned and vomited.

"Weak stomach, huh boy?" the large man said with a chuckle, as he watched Vaten empty his gut. When Vaten was done, the man threw Vaten into the cart and secured him to the same ring as the others. "Sit here and make no sounds."

Vaten did as he was told. He could do nothing else. He was exhausted and terrified and alone. The person he cared for most in the world was lost in the Tentir, if she had survived at all. Once again, he had been too weak to help the ones he cared about. Too weak to find his father, too. And now, he was as good as dead.

Vaten hung his head as the cart rolled down the path.

***

AJEAU WATCHED THE ENTIRE scene unfold. She had not heard what was said nor seen where the men took Vaten, but she noticed how they moved through the forest and the blue paint that adorned their weapons.

As she watched this from her perch in the trees, she remained motionless, concerned scouts may still litter the woods. If no one had seen her yet, she was hidden well enough. So she stayed in the tree as the light from the lantern receded into the distance and disappeared.

*Vaten, wherever you're going, stay alive. I will find you. I will see you again.*

# CHAPTER 3

THE WEEK FOLLOWING THE theft was uneventful except for the delight that spread through the workers' ranks as their plates grew with the newfound rations. Neither the guards nor the Foreman himself acted as if anything had happened at all.

Savique felt relief wash over him. Watching Pachen recover, gain weight, and find her old strength and vigor helped, too. Once again, they smiled smiles of affection rather than conciliation. All was calm, and Savique was grateful for it.

Then, less than a fortnight from the theft, a quartet of Istori Ascetics arrived on the estate. It was a most odd occurrence, not only because there were so few Ascetics left but because they concerned themselves with foretelling weather cycles, the downfall of Lords, and other notable events, not with estate matters.

Savique was in the workshop cutting stone when he heard shouting erupt from the fields. At first, it was only a few voices. But the sound grew until it was clear something was happening.

He left his stone and wandered outside to see what caused the commotion. There he glimpsed Vrai and several guards escorting four people in bright red robes with a black circles on their backs. They carried with them sacks of scrolls. Savique knew who they were the moment he saw them.

The four Ascetics entered the Foreman's residence and remained there for some time. While inside, it seemed no one in the camp worked. Even the guards, who should have ushered the workers back to their posts, stood and gossiped about what they saw.

"I wonder if they are here to anoint a savior," a voice from behind Savique said. "They plucked Lord Balay from the river!"

A woman scoffed. "You believe that?" She shook her head. "We probably need to grow something for them. Or maybe they're here to curse you." She waved her hands at the man, taunting him.

"You'd be foolhardy to question them. They're prophets! They know the future and they'll destroy yours—maybe all of ours—if we aren't respectful."

The woman scoffed again and patted Savique on the shoulder. "What do you think?"

Savique shook his head. "I don't know. I...I've heard the stories too, but it's not hard to hit a target if you shoot enough arrows, right?"

The woman howled with laughter. "Right! Right! Ignore the zealots." She slapped the man. "You see?"

"I wouldn't be so sure," the man grumbled, then walked away.

A few moments later, the Ascetics emerged from Crevir's residence flanked by the Foreman and the Captain of his guard, Vrai. The guards, upon seeing this, quickly began ordering everyone back to their work. The crowd met the words with groans and laughs, but soon enough, everyone returned to their duties.

Savique too returned to the workshop. As he did, he heard yells of 'Are they here to curse us?', 'Am I to die alone?', and 'Is our crop doomed?' He shook his head and sat down at the stone he cut before he was interrupted.

Then the door to the workshop opened and Crevir, Vrai, and one of the four Ascetics entered.

"There is the man you seek," Crevir said, pointing at Savique.

Savique's mouth dropped and hung open. He froze. His heart raced in his chest. There must have been a mistake. But the outstretched hand of the Foreman pointed directly at him. And the longer it did, the more ominous it seemed.

"Savique, up," Crevir continued, raising his hand as if Savique was a puppet he could control. "These people would like a word with you—it's the only way they will leave this place, and I'd rather have them leave peaceably. Who knows what horrors they would unleash if I—" The Foreman shook his head and turned back to the Ascetics, "Anyway, here is the best mason we have."

Savique did not hear the compliment. All he heard was that Crevir would bend to the Ascetics' will out of fear of what they could do. And if they could force the Foreman's hand, they could certainly force his.

So Savique rose and met the eyes of the Ascetics. They looked back at him with plain, unblinking faces. They stared as if they already knew he would come with them. It unnerved him.

Savique, Crevir, Vrai, and the four Ascetics exited the workshop and walked towards the grove. There was no way to be certain, but Savique felt as though every eye in the camp watched his march. It made his throat close, and his mouth go dry. But he kept walking.

After one Ascetic nodded to the Foreman, they all stopped. Apparently, the grove was their destination. Savique glanced skyward at the tree branches and found them calm and unmoving. The opposite of him.

"This will do, then," Crevir said and turned to leave.

"Wait," Savique pleaded. "Where are you going? Don't leave me alone with them."

"They just want words. You will be fine," Crevir said and continued to walk from the grove.

Turning to the Ascetics, Savique's eyes bulged. "W-What do you want with me?"

"As the Foreman said, just words," one Ascetic said, then bowed.

Another Ascetic continued, "We have journeyed far to meet you, mason. We are not of this land, but it is wondrous. Not forever." The voice was calm, controlled, and monotonous. It was like they read the words from one of their scrolls. "That is why we must speak with you."

Savique looked at each face, staring at him. They were still blank, unblinking. A shiver ran through his body. "Why?"

"Because there are things you must hear now. Before all that comes next. The cycle has already begun," the first Ascetic said.

"I don't understand."

"You do not have to. Not yet," the second Ascetic said. "But you must listen. Will you?"

Savique nodded slowly, unsure whether he truly had a choice in the matter.

"Good," a third Ascetic said. She turned to her fellow Ascetic, the one who had not spoken yet, and said, "The leaf will hear us."

The fourth Ascetic nodded and stepped towards Savique. She stopped about an arm's length away and reached into her robe.

Panic flashed through Savique. She was drawing a weapon against him and intended to kill him. He was foolish to believe when they said they were only there to speak to him.

But when she removed her hand from her robe, Savique could see it was not a blade of any kind. He narrowed his eyes, straining to identify what she held. By the time he saw a pink powder in her palm, it was too late. The Ascetic moved it in front of her mouth, then blew.

The pink powder surrounded him. He shut his eyes tight to protect them, but could not stop himself from inhaling the dust. As soon as he did, all went white. And though his eyes were closed, he swore he saw a black specter reach for him.

His eyes shot open. The fourth Ascetic stood in front of him. He was still alive and in the grove. Whatever had reached for him had not grabbed him.

The woman finally spoke. "Be not afraid. The red eye only opens your mind to my words."

Savique nodded as if he could do nothing else.

The fourth Ascetic continued, "There are difficult times ahead. For you, yes. For all, too. Cycles exact a price. Constants, once relied upon, will falter and fail. But you, you will not fail. You will save them all. Do you understand?"

Savique stared at her with his eyes wide, unblinking like the other Ascetics. Again, he nodded slowly. A small part of him knew he did not understand the words spoken to him, but he could not object or ask for an explanation. He could only agree.

"Good," the Ascetic said. "You will lose much before then, gain much too. But it is necessary. You must not lament your losses, forge onward. All happens with purpose. The cycle continues. And when you need it, in your darkest hour, there will be light. You will save them all, you will find the lost, and that is when you will see him again."

Savique looked at the fourth Ascetic and struggled to form words. All he could utter was a monotonous, "W-Who?"

"You," the Ascetic said. "Because only you can. You are the leaf. Remember, save them all, find the lost. Only then will you see him again."

The fourth Ascetic glanced at the other three and bowed slightly to them. They returned with a similar movement and then, in unison, all four bent over, touched their forefingers to the ground, and said, "For Istor."

They rose, stared towards Crevir and Vrai for a moment without saying a word, and then walked through the grove and off the estate.

It took several moments before Savique finally blinked. He still could barely move or think, but the words of the Ascetics echoed endlessly in his mind.

***

AFTER HIS ENCOUNTER WITH the Ascetics, Savique returned to the workshop and continued his labors. Men and women shot him questioning glances as he worked. He knew what they thought. Part of him thought it too—he was cursed or worse—but he refused to give life to the rumors and ignored the voices swirling around him.

But a day later, as he toiled in the workshop, he heard a voice he could not ignore, one that came from a Keeper of Life. The child Pachen housed was knocking on the door, asking to be let out. He rushed to Pachen's hut.

When he arrived, a scream he knew to be Pachen's greeted him. And though he wanted nothing more than to enter and ensure his wife and child were well, he knew he could not.

Another scream came and Savique reminded himself the Keepers knew what they were doing, Pachen was well and strong, and screams were common. They did not need him for this, and his presence would only distract those inside from their work. None of this eased his worry much, but it rooted his feet.

More screams came from the hut. One after another, Pachen screamed until there was no break between them, until they reached a crescendo like the rains during a monsoon. It seemed to last as long as them too.

But then, there was a grunt and all the sounds stopped. Everything was still. For a moment, noise itself did not exist. But then the silence was broken by a loud, high-pitched wail.

"Boy!" A woman's voice—not Pachen's—came from the hut. "A boy lives!"

Savique breathed long and slow. A smile crept across his face even before he was sure what he had heard. Then, all at once, it hit him. His child, a boy, was alive and well.

He reached down, grabbed a fistful of dirt, and threw it in the air. While it fell on and around him, he danced in a little circle—the same dance he remembered his father doing when his third sister was born—and whispered, "Thank you, Eau. Thank you. Thank you, a million times over."

His mind flooded with thoughts, fears, hopes, and pictures of the boy's new life. A baby playing in freshly tilled soil. A child setting the traps to keep the flies, deer, and hares at bay. That same child digging, raking, ploughing, harrowing; laboring in the soil, cultivating the fields, reaping the bounty he earned. A man, working his own land, teaching his own children.

Savique did not cry easily, but that day his eyes gleamed from the tears.

As he wiped away the moisture from his eyes, he moved towards the hut. But as soon as he drew the curtain from the doorway, he was met with yells, "No!" and "Do not enter!" and "It is not ready."

By the time he heard the shouts, it was too late. He saw everything.

Blood, so much of it, pooled on the ground around Pachen's body. The Keepers, themselves stained a dark, black red, worked feverishly at her side with oils and herbs.

None of their work seemed to disturb Pachen, who still lay on the ground, unable to hold the child she just birthed. The child seemed content to suckle at her breast while a woman Savique did not know held him.

Something was amiss. The air in the hut was one of concern and uneasiness, not joy. The Keepers' movements were rushed and increasingly frantic. And Pachen remained unresponsive. Even though Savique knew little about a child's entrance to the world, he knew something was wrong. He was right.

\*\*\*

WEEKS HAD PASSED SINCE Pachen's death, and Savique remained devastated. He spoke few or, more often, no words with those around him. Even to friends who came to console him, he was terse and aloof. He shared his meals with no one and barely touched the extra rations his theft had brought him.

Savique spent most of his time alone, lost in memories. He lived over and over the first time he glimpsed her eyes; a confounding shade of pale green unlike any he had seen before. They had reminded him of the leaves losing the light, though he would come to realize he could not have been more wrong. She was not a dying leaf. She was the red fruit in the tree, vibrant, sweet, and alluring.

The memory, like all the others, would fill his mind for hours at a time. He would stay in every moment as deeply as he could. But after they ended, and each trace faded from his mind, he would always arrive at the same feeling. Confused and angry. It was an injustice that she was gone. He would lash out or scream, then drown in sorrow.

Yet there was a sliver of light in Savique's life. The boy he named Vaten had survived. He had remained resilient to the affliction that cut down his mother and took well to being nursed by one of the Keepers. He ate and slept at regular intervals and, though he howled louder than any beast Savique ever heard, Vaten was healthy.

Savique visited Vaten as much as he could, for his sake and for the boy's, and it gave him immense joy. Even in his darkest hours, Savique knew that seeing his child would lift his spirits. It made days bearable, gave him something to look forward to, and afforded him hope for the future.

And Savique knew it was as important for Vaten to see him. He was his child's only family, the only one who could tell Vaten about his mother. Savique felt that responsibility deeply. If nothing else, he would survive to fulfill it.

Eventually, Savique became accustomed to his new routine. Morning, he would wake early and greet Vaten at the Keepers' hut. Then he would labor at the workshop during the day. After sundown, he would eat quickly, then forsake the night's stories and songs and games for another trip to the Keepers' hut to see Vaten once more.

He did not mind losing the time spent with others. He had better and more important things to do. And his life returned to a new equilibrium until one morning, as he walked his normal path to the workshop, he caught sight of something swinging in a tree.

At first, he could not make it out. Whatever it was, it was not green like the leaves, nor gray like the branches, nor black like the birds. And every so often, it moved with the breeze.

Then he walked a few steps more and turned so he could glimpse the object in full. And when he did, he retched.

It was the hand of Mascheix. The very hand that had patted his chest with respect on the night of their theft. But it was not just the hand, it was all of him. And two others from that night, the small woman and another man. All of them hung from the branches of the tree with a rope around each neck and every hand severed. A sign that read 'thieves' swung next to them.

Savique retched again, this time not because of the grisly sight, but because of the horror of what it meant. They had been found out. Foreman Crevir not only knew that they had robbed him, but he knew who had done it. At least he knew three of them.

Was it only a matter of time before he hung from the tree, as his accomplices did? The thought brought Savique to his knees.

It had all been for nothing. The workers were right; he was cursed. The theft and the extra rations had not saved Pachen nor any of the thieves, except him. And though some workers enjoyed the extra meal, none would have said it was worth anyone's life.

That was not the worst of it. The worst of it was the thought that all would still be alive if they had stolen nothing that night. If Savique had stayed in his hut, never taken his chisel home, or never agreed to the plan, they all would be alive.

He sat in mud, next to his bile, and let the grief overwhelm him. He may never have moved if not for a wail from far in the distance.

It could have been from any of the babies or children in the camp, but Savique was sure it was Vaten's voice. It had to be. The boy's voice was the only thing that would cut through his anguish. And when it did, Savique remembered, he had to survive for his child. He would, Eau damn it.

He was not cursed. No matter what anyone said about the Ascetics.

# CHAPTER 4

AJEAU SAT IN THE tree a long while. She didn't know what else to do. For the first time since she and Vaten left Crevir's Estate, she had no ideas, plans, or schemes. Her mind was a desert, barren.

Though she tried, sleep eluded her. When she closed her eyes, she saw the small man and the large man beating Vaten as he cried out in agony. Over and over, they battered her friend until he was quiet and no longer moved. She forced her eyes open, so she did not have to watch the abuse any longer.

Eventually, the sun began to crawl above the horizon. The new day's birth provided Ajeau with a strange hope, like the night's misfortune was only a nightmare, now fading in the sunlight. She knew it was not true, but she indulged in the fantasy anyway and let her panic retreat.

As it did, a deep exhaustion took its place. She relaxed against the trunk of the tree and closed her eyes. All seemed tranquil, quiet. She imagined remaining in the tree, becoming part of it, letting the branches grow through her. Or maybe she would become a leaf, drink the light, then fall to the earth.

Rocked by a gentle breeze, sleep finally captured her.

\*\*\*

AJEAU, A CHILD, SAT on a wagon that wound through the forests outside Nouv'eau. She was small, less curious, and more afraid than her older self. Several other children sat tied to the wagon with her. She wondered if they were all like her, parentless, unloved, and cast out. They all had the same blank stare as she did.

At the head of the wagon was a short, fat man with long hair tied off at its end. He wore a shawl streaked with white diagonal lines. The clothes were fine, befitting a successful merchant, and the colors on them meant he rode with the protection of the V'eauvians and Lord Balay.

The man looked at the children behind him. "Don't be sad. They don't like sad ones. We'll rest in a bit, and I'll cheer you up." He chuckled as he snapped the horses' reins.

Ajeau shuddered and closed her eyes. When she opened them, she noticed a girl staring at her. The girl was larger than the rest, and Ajeau thought, more mature.

She continued staring at Ajeau, then without breaking her gaze, turned to her left and whispered something to the boy beside her. The boy nodded and whispered something to the boy next to him. Around it went until each child had heard.

"When we stop to rest, we're escaping. I'll attack the driver. You run."

Ajeau's hands trembled, her heart raced. Escape was foolish, rash, and it would get them all killed.

She shook her head at the girl. The girl nodded back. She tilted her head side to side, a sign for Ajeau to look at the other children. Ajeau saw their faces now filled with hope, optimism, and maybe even courage. The girl nodded again, raised her eyebrows suggestively. There was no more discussion.

The wagon came to a stop at a clearing in the brush. The waning light of the sun split through the trees, like it wanted to illuminate only that spot in the entire forest. If Ajeau had not been so worried, she may have seen it as a good omen.

"Here we are," the driver said and hopped off the wagon. "We'll rest here a bit and start up again in the morning. You kids get comfortable."

For a moment, nothing happened and Ajeau wondered if the girl had lost her nerve. It was easy to plan an escape, much harder to see it through. Maybe it was just a fantasy, a way to give them all some hope.

"Sir! Sir! Let me down. I need to pay a visit," the larger girl said.

"Yeah, me too. Me too," echoed the other children.

The man threw a clump of dirt at the cart. "Quiet down! You piss and shit up there, you unwanted scraps."

"Sir. It'll stink up here and draw the vermin out. Might even bring beasts," the girl said.

"Yeah, yeah. Don't worry about that. I'll keep you safe." The man removed a dagger from under his shawl and held it up in front of him. He admired it. Then he lunged forward, miming a stab, and laughed.

The girl nodded at him. "That's right, any of us misbehave and you have your knife. We know the price, sir."

Ajeau's eyes bulged. She could not believe what she heard. The girl invited the man to kill them for the very act she planned. It was beyond reckless. She began to sweat and pant. She squirmed in her seat and looked around in quick bursts for an escape. There were only trees.

The man caught sight of Ajeau's frantic movements and said, "What's going on over there? You going to be sick? Just go already!"

Ajeau met eyes with the man and her heart climbed into her throat. She thought she would vomit, but when she heaved, nothing came out. She groaned, and her hands gripped her legs, pinching her skin until it turned white.

"All right, all right." The man threw up his hands and relented. "Don't need your sick and piss and shit on my cart anyway," he mumbled. Then, turning to the kids said, "Hold the railings. Don't let a finger fall off them if you don't want to lose it."

He began untying the ropes that bound the children. As he did, heads spun. Each child glanced at another, trying to confirm whether this was the plan. Ajeau only looked down at her trembling legs.

After the ropes fell from the last child, the man said, "We'll go ten paces out, as a line. Any of you move out of the line or say anything, I'll cut you. You want to find out how quick I am?"

The children lined up and marched to the woods. The man stared at them like a wolf over sheep. Ten paces came, and they stopped. No one moved.

"Well, what are you—"

The sound of a tree falling nearby drew the man's attention for a moment. The large girl capitalized.

"Now!" she yelled as she jumped on the man. The children scattered.

Ajeau only made it as far as the nearby tree before her legs gave out. Her whole body convulsed, and she felt faint. But she could hear the girl's attacks and could not help wondering what was happening. She turned in time to see the girl strike the driver in his manhood.

As he winced and groaned in pain, Ajeau could not help smiling. Her body was still shivering, her heart still racing, but seeing the man doubled over gave her hope. Maybe it would work after all.

But it did not take long for the driver to regain his footing. And when he did, he threw the girl to the ground. She scrambled to her feet and tried to run, but before she could take a step, the driver grabbed her. He picked her up and hurled her back down again. The girl screamed.

Ajeau closed her eyes and turned from the sight. She implored her legs to support her weight, but when she stood, they shook like a stake pounded with a hammer. She heard the girl scream again.

Ajeau turned and saw the man standing over the girl, kicking her like a doll. The girl's body moved only when his foot propelled it. Ajeau watched as he kneeled next to the girl, raised his hands over his head, and brought them down on the girl's face. Then her chest. Then, over and over, he hit her until he grunted with exhaustion.

Ajeau should have run. That was the plan. The girl knew the consequences; she had even asked for them. But Ajeau could not leave the girl behind. After all, it was the girl's boldness that had given everyone a chance at freedom. And for the first time, her legs steadied and breathing smoothed.

"You stupid stray. You pest! You..." the man screamed at the girl on the ground. His nostrils flared. "I'll never make that back. Those V'eauvians were a year's worth of goods and coin. Stupid..." His yelling devolved into a guttural roar and he kicked the girl in a fit of rage.

From behind the tree, Ajeau saw sunlight reflecting off a small metal object on the ground. It nearly blinded her for a moment until, squinting, she recognized it.

She moved quietly towards the yelling man. As she did, she remembered the girl's bravery, her audacity to think she could save them all. She risked her life for children she didn't know and would never see again.

Ajeau picked up the dagger and, as the man turned around to see what the rustle behind him was, plunged it deep into his belly.

The man shrieked as a trickle of blood ran down his leg. "You—" his words dissolved into shrieks. He grabbed at the dagger and pulled it from his stomach. Then he pointed it at Ajeau. "You!"

The dagger shook, sending droplets of blood flying. He took a step in Ajeau's direction. But he made it no farther. He fell to the ground, blood rushing out of his body, and clawed at Ajeau's feet. Then his arms stopped.

Ajeau looked at the man as his breathing labored, then stopped. She turned, walked to the girl, whose name she didn't know, and knelt beside her. Ajeau pushed at her a few times. The girl did not wake up and, from the vacant stare in her frozen eyes, Ajeau knew she would never wake up again.

After the shock wore off, tears flowed down Ajeau's face. She thought of dragging the girl from the grotesque scene to some place more appropriate. She thought of burying her, as she had seen others do. But she had no tools and even if she did, she had no strength to use them.

So instead, Ajeau collapsed as an image flashed in her mind. A picture of the girl shaking her head yes at Ajeau. What was that look in her eye? Anger? No, it was determination. It was purpose. The girl refused to yield to the will of anyone but herself.

Ajeau lay there, determined to never forget what she learned. *Always fight to control your destiny.*

***

AJEAU AWOKE WITH THE sun still high in the sky. Despite the images from her past still circling her mind, she felt renewed. Her body no longer wilted from exhaustion, and she no longer feared the previous night's events. Yes, they were awful, but she knew her strength.

Still, questions streamed through her head. She knew nothing about those who took Vaten, why they did, or where they were going. Was he even alive?

He must be, she told herself. Until she knew with certainty that he was dead, she would not allow herself to consider the opposite. He was alive, and she had to search for him. No, not just search, she had to find him.

Her first instinct was to follow the direction of the caravan. They went south, heading back in the direction Vaten and Ajeau had traveled. She knew some of the terrain now and might pick up their tracks easily.

No, she told herself, that was stupid. The caravan was gone. And it was heavily defended, anyway. She'd more likely get herself captured than save anyone.

Ajeau slammed the tree in frustration. She had no resources, barely enough provisions to last the week, and no help. She was one person. Alone, again. It had been a long time since she had been abandoned, but the loneliness settled in like it had never left. Like it was back where it belonged.

She shook her head. No, she would not allow herself to fall into self-pity. Remember, always fight—

The fight. The attack. That was her answer. Or at least a starting point. Those who abducted Vaten shot arrows at them before they took him. She could look for the arrows and see if they held any clue about who those people were.

She hopped down from her perch and tried to backtrack her steps from the previous night. They must be around here somewhere, she told herself. But she wasn't sure where she was now and where she had been when the arrows flew by her face.

And it did not help that all the trees looked alike. They were all brown and cracked, with leaves scattered around their bases. Sure, some had vines twisted around their trunks, or were broken halfway up, but nothing disrupted the pattern enough to be distinctive.

She looked around for something out of place near the trees. A bright color, a fleck, a glint. She followed her eyes to feathers and rocks, but no arrows.

She wondered if they picked them up. It was an odd notion, but materials ran in short supply these days. Perhaps they reused them.

Regardless, Ajeau would not give up. She continued to look at the trees from all angles, walking them in circles, until she tripped over something. She stumbled and looked back to see the pack she placed on the ground the previous night.

They had been there. It was where the first arrow had broken their conversation.

Ajeau looked at the surrounding trees. At the base of the third one she saw, laying disguised among the dirt, an arrow.

Ajeau reached down and picked up the arrow. She held it in her hand, like it was some priceless jewel. And in some ways, it was.

A reed—once common in Bas but now rare due to the drought—formed the shaft. The entire thing was painted blue, just as she had seen on their blades the night before. She did not know why blue paint, but she was sure that the arrow belonged to that group.

More impressive than the painted reed was the arrowhead. The rock was blue, gray, and white, banded together in layers like it had been weaved by some divine artist. It was magnificent. And unlike anything Ajeau had ever seen before.

But it led her back to the same questions she had earlier. Who were these people? She could not even venture a guess. Instead, all she could think of was who they weren't.

They were not V'eauvian, at least they didn't bear the white color of the Lord. And they took nothing—except for Vaten—so they weren't common raiders or thieves. They were too heavily armed to be merchants or traders. Besides, no smart merchant or trader traveled through the Tentir Forest these days.

And she knew they were not Noye. They did not attack on horseback. For the Noye not to be riding, to not have horses with them at all, would be like a lake without water.

So, it was no one familiar to her. That was no problem. If she didn't know them, then she would just have to find someone who did. And there was only one place to go to do that. The largest city in Bas. The place she was already going. Nouv'eau.

It was not much, but it was progress. She had a place to go and a reason to go there. If she was honest with herself, she would have known the reasons went far deeper than just Vaten. Her family. Her abandonment. Those strange scars on her arms. Yes, there was much that Nouv'eau might tell her.

But she told herself it was for Vaten and used that as a door to keep out all other thoughts.

Ajeau did not know how far she had to go or the perils that may be ahead. She had already encountered one gang of armed individuals and there was likely to be more. But that did not bother her. She had a goal; get to Nouv'eau. Find Vaten.

Arrow in hand, she stood and began her trek.

***

As he did every day, Seule walked out of his hut in the Tentir Forest and smelled the dry, earthy, and faintly sweet morning air. The sun, as it had been for years, was bright and hung in a cloudless sky.

"You speed the decay today," Seule said as he looked towards the sky.

He chuckled, shook his head, and began his daily ritual of foraging for food. Mostly, he found grains, nuts, berries, and seeds. But there was always a chance he could come back with some meat. Those were joyous days, though they were becoming far less frequent.

Still, his food supply always remained enough for him. And there was no one else to worry about. No visitors would come there, and that suited him fine. He would remain in the forest alone until his death. Then he could return to the earth and provide it with the sustenance it needed to return to its former glory. At least, that was his hope.

As with every hunt, Seule planned to return home with whatever he had found. But on that day, he did not return with food. No, he returned with a girl—unconscious but still breathing—who had collapsed in the brush.

# Chapter 5

The cart rolled along the dirt path, shaking its passengers. A faint light, cast from a lantern affixed to the cart's frame, illuminated faces covered with dirt and sweat. They all pointed down towards the wood their feet rested upon, as though each could no longer muster the effort to hold their heads upright.

When the lantern swayed to the right, the light exposed Vaten's face. It showed a man gritting his teeth and holding back tears. It was not just the pain radiating from his wrenched shoulder, but the pain of losing his friend, his purpose, and everything that was familiar.

And the thirst. He had had no water for what felt like ages. His lips were rough, his skin was cracked, his eyes burned, and his head throbbed mercilessly. The pain hurt, but the thirst tortured him.

Vaten had not said a word since being taken to the caravan and tied to the cart. But he was desperate. "Water!"

No one responded or even bothered looking at him. He tried again. "Sir, please. Water."

"Shut up over there!" someone walking near the cart said. "No noises!"

Before he could protest, Vaten heard a thump from the wagon floor. He looked down to see a small waterskin at his feet. He glanced back up and saw a man staring at him. "Here's some water, kid. But for Sol's sake, don't talk so loud."

The man was no taller than Vaten but commanded a much different presence. He was solid, muscular, though not large. If the drought, or his capture, had affected him, it was not clear how. And although his hair was unkempt, Vaten could detect the neatly cut lines that had once been present. They were lines only a man of wealth would possess.

The man's clothes substantiated Vaten's guess. They were dirty, faded, but they were colored. He wore mostly amber with flecks of brown and green. There were no patterns or symbols, but that there was color at all, and they were not the tatters that Vaten and the other prisoners wore, was proof of the man's means.

Vaten stared at him, wondering how a man of wealth ended up captured and chained to a wagon. Regardless of the answer, he took solace the man was there. Even men bigger and richer than himself shared the same fate as him.

Vaten maneuvered the bag with his feet to his lap. He opened it with his teeth, holding the bag between his legs, then put his mouth over the opening and gulped the fluid. He didn't even check to ensure it was water. It was.

As he drank, Vaten thought of the words the man spoke. Not like the people who captured him—this man's rhythm and inflection were precise—but he had said 'Sol's sake.' Vaten hadn't heard the phrase since the estate. But his memories failed him, and he couldn't recall who said it or where the man was from. Somewhere south, he thought.

"Hey! Don't drink it all," the man who offered him the water said. "We don't get much water and we won't refill it until the next stop. Maybe longer."

Vaten swallowed. "Sorry, I haven't had anything to drink in more than a day."

"Get used to it," a different prisoner said. "You'll get a few sips of water a day and that's if you ration well. If you don't, you'll—."

"I told you to stop making noise! Last warning until I get Aloc over here to make sure you never make any noise again," the man walking next to the cart said.

Talking on the cart ceased. The man walking beside them gave them an approving look and then continued marching ahead.

The man who passed Vaten the satchel pointed at it, then at himself. Vaten nodded, sealed the pouch, and flicked it with his foot at the man. It landed between his legs. The man bowed his head. When it rose, he said, "I'm Levitien."

"I'm Vaten." The man next to him admonished Vaten with a stare.

Levitien put his hand over his mouth, miming silence. Vaten nodded once more and closed his mouth. He didn't need to find out the punishment for disobedience.

As the caravan continued to move south, days passed. The trees faded and gave way to mossy grass covering rocky hillsides. The rocky hillsides gave way to steep cliffs and jagged ridges.

It was the first time Vaten had glimpsed the Quimper Mountains at close range, and their beauty struck him. He finally believed all the stories of Entier, the mason who, like Vaten, lost his father when he was a boy. Only Entier went on to create these peaks rather than being captured.

As they traveled over ravines, around boulders the size of buildings, and next to cliff faces that seemed to have no end, Vaten wondered why there were no stories about those who created the paths. They were just as impressive.

It was the kind of thing he would say to Ajeau, who would undoubtedly have a story to explain it. "You haven't heard about Ophique? She carved her way through the mountains with an axe so the Balafre could escape the specters of the Tentir."

"That's not true," Vaten would say.

"Of course it is. I'll prove it. Let's climb the mountains right now! I'll show you their marks."

Then she would wait and watch, with a mischievous smile on her lips, as fear slowly grew in Vaten's eyes. Then she would laugh. "Gotcha!" she would say.

"Shut up, you did not. I knew you were lying."

And for the smallest moment, Vaten felt warm. Until he remembered it was a dream. The conversation never happened. He was alone, sitting in the same cart he had been in for weeks. And he may never see Ajeau again.

\*\*\*

THE CARAVAN CAME TO a stop on a narrow pass. A group of captors the prisoners had nicknamed 'riders,' simply because they always rode on a horse rather than walked, huddled together. Vaten could not hear their discussion, and he would not have understood their language even if he had, but he could see they were animated. Everyone seemed to point in different directions.

As Vaten continued to watch the debate, a stone jutting out from the steep cliff drew his eyes. It would not have looked out of place from a quick glance. But the more he stared at it, the more he became convinced it was incongruous to the surroundings.

A voice interrupted his thoughts. One of his abductors spoke. "You. All of you. We're camping here. Prepare to be moved to the ground."

As Vaten glanced back at the oddly shaped stone, he finally realized what about it caught his eye. A small strip of blue ran lengthwise around the center of the boulder. It was extraordinary and unnatural, but nearly imperceptible. And, Vaten thought, a familiar shade of blue.

"Hello again," a man said, chuckling. Vaten looked up to see the large man who had captured him. "No movements or speaking, or I will break your arm this time."

Vaten did as he was instructed.

The large man unchained Vaten, then carried him to a small circle drawn on the ground. The large man was so confident in his abilities, he hadn't even bothered to restrain Vaten for the walk.

Of course, there were no options for escape. The sides of the path were sheer cliffs and if Vaten ran on the path, he would have been seen easily and recaptured or killed. It was best to accept his fate.

The guards brought Vaten and the other prisoners to a small circle where they were bound together and then to the ground so tightly that they could barely move. A few paces away from them, one captor stood watch. His instructions were simple: "No one moves outside the circle." None of the prisoners asked what would happen if they did.

As the prisoners sat huddled together, trying to stay warm in the cooling air, Vaten noticed something strange. The number of people in the camp quickly thinned. It was not subtle either. The man watching the prisoners remained, but the caravan had lost nearly half its members. Even stranger were the ropes that now hung down the cliffsides.

Then he seemed to understand all at once. "Have they climbed the cliffs?" Vaten said.

The guard perked up but said and did nothing. He just stared at the prisoners with a hand on his sickle.

Vaten continued, "Why would they do that?"

For a long moment, no one said anything. Then Levitien broke the silence, "Who knows, kid? But it looks important. They took a lot of their hands with them."

"Yeah." Another man nodded. "I bet they're looking for the night's kiss."

A different prisoner laughed quietly and said, "Don't be ridiculous, that's just a myth. It's not true."

"What's the night's kiss?" Levitien asked.

"Oh, here we go."

"It's a flower that supposedly makes you ageless and unable to die, but it only blooms on the night of a red moon," Vaten answered.

"Haven't seen one of those." Levitien chuckled and looking up said, "And there's nothing red about tonight's high moons."

"It's a stupid story for children. It's not real."

"What about the wind petal?"

"A plant that allows you to fly? An even dumber story."

The banter ended. And now that they had spoken, and there had been no consequence, the prisoners felt emboldened to talk more. And as the night darkened, sporadic discussions rose and fell. There was only one topic on their minds though, their captors.

No one knew much for certain about them. Yes, they spoke a strange language, moved swiftly, and kept their prisoners alive. But Vaten knew all of that already.

What he didn't know was who they were, where they came from, and where they were taking the prisoners. They all had guesses or assumptions, but most were bleak and ended with them all dead or forced to serve some awful foreign lord. In some ways, it was a good thing no one knew for sure.

All the while they spoke, the man that guarded the prisoners continued to stare at them, his attention unwavering. And his hand never moved from the hilt of his sickle.

Soon, some prisoners fell asleep. Vaten would have joined them, but before his eyes could close, he heard Levitien's voice. "Hey kid? Vaten. They captured you in the Tentir, huh? What were you doing there?"

"What do you mean?" Vaten yawned. "I was travelling, heading north to look for something, when I was ambushed."

"You were heading north? To Oyonnax?" Levitien nodded slowly. "That's where I was when I was caught. What were you looking for?"

Vaten shrugged and shook his head. "What does it matter? I was looking for something. And I was heading north to Nouv'eau for help finding it."

"Oh, Nouv'eau? What's there?"

"I don't know. It was a guess. Maybe someone in Nouv'eau would know where to find my—" Vaten stopped speaking. He had not decided whether he would tell everything to this man who had suddenly taken a keen interest in him.

"Find what?"

Vaten hesitated, then said, "Someone I was looking for."

Levitien stared at him through narrowed eyes. "That person is in Nouv'eau?"

"No. Well, I don't know, he could be. The Noye took him and—"

"Ah, yes. The Noye. They looted villages in Versud too, though not in a while. But there's no Noye in Nouv'eau, you should know that. They get along about as well as two packs of wolves."

Vaten's heart skipped a beat. The man knew something about the Noye. If Vaten made it out of his imprisonment alive, Levitien might even help Vaten find his father. The chance was too great to lose, and Vaten abandoned his cautiousness.

"Well, we thought it a good place to get help. I was looking for my father. He was captured by the Noye not long after I was born. And I intend to make them pay for that," Vaten said with conviction. Then he sighed, "Or at least I did. But, what else do you know about the Noye?" Vaten leaned his head forward with anticipation.

"Your father? Hmm," Levitien said, still staring at Vaten. He paused a moment, then continued, "Not much. I suppose what everyone knows. They are wandering raiders. Or they were. Not too many around these days. I've heard they died off with the drought. I don't know if it's true but, I don't suppose they'd be easy for you to find."

Vaten nodded, discouraged. After a moment of quiet, he said, "You're from the South? What were you doing in V'eauvian territory?"

"I'm from the south. And I traveled north to find something too. I guess we have that in common." Levitien laughed, an infectious chuckle that reflexively brought a smile to Vaten's face.

Vaten pointed to Levitien's clothes and asked, "Are you a noble?"

"No, no." Levitien shook his head and held up his hands. "Not a noble. A humble steward like my father. We helped run crop and manage the estates. That was before the drought, though. The storehouses have been empty for a while. No Vizier can withstand that."

Vaten stared at Levitien, wondering what the man meant. Not about the drought or the storehouses, but about the Viziers. He should have known they prevailed despite it all.

But before he could ask a question, Levitien said, "Time for me to get some rest, kid."

After a few slow blinks, Levitien fell asleep. Vaten followed soon thereafter.

*** 

VATEN AWOKE TO A commotion in the camp. The sun hadn't yet completed its climb over the mountains, but the caravan appeared back to its original size. Those who left so suddenly had returned.

There were celebrations among the camp's members. They embraced each other as if they won a hard fought battle. But Vaten saw no wounds, no injured fighters, no evidence of a battle at all.

What he saw were two men moving something draped in black cloth. It was impossible to tell what was under the cloth, but Vaten knew from the smiles on his captors' faces, it was valuable.

Vaten threw dirt to wake up the other prisoners. "Hey. They're back."

"What?" one prisoner groaned. "Who?"

"The camp. The camp is back to full," Levitien said. "And it looks like whatever they did was a success."

"They're carrying something. Can anyone see?" Vaten asked.

"It's something round, but it also has points. Think it's an ox or stag's head or something?"

"No, no way. Too small and too many things poking out. They're not antlers. Plus, I don't see blood anywhere."

The object, covered in its sheet, continued to be paraded through the camp. All who observed it reveled in its glory.

"I think they're putting it in the boxes from their carts. Maybe they'll bring it past us," one prisoner said.

The man was right, at least about the boxes. Their captors put whatever they found in boxes and then walked each box securely towards the cart as though they were full of glass.

Not only did they revere the object, but it was fragile. They wanted to take care of it and ensure its survival. Vaten wondered if it was alive.

The guard who had watched them overnight loomed over them. "No more talking," he said. "We are moving on. You will be loaded back on your cart. No movements."

In a series of coordinated movements that reminded Vaten of birds' murmuration, the guards hauled the prisoners back on the cart, bound them once more, and then stood beside them. A few moments later, the caravan began moving. As it did, Vaten imagined what he might find if ever looked under the black cloth. None of the images gave him any hope.

# CHAPTER 6

THE THIEVES HAD HUNG from the trees for less than two days before the vultures began to circle and take their meal, the smell of decaying flesh leading them to their prize. The squawking and pecking upset the workers who saw it, but that was the purpose of the display. Yes, the message had been sent; if you steal from the Foreman, you will end up as feed for the carrion.

With no more use for the bodies, Crevir sent his guards to remove them from the trees the next day. Savique and many other workers watched as the guards fished the remains down from the branches, then hauled them off to be salted so that their flesh could not return and nurture the soil that had sustained them. There was no greater insult, but thieves were not offered mercy in life or in death. And no one would be foolish to demand otherwise.

But Savique knew those in the trees were not wicked nor malicious. They were not raiders looking to enrich themselves or ruin Crevir and his estate. They were workers who wanted to see their friends, families, and any fellow hand, have enough to eat. "That benefits the estate," Savique could hear the small woman say.

When it was done, after guards loaded the bodies onto the wagon and pulled it out of sight, Savique lingered. Even after the light of day faded, Savique remained staring at the now dark grove.

It was not sadness or anger that kept him there. No, it was duty. He was alive, and the rest were dead, so he gave them what he could. A vigil. There was no reason he should remain standing while all those around him fell to the earth.

*You will lose much...* The words of the Ascetics burst into his mind like they were a seed planted there, ready to sprout on such an occasion. *All happens with purpose*, the voices continued. Savique grabbed and shook his head. Nonsense!

A rage sparked in his gut. The Ascetics had the impudence to talk of purpose as a child lost his mother, as friends died to save their kin, as righteous men and women scraped and clawed only so they would not starve. He wanted to scream, but knew he would be the only one to hear the words.

Instead, he hung his head and decided there was no purpose to it. He was alive because of chance. Coincidence alone. There was nothing more to believe in.

As a deep, dark night descended around him, Savique felt the ground shake under his feet. He steadied himself and wondered what madness approached now.

*** 

"The Noye ride for the western fields," Vrai said.

Foreman Crevir stood in his residence across from the Captain of his guard and felt the ground rumble. He watched the pictures on his wall shake. The jewels on his table clinked and the padded chair rattled against the wooden floor. He scowled. All the luxuries he had procured—the fine food and drink, the jewels, the rare games, the lavish cloth—were under threat.

He felt the ground rumble again. But this time, it did not stop. It only grew louder and stronger, like the sound of the thunderous rivers that flooded during the wet season.

"And? What are we to do?" Crevir replied, sharply.

"You won't like what I have to say."

"Out with it!" Crevir waved his hands, gesturing for Vrai's words. "We don't have much time before those barbarians arrive. I want a plan."

"We should let them have it."

Crevir scowled at Vrai. "Let them have the western fields? In their entirety?" He clenched his fist. "Do you plough in circles?"

"No, sir." Vrai shook his head. "But the Noye are likely here for the yields. They—"

"I know what they are here for!" Spit flew from his mouth as he spoke. "The bastards want to rob us. I will not allow that."

"Sir, if we let them take the crop, we won't—"

"No." Crevir slammed his fist on a table, causing his ivory cups and bowls to rattle. A bit of wine spilled. Even if he had noticed it, Crevir would not have cared. "That is unacceptable. We will not reward their raids with our harvest. We are not cowards!"

"No sir. But the Noye are formidable fighters. If we rally the guard to meet them, we will lose many. And there is no assurance we would be victorious."

Crevir moved to a chair and sat. If Vrai was right and the Noye defeated his guards in battle, the estate would be in chaos. They would lose the crops anyway and the Noye might even burn the entire place to the ground as they did in Lavieux.

Yet, he could not present the harvest of the western fields to the raiders. There was not enough in the stores to replenish their supply. And he could only restrict the workers' meals so much. At some point, they would stop working because of poor treatment or exhaustion.

Crevir rubbed at a bead of sweat forming on his forehead and closed his eyes. He implored himself to think of some way to avert the oncoming disaster.

Vrai paced in front of Crevir. "Sir, they are—"

"Allow me a moment!"

Crevir watched Vrai walk to the window and stare at the black fields beyond. The man crossed his arms behind him and stuck out his chest.

Then, in a quick burst, Vrai turned back to Crevir. "Sir, I have a new idea."

"I said I am trying—" Crevir stopped himself and shook his head. "What? What is it?"

"If they ride to the western fields, perhaps we can direct them to the edge of the barley. There would be nothing there for them to steal—"

"Yes," Crevir said with a sigh. "And then they would simply turn and make their way in deeper until they found something worth taking." His voice grew in frustration.

Vrai held up his hand. "Not if we lit a row or two on fire. That would—"

"Now you want to burn the fields?" Crevir breathed deeply. Then yelled, "Why not the entire estate then? Or should we just cede it to the raiders without a fight?"

Vrai bowed his head. "No, sir, not the entire field. A row or two at most. So the flames lie against the aqueduct." He raised his head. "Don't you see? It would trap them. They would have to either retreat or risk riding through the fire."

Crevir pursed his lips together, then glanced at the ceiling. He opened his mouth, then closed it and stood. He took a deep breath and exhaled. It was a show; he had already decided the plan was a good one. A great one. It would stem the losses—both in guards and in crops—the estate would suffer. And the barley that was lost could be seeded to grow again in the next harvest.

"It is an interesting plan." Crevir rubbed his forefinger against his thumb. "And how would you direct them to where the barley grows?"

"The guards will flank them as they ride in." Vrai described the action with his hands. "From inside the camp. They can remain hidden until the Noye break the line of the fields. Then they emerge and drive them south. It should require little direct fighting."

Yes, it was an excellent plan, Crevir told himself. There was a reason Vrai had been his captain for so long. The man was smart. He could think himself out of a noose. But the man would likely never find himself caught in one.

"And if they want the camp," Crevir said, knowing Vrai would have an answer.

"Yes. And they may put torch to some huts, but they are not here for the camp. We both know that much."

Crevir could not help letting a smile walk across his lips.

"You are right. And your plan is sound. Now let us gather the guards and send these bastard Noye back to whatever plague-infested pit they call home."

Vrai and Crevir left the Foreman's residence and mounted their horses. Crevir rode to the northern end of the estate while Vrai rode to the southern end. They would gather all the guards stationed at every outpost. Then, they would meet in the middle of the camp on the edge of the western field. If they rode swiftly enough, they could beat the raiders there.

And, for a moment, when they arrived at the camp, that is what Crevir thought; they had beaten the Noye and now only needed to wait for them to appear.

Guards sat atop their horses with their spears pointed towards the sky, ready to meet the assailants. Bowmen stood beside them with their arrows notched. They all waited to hear Crevir's call. But no call ever came.

The Noye never appeared. Not a single one. And the hoofbeats that once sounded so close receded into the distance and then disappeared.

Crevir turned to Vrai and said, "Strange. It is quiet. Are you sure they rode to the western field?"

"Yes," Vrai said, craning his head in all directions. "That is what the scouts told me."

51

"Then where are the Noye? I know better than to think they retreat." Crevir joined Vrai in scanning the area for any sign of their foes. "Do you believe they wait us out?"

"Perhaps. If they saw our approach to the camp, they may have double backed and—"

"Sirs!" A scout ran up to Crevir and Vrai. "Noye have been seen riding through the eastern field!"

"What?" Crevir's body tensed and the veins in his neck bulged. He turned to Vrai, shaking with rage. "The eastern fields? They will sack our wheat or pulses or—"

"No." Vrai said, a smile flickering on the edges of his lips. "They cannot be allowed to raid the eastern fields. Guards—"

"What is your plan now?" Crevir asked.

"Now, we must fight." He angled his spear forward towards the eastern fields. "We must protect our crop. There is no other option." His tone was flat, uninspired.

Crevir nodded, then glanced at the men and women around him. "You are all heroes tonight," he said. "Drive off this pestilence and find extra bread and wine in your rations!"

Men and women pounded their spears and feet on the ground in support.

Crevir smiled. "Now, follow your Captain! To glory!"

The horde of guards rode through the camp back towards the eastern fields. Their hooves rocked the earth. The thunderous sound woke the camp with fear that the world itself was being torn apart.

As the guards arrived in the eastern field, they encountered only a handful of Noye. And, to their surprise, the raiders seemed uninterested in battle and even less interested in the crops below them. Instead, they rode swiftly away from the estate.

"We have scared them off!" Crevir yelled to a raucous cheer as the final Noye rode out of sight.

For a moment, he thought about sending his guard after them. He could make an example of the heathens, he thought, and teach them never to return to his land.

But he didn't. He had won against the mighty Noye and he would have to be satisfied his fields remained unplundered and he and his guards remained alive. If the Noye returned, he would be ready.

Then he felt a tap on his shoulder. He turned to meet Vrai's face, a scowl plastered on it. He saw the man's outstretched arm pointing at a small light in the distance.

"What is..." Crevir began, but before he finished the thought, he knew what it was.

He could only look on in horror as his residence went up in flames.

***

SAVIQUE HEARD CRUNCHING AND creaking noises coming from the grove. He walked forward and peered between the trees, but saw nothing in the darkness. The world had stopped rumbling, but now something was in the wood. And it sounded as though it was coming toward him.

He backed away, his hands shaking, and then turned to run. As he did, the noise stopped. Savique froze and glanced around. Then, after another moment of silence, he chuckled to himself. He had let a bird or a rat terrify him. He shook his head, picked up a rock, and hurled into the trees. Then he turned and walked back to his hut.

A moment later, something hit him on the shoulder. He glanced down and saw it was a small rock. He was not sure, but it appeared to be the one he had thrown. His body tensed. Birds and rats did not throw stones.

He turned around and found himself looking at with a tall woman wearing a green cloak riding a horse. In the darkness, against the wooded background, she looked nearly invisible.

What he could see—metal glistening in the moonlight—disconcerted him. She held a spear in her hands and a dagger and a sickle hung around her hips. On her back, looped through her arms, was a small wooden shield.

Savique knew immediately she was Noye. The green robe, the weapons, the woman's height, and she sat on a horse. There was no doubt. His heart rose into his throat, his breath became ragged, his world spun.

Savique had heard stories of the Noye. They stole without mercy, took food from the starving. They burnt entire villages and camps to the ground to get what they wanted. If you valued your life, you stayed out of their way. Even that was not always enough.

He thought about running, but his legs shook, and his feet were fixed to the ground. He was as likely to move as the trees in the grove.

"W-What do you want with me?" Savique said.

"You, *cochon*?" The Noye woman shook her head. "Whatever would I want with you?"

"I-I don't know."

"If you don't know, then surely I don't either, *cochon*." A quick smile flashed across her face.

There was that word again, cochon. Savique wondered what it meant and whether it portended good or bad.

He swallowed loudly. "Then what do you want?"

The woman laughed in short staccato bursts. "I want many things. I want the sun to rise. I want the rain to fall. I want the crops to grow. I want the horse to run. I want the spear strong. I want—"

"I mean, why are you here? Tonight," Savique said, concerned she would list everything she had ever wanted. "Why are you attacking us?"

"We are not attacking you, cochon. We are here for what is ours."

"What is yours? The food here is ours." Savique brought a hand to his chest. "The wine and water, too. We work hard—"

"You misunderstand me. We do not come to steal from you. The Foreman and Vizier take enough from you." The woman spit on the ground. "We are here for a gift. Something the Foreman stole. It is important to us and will provide us direction in the years to come. You will know that too soon enough, but not yet. Only when the time is right."

Savique shook his head. "I don't understand."

"Of course. You are not meant to. Not now. There is simply no time." She picked her head up and gazed at the fields. She squinted and leaned forward, then nodded. Without glancing back at him, she said, "It is time for me to leave. I will explain more when we meet again."

"What? We will see each other again?"

"Oh, yes." The Noye smiled. "The winds that blow will not always propel the Foreman. They will hinder him too. I do not know when, but our paths will cross again. And do not forget to enjoy the warmth by the fire tonight." She laughed loudly as the horse reared on hind legs and roared.

Savique thought the horse laughed too. At what, he wondered. But before he could speak, the Noye was gone and with her, any chance of answers.

Except he solved one of her riddles when, later that night, he saw the Foreman's residence ablaze. *Enjoy the warmth of the fire.* She had told the truth. He wondered what else she knew.

***

IN THE WANING DARKNESS before morning, a woman atop a horse galloped quickly through the grasslands. Within moments, other horses with men and women atop them surrounded the woman.

She was unbothered by their presence, for they were like her, armed and dressed in green. They were her brothers and sisters. And they all continued to ride through grasslands, around trees, and over streams. They did not slow or stop. They rode as though they were being chased, but no one was behind them.

When they reached a small unassuming clearing in the woods, they dismounted and embraced each other. They patted and rubbed their horses proudly with radiant smiles stretching their mouths wide. With fists clenched and shaking, they rolled their heads to the sky and celebrated as though they were the heroes in the stories they had been told.

A man was there too. He had waited for their arrival and though he was not dressed in green like the others; he was every bit their brother.

One woman took something out of a sack. She held it in front of the others and their excitement grew. There were more smiles and more embraces. The cheers now would have been audible to anyone else nearby. No one was.

The woman with the object then raised it up towards the waning moons as if it was an offering. But she only inspected it. Such a powerful object in such a small box. It was magnificent.

Then, as if she had gleaned the information she desired, she lowered the box and turned to the man not dressed in green. She bowed her head and said, "Thank you, Vrai. Without you..." She did not need to finish her sentence. Everyone knew.

He did not respond to her, but bowed his head. A sign of respect and modesty. He had only done his duty, his responsibility. It was why he was there.

But that night was the culmination of many days and nights' work. Without Vrai, there was no raid. There was no box. There was no direction or purpose to come. He may have been modest, but the Elders knew what he had done. What he had given up. His sacrifice for their success would never be forgotten.

A woman asked, "And the other? Is he here?"

"Not yet," a man replied.

"Do you believe what the Ascetics say?" the woman asked Vrai. "I am to understand you heard them."

"I did. The words are those you know, but whether they are truth..." Vrai shrugged.

"No matter," a different woman said. "He is not here. And we have what we need. Let us discover its purpose. If the Ascetics' words become real, then so be it."

"Yes. For now, we will return to our tribes," the woman with the box said. "We will let fate take its turn. Keep your eyes on the trees. I will see you all again soon."

The riders embraced each other once more. Then they mounted their horses and rode in different directions. Nearly imperceptible to all but the closest observers were strange symbols carved into the trees. The riders darted past the symbols, noting them as they did.

Two riders, a man and a woman, rode together, then eventually separated. They said no words as they did, but they understood each other. One rode north back to an estate. The other rode east to wait for a sign. To wait until she met the mason again.

# CHAPTER 7

AJEAU WALKED THROUGH BRONZED shrubs and over collapsed trees. She tore at vines that turned to dust in her hand. She licked droplets of water from dead leaves. She slept on branches that barely supported her dwindling weight. She followed paths and wandered away from them. But throughout it all, she kept telling herself, get to Nouv'eau. And find Vaten.

One day, while walking, Ajeau heard a wondrous sound. Trickling water. It was faint and pulsed in and out of her awareness. But she resolved to find its source. So she devised a crude, if not tedious, plan.

She would take a few steps and then listen. If the sound was weaker, she would take a step in a different direction, then listen again. If the sound was stronger, she would continue in that direction. Ajeau repeated the practice again and again with the hope she would eventually find water.

It took nearly two days for her to find the stream. But when she did, she nearly wept.

She had exhausted her supplies long ago and had survived on insects, leaves, and the occasional nut or seed. And though the forest's never-ending reach demoralized her at every turn, the stream revitalized her, both in body and spirit. She drank, of course, but also found tadpoles trapped in pools and stores of berries among its banks. Perhaps best of all, she now had a direction. She could follow the stream out of the forest.

Though she would have loved more time to rest alongside the water, she would not delay her travels more than necessary. She regained her strength and replenished her supplies, but once they were full, she followed the stream wherever it would lead.

Before she saw the sunset, the water had run dry. It did not surprise her; the drought dried everything. And she could still follow the indentation the river left in the earth.

But then she ran out of food and water. After another few days, she became unsteady on her feet. The world spiraled around her, and she no longer had any sense of direction. Even as her legs became cut and bruised from the undergrowth, she forced herself onwards alongside the riverbed.

Until she saw something in the forest. A young man moving between the trees. He turned and glanced in her direction. She recognized him immediately, and her heart sang with joy.

"Vaten!" she called. "Vaten! I can't believe I found you."

The young man stared at her as though he did not recognize her.

"Vaten, it's me! Ajeau. Are you alright?"

The young man turned his back and walked away from her. He made no sound.

"Vaten!" Ajeau followed him. "Say something. Anything. Please."

He moved faster—too fast for her to keep up—and fell in and out of view. Then, a moment later, he was gone. Except for a gentle breeze, the forest was still.

"Vaten!"

When Ajeau spun around she saw only forest, only the same tree repeating as if planted everywhere, forever. The dried riverbed that would deliver her from the Tentir was nowhere to be found. She was lost.

She ran a few frantic steps in one direction, then another. She put her hands on her head and closed her eyes. Her breathing labored. She sat on the ground to catch her breath. That was all it was. She was not giving up, she only needed to rest. A brief rest and then she would be ready to walk to...wherever it was she was going. She would remember that too, when she woke.

If it were not for a man foraging near his hut, she would never have opened her eyes again.

***

AJEAU AWOKE IN A dark hut with an unfamiliar man by her side. It was night, and the man was asleep, but she could see an outline of his body through the darkness. She was too tired and weak to move or worry about where she was. Even though she had just woken, her body craved more sleep. And she surrendered.

When Ajeau woke again, she was alone. And in the light of day, the hut appeared less threatening. She noticed a bowl next to her head and a small pile of nuts on a stump by her feet. Some kind of animal skin covered her shins and knees. It was soft but provided resistance as she tried to move. That she could move at all was a good sign. She was healing.

Whether because the man she had seen in the night assisted her, cared for her, or not, she did not know. But someone had taken her to the hut and laid out the food and drink for her. She knew that much and was grateful for it.

Ajeau stretched and found she was no longer exhausted and weak. Her legs were sore but alive, not the unstable stalks she had dragged through the forest. And her stomach didn't burn with hunger or thirst.

Then, she had a most hopeful thought. Perhaps she was out of the forest. Yes, she was in a hut. And no one built huts in the Tentir. She had food and water as though it was a home. No one would make their home in such a place.

But when she sat up and glanced out the window, she saw only trees, bushes, and vines. It was the same view that had followed her for months, maybe longer. Her head dropped. The woods were not done with her yet.

Trapped, doomed to walk the forest forever, she would never make it to Nouv'eau and never find Vaten. She clenched her fists and screamed. No words, not at anyone, just rage hurled into the world.

A moment later, a man hurried into the hut, holding vines, leaves, and bark. "Are you all right?" he asked her.

Ajeau stared at the unfamiliar man in front of her. He was lean—she could make out the sinews holding his body together—as though he had not eaten in ages. His hair was bonded together in clumps, his beard uneven. He wore tatters, barely anything above his waist, though leather moccasins covered his feet.

She eyed him. "Who are you?"

"My name is Seule." He continued to walk to her side. "Are you all right? What was that yell?"

"Yes," Ajeau said. "I'm fine. It was nothing." She watched him sit down next to her. "Seule, are you the one who took me here and bandaged my legs? Did you give me food and drink?"

He smiled and nodded. "Yes. I did those things. I found you very near death in the forest during a forage and brought you here nearly a week ago. You—"

"A week?"

"Yes, like I said, you were unwell. I couldn't wake you. Your breath was very shaky. So, I carried you back to my hut. Here," he said, gesturing to the surrounding walls.

"And you fed me?"

"Of course! I could not let you die in my hut. I wrapped your injuries and gave you some tea. But you spit it and shook so violently. It made me very nervous. After that first night, though, you settled, and I heard you talking about someone."

Ajeau furrowed her brow. "Who?"

"A...Vaten? I think that is what you said." He shook his head and shrugged. "But you smiled after calling for him. I thought it was a good sign."

Ajeau glanced away from Seule's eyes. She wondered what she had said in her sleep and what else he might know about her. Anything was unsettling.

Even if Seule appeared friendly and had saved her life, she did not know what he wanted in return. Until she knew why he did what he did, she wanted to keep as much from him as possible.

Seule continued, "I gave you more food and water and tea and every night you got a little better. Your breath came back strong, your rest was calmer, you stopped shaking, and your cuts even began to heal." He began unwrapping the skins that had covered them.

Ajeau remembered the gashes and bruises littering her legs. Now, she saw scabs and scars.

Seule pointed, nodded at her, and said, "See." He smiled softly at her, revealing long wrinkles around his eyes and mouth. "And today you woke up." He recovered her legs with the skins, then sat with his hand on his lap.

"Thank you," she said. "I don't know what to say. You saved my life. Provided me food and water from your supplies. But..." Ajeau shook her head. "Why?"

"Because your life needed saving."

Ajeau's eyes narrowed. "And that's it?"

He glanced at the ceiling of his hut and scratched a clump of hair. "Yes, I think that's it. Life is a valuable thing. It must be cultivated and nurtured, much like a tree." He gestured behind him, outside the hut. "There is too much death in the world now. I saw a chance to restore life rather than let it expire. That was enough for me."

"But what if I meant to do you harm?"

Seule chuckled. "You are not as tough as you look. I think I could protect myself. And if not, then that is my fate. I would return to the soil and nurture the forest. Cultivating more life."

Ajeau frowned at him, confused. His kindness was strange, like those colorful butterflies on the estate. They were too fragile to survive. Yet, they did. And like those butterflies, she didn't think such things could exist before she saw them with her own eyes.

"All right. Thank you. I mean that genuinely." Ajeau bowed her head. "But how can I repay you that debt?"

"No. No. There is no repayment needed." He laughed through his nose. "I am happy my supplies didn't go to waste."

A calm filled the hut. Ajeau lay back down on the ground, closed her eyes, and breathed a sigh of relief. She was still in the forest, but at least she had someone to talk to and help her. It was an unexpected piece of luck.

Seule stood up and walked to the doorway. Before leaving, he turned and said, "I rushed back so soon after hearing your screams, I forgot to bring in our latest haul." When he returned, he held a handful of small yellow fruits that resembled tiny apples. "*Pouple*!" he said. "We are living good fortune today."

Ajeau and Seule shared a snack of the pouple and water. The fruits energized Ajeau, and for a moment, she thought she could stand. She felt strong and knew the only way out of this place was to walk.

But as soon as she rose to her feet, she fell back to the earth. It was as demoralizing as it was embarrassing. There would be no quick recovery for her. It would require patience. She hated that.

"Do not rush these things," Seule said, patting her shoulder. "Slow progress. That way, you will be able to walk without exhausting yourself again. You do not want to end up on the ground as when I found you."

Ajeau let out a frustrated sigh and said nothing.

Seule took a bite of fruit, chewed it loudly, then swallowed it. He rubbed his stomach. "Mmm," he said. "I was like you once too, excitable and—"

"I don't think you know me at all. You don't even know my name."

Seule smiled and nodded. "Then maybe you want to share it?"

Ajeau sighed. "Ajeau."

"Very unique. V'eauvian?"

She nodded.

"Interesting," Seule said. "How does a young V'eauvian woman find herself near death in the Tentir?"

At first, Ajeau said nothing. But then she decided there was no harm in letting the old man know about her travels. She did not have to reveal every detail, but she did not need to lie, either. Partial truths would suffice.

She told him she traveled with Vaten to help him find his father and about the assault in the forest. Afterwards, she wandered in search of help. "I found that, I guess," she said, smiling for the first time since Vaten had been taken.

Seule nodded. "Ah, so there is a reason you are rushing. This man, he is your partner?"

"Friend," she said. "Almost family. We've known each other since we were young."

"Wonderful!" He put his hands up in the air. Then he let them fall back onto his lap. "Not about his capture, of course—I hope he returns to you soon. But it is good that you two vagrants survived together this long. Most—"

"No, no. We are not wanderers like that." She paused, thinking perhaps they were. "We grew up on an estate together, but we left a long time ago."

"You left an estate? In this drought?" Seule's eyes grew big and he leaned forward. "What were you thinking?"

Ajeau shook her head. "We had to. The place had become a nightmare. He—" Ajeau stopped herself. No matter how much she trusted Seule, she would not reveal the Foreman's name to him. It would be too dangerous. "The drought did not spare us on the estates. People starved even before we left."

"On the estates too?" His voice grew somber. "I thought the supplies would last the worker for, I don't know, but longer than this. So many will..." He closed his eyes and rested his forehead on his hands. Without looking up, he said, "Tragic."

"I know. It is like Eau has abandoned us forever."

"No." Seule's head jerked up. "I don't believe that. They have always come back before. Maybe they have been led from our world. It is not unlike the story of Olemic. Have you heard it?"

Ajeau shook her head. "No."

"Too bad. It is a good one and I am not a storyteller." Seule sat up straight. "But, in it, Olemic is told she must protect Eau's son Zerois from Pyrale, the source of all blight. You've heard of him, right?"

"Yes. Of course."

Seule nodded. "Good. Pyrale wants to kill Zerois to take his place and unleash chaos on the world, but he cannot overcome the great Olemic. At all turns, the great light thwarts Pyrale. So he hatches a devious plan to lead Olemic into the cave of the unending serpent.

"Pyrale challenges Olemic to illuminate the cave. If she can, he will stop his pursuit of Zerois and submit to her forever. Olemic agrees and brings light to each part of the cave. But as she traverses its endless tunnels, she gets lost and cannot find her way out.

"Pyrale seizes on this opportunity and captures Zerois. He takes Zerois' place and spreads blight everywhere. Eau's world is ruined forever."

"Not a cheerful story, is it?" Ajeau said with a smirk.

Seule smiled and held up his hand. "I am not done yet. Olemic, aided by the serpent herself, eventually escapes the cave. She is too late to save Zerois, but she confronts Pyrale. She has lit the cave, so he must relent and submit. With him defeated, her light drives the blight from the world. Eau's world is reborn, ready for her second son."

Seule stared at Ajeau as though he were expecting some ovation. When none came, he said, "Well, there is far more action in it when performed by the tellers."

"But what does that have to do with the drought?" Ajeau said.

"Maybe nothing." Seule shrugged. "But see, even things led astray can find their way back. Olemic returns and so can the rain. So will Eau. Their world is not yet ruined."

"I don't know. If you had seen what I saw, you might not believe in old fables," Ajeau said.

"I have seen much and I believe in much too," Seule said, his tone serious. "It is the reason I believe in the old fables."

Ajeau remained quiet. She did not find Seule's belief surprising, even if she did not share it. She had seen the stories give hope and purpose to those on the estate. But Ajeau never found solace in any story. They had not saved her before and were not saving her now.

And she knew that was because the stories were not for her. No, she was not Eau's second son. She was their first. Abandoned, unprotected, and disposed of. The world was not reborn for her and there was no place for her in it.

Seule noticed the change in Ajeau's expression. "What is the matter? Are you ill? Are the pouple rotten?"

"No." Ajeau's voice was quiet. "Nothing is the matter. Everything is as it should be."

Seule only stared at her in response.

His glance felt like the gaze of a thousand eyes, every one of them scrutinizing her for some flaw she tried desperately to hide. She would never let them see what she knew; she had no people, no place, and no purpose. She belonged nowhere.

So, to distract the onlookers, she turned their attention onto the only other person with her. "You haven't told me what you are doing out here alone in the forest?"

Seule's eyes fell from Ajeau to the ground. His words were barely audible. "Making amends."

"To who? For what?"

"That...that is a story for another time." He rose and walked from the hut.

# CHAPTER 8

THE CARAVAN CELEBRATED. THEY descended the mountains while men and women sung, danced, and embraced one another. It was not garish, the caravan still moved with efficiency, but the mood was jubilant.

The prisoners watched with curious interest. Not only were the songs and dances unfamiliar to them, but the attitude among their captors was strange, too. Once they had walked beside the carts with an unshakeable focus, never a step out of line. Now, they were laughing, smiling, and clapping each other on the back. It was like seeing a snake walk upright.

Not that the change in temperament was unpleasant. The guards were more lenient with the prisoners. Rations had increased, threats of violence and harm had decreased, and talking was now permissible. The prisoners were still chained, but their days improved. Even Vaten's arm no longer hurt.

All enjoyed the improved treatment, save for Levitien, who seemed to greet the change with suspicion rather than appreciation. The man was a hawk and remained vigilant of the guards' movements, their lapses and missteps too.

After a few days of this, Levitien started to scratch light marks into the wood of the cart with his fingernails and mouth words to himself under his breath. He furrowed his brow intensely, as if he was in some great debate with himself.

As night fell on the caravan and the prisoners ate their daily rations, Levitien finally spoke to his fellow captives. "It is odd, good, but odd. Since they found—whatever they found up there in the mountains—the guards have become careless. At least far more often than before."

"Yeah, they are finally giving us a little time to ourselves," one prisoner said with a chuckle.

"What do you think they found up there?" another prisoner asked.

"I'm not interested in what they found," Levitien said. "It could be something they use in one of their rituals for all I know. It doesn't matter what it is, I only care about what it means for us."

"More food?" Another chuckle.

"Yes, and a chance to escape." Levitien met each prisoner's eyes to show them he was not joking.

The other prisoners glanced at each other warily.

"It is impossible," one man said. "We are bound and watched. They are armed and stronger and—"

"And no one would take us in," another continued. "Where would we go?"

"At least we have food and water here. I'd rather live than take a chance running."

"This is not a life," Levitien said. He held up his hands to show the ropes holding them. "They control everything we do. And you wish to surrender to that fate?"

The caravan went quiet.

Vaten locked eyes with Levitien and felt the man's confidence radiate through him. They had a chance. Levitien was not just saying it, he believed it. And if he believed it, then perhaps it was possible. Could they escape?

At first, it was only a nagging question. But it didn't stop. And the more Vaten thought about it, the more the question became a statement: they *could* escape.

After all, Levitien was savvy and strong. He was a steward. And though that did not mean he was beyond all scrutiny, it carried weight. A steward would not throw his life away on a foolish gamble. If he said they had a chance, then they did.

And if they escaped, Vaten could find Ajeau and resume the search for his father. Dreams and possibilities Vaten had extinguished at his capture roared back to him. They flooded his mind with images of reunions and vengeance. He smiled. *They could escape.*

Before anyone else could break the silence, Vaten said, "How do we do it? Do you have a plan?"

"See, even the kid's with me," Levitien said, admonishing the others as much as praising Vaten. "Here's the way I see it. The guards have been...unstable the past several nights. Even now, we can speak because they're too loud and too busy with their celebrations."

The men looked around and saw he was correct.

"So, how do we escape? What do we do?" Vaten said.

Levitien smiled at Vaten. "We start a fight."

"What?"

"You want to fight us?" a different prisoner said. "How is—"

"It won't be real," Levitien said. "It's a ruse."

Vaten shook his head. "I still don't understand. How will a fake fight help us escape?"

The third prisoner's eyes opened wide, and he nodded as he began to understand. "Because it will bring the guards to us."

"Right." Levitien pointed at the man. "The guards will come to us—"

"We don't want them to come to us if we are trying to escape," the first prisoner said.

"Shut up and let me explain. When we fight, guards will come. When they come, we will throw this in their eyes." Levitien grabbed a handful of dirt from the ground.

"Blind them," Vaten said.

"That's right. They won't be able to see a thing. And while they are blind, we will lift their blades from their sheaths and cut their legs so they can't follow," Levitien said.

The third prisoner nodded. "And we'll have the blades to cut us free of the ropes."

"Now you see it." Levitien nodded. "Once we're free, we run fast and far in whatever direction has cover. I assume you—"

"What if they call for someone?" the first prisoner asked.

"The sound of their celebrations will make it hard for them to hear," Vaten said. "The calls might not be heard."

"And if they are heard?"

"We will move quickly," Levitien said. "Even if they call out, we'll be free before anyone can get to us."

The prisoners glanced at each other in silence. That was the plan. No one knew whether it would work, but at least one of them believed in it. Vaten would've agreed to nearly any plan. He was already living in the fantasies of his freedom, ones he once thought impossible.

"I'm in," Vaten said.

"That's right, kid." Levitien nodded at him. "The rest?"

"You're crazy." The first prisoner shook his head. "It'll never work."

"I don't—"

"It will!" Vaten scowled at the man. "And it's our only chance. You've seen the guards. They've been falling over themselves with whatever they're drinking."

"What do you know? You're no bigger than a sprout. I'd rather stay here and live."

Vaten drew in a breath sharply. "With these monsters? Levitien has a good plan. Do what he says and we can be free. Are you that—"

"All right, look," Levitien said, trying to soothe the rising tension. "I don't know where we're going. Or what they're going to do with us. Servitude, torture, sacrifice, who knows? I don't want to find out, though. I want to get out of here. And this is our chance."

It broke the last of the resistance. To be against the plan—to stay—meant damning them all to a horrific fate. And no one wanted that. It was deeply convincing, so much so that no one recognized the deception.

"Well, he's right about the drinking and the noise," the third prisoner said with a slight shrug of his shoulders. "They've been loud and clumsy the past few days… All right. I'm in too."

"Yup," another prisoner said.

The first prisoner glanced at the rest. But then he sighed and said, "Fine. But I'm not fighting."

"Then you two." Levitien pointed at the other two prisoners. "You grab the dagger and cut them. Once they can't follow, you cut us free. You can do that?"

The men nodded.

Levitien continued, "I'm the last one to go. It's my plan and I'll make sure the rest of you made it out safely. I'll watch over the kid too."

"And when will we…" Vaten said, eagerly.

"The next night they are drunk, we will be free," Levitien said with a glint in his eye.

Vaten had no reservations. The plan would work. It was a certainty. And having Levitien with him felt even more reassuring. Vaten thought, it must be how a son feels when his father protects him from the dangers of the world. If only he knew.

***

A FEW DAYS AFTER they had agreed to the plan, not yet a week since the caravan descended the mountains, the prisoners moved through a withered field under moons that seemed brighter than the sun. Eventually, the caravan came to a stop, and they set up camp. As the guards moved them from the cart, Levitien smiled at the other prisoners and nodded. Tonight was the night.

As the captors continued their triumphant celebrations, the prisoners sat on the ground antsy and jittery. Their fingers twitched and legs shook. They glanced too often at each other. Vaten's stomach ached, and he worried he would be sick and his vomit would ruin the plan. Even Levitien, who had seemed so sure of his idea, chewed on his lips, as nervous as the rest of them.

Screams broke the quiet of the night. It took a moment—a moment where his heart did not beat—for Vaten to realize they were shouts of delight. They emanated from a fire some ways from the prisoners. One guard wandered to see what the commotion was about, leaving only a single woman to guard them.

Vaten smiled and glanced at the other prisoners. Their eyes met his with the same knowing smile. It appeared they shared the same thought; only a single guard now. It was perfect.

Levitien seized the moment. Before anyone could think otherwise, before the guard who left could turn around, Levitien said, "Now."

In an instant, the man next to Vaten and the one across from him started yelling frantically and grappling with each other. It was convincing. They kicked each other then punched, then Vaten thought he saw one bite the other.

The more Vaten watched, the more he panicked. His heart in his throat was the only thing keeping the bile down. He peeked at Levitien for some reassurance but found him staring at the two men with a blank face.

The guard watching them let the melee go on for a bit. Then she rose and shouted at the prisoners, "Enough. Stop. Stop! Or I will end your fighting for good."

Like a reflex, the prisoners stopped fighting. They glanced at each other, and after a moment of shared understanding, continued.

"I said stop! You crazed fools," the guard shouted as she walked towards the prisoners. She peeked over her shoulder at her partner, then stepped forward and kicked a prisoner in the back. The man exhaled sharply, groaned, and started retching.

Dirt from Levitien's arm flew at the guard. It struck her in the face and she flung her head back, closed her eyes, and began rubbing at them. She staggered for a moment, then bent down, as if she expected another attack on her face. As she did, the prisoner charged with lifting the dagger, grabbed the guard's belt, snatched a dagger from its sheath, and plunged it into her leg.

The woman cried out in pain. She tried to rise and fend off an attacker she could not see, but collapsed to a knee. She screamed again as the prisoner withdrew the dagger from her leg.

"Hurry, cut us free."

The prisoner moved quickly to cut the rope that bound them. He started with himself, then the man he fought with, and down the line he went.

To Vaten, it all seemed like a dream. Everything slowed and then sped up again. One moment he was looking at a fight and the next he was looking at his hands. They were free.

"Shit!" one prisoner said. "They heard her. Run. Run!"

Vaten felt a slap on the shoulder as a prisoner ran past him. He should have followed. His feet should have moved. But nothing happened. Vaten just stood and watched the other prisoners run into the field.

But only three of them. There should have been another. Vaten turned and saw Levitien still bound to the stake in the ground.

"Go," Levitien said as he tried to pull the rope from his arms. "You need to run now. Quickly. Run!"

But it was too late. The prisoner was right. The guards had heard the screams. And before Vaten could move, he felt a knife against his neck.

Then he saw the arrows in mid-flight and the prisoners drop to the ground. They had not even made it a hundred paces from their bindings. Trees swayed mockingly in the distance.

Vaten could not breathe. His hands trembled. They were all dead. He had gotten them killed, even the one that had resisted the plan until the end. And now he was next.

He glanced at Levitien on the ground next to him. The look on the man's face was odd. Not shocked or sad. Not even scared. It was almost as if he was indifferent, like he listened to a story he already knew the ending to.

***

THE CARAVAN WAS DOUR. The attempted escape had ruined their celebrations and gone were the songs and dances that had filled the camp earlier that night. Now there was work to be done.

They cleaned and secured the area. Even while inebriated, they were far more adept than the guards Vaten knew. They tended to the wounded woman, collected their arrows from the field, and again bound the two surviving prisoners without a single order.

The guards' final act was to retrieve the dead men. Vaten and Levitien watched as the prisoners were carried into the camp and thrown into a fire.

As Vaten watched the bodies slowly turn to ash, guilt flooded him. It was he who had agreed to the plan and supported it so fiercely, while others questioned its soundness. And he didn't even run with them, couldn't even move his feet. Again, he had been too weak to help anyone.

A woman approached, and it shook Vaten from his self-admonishment. He had never seen her before, but when he saw she wore the dress of a rider, a long dark robe with a blue insignia on it, his legs shook. He stared at her, agitated by her presence.

The woman who stood in front of him was lean, and tall with round, soft eyes that had a hint of familiarity in them. They were in stark contrast to her face, which was full of sharp lines and defined bones. It was the face of influence, Vaten thought, warmth and strength as needed.

The woman's hair moved delicately with the breeze, obscuring her face momentarily in a veil of white and black. She didn't move, unbothered by the curtain of hair, and waited for the wind to stop as though it was under her control. Eventually it did.

"I am Zejela. The Elder here." She gestured at the camp.

The words Zejela spoke were perfect Bassian. There was no accent, no rhythmic difference to her speech, like the others in the caravan. It was strange, but Vaten was more concerned with the words she spoke, rather than how she spoke them.

*An Elder.* The woman was a person of power and consequence. She decided fates and delivered justice. And she did not appear to be old enough to have earned the title through age. No, she earned the title for her actions. Vaten hoped it was not for her ruthlessness.

She continued, "Your plan to escape was imprudent. Our arrows do not miss. Though I suppose you know that now." She glanced at Vaten, "You are lucky you did not run. It saved your life."

"And you," Zejela said, turning to Levitien. "You threw the dirt. Your time with the Sentries will not be pleasant." She paused for a moment, glancing at one man, then the other. When she was done, she continued, "This will be your only warning. If you want to keep your lives, do not try to escape again."

Levitien laughed. His head flew back, eyes closed, mouth open wide, and loudly, mockingly laughed. "Our lives? What lives? You stole our lives. And you think we'll just ride along pleasantly as you beat us and starve us? Until what? You sell us to some merchant or trader or landowner. Or just get sick of us and kill—"

A Sentry stepped forward and shoved the butt end of his sickle into Levitien's stomach. Levitien exhaled sharply, lost his breath for a moment, then turned his head to hide his pain.

Zejela patted the Sentry on his arm. It wasn't clear whether she did it in approval or in condemnation. Either way, the man stopped and stepped back.

"Your treatment improved, no? We gave you more water, more food, even more time to talk. We have kept you alive amid this..." she waved her hand in small circles, gesturing at the ground, "this dying earth. And still you try to run."

"Did you expect us to stay obedient? You abducted me, nearly broke my arm, and separated me from my friend," Vaten said. "You want us to be submissive until our death?"

"Yes, we did those things. We had to do them and would do them again. But there are many things you do not know about us. About our journey. Know this though, we do not intend to kill you. We did not intend to kill the others either, but we had no choice. We will do what we must." Zejela stared deep into Vaten's eyes. "We keep you because we cannot let you go."

Vaten hung his head and said nothing.

Zejela continued, "You may understand someday. Until then...obedience, as you said. That is what's expected."

Levitien who could now breathe again, scoffed. Then asked, "What's in the boxes?"

"This conversation is over. We will move again shortly."

Zejela turned to leave and as she did, Vaten noticed a scar beginning just below her ear and running the length of her neck. The wound had long since healed, though the skin remained discolored. It reminded Vaten of a scar on Ajeau's arm. Like a river through the forest, she had said.

But all the rivers were dry now.

# CHAPTER 9

"Savique, get up!"

Savique opened his eyes to find bright light had infiltrated his hut. It was morning. For a moment, he wondered if he had dreamed his encounter with the Noye woman. Maybe the entire raid was a dream and the Foreman's residence was intact.

As soon as he sat up and saw one of the Foreman's guards standing in front of him, he knew it had not been a dream. Disturbing, terrifying, mysterious, but real.

"I said get up!" The guard pushed him with his foot. "The Foreman wants to see you."

The word jolted him awake. He was still a thief, and he worried he would suffer the same fate as his friends.

"What?" He shook his head. "Why does the Foreman want to see me?"

"Don't you know?" The man eyed him suspiciously. Savique's hands trembled. "The Noye were here last night. Did you sleep through the raid? They destroyed the Foreman's residence."

Savique nodded. "Yes. Yes, I am aware of that. But why does he want me?"

"The Foreman's residence is destroyed." The guard paused and stared at Savique as if his meaning were obvious. But he saw no understanding on Savique's face, so he continued, "That means you are needed to fix it."

"Oh, right. Of course." Savique breathed a deep sigh of relief.

To the guard, and the Foreman, he was still only a mason. Not a thief or a conspirator with Noye interlopers. And he was only necessary because he would provide the stones and help lead the construction of a new residence.

"Well, hurry and get ready then." The guard gestured for Savique to get to his feet. "I am to bring you to the Foreman immediately."

Savique stood and smiled as he gathered his tools. A chance to work stone was calming. It was normal and routine. There had been too much chaos, mystery, and grief in his life lately. The work would bring him joy, or at least some peace.

But once he reached the work site, Savique quickly realized the calm and peace he sought would not be found. The whole place stunk of suspicion and mistrust. And while some guards sorted through ashes, others accosted workers. Where were they? What did they see? Who did they help?

It was not just questions, either. Guards grabbed workers, shoved and struck them when their answers were not satisfactory. Even if they provided reasonable responses, they were met with antagonism and threats.

"Go ahead and leave," one guard shouted. "Where'll you get your food? You want your family to starve?"

"The Foreman treats you well," another guard said. "If you do not want that to change, tell me what you know!"

Yet another guard simply kicked at a man scurrying away, and said, "Get out of here, you worthless drudge."

The man escorting Savique brought him through the site and up a set of stone stairs to a platform where Crevir and Vrai stood looming over a man who had bruises and cuts on his face. Savique recognized the man as a guard, though he didn't know the man's name, and wondered what had brought him to his knees in front of the Foreman and his Captain.

"Wait," the guard at Savique's side said and held out his hand to prevent Savique from walking forward.

Savique obeyed without saying a word. He stood with his arms at his side while the man in front of Crevir and Vrai dripped blood onto his shirt, his face a picture of shock and fear. Tears rolled down his face. Crevir made no attempt to keep his words quiet.

"I will ask you again," Crevir said. "Why did you lie to us?"

"Sirs, I did not." The guard shook his head frantically. "I reported only what I saw."

"You say you saw the raiders ride for the eastern fields?" Crevir asked.

The man nodded. "Yes, that's right." He glanced at Vrai and then Crevir. "When they breached the barrier—I did as I was told!" He stared at Vrai. "I told you, they rode for the east!"

Crevir shook his head in disappointment, then turned to Vrai. "He calls you a liar to your face and you remain calm. You are steadier than me."

Vrai bowed his head. "A mistake, I am sure. Perhaps he mixed his words or lost his direction or—"

"Or he conspired with the Noye all along," He bent down and grabbed the man by the hair. He pulled, stretching the man's neck taut. "What did they promise you? What did you earn for letting them defile my property? You fool, you do not know what you have done!" He screamed in the man's face.

The guard shook in Crevir's grasp. "I...I told him. The mistake was not mine."

Crevir let go of his hair, then struck the man on the chin, sending him toppling to the ground. The Foreman walked to Vrai and held out his hand. Vrai hesitated a moment, then placed a dagger in the Foreman's hand. Holding the dagger, he walked back to the man on the ground and stood over him.

"I will give you a last chance to save yourself," Crevir said. "Tell me of your mistake or I will return you here and now." Crevir pointed the dagger at him.

The man coughed and spit blood on the ground next to him. He didn't sit up, but he opened his eyes and stared up at Crevir. "Fine..." he said. "I lied."

Crevir spit on him. "Traitor," he said. "Do you know where they took it?"

"What?" The man's eyes narrowed in confusion. "Took...what? I only mis-spoke."

Crevir moved closer to him and placed the dagger against his throat. "Tell me, where did they take it?"

The man shook his head. "I...I don't know. It was—"

Crevir plunged the dagger into the man's throat. The man coughed as blood poured from his neck and pooled in the dirt. It ran in small rivers past Savique and down the small slope towards the site where the Foreman's residence once stood.

Crevir stood, walked back to Vrai, and handed him the bloody dagger. "Stained my gloves," he said with disdain.

Vrai wiped the dagger on his pants. "And he didn't know a thing."

"Of course not," Crevir said sharply. "He was a fool. They would not have shared a word with him."

Vrai nodded. And silence fell over the two men.

Crevir sighed and patted Vrai on the arm. "Clean this mess." Then he walked to where Savique stood and dismissed the guard at Savique's side. "I am sorry you were witness to such insolence." He gestured to the guard bleeding on the ground. "Most in my guard are righteous and worthwhile. But sometimes..."

Savique did not look down. He kept his eyes on the Foreman. "I am sorry," he said with no emotion.

Crevir waved his hands. "Anyway, what do our building supplies look like? Do we still have limestone or sandstone remaining from the towers?"

"We have an abundance of bricks but—"

"I did not ask about bricks," Crevir interrupted, annoyed. "This place burned like kindling because of those bricks. What about the stones?"

"Yes, sir. We only have two large limestones and a handful of sandstones. We used many of the blocks repairing the storehouses. There is not enough to make a new residence."

Crevir glared at Savique and clenched his fists. He inhaled deeply, then exhaled without ever taking his eyes from Savique. "Another insult," he said through grit teeth.

Vrai appeared beside Crevir and whispered something in the Foreman's ear. Crevir appeared to consider the information, then nodded.

"Build a temporary structure from the bricks," Crevir said, resigned. "Save the stone for now. After the harvest, I will trade for more and you will cut them. Then—"

"Sir!" A guard ran up to Crevir. "Is this it? What you're looking for?"

The woman held a stone chest up to Crevir as if it were an offering to a god.

"No." A look of disdain fell on his face. "That is far too big. I am looking for something small that you can hold in a single hand. Keep looking!"

Turning back to Savique, he said, "Where was I?" He paused for several moments, then continued, "Right. I will trade with Balleum for more stone, and then you will build a residence that will not fall to some vile raiders. Do you understand?"

"Yes, sir," Savique bowed his head.

Savique knew what Crevir would trade to Balleum for the stone. Crops. Balleum had once told him that food was the only indispensable good in this world; everyone valued it, Lord to worker. Savique shuddered as he remembered the dwindling supplies he had seen in the storehouse.

As he stared at his feet, he wondered how much the shares would be cut to make the trade and who would suffer from it. Too many. He exhaled.

Savique brought his head back up and stared at him. Crevir grinned back.

***

ON THE LAST DAY of the harvest, Crevir noticed a terrifying sight approaching his estate. A woman wearing a bright white shawl over her leather gear rode quickly through his fields.

It was not the horse, nor her pace, nor even the weapons the woman carried that alarmed him. It was the color of her shawl that gave him a sense of dread. White. She rode for the Vizier in Nouv'eau. And there was no doubt the message she carried brought unwelcomed news.

He slammed his fist on the arm of the chair he sat in. She came today of all days, asking what, he wondered. The Vizier already had taken so much.

Crevir stood, then exited his residence and called Vrai to his side. They met the Vizier's steward with bowed heads, as proper decorum dictated. The Foreman had standing in his estate, but he knew his place in the world. He knew not to provoke the Vizier, else he wanted to lose that standing.

"Welcome friend." Crevir lifted his head and extended his arms towards the messenger. "We are honored to receive you on behalf of the Vizier."

"Thank you, Foreman. I am here to inform you that Vizier Desait orders an increase in commissions this harvest. Your estate will be required to provide—"

"Another increase?" Crevir said.

The woman put her hand up to stop his objection. "This is the Vizier's orders. If you would like you can go to Nouv'eau and speak to him—I will take you myself. But we both know how that ends."

"Of course. My apologies." Crevir brought his hands together and bowed his head once more. "The Vizier only asks for what is his and I will gladly meet his requests."

Crevir saw the disdain in the woman's eyes. Courtesy and decorum would not pacify her. Then, he thought, perhaps it would be best to let her talk. Say her peace, then leave. He could manipulate the tallies later.

"Yes, you will," the steward said. "Now, the Vizier wants you to keep steady the onions, radishes, and garlic. Increase one and a half times over the barley and wheat. Double the grapes. The Lord has grown a taste for sweetness."

The increase was unreasonable. It would stretch the estate beyond what even the most fruitful harvests would provide. If they met it, there would be no reserve should harvests be less plentiful in the future. And worst of all, he had already traded a substantial portion of his grapes.

But it did not matter how extravagant the demands were, his response was the same. "So it will be. Is there more?" he asked.

She stared at him as if to say, 'of course there was.' Instead, she said, "Don't forget, you haven't paid the entirety of your previous levy. Vizier Desait is kind. He will not extract any punishments if you make up the difference with your next delivery. If you choose not to do so, you will find that kindness evaporated."

"Of course." Crevir smiled. "The Vizier will find our next payment erases all debts."

"I will relay that message to the Vizier. Ensure it is the truth." The woman paused and brought her hand to her chin as though she was trying to remember if there was anything else she should tell the man. She shook her head. "Well, I suppose that is all. Now—"

"You are, of course, welcome to our hospitality." Crevir stretched his arm towards the rest of his estate. "You can eat, drink, sleep, and rest comfortably here."

"Thank you, Foreman. But I must continue my journey. There are other estates that must heed the word of the Vizier."

"I understand. You do your duty with great care. The Vizier is lucky to have such committed stewards."

Crevir again saw something like disdain pass across the woman's face. And without saying another word, she walked to her horse, mounted it, and rode back through the fields she had come. Within moments, she was out of sight.

Vrai had heard the entire exchange and once the Steward passed the fields, he asked, "What will you do? We do not have the Vizier's shares."

"Do you think I am unaware of that?"

"No." A brief smile crossed Vrai's lips. "But I know you have thought of something."

Crevir chuckled. "You know me well, or have a good intuition. Perhaps both. Anyway, yes, there is a plan. The Vizier wants his due and though we cannot give him enough crop to satisfy his increasing lust, we can give him something he prefers almost as much as food."

"And what is that?" Vrai asked.

"A thief. Someone who took his crops and made it impossible for us to meet his demands."

Vrai frowned. "The Vizier cares about such common criminals?"

"Oh, yes." Crevir nodded enthusiastically. "Thieves are a plague on the Vizier's lands. He cannot stand their existence. If I were to deliver one into his hands, well, it may not eliminate our obligations, but it would likely reduce them. At least, it would buy us time. Perhaps enough for another harvest to come and go."

"It is too bad, then, that we already dispatched of those who took from the eastern storehouse."

Crevir stared at Vrai through thin eyes, somewhere between angry and suspicious. "All except one, you mean."

"What?"

"Do not feign ignorance, Vrai. It is not a good look on you." Crevir pointed an accusing finger at him. "I know you withheld one name from me. The one some called cursed. The man who spoke with those zealots. That outsider. Our mason."

"Savique?" Vrai shook his head. "I had no—"

"Do not protest it. I know you take pity on him and his child because of their loss. But I have held my hand long enough and maybe, had this fate not befallen us, I would've let him stay. He is a good stone worker. Now, though...his sacrifice will be for our greater good." Crevir smiled. "Isn't that what the old man said about why they stole? 'For the greater good.'" A fiendish laugh followed.

Vrai took a few deep breaths to compose himself, then said, "If he is a thief, let him hang." Vrai gestured to the grove. "Here. In front of the camp. So no one crosses you again."

Crevir's laughter stopped. "No. That would be a waste. And you know that." Again, Crevir narrowed his eyes in suspicion. But almost as soon as they did, they widened as though he gained some insight. "Ah, perhaps this is about those Ascetics. I know you believe in that Istori nonsense, but you know how I feel about it. Get it out of your mind. That would be my suggestion."

In subtle movements Crevir never saw, Vrai grasped the hilt of the blade hung above his backside and drew it halfway out of its sheath before he stopped. He caught his breath in his mouth, then removed his hand and let the knife slide back into its holster. He frowned and exhaled.

Crevir patted him on the arm. "Forget it. And bring me Savique." Crevir smiled like he tasted the sweetest fruit.

***

SAVIQUE SAT ON THE ground near the new residence he built for the Foreman and begged Vrai and Crevir for his life.

"Please do not do this!" Savique said. "I have a child! I am a good mason! I did nothing wrong!"

"Do you deny you stole from the Foreman?" Vrai asked him.

"I-I-I only took to feed my wife. She was starving and with child. She needed the food!"

"Little good it did her," Crevir said to Vrai with a grin on his face. Then to Savique he said, "You admit it! You stole from me and now you must accept the punishment."

"Please." Savique glanced at Crevir, then Vrai. "I will make restitution. You can cut my shares. I will work without pay. Please, don't take me from my son."

Vrai stared at him, emotionless. He did not blink or hesitate. He said, "Your fate is already decided," then lowered the brand onto Savique's hand.

To Savique, the long metal pole with the estate's mark on it moved at a snail's pace. He stared at it as though it was not real. But it was. And it meant he would never work again, never see Vaten again, perhaps never breathe again.

Then, something inside him shouted for him to fight, struggle with all his might and he could avoid the brand. He could avoid his fate. But it was the frantic throes of a panicked mind. No matter how hard he tried, he could not move his hands.

When the brand landed, pain replaced everything. Savique screamed but never heard a sound. His head swung violently, but he never felt the hands grabbing to control him. His skin bubbled and smoked, but he did not smell burning flesh.

Vrai lifted the brand off Savique's hand and thrust it back into the fire. He waited a moment. Then he picked up the brand and plunged it down on Savique's other hand.

More pain. More screaming. Savique wished for unconsciousness, but it did not come.

Crevir grabbed Savique's writhing head and looked into his eyes. A film of tears glazed them.

"You should not have taken from me," Crevir whispered into his ear. "I gave you a home and work after all your travels. And you turned out to be scum like the rest of your people. And, just like them, your suffering will soon be over. Oh, and don't worry, I will see that Vrai takes good care of your son."

Savique's eyes opened wide, but he couldn't speak. Crevir's words were the first things to cut through the pain, but he found his body unresponsive. He could only think of his child in Vrai's hands, suffering the same fate as his friends.

Whether it was the agony in his hands, exhaustion, or the thought of his son's demise, Savique finally collapsed. It was a relief.

Crevir faced Vrai and said, "Get him bound and on the way to Nouv'eau with our shipment."

"Yes, Foreman," Vrai said. "I will relay our story to the Vizier."

"No," Crevir shook his head. "Listen. You will remain here, send one of your subordinates. I will not chance you acting on your pity once more."

"Sir, I would never disobey—"

Crevir held up a hand. "My mind is made up. Make it so."

"Yes, Foreman," Vrai said and began tying rope around Savique's arms.

\*\*\*

THE CART SAVIQUE SAT atop rolled through the wood. With each turn of its wheel on the path, his head jostled against the wooden railing. The barrels that surrounded him—full of the Vizier's payment—sprung into the air and then landed with a heavy thump.

Whether it was the sound of the barrels or the force of his head hitting the railing, Savique eventually awoke. He opened his eyes and the bright light of the sun obscured his vision. He wasn't dead, the ache in his hands and head convinced him of that, but he knew little else of his predicament.

As his vision cleared and the disorientation lifted, he looked around to see where he was. Though the barrels made it hard to see much, he could tell he was in a dense thicket, but not one that was familiar. The trees and shrubs all looked different from those near the estate. He must have been unconscious for some time.

He wondered where he was going. But then he decided it didn't matter. Wherever the Foreman sent him, his fate would be the same. And there was no going back to the estate or his son.

The cart hit another bump and it sent Savique off his seat and into the air. It was not much, there may not even have been enough room for moss to grow between him and the wood, but it was enough that when his flight crested, he could see over the barrels for the first time. Ahead of the cart were several guards—Savique counted six in the short time he had, though there could have been more—riding on horses, one of which was attached to the cart.

He saw familiar faces among the group, but no one he knew by name. He had hoped, if there was a familiar guard, he could reason with them. After all, he had helped build some of their quarters and repaired some of their stone axes and sickles. And he had always treated them well.

It was a foolish thought, and he knew it. The guards, friendly or unknown, would not help him against the Foreman's orders. It would trade their deaths for his. It was not a trade anyone would make. No, he was stuck on that cart, his future set.

Savique crashed back to the cart. He tried to brace his landing with his hands, forgetting for the moment that they were bound, but failed and fell onto his stomach. His hands screamed out in pain. When he righted himself, he gazed down at the gruesome sight.

The back of his hands were crusted black and red. Pus oozed from underneath fresh scabs. The skin around his wounds was cracked like flakes from a crust of bread. They pulsed in short, painful bursts.

But worst of all was he had to bear the Foreman's crest until his death. Even after it. As long as anyone saw his body, they would see the mark of a man Savique despised.

As he stared at the insignia, his hatred grew until it exploded. He shook his hands futilely, as if thrashing would soothe him. When it didn't, he lifted his head to the sky and screamed loud enough for the birds to flee the trees. Then he breathed long, slow breaths.

And eventually the rage disappeared, but in its absence, he found only despair. Crevir had taken everything from him—his friends, his wife, his work, and now his home. He hung his head as an image of his young son came to mind.

Vaten, the only thing that gave him purpose, was gone. Tears formed in the corner of Savique's eyes. The boy had lost both his mother and his father before he could even walk. He would know nothing of his family and their love for him. If he survived the Foreman and his estate at all.

The boy was alone.

No. Savique stomped his foot against the cart and pledged to himself if there was one breath left in his body, he would use it to return to Vaten and ensure his son knew he had a family. He would not abandon the boy.

Like rain on a sunny day, the words of the Ascetics floated into his mind unexpectantly. *That is when you will see him again.*

The sound of a distant thumping interrupted Savique's thoughts. The beats, short and quick, grew closer. It took Savique a moment to place them, but then it was clear. Horses approached the cart in full stride. Whoever they were, they would be upon it soon.

The cart stopped and Savique heard the guards say, "Ready your blades. Sounds like bandits ride on us..." There was a pause, then another shout, "From behind. And the left!"

As soon as the words came out of the guard's mouth, there was a clashing of metal, braying horses, and groans from men. Shouts and screams followed. More cracks and thuds. Then the earth next to the cart shook. Savique could see nothing, but heard and felt it all.

And just as quickly as the noise appeared, it stopped. All appeared calm. The bandits must not have been an organized bunch, Savique thought. Perhaps they were only looking for an easy prize and rode off once they saw the squad of guards.

If that were true, though, the guards should have said something. But they didn't. There were no cheers for their victory or calls to tend to the wounded.

Now the silence had gone on too long and it was troubling. Savique wondered if anyone was out there. Or was he to be left to rot tied to the cart in the middle of some unfamiliar forest?

Finally, a horse neighed. Then a whistle. Then footsteps on the soft dirt approached the back of the cart. Someone was alive and coming towards him. Coming *for* him. Savique panicked.

The gate lowered. Savique looked up and saw a familiar face, but the last one he expected.

The woman held out a hand and said, "Sooner than I expected, cochon."

# CHAPTER 10

DAYS AND NIGHTS CRAWLED by as Ajeau rested in Seule's hut. She woke most mornings, still tired from the night before and craving food. Seule would bring her water and whatever food he found foraging or something from his dwindling supply.

Ajeau would eat, drink, and feel her energy rise. She would stretch her legs, stand, or walk around the hut, anything to feel like her recovery was progressing. But her strength would soon drain and she would find herself back on the floor resting, frustrated by thoughts of never making it to Nouv'eau or finding Vaten. Not even the stories Seule would read from his ancient scrolls would soothe her.

But her strength and endurance grew every day. And one day, she found herself able to pace the hut for most of the day. Then later, she joined Seule on a brief excursion not far into the forest. And when she felt healed, she asked to join him when he foraged.

"My trips are not simple walks. They are purposeful and laborious. It is not without a fair amount of difficulty," Seule said.

"I know, but I am ready. I feel strong." Ajeau jumped twice as if to demonstrate her vigor.

"That may be so, but we will have to leave early. There will be few breaks and, depending on our haul, there might not be much to eat or drink."

"I can manage," Ajeau said. "I have to try at some point."

"Why not rest for now?" Seule gestured to the bed of leaves and chaff on the ground. "There will always be another day to join me."

Ajeau shook her head in defiance. "And there will always be another day for me to rest. But Vaten may not have those days. I cannot waste time while he is a prisoner somewhere. I have to continue my journey. To do that, I must test my strength. Foraging will do that for me."

Seule paused a moment to consider her words. Then he nodded. "All right. If you believe you are ready, you can join me tomorrow. Rest well tonight."

To his word, the next day, Seule led Ajeau into the woods.

It was unlike anything Ajeau had previously known. She had foraged before—she and Vaten often searched for food during their journey—but what Seule did was different. It was systematic. She thought comparing her previous experience to this one was like comparing splashing water with swimming.

But Ajeau's memory of that day would not be of Seule and his restless head or the winding course they walked through the woods. It would not be of the instructions Seule provided on where to go and how to search. No, what Ajeau would remember from that day was the strength she returned to the hut with. Or perhaps the dead rat they found.

Ajeau and Seule returned to the hut at dusk and set to work building a fire to roast the day's wondrous find. The smell of flesh nearly brought tears to Ajeau's eyes. She had been without meat for so long, and though the fruits, nuts, and roots she ate sustained her, they did not provide the same comfort as a good piece of meat.

They ate slowly, savoring the meal. Seule, unable to leave a moment in silence, said,

"A rat is dead,and we are fed.We ate it all, it was not small.So thank you Eaunow we must go,to sleep."

Seule closed his eyes, threw his head back, and snored loudly. Then, nearly in the same instant, began laughing loudly.

Ajeau chuckled, and said, "Well, at least the rat didn't make me sick." They both laughed.

Spirits were high around the fire, not only because of the meat but also because Ajeau was well. She had recovered completely and part of her wanted to run off into the night right then. Or at least walk. Either way, she was eager to resume her journey.

So as the fire warmed her body, and the meat satisfied her hunger, Ajeau said, "This will be my last night here. I am ready and I need to leave."

Seule gazed at her, not surprised or happy or even angry, but concerned. "Are you sure? You have only foraged once with me. There can be more, we can travel further, ensure you're rested and that your endurance has returned. Besides, you are good luck." He held up the stick that had roasted the rat.

Ajeau smiled and nodded. "Yes, I'm sure. My strength has returned; today's trip confirmed it for me. I feel like I could walk to Nouv'eau without stopping and I have you to thank for that. But I can't wait any longer. I must go."

"Nouv'eau? You're going to Nouv'eau? You never said that before." Seule leaned back and frowned.

Ajeau shrugged. "Yes, well, that is where I'm headed."

Seule shook his head. "That's more than a week's walk north without detours. If you get lost...I do not think you are ready for such a trip."

"I am," Ajeau said, in a tone more defiant than she intended. "I need to get to Nouv'eau. It might be my only chance to find Vaten."

"Ah, yes. Vaten. You think he is there?"

"I don't know. I don't know where they took him, but someone there might know about..." She inhaled sharply and frantically scanned the hut. "Shit! Did I lose it?"

"Lose what? What is it?" Seule met the panic in her eyes.

Ajeau stood, took a few steps in one direction, then stopped. She spun around and took a few steps in another direction. She threw up her arms. "It was an arrow with a tip made from a blue rock. I found it on the ground near where Vaten and I were attacked. It belongs to those who took him."

"Oh." Seule brought a hand to his chest and exhaled. Then he smiled and said, "The arrow. Right! I forgot." He walked to the back of the hut. Hidden in a mess of rocks, pelts, and a few sticks, was Ajeau's arrow.

"Here you go," he said. "I found this with you in the forest. I didn't know if you wanted it or not, but I thought it would be smart to hang on to. Then I forgot about it, just like you did." He chuckled.

She heaved a deep breath and let a relieved smile cross her face. "Thank Eau you have it. Have you seen anything like this blue rock before?"

Seule shook his head. "I haven't, but it's magnificent, isn't it?" He leaned his head close to the rock, scrutinizing it. "It looks like the sky itself colored it. And it's solid, it feels like it could pierce metal. This is from Vaten's captors?"

"Yes."

He frowned and crossed his arms in front of his chest. "And that is all you know about them? The only clue you have?"

"There was something else. Something I can't remember. They..." Ajeau's voice trailed off as she struggled to think of her attackers. "I wish I could remember what it was."

"Hmm. Well, you can try chewing on some buscade root. It'll help bring back memories."

"What root?"

"Buscade." Seule said. "You've not chewed it before? I thought everyone did!"

Ajeau eyed him, confused. "No, I've never heard of it."

Seule held up a finger, then turned and walked to his supply. He rummaged through the food and leaves and pulled a small stick with branches still attached. He broke the branches off and shaved the bark at the end.

"Here, try this," he said, handing the root to Ajeau.

Ajeau took it and held it in her hand. It could have been anything. "This won't kill me, right? On my last night here."

Seule laughed. "No, no. You will be fine. I will go first if you want me to."

He extended his hand towards Ajeau. She disregarded it and put the root into her mouth. She chewed. It tasted faintly earthy, reminiscent of a carrot.

"When do the memories come?" she asked.

"It takes a little time. Chew slowly and rest your mind." He gestured to the seat behind her. "They will come."

Ajeau did as instructed. She sat down on the ground and continued to gnaw at the root until her mouth went dry. Still, no memories flashed before her eyes. She wondered if this was one of Seule's bad jokes. But then her tongue tingled, and a heat built inside her ears. Her eyelids became as heavy as stones.

Something appeared in the fire but it was mixed, vague and fuzzy, as if she couldn't focus her eyes on the image. She knew it was her younger self. She tilted her head to the side and looked on with wonder. The memories came.

Ajeau, tiny, afraid, and blinded by sunlight, bawled as a woman picked her up and cradled her gently. She did not recognize the woman and could not see her clearly, but knew the woman's smell, felt comfort from her touch, and was soothed by her voice. She ate at the woman's breast. Hunger rose like a wave, crested, crashed, and retreated out to sea. A warmth grew within her. She slept.

Ajeau, a small child now, tried to run. A hand gripped her arm tightly and held her back as she tried to wriggle out of its grasp. She yelled something inaudible. The woman who fed her looked on with horror, but she made no movements to help. A man lay motionless on the ground, a growing red lake saturated the soil underneath him.

She glanced upwards at the person grabbing her arm. She saw long gray hair, a short skeletal nose, and a face covered in wrinkles and scars. He smiled at her and panic stabbed her heart.

Then, agony. Pain radiated from her limbs but infected her whole body. She looked down to see her arm cut open, blood collecting in some small flask. She screamed as tears ran down her face.

As soon as it had come on, the pain stopped.

Ajeau, no longer a child but not yet an adult, stood on the edge of the vast fields of Crevir's Estate. Clouds roared overhead. She broke into a sprint and ran through the fields as fast as she could. Her heart pounded. The skies thundered and water pelted her ruthlessly.

By the time she arrived at a small hut, the water had soaked her. She walked inside and saw a young man, about her age, sitting with an older woman. Vaten and his keeper, Tille. The Ajeau who watched these memories smiled as wide as her younger self had.

Now a young woman, Ajeau stood on the edge of the same fields she had just run through. They were dying. The storehouses were ruined. Vaten stood next to her and viewed the scene with the same tortuous expression. They turned and began walking, heading north along a trail.

Ajeau climbed a tree in a frantic scramble. It was dark and she was scared. When she seated herself on a stable branch, she stared down at the ground and saw someone fall. She wanted to cry out or leave and help him, but fear kept her rooted to the tree. Then, as now, the shame and remorse tore at her.

A large man, too graceful and agile for his size, followed and picked up Vaten. He made no sound as he joined his companion. They were so lithe, their movements so rhythmic through the forest, it was as though they knew every root and stick on the ground.

While the large man carried Vaten away, Ajeau noticed blue paint on their weapons, glistening in the moonlight. Then they were gone, leaving her alone in a tree.

In Seule's hut, Ajeau opened her mouth as if to speak. No sound emerged. Her mouth closed. Soon thereafter, her eyes shut and her breathing steadied. She was asleep.

Seule chuckled to himself, wondering what she had seen. The visions could be powerful or insignificant, the root only provided the chance to remember something. What she remembered, he knew, was left to fate.

***

BEFORE THE SUN BROACHED the horizon, Ajeau awoke. She stood and stretched, ready to begin her journey. She walked outside and found Seule staring into the forest with a pack of food and a canteen of water resting beside him.

When she stepped on a leaf, he turned to her and grinned. "You're awake," he said. "I hope you had a restful sleep. You feel well?"

Ajeau breathed, then said, "Yes, and I had no dreams. That must be a good sign."

"Well, the root has been known to—" Seule threw his hands to the side of his head and mimed being unconscious.

Ajeau smiled and chuckled softly. Another bad joke, but she again humored him. She did not know when he would be able to tell a joke to someone else again.

"Did you remember what you wanted?" Seule asked.

"Yes, I remembered a lot of things..." Ajeau glanced at the ground and stared at it a moment. Then she looked at Seule. "But most importantly, I remembered about the people who took Vaten. They moved with a grace and speed that was unnatural and they covered their weapons in a blue paint."

Seule frowned and shook his head, confused. "Strange." Then his eyes widened, and he pointed at Ajeau. "Like the rock!"

"Yes. Though the rock is real and its color natural." She shrugged. "I'm not sure what any of it means. But maybe I can find out who they are. And if I can do that, then, hopefully, I can find Vaten."

"And you leave now?"

Ajeau smiled and nodded. "There is no need to wait anymore. I am ready. I promise you that."

Seule bit his lip and averted his eyes.

"Seule—" Ajeau began.

"I know, I know. It was just nice—"

"No, Seule."

"—having company. And I worry about your journey. But I know you must—"

"Seule!" Ajeau yelled to stop the man talking.

"What?" he said, meeting her eyes with tears rolling slowly down his cheek.

"Why don't you come with me?" Ajeau said. "We can travel together."

"No." Seule inhaled deeply and shook his head. "I cannot do that. My place is here. I must make amends."

"Why?" Ajeau stared at him, confused. "Why do you have to stay here? Why can't you travel with me or even seek others? What amends keep you here?"

"That is a long and complicated story."

"Before I go, I want to hear it."

Seule smiled, then let it fall slowly from his face. "Perhaps the short version, then, so that you may proceed with your travels. I ran from my people, my place of birth, and sought a place to live alone without others so that they could survive. The Tentir seemed as good a spot as any. And it was until the streams dried up and—"

"No," Ajeau said, unimpressed. "That answers nothing. Why? Why did you leave? How does staying here make it easier for anyone else to survive? What does that even mean?"

Seule sighed. "I know. The truth is..."

"Please," Ajeau said.

"If I must."

Ajeau nodded.

"Many harvests ago I worked the land east of here. The community thrived and there was plenty for all. We even had a good trading relationship with Nouv'eau!

"But as our yields increased, so did the pressure to account for them. We needed scribes to tally the incoming and outgoing shares. Who got what, and when. These people, once humble workers like everyone else, gained standing in the community. With that standing, came power."

"You speak of Viziers." Ajeau spat on the ground in disgust.

"Yes, though we did not use that term on our land." Seule waved his hand. "Regardless, these people gained power over food, goods, and the community. Some could not shoulder this power respectfully. Some of these people stole and became wealthy. They used those riches to trade for weapons, weapons they used to force more work, to give them more supply and enrich them further."

"So, these Viziers forced you away from your people, out of your home, and you came here?"

"No. No Ajeau." He met her gaze and kept it. "I was one of those people. I was a Vizier."

"What?" Ajeau shook her head. "How is that possible?" Viziers were people of wealth and power, not disheveled recluses searching for scraps in the forest.

"Yes, I did those things." Seule hung his head in shame. "Then the drought came and there was nothing left to steal. No riches to gain. The land deserted me because I took advantage of it. And the workers, my friends in my youth and no longer afraid of my dwindling power, came to return me to the earth. So, I ran and made the forest my home."

Ajeau's mouth hung agape. She would have dismissed the tale as a lie if it was not Seule who spoke it. He was too truthful and the emotions he wore on his face were not those of deception. That such an honest man was a Vizier only confused her further.

But then her mouth closed, and she smiled. He had saved her and kept her alive. It was just as he said. He was making amends.

Ajeau walked forward and laid a hand on his bony shoulder. "I am sorry you must live out your days here alone," she said. "I hope you can make good soon enough."

Seule only stared at the sky as though he was lost in thought.

Ajeau thought it was the first time she saw him without a smile on his face. Even if it wasn't, it bothered her. She had not wanted her last moments with the man to be filled with such seriousness. But there was no changing it now.

"I think it is time for me to go," Ajeau said. "I—"

"Wait! I almost forgot." Seule sprung to life, leaving behind whatever trouble that ran through his head just moments before. He turned, walked to the back of his hut, and rummaged through a small pile of tools on the ground.

"When you reach Nouv'eau, look for a woman named Aube. I knew her once, before I left my home. She tried to warn me about the... Never mind." He grabbed Ajeau's hand, opened it, and placed a smooth, round stone in it. He held her hand as he said, "She is a good woman. Smart. She might not know much about the people you're looking for, but she'll know something. If she's alive and you find her, tell her you know Seule from the coast and give her this rock." He let go of her hand.

Ajeau put it in her bag next to the arrow. "Thank you," she said.

Seule nodded, but his expression was one of concern and seriousness. "Know that Nouv'eau can be a dangerous place and the people there wary of outsiders. Vaten's captors do not seem like fools either. They put time and care into their weapons and actions. I hope Vaten is safe and returned to you, but do not play with these people. You may not survive it."

"I know," Ajeau said. "But I won't abandon my friend."

"Of course, I..." As if he knew his words would make little difference, Seule stopped talking, bent down, and picked up the goods he packed for her.

Ajeau took the packs and bowed her head in appreciation for all that he had done for her. It was in that moment that she realized she did not care about his past. Regardless of if he was a Vizier, a hermit, or neither, he was a friend. The only one she had found since Vaten all those years before.

And as it did then, her heart filled with joy.

Seule smiled his humble grin and said, "You do not need to bow. But thank you. Your presence will always be welcomed here. Long ago, we used to say this to kin and today I say it to you. As long as I have something, you have something."

"Thank you," Ajeau said. "For everything."

They embraced.

After they separated, Ajeau turned and walked into the forest. She could not bring herself to look behind her. If she had, she would not have seen her friend, his warm smile, or his jaunt frame. No, she would have seen the same scene that lay ahead of her, the emptiness of a lonely forest.

# CHAPTER 11

LEVITIEN KICKED VATEN'S LEGS and said, "Wake up, kid."

Vaten stirred, but his eyes didn't open. He wasn't asleep and felt Levitien's kicks, but he hoped by ignoring them, the man would leave him alone.

The two prisoners had said little to each other since the night of their failed escape and that had suited Vaten fine. There was no purpose in speaking, anyway. There was no hope, no chance for escape, nothing to do but obey their captors.

Vaten did not eat, his appetite abandoned him for long stretches, and he did not sleep. He sat in the cart with his eyes closed and surrendered.

"Sol's sake, kid. Wake up. You will not want to miss this." Levitien again met strong resistance.

He rolled his head to sky and sighed. "All right, kid. I'm sorry. I'm sorry the plan didn't work. I'm sorry we're still trapped on this cart. I'm sorry you almost got killed. But you're alive. We both are. You can be mad at me, ignore me—I know you're not sleeping—but you should at least be happy you're alive. And I mean it when I say you will not want to miss this."

"Sorry? You're sorry? I'm the one that got them killed," Vaten said, as though he was responding to a challenge, not an apology.

"Is that why you're upset? You think you killed them?" Levitien scoffed and shook his head. "They made their own decisions. You didn't do anything."

"That's right!" The words burst out of Vaten's mouth with an unexpected viciousness. The anger directed at himself more than Levitien. "I didn't *do* anything. I didn't help them. I just watched as they were killed. Killed because I convinced them to go along with some wild plan like it even had a chance."

"Quiet down over there!" A Sentry yelled at them.

Levitien shrugged and whispered, "There was nothing you could do. You going to fight the whole caravan by yourself? Going to overpower the Sentries? Stop their arrows in mid-flight? If anyone killed them, it's them over there. All we could do was try to get away. The others knew that. That's why they ran."

"They ran because they had to and I..." Vaten slammed the cart with his fist. "I never even moved my feet. All that time spent dreaming about the possibility of escaping—I should've never said anything. It was hopeless, and I was stupid to believe otherwise."

"Kid, you can't beat those stronger than you head on. It doesn't work. You need to be patient. Things change. Just look at this soil." Levitien spit on the ground and watched as the cart's wheel rolled over it. "Not long ago, it was rich and soft. Now it's dry as dust. Planting your seed now would yield nothing. Wait for the right time. It will come and your hope will be rewarded."

Vaten responded only with silence, his hope had been abused enough. He closed his eyes and hung his head, content to wrap himself in a coat of guilt.

But unlike his body, his mind could not remain still. It leapt from image to image, thought to thought, like it was trying to find something lost. He thought of the men who died, the Sentries' arrows arcing in the air. It was familiar.

Then, words called out to him from the past. "Wait for the right time..."

His mind had found for what it searched. The words spoken by Levitien a moment ago, but in a different context, said by a different voice. Vaten knew whose it was. He had heard it so many times.

And then, in his mind's eye, he was no longer in the cart. He was in a field with men and women that he knew. That he trusted. The voice came again and unleashed a terror in him.

"Wait for the right time. Wait for the right time. Now!"

***

VATEN STOOD ON A dirt path surrounded by tall, healthy grasses. That it had grown at all was a miracle. That's what the workers on Crevir's Estate had called the brief shower that fell over them during the prior planting season. A miracle.

Rain had not come for years until it did. And all rejoiced at its emergence. But even then, the showers were weak and moved on quickly. They barely refreshed the ditches that brought water to the crops. The decay of the estate had been postponed but not halted.

Though as Vaten stood watching the workers in the grass, he did not think of the fields' decline, but of their growth. A fresh harvest was in front of him, and it would bring food for all, perhaps even the storehouses, if they rationed well. Those who were worried they would go hungry were only pessimists.

But there was one worker whose constant worry about the state of the fields was most annoying. Ajeau thought a day without rain meant another drought, and the shares would be cut again. And even on that day, in front of an abundant yield, she approached Vaten and said, "If we stay, we'll starve. Let's run. Today. And find someplace better."

"These are the most fertile fields on Bas," he said, trying to soothe her concerns. "We have plenty here. And there is no other place to go. Certainly, no place better."

"But you're a guard, Vaten. You don't understand what it is like for us. You are cared for like Crevir himself."

"That's not true. You know I wasn't always a guard. I wasn't always cared for here. I lost..." He sighed. Then, as if finding a new line of thinking, he started again. "Look, I know it's not perfect here, but the rains haven't left us. When they come back, this place will provide for us all once again."

Ajeau rolled her eyes and said, "It can. But not when most of the shares go to you and the F—"

"Careful Ajeau." Vaten held up his hand and turned his head from her. "We are friends, but you know my duties. You'll be punished for speaking like that."

Ajeau shook her head. "Come on. Where did that fun kid go? Remember, you used to sneak autel berries from that trader's cart. I think you used to say, 'They're sweeter when you don't have to pick them yourself.'" Ajeau imitated Vaten's voice poorly, then broke out in laughter.

Vaten grinned at the memory. "They were sweet, but that was a long time ago. I can't do that stuff now. I have to be tough. That kid is gone."

Ajeau paused and narrowed her eyes at Vaten as though inspecting him. Vaten thought it a rare moment of silence from her, but as soon as he finished his thought, her eyes opened. She smirked and said, "Nope. I don't believe it. You're still that kid in there somewhere. I'll find him one day."

The response annoyed him. The entire conversation did. He wanted to lash out, scream at her about who he was, who she was, but he knew that would only prove her point; kids lash out.

Luckily, Vaten heard his name called from across the fields. He couldn't see the man calling him, but recognized the voice as the Captain of the guard. From the tone of the man's voice, Vrai appeared irritated.

Ajeau pushed Vaten with her hands and said, "Go. Go."

Vaten ran to the wiry man, who stood as if his back was made of wood. It was not uncommon for him to be rigid—Vaten often wondered if the man's shoulders could sag—but today, Vrai's heavy beard and round eyes could not hide his scowl.

Vrai grabbed Vaten by the shoulder and pulled him close. "Stop distracting the workers from their task," he said. "You are to oversee, not interrupt. And you need to see all. You can't do that if you are talking with one. Now let's go, the Foreman wants to see us."

Vaten nodded. Vrai had reprimanded him before and he knew well enough not to say anything in return. Besides, he didn't mind it. Vaten figured it was good to learn from the man. Vrai could command men with just his voice. That was power. That was strength.

Vaten made it a priority to listen and observe Vrai, hoping one day he could emulate the man. At the time, that was reason enough. And though it wasn't his intention, it was shadowing Vrai that led Vaten to his true prize.

A week later, while drinking wine with his fellow guards, Vaten found himself alone with Vrai. He remembered little of what they spoke about before Vrai shattered his world.

Without warning, the man said, "Do not believe the Foreman. Your father is alive. He cannot see you yet, but there will be a time. Be patient until then."

Vaten only stared. He blinked as though he no longer controlled his eyelids. He wondered whether it was a joke, a lie, or—his heart raced—real.

Before Vaten could respond, Vrai nodded and continued, "Believe me. Have patience. The Noye will not keep him from you forever."

Then Vrai walked away and said nothing more of Vaten's father.

The Noye. Vaten seethed at the words. He thought of his father struggling against bindings while some giant beast insulted and tortured him. Yes, the Noye would not keep his father from him forever. That was because he would take his father back. And end those vile Noye.

It was just like Crevir had told him. The Noye were to blame for it all. And though the Foreman may have lied about whether his father was alive or dead, the Noye still had him. And so, like a mole that burrows underground and waits patiently to emerge, so did Vaten's hate for the Noye.

From that day on, every interaction with Vrai took on an outsized meaning. Even when he did something wrong. He took his scoldings with a side of hope Vrai would deliver him to his father.

But not long after the harvest, the pessimists' fears materialized. The rains stopped, the crops failed, the supplies disappeared, and the shares were cut. Not much for the guards or the Foreman, but those who worked the land, Ajeau among them, faced starving conditions.

It horrified Vaten. He watched his friend whither, her brashness fade like the crops she worked, until he gave up and agreed with her. It became so dire he shared most of his rations with her and other workers.

It may have saved Ajeau, but it was nowhere near enough.

As more workers faced the brink of starvation and death, the estate became unruly, rebellious, and violent. Workers targeted, beat, and bloodied guards. In return, Crevir burned huts, armed the guards with new iron swords and daggers, and punished all infractions with cruelty.

"They are angry because they have no food." Vaten would yell at the unsympathetic guards. "When the rains return, we won't have anyone to sow the fields or harvest the crops. We won't have any food for anyone!"

Then one morning, when they should've been in the field or the workshop, the workers formed a mass in front of the Foreman's residence. The horde yelled and chanted insults at the Foreman. They threw sticks and rocks at his dwelling.

For a while, there was no response. Vrai had called back the guards to stand ready near the storehouses as the uprising carried on.

Crevir raged at his Captain. "What are you doing? Have the guards send them back to work or make an example of them! What else are your shiny new toys good for if you don't use them?"

Some guards made their way to the door before Vrai held out an open palm. When they saw him, they stopped.

"Let the crowd yell," Vrai said to the Foreman. "They will tire and we can return to our day."

Crevir inhaled and leaned back in surprise. "You would let such insolence go unpunished? What is to stop them the next time their bellies rumble?"

"Yes, they are hungry," Vrai said. "And they are angry. But there is only one way to soothe them. It is not with violence."

"What have you planned?"

"No plans. It's simple nature." Vrai gestured behind him at the fields of the estate. "The workers will go back to the land and pick whatever food is left. That is the only way they eat. It is the only way they survive. Fear of death will drive them from this house."

"I do not like this, Vrai." Crevir said.

Vrai leaned close to Crevir's ear. "You know we cannot return them," he whispered. "We *need* them, we are behind on the Vizier's—"

"I know our status!" Crevir grabbed the man's arm. He struggled to wrap his hand around it. "But they will—"

"They will not," Vrai said. "Watch."

Crevir relented. But the crowd outside did not.

With the guards and Crevir still absent, a few workers began chanting that the Foreman had left, and the estate was now theirs. It began as a fabrication—no one really believed Crevir and the guards would leave—but it satisfied something bleak in their hearts. And violence followed.

The fields, dry tinder, were set ablaze. Empty huts and workshops followed quickly thereafter. The crowd of workers pushed their way into the Foreman's dwelling looking for something that might save them. Food. Drink. Riches. Calls of 'take whatever you can carry' and 'it's ours now' reverberated through the house.

"This had gone on too long!" Crevir shouted at Vrai. "You have lost me the fields—fine, they can be replanted. But I will not lose my home to these pests. I have worked too hard for it. Now, return these insects to the ground and restore order to my estate!"

Vrai sat motionless, ignoring the man screaming at him.

"Did you hear me?" Crevir stood over Vrai and yelled. "I said, clear my home! End this revolt!" When no words came, Crevir reached down and shook Vrai's shoulders with both his hands. Still, the man did not move.

"So be it." Crevir spat beside Vrai, then spun around to face his guards. "We will take back this estate, starting with my home! Flush them out from the back, then flank them from the sides. Simple pincer!" No one moved for a second. "Now!"

The guards rushed into formation. Vaten eyed Vrai on the ground, but did not linger. He followed the orders and moved towards Crevir's residence.

The plan worked flawlessly. Guards easily cleared the workers from the building. And when they exited out the front, they found themselves trapped by guards on either side.

The workers had no plans; they were not soldiers nor aware of the tactics of combat. They froze, regret in their eyes, fear in their hearts. Their hands, full of fruits from far-off regions, metal pitchers of wine, and the skins, furs, and clothes of a rich man—all of it paid by their labors—trembled.

"Wait for the right time!" the Foreman said to the guards.

Vaten stared at the workers. He pleaded with them in his mind to drop what they had taken and run. Nothing they had was worth returning to the earth for.

"Wait for the right time!"

The workers glanced around, panicked, begging for mercy from the guards. Some bent over and put their pickings on the ground while others put their hands up in capitulation. But none of it was enough for Crevir. He had won but not yet secured his vengeance.

Vaten's body shook, his arrow rattled against his bow, his nerves were fried.

Then one worker ran towards the house for cover. It was a foolish move. The guards in the house closed the door, and with their spears, impaled the man. A cry went out from the others. They scattered.

"Now!"

Arrows arced in the air. Men and women fell to the earth.

Vaten dropped his bow, his arrow falling with it, and ran. He didn't know if anyone saw him or if arrows were coming for his back too, but he ran as fast as he could to the camp and the hut of a friend he hoped had not joined the mob.

Shaking and weeping, he called out for Ajeau. He begged for her to appear. She did not. He left her hut and frantically searched others, diving into and out of every structure he could make it to. She was nowhere to be seen. He retched at the thought of her in the crowd, pierced by some guard's arrow.

But then a familiar voice called from the trees of the grove. "Vaten, you idiot. Shut up and come here."

"Ajeau?" he said, stunned. He walked on trembling legs to her side. "You weren't there?" He grabbed her to make sure she was real.

"No, I'm not dying for some stupid Foreman and his stupid estate."

Vaten exhaled. "Thank Eau."

"But," Ajeau said, her voice more serious than just a moment before. "I'm leaving now and you need to come with me."

"I-I can't. Vrai knows my father. He can help me find him; I know it. And I can't let that go."

"The Captain?" Ajeau said in disbelief. "You would stay for that beast? You would choose his canings over my friendship? No matter if he knows your father or not, he is wicked."

Vaten averted his eyes to the ground and whispered. "He's different from the guards. He's fair and thoughtful. Yes, tough, but not cruel, at least not to me. He looks after me. And if he knows my father..."

Ajeau put her hand under his chin and lifted his head up so they stared into each other's eyes. "We'll find him ourselves." Her eyes sparkled with adventure. "We don't need Vrai, nor this place. We'll walk all of Bas to find your father. To the ground if we fail."

Vaten remained silent, unsure.

"Anyway," Ajeau said. "The Foreman is likely to kill if you go back. Now, come on." She punched him lightly on the shoulder. "Let's run. Today. And find someplace better."

When she turned and walked towards the trees, Vaten followed.

\*\*\*

"AH, THERE WE ARE," Levitien said and then inhaled deeply through his nose. "Quit your whining, kid, and look at that." He pointed with his head, showing Vaten whatever he should see was behind him.

Vaten glanced at Levitien but missed the signal from the man's head, and said, "What is it?"

"That." Levitien again nodded his head toward Vaten.

Vaten turned his head and gazed at a wondrous sight. Infinite blue. Like a sky, but alive and moving. It seemed the opposite of the brown scenes of desolation which surrounded them. Instead, it was creation. Undisturbed by drought, water rose and fell, as far as the eye could see.

"Is...Is this the sea?" Vaten said in awe, forgetting the guilt, the misery that so enveloped him only a few moments ago.

"Never seen it before, huh?" Levitien smiled, chuckled softly. "Now you'll never forget it."

"I've only heard stories of it. I half thought it wasn't even real."

"Oh, it is real, kid. And every time you see it, you'll have the same feeling of wonder."

That may have been true but, in that moment, Vaten thought of the tales he had heard of the sea. Tales full of marauders arriving to conquer, endless trips of insane men, the attacks of strange beasts, and unfamiliar lands nurturing all kinds of terror. He wondered which was he fated to live.

The caravan stopped atop a hill next to a rocky cliffside and the prisoners were moved to the ground. Then they watched as their captors deconstructed everything. They turned every plank of wood, metal rivet, and stretch of rope into storage and packed away everything else. Nothing was discarded or wasted. Even the boxes that carried the mysterious prize the people of the caravan worked so hard to obtain were readied for transport.

Zejela strode towards the two prisoners. She acknowledged the guards that kept watch and then turned to Vaten and Levitien. "You will board boats soon. Do not resist the Sentries and your trip will be a pleasant one."

"What trip?" Levitien asked.

Zejela eyed him contemptuously. "If you must know, we are sailing for Zevaco and will land within a month if the weather holds."

Levitien furrowed his brow as he gazed at the woman. "Where?"

"Zevaco, our home." Zejela paused. Then she shook her head. "You will know more upon our arrival."

"Wait. What? Zevaco?" Levitien said.

Vaten's face dropped. "A month?"

Zejela had already turned and left. The Sentries pulled on the ropes binding the prisoners and pushed them to walk forward.

Levitien turned to Vaten. "You ever hear of Zevaco, kid?"

Vaten shook his head. "No."

"Of course not." His eyes glimmered, lips curled into a smile.

Vaten did not smile. He hung his head and wondered what would greet him on those foreign shores. Captivity? Servitude? He had lived that life and been too weak to change it. Now was no different.

Vaten heard Levitien's words again—*wait for the right time...your hope will be rewarded*—like bait in a trap closing around him. As the boats departed, Vaten saw, for the first time, land receding into the distance. His dreams retreating with it.

# PART II

*The tree survives.*
*Tall, in the sun.*
*Fruit, as night.*
*Within, a seed.*
*Reverence, as at home.*

*The land expires.*
*The sky halts.*
*A growth begins.*
*It is the end of plenty.*
*It is the beginning of one.*

*It will be known.*
*It will be sought.*
*It will be found.*
*It will be wielded.*

*Do you forget the payment of your ancestors?*
*Refuge comes to those who heed their elders.*

–Istor Bouton

# CHAPTER 12

IN THE NIGHT'S DARKNESS, Savique and the woman who had rescued him rode atop a horse. It sped through the forest as furious as ever, darting, weaving, and jumping to avoid the obstacles in its path.

Savique was relieved to be free of the Foreman and the cart, but he knew he had not yet been saved. This woman—the same one from the night of the raid—was a stranger. And Noye. Though she had rescued him, he had no idea why. And no idea where they were headed.

With the brands he wore, nobody with ties to the Lord would welcome him. And if he came across anyone familiar with Crevir or Vrai, his life would be over. Maybe Vaten's too. But at least he was alive.

His heart thumped in his chest. Yes, he was still alive. And he had to remain that way if he was ever to see his son again. In that moment, Savique mumbled a prayer to himself while his fingers dug into the side of the Noye he rode with. It may have saved him.

After his plea, the horse tripped. It stumbled and tilted sharply to the left. Both riders pitched with the beast, in danger of falling under it and being crushed beneath its weight. Savique let out a soft scream and winced, bracing for impact.

In a sudden and swift move, the woman in front of him pulled her spear from the right side of the horse's body, crossed her arm in front of her and stabbed it into the ground on the left side of the horse. Using the spear, now stuck in the ground, she braced the horse, herself, and Savique, and allowed it to regain its balance.

Savique's mouth hung open as if he was screaming, but no sound came out. He blinked like it was his first time. If not for the spear sticking out of the ground, he would not have believed it had happened at all. But it was there, shaking like a branch in the wind.

The horse whinnied. Savique thought it sounded like an apology, and it received a few firm pats in return from the woman who had saved their lives.

Then the horse, without instruction, reversed to allow the woman to retrieve her spear. She did so and turned to Savique. It was the first time she had looked at Savique since she helped him off the cart.

"Close," she said, then grinned a wide, open-mouthed smile. "We'll be arriving soon. Don't worry, cochon, you'll get your rest there."

She omitted, Savique noted, the location of their arrival.

***

As THE SUN CRACKED the horizon, spraying the first rays of light on the world, the horse stopped beside a large swatch of grasslands. Savique stared at the endless lines of plowed fields, planted crops, irrigation channels, and the storehouses rising into the sky. There were no people in the early sunlight, though it was obvious someone worked the land.

Savique felt a soft tap on his arm. Then a few more, harder. Finally, he turned and found the Noye woman looking at him and gesturing for him to dismount.

He did, and after landing, realized they were not alone. A pulse of terror ran through his body. The Foreman had found him. He would be returned to the estate and killed. Perhaps forced to watch his son's death.

But then he noticed the other woman's tall stature and dark green dress. She was nearly identical to the woman he rode with. She was another Noye. Though his heart steadied, he still did not have answers to any of his questions.

The two Noye embraced, and the woman Savique rode with said, "It is good to see you again. You are well?"

The other woman smiled and nodded. Then she inspected Savique. Though her gaze may have lasted only a minute, it felt like a year.

Upon finishing her examination, she turned to the first woman and said, "That is the man you brought? He does not look worthy of knowing, even less so than I imagined. I do not trust him. He is a man of the estate."

"He knows stones, Eyvo," the woman Savique rode with said. "Knows them well. You worry about his loyalty, but he has nowhere to go, no—"

"I can vouch for myself." Savique stepped forward. "I hold no allegiances to any estate. Certainly not the one that provided me with these." Savique held up his hands. "But who are you people? And what do you want?"

"Yes, perhaps introductions are in order here," the woman Savique rode with said. "I am Navo of the Ille. Elder of the great nomads. And this is..." Navo-Ille gestured to the other woman.

"Eyvo, also of the Ille. But you will get no more from me until—"

"She is also an Elder," Navo-Ille said as though she expected Eyvo-Ille's wariness.

"Navo!" Eyvo-Ille sighed, then pointed to Savique. "You know nothing of this man. He could spy for the Lord or some other evil."

"Do you distrust Vrai too? He has told us everything we—"

"Vrai? What does that bastard have to do with anything?" Savique asked.

"That bastard," Eyvo-Ille loomed over Savique, "is why you are alive. Do not tarnish his name with insults."

"What? No." Savique shook his head. "I think you are mistaken. Vrai is the reason for my brands. He was the reason I was in that cart, travelling to my death."

Navo-Ille raised her eyebrows and smiled. "No cochon, it is you who are mistaken. Vrai may have branded you, but he is our brother. He told us of your fate."

Savique's face dropped. It was preposterous. Vrai was the Foreman's Captain. He commanded the guard. He could not be a Noye. But there was no reason for these women to lie to him. Nor for them to know of Vrai at all.

"See, he doesn't even know the horse who carries him. You think him ready to be told?" Eyvo-Ille frowned and shook her head. "No, he is unqualified."

"I remember you saying the same words about Vrai. And we would have nothing without him. Not all outside us are against us," Navo-Ille said.

Eyvo-Ille glanced at the ground and pursed her lips. Then she said, "That is not the same."

"But why?" Savique said, gazing at his brands. "If you were going to rescue me, why force me to be branded? Why not take me the night I saw you in the camp?"

Navo-Ille sighed. "Yes, in hindsight, I would have preferred that, too. But we did not know then. Your rescue became necessary the moment you were caught between the Foreman, the Vizier, and the Lord. You were an offering we could not let be made."

Savique looked up from his brands and let his hands fall to his side. "And why was that?"

"That is a good question." Navo-Ille glanced at Eyvo-Ille. "We have—"

"Navo!" Eyvo-Ille shouted. "We have made no decisions here. I said I do not trust him. And that has not changed. You will not speak of it to him."

"Do not trust me?" Savique chuckled and ran his hand through his hair. "You raided my estate. You are of the same kin as the man who branded me. I have done nothing but trust, and you won't even tell me why I am here?"

Navo-Ille glanced at Eyvo-Ille. She returned it with a glare but then sighed and said, "I am sorry but I do not know you nor where your honor lies. But as you said, you have trusted us and I will return the favor. You are here because Vrai believes what the Ascetics told you. He believes you are...important for what lies ahead."

"The Ascetics?" Savique said, confused. "You believe that nonsense? I think I am more likely cursed than able to find anything lost."

"Vrai takes seriously the words of the Istori," Navo-Ille said. "He is a traveled man and knows much."

Eyvo-Ille scoffed. "He is sentimental and credulous." A brief smile crossed her lips. "But I trust the man as much as I do any of my tribesman. Perhaps more. He believes their words, but I am not so sure."

"And what does he think I will do?" Savique asked.

"That is a question you would have to ask him," Eyvo-Ille replied.

Savique would have liked to do that. But it was not the first question he would ask the man. There were plenty more he needed the man to answer to.

Eyvo-Ille squinted and pointed towards the rising sun. "Sun is up, Navo. Time to prepare."

"Wait," Savique said, glancing around. "If you won't tell me why I am here, at least tell me where we are."

"Planning to run, cochon?" Navo-Ille said, grinning.

Savique said nothing. Even if it was meant as a joke, the idea had crossed his mind. As improbable as escape was, it may be better than his fate with the two Noye.

"We are east of Morvan, alongside Lord Balay's personal farms." Navo-Ille pointed to the extensive fields in the distance. "You see how fertile they are, yes? There is food of all sorts here, barley, fig, wheat, even olives. A delicious assortment!"

"Lord Balay's fields? What are we doing here?"

"Getting food," Eyvo-Ille said, as though the answer was obvious.

"Yes, the fields have few guards today. We have gotten word that the Lord's Guard has conscripted many in their search for—well, us," Navo-Ille said.

Savique's heartbeat quickened. "They search for us?"

"Do not worry." Navo-Ille waved her hand. "They have been after us for some time. You see, the Foreman was displeased to lose a certain possession. Now, it appears the Lord has taken interest—"

"V'eauvian scum," Eyvo-Ille added. "He would use any excuse for a crusade against us."

Navo-Ille nodded. "Yes, that is undoubtedly true. But their conscription is only evidence of their desperation."

Savique did not understand most of what the two Noye said. And what he understood did not reassure him. "We are raiding these fields? Stealing the harvest?"

"Some of it, yes," Navo-Ille said. "We will wait until night, ride through the farms, and take what we can. After that, we will return to our tribe and share our bounty with them."

"You are raiders, then? Thieves!" Savique's entire body tensed. "The stories of your kind are true?"

Eyvo-Ille and Navo-Ille glanced at each other, annoyed at the question.

"People will speak about us how they may, tell tales of the true and the untrue. The untrue benefit us as much as the true. Yes, we take food. But Lord Balay has plenty." Navo-Ille pointed to the storehouses. "He will not miss what feeds our entire tribe."

"Right, stolen food does not hurt the Lord. It hurts the workers," Savique said, his voice rising with frustration. "Their shares are cut. Their work increases. Their lives are taken."

Eyvo-Ille nodded. "That is true, but only because those who labor in the fields do not understand their power. They can't in comfortable times. Only when they are made to be uncomfortable will they be able to put an end to their plight."

"You want to make us uncomfortable?" Savique stomped the ground and gestured angrily at the Noye. "We are starving! We are killed if we reach for more food. Your raids do not make us uncomfortable; they make us suffer!"

Navo-Ille placed a hand on Savique's shoulder. "Our allegiances are to our own. We are not saviors for those who toil for the Lord. They are their own masters. Maybe they will realize that one day, maybe they won't. But it is not our concern. We have far more important obligations."

"Enough of this," Eyvo-Ille said. "We must go now."

The Noye mounted their horses as Savique remained still on the ground. He glanced up at them with clenched fists. Navo-Ille met his gaze while Eyvo-Ille ignored him.

"Are you coming?" Navo-Ille held out her hand. "You can ride with me."

Savique wanted to lash out. Yell again at the thieves in front of him. But he knew it was futile. With or without him, the fields would be plundered, the shares would be cut, and the workers would be punished. He sighed, resigned.

"I don't know," he said, shaking his head. "I don't know if I can cause them to suffer, like I have suffered. Whether purposefully or not."

"I understand. Then our paths part here," Eyvo-Ille said.

Navo-Ille turned to her fellow Noye. "Eyvo..."

Eyvo-Ille shrugged and patted her horse's neck. Then she inhaled deeply and said, "Savique, those I trust believe you can help our people. On the chance that is true, I wish you to ride with us. And if you do, on my honor, I will help you return to the estate and your son."

"How did you..." Savique began. But he realized the answer did not matter. If he was to see his son again, he would need help. Not from men and women like himself, but from those of consequence. Elders. Warriors who rode against people like the Foreman.

"On your honor?" Savique asked.

Eyvo-Ille nodded. "Yes."

Savique did not wait to consider the proposal. It was assistance in returning to the thing he cared about most in the world. He nodded, and said, "All right. Then I will ride with you."

He grabbed Navo-Ille's outstretched arm and felt the familiar tug of the woman as she helped him mount her horse. The two of them sat in the same position as they had when they came upon the clearing.

"Good. We will get you a horse. But for now," Eyvo-Ille passed Savique a small metal blade, "if we should run into any trouble."

He held the dagger in his hand and maneuvered it through the air, remembering a time long ago when that action was common. But that was different, he thought. That was nothing like this. That was not for something, not for someone. It was not to go home, but to leave it.

# Chapter 13

More than two weeks since she left Seule, Ajeau finally saw the lights that illuminated the great wall of Nouv'eau. She smiled as though each flame was a drop of water for her parched throat and then collapsed to the ground.

Ajeau had run out of rations days ago. Though foraging had sustained her, there was little strength left in her body. Her legs shook, her vision spun, and her mind wandered. But it was not until she saw the lights high in the sky—but lower than the stars—that the exhaustion caught her. Maybe she let it, knowing she had finally made it.

When she awoke, the sun was overhead and she could see fully what she had only glimpsed the night before. And it stunned her.

A large stone wall rose from the ground and stretched taller than any tree Ajeau had ever seen. Halfway up the wall were the lights she had seen the previous night. Torches and lanterns hung in windows that extended the length of the wall, illuminating the world in front of it. But still it grew higher. For all Ajeau knew, its crest touched the clouds.

She wondered if giants built it. Or worse, giants resided within it. She resolved to find out. She only needed a way inside.

There appeared to be only two options. The path leading to a large gate or a river flowing into the city from the west. She could not even see its terminus because of the height of the wall.

So Ajeau walked the path until she could see activity at the nearest gate. Guards stationed outside large wooden doors attached to pulleys by rope sat lazily throwing rocks at birds. She counted four, but in the same breath ignored the number. She was not invading the place, she only wanted to enter.

For some time, Ajeau watched as the guards worked, if what they did could be considered work. They rested for long periods and when they opened and shut the city's gates for merchants and traders, they did so with as little effort as possible. They did not even speak to most moving through the entrance.

It gave her hope she could enter the city without trouble. Even if the guards stopped her, she had a V'eauvian name and blood. That should be enough to allow her access.

But she realized she had no evidence of her blood, no relatives or friends who could vouch for her either. And she did not transport goods, nor have the fancy robes and tidy appearance of a merchant. She looked like a worker escaping an estate. No guard would allow her inside the city on her word alone.

Then she considered the river. It was full of boats moving in and out slowly, like ants marching to and from a fallen piece of fruit. She knew the docks would be full of workers who looked like her. She could steal a ride on a boat, blend in with the workers, and not have to worry about guards at all.

But there was no easy way to sneak aboard a moving boat so close to shore without being seen. Even if she waited for nightfall, there would be lanterns shining everywhere. And if the crew found her, they'd label her a thief. One wrong step and she would be killed. No, the odds it went bad were too high.

She kept thinking, but there was no solution without problems or grave risks. She kicked at the dirt, snapped branches, and even let out a few silent screams when another plan collapsed in her mind. So close to her goal, her last obstacle appeared insurmountable.

Tired, hungry, and now out of patience, Ajeau threw up her arms and walked across the open grasses towards the nearest gate without a plan.

Her hastiness led to an unexpected overconfidence. Of course, she could think of how to outsmart the guards when she arrived at the gate. Her best plans were always improvised, and the guards were always dumber than they looked. So she walked as quickly as her tired legs would allow.

As she approached the wall, the ivory behemoth seemed to grow in front of her. Its true size, as well as her smallness, became apparent and her confidence waned. She was an ant approaching a boulder. But unlike the ant, she understood it could crush her.

The realization came too late. Ajeau looked up and found herself within eyesight of the guards. She could not run; they would catch her. Her only option was to think of a plan, or her journey would end outside the wall.

The guards saw Ajeau approach, and she met their gaze. She thought them hardly an imposing group and their outfits made them appear naïve and inexperienced. They wore dirtied white shirts with no sleeves, leather kilts with faded white stripes down the side, and broken sandals that couldn't protect their feet. Crevir had treated his guards with more care. Even if the belt wrapped around their torso was leather, it was thin and held no blades.

They were not unarmed, however. Each one held a flimsy spear and a cracked wooden shield with heavy chips taken out of its center. Their grips on each were shaky, and they appeared encumbered by the weight when they moved. It was clear they were not warriors, only there to ensure those entering the city were supposed to be there.

"You. Stop there!" one guard yelled at her.

She took another step forward, still trying to create a plan for getting past the guards and the wall.

"I said stop!" The same voice.

"Me?" Ajeau said, surprised to see only a single guard approaching. Even though she was not an intimidating sight, she thought more guards would have come to turn her away. Their loss, she thought as an idea started to take root.

"Who do you think? There's no one else around." The guard looked around mockingly. "Now, what is your business in Nouv'eau?"

"I-I am searching for my family." Ajeau's mouth went dry. The truth was not part of any plan, but it had fallen out when nothing else would, as though she had plugged all the small holes in a wall and forgot about a large one.

The guard chuckled. He turned to his partners and said, "A stray!" Then he turned back to Ajeau and said, "Shouldn't you be working the fields then?"

"But I'm V'eauvian," Ajeau said. "They—my family—might be inside."

"Oh, I didn't realize you were V'eauvian! Right this way, Master." The guard could barely contain his laughter. The others didn't, and Ajeau heard their howls. She fumed.

"Shut up, *hublon*."

"What did you call me?" The guard raised his spear and pointed its head at her. "Get out of here, orphan. Go back to the fields. You'll never get into Nouv'eau or find your family." He taunted her with a face feigning tears. "Poor girl."

Ajeau stared at the spear pointed directly at her and wondered if the guard had ever actually stabbed anyone with it before. It didn't matter, she would not allow this cretin to kill her. And in that moment, a plan finally emerged.

"I'm not leaving until you let me in," Ajeau said.

"Good with me. Stay right here until you return to the ground. You look halfway there already."

Ajeau took a step towards him and grabbed the spear, holding the wooden shaft just below the metal point. She looked the guard directly in the eyes and spit in his face. The guard grunted and recoiled. The very moment he did, Ajeau swung her foot, catching the guard in his groin.

He groaned loudly and bent forward, head over his feet. When he did, he released his grip on the spear and it fell into Ajeau's hand. She quickly reversed its tip and pointed it at the guard's neck.

The guards near the wall laughed wildly at this turn of events. They hadn't seen a fight, especially one such as this, in quite some time. One even fell on the ground, his tears leaving a small pool of mud in the dirt next to him.

"Now," Ajeau said, pressing the spear into the man's flesh. "Let me in."

The guard, still doubled over in pain, said slowly, "There's still...three others. You...you kill me...you die too."

"Oh, I won't kill you. I'll just run off with your spear. Find the nearest trader and make a deal. You'll have to explain to your superior how you lost your weapon. I know you can trust your fellow guards to lie for you, right?"

Whether he weighed her comments or was in too much pain to respond, the guard remained silent. Then, after he held his hands out in submission, Ajeau allowed him to rise slowly. He stared at her with lips pressed together and said nothing.

Ajeau smiled mockingly at him in response. Then she said, "Let me in and no one will know. I'll give back the spear and I can defend you when those guys lie to everyone about how that stray girl stole it right out of your hands."

The guard clenched his jaw and ground his teeth. His brow fell over his eyes, creasing the top of his uneven nose. Ajeau wondered whether the man would retaliate, try to hit her with his shield or hand before she could slash at his neck. But the guard made no movement.

"Yes. All right. I will let you in," the guard said, more interested in protecting his pride than his city. "But you keep your mouth shut and give me the spear."

Ajeau nodded, relieved. "As soon as I pass through the gates."

She tapped the guard with the spear and gestured for him to turn around. When he did, Ajeau placed the spear tip tight enough to his lower back to leave a scratch. "Don't try to run, or I will force this spear through you before your foot hits the ground."

The guard said nothing and continued to march slowly to the gate.

As they arrived at the wall, Ajeau disappeared behind the guard she escorted. Her hands shook, and she wondered if the other guards would attack her. If they did, she was ready to spear the man in front of her and run in the resulting chaos.

But when she peeked out from around her hostage, she saw a mix of shock and delight on their faces. They were enjoying the scene. And appeared as if they had no interest in stopping her.

Still, the gate remained closed.

Ajeau prodded the guard with the spear. "Open the gate." When nothing happened, she gave him another jab and said, "Now."

"Primund! Open the gate," the guard said. "This one belongs to Morillon. She got lost during one of his...expeditions."

"Morillon? Again?"

"Yeah, you know, he can't hold on to his figs and they hang between his legs," Ajeau's hostage said.

Laughter broke out amongst the guard.

But as they laughed, one moved to the wheel holding the gate closed and spun it. The door creaked under the pressure of its roped hinges and, though it had only opened a crack, that it had opened at all made Ajeau exultant.

As she walked past them, the cohort of guards inspected Ajeau like she was a strange colored bug that had landed on their arm. She did not know what to do, so she jabbed the guard, thinking it would make her look more formidable.

"Yeah. She looks like one of Morillon's alright. Barely any skin left on her. What does he even feed them?"

"I think they get it worse than the pigs." More laughter.

"Still, she knocked you around pretty good."

"And took your spear! How thick are you?"

The raucous laughter reached its crescendo, peaked as the gate thundered to a stop. Ajeau turned and glanced at the opening. The city beckoned. A smile passed over her lips without her realizing it. She had arrived.

Then, from above, a loud, deep voice broke through the laughter and brought the guards to a standstill. "Enough of this, you idiots! Get your spear back and get back to your post."

With a move more graceful than Ajeau expected, her hostage spun away from her and then seized the spear with one hand. She tried to shake it free of the man's clutches. When his grip did not relent, she tried to stab the man. The spear did not move. He easily overpowered her.

Once she realized this, she dropped the spear and ran. It caught the guard by surprise and by the time he realized what happened, Ajeau had made it inside the city gates and nearly out of sight of the now humorless guards.

None of them followed her.

\*\*\*

THE EYES FOLLOWED HER. From high above, lurking in a window in the wall, the Eyes saw all. Heard all too. And she raged at the guards tasked with protecting her city.

How could they let this girl—an outsider—into the city? Such people only come here to take, and because of that, Nouv'eau now had too little. The next cut would come out of the gate guards' rations, she concluded. It was only fair.

But as the girl walked through the gate, the Eyes saw something she had not expected. On the girl's arm, there were marks broken and discolored. Some may have thought it a brand or scars from wandering the forest. But the Eyes knew. Something—someone—had made a cut there. No different than the Arboricole had done all those years ago.

The Eyes smiled, licked her lips slowly and said to no one, "So you are not an outsider after all. But are you the one I was promised? The Hijeuse?" Her grin revealed all her teeth. "Yes, all is clear now."

# CHAPTER 14

VATEN STOOD ON THE ship's deck, listening to the sound that had become so familiar to him: waves slapping at the hull. But today he saw something unusual above the vast blue expanse. A strange bird drifting overhead. Its wings were static, unmoving, as if carried by some invisible hand.

He stared at the bird, wondering where it was going, where it was from, and whether it would survive its journey. Perhaps it would not. Still, he marveled at the creature, flying so far from its home. If nothing else, it was a welcomed break to the monotony of his trip.

Vaten's days at sea were not always dull and repetitive. His first days on the ship were remarkable in so many ways. The lurching of the boat, the creaks and moans, the smell of salt that stung his nose, the unrelenting sun, the wind that whipped his face raw, the sickness, and the waves both small and large were incredible, though not wholly enjoyable, experiences.

But the novelty wore off quickly and after only a few days the scenery had become static, the changes only brought on by the sun's light or its absence. Days extended for what felt like weeks. Not even thoughts of Ajeau or his father would pass the time. And they would cause him great anguish. So, he gave up thinking about them.

If there was one source of amusement on the boat, it was Levitien. Now that the two men had no ability to escape, they were free to walk the ship and talk privately. If they didn't cause problems for the crew, they were free to do as they pleased. Their hands were still bound behind their back—their freedom was not absolute—but it allowed for a modicum of independence. And they used it as best they could.

The two men made up games to pass the time. They were silly little competitions, like kicking each other's feet or grabbing one man's bindings while the other tried to avoid it. But they made the prisoners happy. And they played as two young kids might when there was no work to be done. Vaten had long forgotten those days.

Their play also disabused Vaten of any previous skepticism of the man. In Levitien, Vaten found a friend who understood his plight but managed it far differently.

Levitien was curious, not solemn like Vaten. He was brash and clever, too. And the more time Vaten spent with the man, the more Levitien reminded him of Ajeau. Perhaps he was a little more arrogant than her, but the similarities were there. Losing Ajeau to gain Levitien was not an equal trade, but it was a minor consolation.

And like her, Levitien steadied Vaten's spirit as he needed.

"I still see them dying in that field," Vaten said on one day, indistinguishable from the others.

"Who?" Levitien replied.

"The prisoners. The ones killed by the Sentries."

"I've told you, kid, you have to let it go. People make their own decisions. It's terrible they were killed, but it is not our fault."

"You don't feel responsible, even a little?

Levitien sighed. "It's complicated. What are we responsible for? An idea?" He shrugged. "Yes, maybe that. But you did not force them to run. You did not capture them and take them from their people. You did not shoot any arrows."

"But I convinced them. Then I did nothing to save her—I mean, them." He closed his eyes and turned his head from Levitien.

"Don't you see that you're contradicting yourself? You cannot be both responsible and powerless. And in this case, I think you were powerless. But that also means it was not your fault."

It did not happen then, but the words eventually seeped into Vaten. He forgave himself for the death of his fellow prisoners, for abandoning Ajeau, and for the errors of his past. The weight of those responsibilities, he dropped into the sea where they would sit, unknown to all. Except perhaps a bird drifting overhead.

***

A LOUD YELL ECHOED through the ship. Then another. Movement followed. Vaten and Levitien watched from the bow as the crew ran through the ship, nearly knocking into each other as they did.

Zejela approached them and smiled. She stood there a moment with her hands cupped in front of her stomach as though she received welcomed guests.

Vaten noticed she no longer wore the dark robe she had on Bas, but instead a light dress cinched at the waist. The outfit was somehow both more and less formal. And the look on Zejela's face reminded him of their first meeting, when he first gazed at her and found her able to warm his chest or cave it in. Familiar, warm, and severe.

Her hair, streaks of black and white, danced around her face as she said, "I hope you both have tolerated the journey well. Even under the circumstances. You should know—"

"Wait. You said 'tolerated.' As in the past. The trip is over?" Levitien asked, glancing around.

"It will be soon," she said. "The loud yell you heard was our barrelman spotting land. The crew behind me works to ready the ships for our arrival. We will land on Zevaco within the day."

Vaten swallowed loudly and stared at Levitien with his eyes open wide. The ship was known and comfortable. But now the unknown was upon him and with it, fear.

Levitien ignored Vaten's gaze. "And our fates when we get there?"

Zejela inhaled deeply through her nose, pursed her lips, and nodded. "Yes, I knew that question would come. And you have no reason to fear. You will be free men on Zevaco."

Vaten's heart pounded. He felt his blood pulse through his ears like a drum. It was unbelievable. A free man? He was not sure he knew what that looked like anymore.

Zejela continued, "There is no indentured work on the island, no slaves. All people are free to work the land, trade, create, or assist the nation in other ways. If you work, you will be paid, be fed, have shelter, and be an equal to others."

Not only a free man, but the chance to be an equal. He could not believe what he heard.

"If you do not work or assist in some capacity, you will starve, without shelter and remorse, like you never lived. Like I said, you are free to choose." Zejela extended her hands towards them as if weighing the choice.

"And if we choose to take up arms, fight, kill as many as we can. What then?" Levitien asked smugly.

Zejela glared at Levitien as if he were a petulant child. "If you commit such atrocities, you will face our penalties. Our punishments are harsh but fair, and I do not recommend you discover them."

"What if—" Levitien began.

"And, if a question of escape is to follow from your lips, let me displace it with these words. There is no leaving Zevaco or returning to Bas. Even if you stole a ship, you would die at sea. But you are welcome to try." Zejela chuckled to herself. "You are no longer our prisoners."

Vaten stared unblinking at Zejela. The conversation intrigued him as much as it confused him. "If we are not your prisoners anymore, why take us at all? Why remove us from our lives to place us in yours?"

Zejela met his gaze. "All I can say is that it was necessary. But heed my words. You would do well to settle and live your life on the island. I was once you. Born on Bas. A V'eauvian. Captured. Your life can be born anew here, and it can be worthy."

A Sentry marched to Zejela, and whispered words Vaten did not understand. She nodded, whispered back, and then returned to face Levitien and Vaten. "I am needed elsewhere at this moment. You may have questions about our customs or language or land. I will do my best to answer those another time."

And with those words she strode off, pointing and talking to men and women that had kept Vaten in binds all this time. Equal to them, he wondered, how would that be possible?

Vaten and Levitien turned to one another. "What do you think of that, kid?" Levitien said. "You believe it, or are we walking to the hangman's noose?"

"I think I believe her," Vaten said without conviction. "Why would she lie? She's kept us alive this long. If they were going to kill us, they would've done so long ago, right?"

Levitien scratched his chin with his shoulder. "I don't know. I believe her too, but it seems odd, no? Why bring more mouths to feed? Why keep outsiders to work fields that are dying? Why expend resources on us and not save them for themselves?"

"I don't..." Vaten shook his head as his voice trailed off.

"Take care, kid. Keep your eyes open. Let's see what happens when we arrive on this Sol damned land."

\*\*\*

VATEN TOUCHED ZEVACESE SOIL first. Levitien followed soon after. During their time on Zevaco, the two men would argue and laugh over who exited the boat first—a pointless battle of pride—but the truth was, both men were forcibly removed from the ship. They had no say in the matter. And standing as free men on the shore of some unfamiliar land, they were more apprehensive about their position than excited.

The ships arrived at the port village of Erauke on the western edge of Zevaco. The similarity of Erauke to any small village on Bas surprised Vaten. Not only did the huts appear to be made from the same clay bricks, but they were also the same shape, size, and organized in the same small blocks. Even some decorations looked remarkably like those found on huts on Crevir's Estate.

But it wasn't only the huts. Fishing nets and angling hooks, ploughs, and scythes were all near exact replicas of those Vaten had used on the estate. It was as if the two societies mirrored one another and the advances from one found its way to the other.

Beyond the tools and huts lay fields, hills, and small mountains covered in trees. All was green. Lush. Thriving. As similar as the huts were to those on Bas, the landscape was the opposite. It had been so long since he observed such a fertile place, Vaten forgot how land was meant to appear.

And that's when Vaten realized there was water there. The rains that stopped on Bas must not have done so on Zevaco and the land to flourish.

Vaten shuffled towards Levitien, eager to share his conclusions, when he was preempted by his fellow free man. "No drought here, huh, kid?"

Vaten's smile faded. Annoyed the conclusion was no longer his, he simply nodded and stared straight ahead.

It was there Vaten saw the boxes so coveted by the people of the caravan carefully loaded back onto carts. All the while, Sentries stood protecting the area from any undue attention from the local villagers. Those caught gawking were directed to move at bladepoint if necessary.

Once they loaded the boxes, the Sentries mounted their horses and, on Zejela's orders, departed before any more eyes came their way.

After giving the commands, Zejela walked towards Vaten and Levitien.

"I must ride with the rest to Soccia, the Seat of Elders. I have left horses for you with the stablemaster." She pointed over her shoulder at a small hut next to a large, muddied field.

"She speaks little Bassian, but expects you. You can ride the horses wherever you please. Venture across our land. Find a settlement that offers you work. Or, if you choose, you can follow this path to Soccia and pledge in front of the Elders. As I said before, you are free men."

She turned to leave but was interrupted by Levitien's voice. "Zejela! Would we not be of some help on this journey?"

Zejela smiled, seeing through Levitien's poor guise. "My business in Soccia is personal. Between me and my fellow Elders. I appreciate your offer of assistance, though I assure you it is not needed. Now, I must be off."

"What if we—"

"Levitien, I must go," she called back as she mounted her horse. "If your questions remain, seek me out in Soccia. Or look for answers among your new brethren."

Then Zejela, atop her horse, galloped away, leaving the two men standing next to each other in a world both familiar and strange, amongst a people who were now theirs but entirely alien. As the people of the village moved around them, Vaten glanced at the sky and saw a most desired sight. Rain clouds.

***

THE RAIN FELL HARD and fast; the clouds unleashing their torrents before Vaten and Levitien could find cover. Though they tried to run towards the stablemaster, they lost their way. The rain obscured even that which was within an arm's reach. But eventually Vaten saw a tree near him and gestured for Levitien to follow.

The two men sat under the full branches as the rain relented. Drips of water still fell on their heads through the leaves, but they could once again see the fertile land around them. It was green as far as the eye could see.

Vaten pointed to the hut in the field Zejela had shown them and said, "Should we go? We are free men, after all." He grinned and turned to Levitien but was met with a blank stare. "What's the matter?"

Levitien stared at him for some time, then sighed and said, "I just want to go home. Back to Rigolade. Back to my family." He closed his eyes and added quietly, "I'm sorry."

"I want to go back home, too. I need to find Ajeau. And my father. But this land is amazing, isn't it? We won't have to hunt for scraps anymore. And we are free and equal."

"Yes, compared to Bas, it is incredible," Levitien said, wiping the rain from his brow. "No drought. Food and resources enough, it seems, for everyone. But it is not ours. Not mine, at least. And no matter what Zejela tells us, we will not be equals here. I know how too many places treat outsiders. Noble or peasant, they are never equals."

"So, you aim to leave?" Vaten shook his head and shrugged. "How?"

"I'm not sure yet, but there must be a way. Zejela told us she herself entered this land as a captive and she ventured to Bas. If she can do it, why not us?"

"I don't know," Vaten said. "She is an elder here and has all the power that would entail. All the resources too."

"Yes, but she became an elder. How?" Levitien exclaimed as if it proved some point lost to Vaten. "And not all who were in the caravan were elders. Perhaps we may be able to join another journey to Bas as a Sentry or something else."

"It's possible the Sentries are from here. On the trip to supervise Zejela."

Levitien scoffed, then shook his head. "Supervise an elder?" he said. "That seems unlikely. But regardless, I'm going to find out what is real." He leaned in towards Vaten and spoke with a conviction Vaten had not seen since the night he told them of his plan to escape. "I won't force you to come with me. It's your choice. But I want you to. I never expected a trip like this to bear a friendship, but it has. So, I ask, are you with me?"

Vaten did not hesitate. He embraced Levitien and said, "Yes. I am with you."

"Then listen. I have an idea. If we can find out why these people came to Bas, we can concoct a reason for them to go back. Once we do that, we ensure we are a part of it."

Vaten's eyes narrowed. "And how do we do that?"

"I'm not sure yet." Levitien glanced at the tree, then Vaten again. "But the answer lies in those boxes. I don't know what's in them, but it's why they came to our land. We find out what is in the boxes and we can go home."

"I don't—"

Levitien grabbed his shoulder and stared into his eyes. "I know it's light on specifics, but it will get us home," he said. "Unless you have a better idea?"

Vaten shook his head. He did not. Still, Vaten remembered the last time he agreed to one of Levitien's plans. The look on his face said enough.

"Kid..." Levitien held out his hands. "There's no hurt in trying to find out what is in those boxes. All we do is ask. We don't have to break any customs here to ask, right?"

"Right...but..." Vaten hesitated. Then relented. "All right."

The two men stood, their feet sinking into the muddy ground, and walked to the stablemaster. They secured their horses from the woman and then readied themselves to ride to Soccia, the Seat of Elders, and pledge themselves to a land they had every intention of leaving.

As the horses dashed along the path, Levitien yelled, "First, we must find Zejela!"

# CHAPTER 15

THE ENDLESS BICKERING EXHAUSTED Savique. It seemed Navo-Ille and Eyvo-Ille argued day and night. Regardless of where they were going or what they were doing, the two Noye disagreed over some matter.

It had been weeks since Savique first agreed to join them and in that time, there had been few constants. They never rode in the same direction for more than a day. They raided some fields but passed by others without incident. They stopped to camp amid large trees, open spaces, or tiny hovels hidden from view.

But the two Noye always argued.

Savique learned much about his companions through these disputes. They voiced their opinion openly, told fantastic stories, loved fruit over grains, were expert trackers, had unique senses of humor, loved their horses as people, and were stubborn as mules.

Despite the frequency of their disagreements, nearly all of them were trivial matters and always ended with smiles and laughter. There would be cordial insults and sometimes even friendly wrestling before then, but the two Noye never allowed their bickering to become personal or linger into their duties.

On this day, however, their voices were louder than usual and the air charged with a hostility that concerned Savique. He sat off to the side, wondering what could have caused such a change in their attitudes and whether they were truly angry this time.

"Savique, come settle this." Navo-Ille waved Savique over.

"Yes," Eyvo-Ille said. "We have an urgent matter that you may be able to help with. Navo and I have been discussing the ability of a—"

"Savique, what do you know of the date?" Navo-Ille asked. "Have you eaten such fruit?"

Savique rolled his eyes and sighed. "Yes, I know of it," he said, mildly annoyed. "I ate one a long time ago. Very sweet, I think."

"Do you know where those fruits come from?" Eyvo-Ille said. "Have you ever seen the plants that bear them?"

"I've heard they come from trees with long bushy leaves at the top. Though no, I have never seen them."

"Trees!" Navo-Ille glanced at Eyvo-Ille, cocked her head slightly to the side, and said "I told you."

"The issue was not whether they come from trees." Eyvo-Ille glared back at Navo-Ille. "Though even he says he has never seen such a tree, the issue was where such plants may grow." She turned to Savique and continued, "If it is a tree, do you know where to find them?"

Savique shrugged. "I believe the south. I've been told dates and figs like the warmth—"

"The south!" Navo-Ille exclaimed loudly as if Savique's words were punches in a fight.

"Versud is a large place," Eyvo-Ille again countered, undeterred by Navo-Ille's confidence. "The trees may grow there. But they do not grow in the desert! Nothing grows there. It is infertile."

"Why?" Savique said. "Why does it matter? Who cares about what bears a date or where the tree grows?" He matched the volume of the two Noye, if not their animosity.

The Noye remained quiet, but their faces betrayed their silence. There was an answer to the question, Savique was certain, and if neither would provide it, then it held some significance for them. Perhaps it was not a trivial matter after all.

The argument ended there, peculiar as it was. Typically, there was a natural progression from disagreement to resolution, from passionate to disinterested, from frustration to amusement. But no such progression occurred here. The discussion was severed prematurely, leaving a heavy silence, like a thick fog, over the riders.

Until a buzzing noise broke it, as though a bee had flown by them.

Navo-Ille fell over without warning. As she hit the ground, she cried out in shock and pain. Savique glanced at her and saw an arrow sticking out of her shoulder.

He froze. The sight was so unexpected that it took Savique time to understand what was happening. Then, with a surge of panic, he knew. They were under attack.

Before he could think about it any longer, Eyvo-Ille grabbed him by the back of his shirt and threw him to the ground. He landed with a groan as the impact knocked the air from his lungs.

"Shh," Eyvo-Ille said as the two of them lay on the ground only a few steps from the writhing Navo-Ille. "The Guard are here."

"How do you know?"

Eyvo-Ille nodded her head in Navo-Ille's direction and whispered, "Arrow."

Savique turned and marveled at the ornate white markings lining its reeds. It was like a work of art, labored over and valued by those who created it. And he knew it could only have belonged to the Lord's Guard.

By the time Savique turned back to her, Eyvo-Ille had crawled towards her horse, where her spear and shield rested. As she did, Savique ran his hand down his leg and felt the handle of the dagger sheathed there.

Navo-Ille clenched her teeth and grunted as she grasped the arrow sticking out of her shoulder and pulled. The metal tip came dislodged, and she exhaled loudly once it had been fully removed. Holding the weapon in her hand, she stared at it, then threw it on the ground in disgust.

All the while, Savique continued to hear sticks snapping, leaves crunching, and voices whispering on the wind. The Lord's Guard approached.

Then another arrow. It glanced off a tree near Eyvo-Ille's horse, hitting no one. The horse whinnied in response but was otherwise undisturbed, as though the beast was unfazed by the passing projectile.

"Savique!" Eyvo-Ille said urgently. "They are coming from the East. Be ready! You will have to fight."

Savique, unsure which way was east, spun around, hoping to see someone. He didn't, but he was ready. He could fight. He had done it before.

But then, like a thunderclap exploding overhead to announce the rain, Navo-Ille's voice announced her charge. "I see you there, slave to the Lord!"

Savique glanced up from the ground and saw Navo-Ille holding her shield in front of her torso with her damaged arm. Blood still ran from her wound. Her undamaged arm held the spear horizontally, pointing in the direction of the guards she saw. Then she squeezed the horse with her legs, crouched atop the beast's back, and whispered something in its ear.

The horse burst forward and was upon two guards before they could even draw their swords. To the first, Navo-Ille shoved her spear through the man's eye with gruesome precision. The guard did not muster a shriek or scream in defense, only fell to the ground with a whimper. The horse, unharmed and without a rider, rode away quickly to escape the encounter.

With her spear lodged in the first man's skull, Navo-Ille dropped it, drew her sickle, and continued to ride past the second guard. The guard, instead of riding away from Navo-Ille to gain space from the woman, tried to turn his horse and follow her. It was clumsy, a move made by a novice, but Navo-Ille took no mercy on the man. She rode around him, stopped, and as the guard turned to face her, she removed his head in a single strike.

Like his slain partner, the man's body fell lifeless to the ground, and his horse rode off.

Navo-Ille moved to retrieve her spear, laying with the first man, when she saw her mistake.

The two guards had been decoys, purposely placed to draw the Noye into a trap between two sets of guards. Now, instead of facing a group of enemies at the front, Navo-Ille was flanked on both sides by them.

She cursed her recklessness. She should have known the decoys were too obvious, their tactics too foolish. They were not warriors; they were simply men holding weapons without understanding their meaning. It was a costly error in judgment.

***

FROM WITHIN THE TREES, Eyvo-Ille saw the ploy unravel. And unable to stop Navo-Ille's charge, she mounted her horse and rode laterally from where her tribeswoman stopped. It did not take her long to find one of the flanking parties.

There she glimpsed a woman dressed in white, skin as dark as hers but with hair as golden as the sun. The woman sat on a gray horse, a bow notched with an arrow clutched in her arm. She stared at Navo-Ille as Eyvo-Ille quietly dismounted and advanced on their position.

"You have something that belongs to us," the woman in white shouted at Navo-Ille.

Navo-Ille said nothing in return.

"There is no escape. We have you surrounded," she said. "One word and arrows will pierce your chest and return you to the earth,"

"So be it!" Navo-Ille yelled back.

"Give us what we want, and you can leave with your life. We will take..." The woman in white paused and glanced to her left. "Only a hand for your theft."

Navo-Ille responded by spitting on the ground.

"Have it your way. We will torture its location out of you." She turned to the party of guards and said, "Do not kill her, capture her. We need the—"

Eyvo-Ille, near enough now to her adversary, whistled loudly. The horses, surprised, reared on their hind legs. It was only a momentary distraction, Eyvo-Ille and Navo-Ille both knew it, but it was long enough that Navo-Ille could charge. And she did.

As she rode, Navo-Ille swung her spear—still coated in the blood and sinew of the man she impaled—like a madwoman. The arrows flew from in front of her and behind her. They landed on the forest floor, on her shield, on her horse, and on her. The impact sent a surge of pain through her body. She lost feeling in her legs. She could hardly breathe. But she rode forward to take as many as possible with her.

Eyvo-Ille swiped from the ground at the legs of horses and people alike. She speared those that did not see her. Those who saw her and took aim at her found her gone before they could land a strike. Eyvo-Ille, nimble as a fly, maneuvered through the horses, disappearing and reappearing as needed.

"Fools! Off the beasts and get her," the woman in white said.

Without delay, the guards dismounted to fight Eyvo-Ille. But when they did, they saw their ranks had already thinned considerably. They shared tentative glances as they searched the ground for their enemy.

Their caution made them an easy target for Eyvo-Ille. Her speed and grace unmatched by any of the guards, she cut them down as though they were saplings.

Then, she looked up where the woman in white had been and found her no longer there. She glanced from side to side but saw no one living. If not for Navo-Ille, it would have been a complete victory.

Eyvo-Ille rushed to her sister's side. She lay in the field with arrows fixed to her back and legs. "How could you have fallen for that trap?" Eyvo-Ille said as tears formed in her eyes.

Eyvo-Ille tended to Navo-Ille in the field as best she could, but she was no healer. She only knew what had been done to her. She removed each arrow, placed leaves over the wounds, and pressed on them. Navo-Ille groaned when she did. There was still life in her sister's body, though it was faint.

"Savique, where are you?" Eyvo-Ille said without taking her eyes off her sister. "Come help me with Navo already. We need to get her—"

A bow string tightened around her neck and stole her words.

"Where is it?" an unfamiliar voice from behind her said.

Eyvo-Ille flailed, but hit only air. She tried to headbutt whoever was behind her, but again made no contact. She tried pulling the string with her hands, but it did not budge. Her eyes began to swell and bulge from their sockets.

"Where is it?" the voice said, growing enraged. "Tell me!"

Eyvo-Ille's chest heaved, trying desperately to gasp for life. Her vision narrowed and blackness crept in. She jerked. And again. The last thing she saw was a lock of golden hair, and then the blackness consumed her.

"Where is it?" the voice screamed.

\*\*\*

SAVIQUE STOOD BEHIND THE woman in white, looked at his dagger, and plunged the blade into her. He pulled it out and stared as the white vestments the woman wore turned red. She dropped her bow—the string loosened from Eyvo-Ille's neck—turned and stared at Savique. She tilted her head to the side, confused, then reached out to strike him, but missed and tumbled to the ground.

She lay still for a moment, then frantically clambered away from him. Even with the wound, she was quick and made it to her horse before Savique thought to stab her again. She mounted her horse with a scream, blood dripping from her onto the beast's back. Then she rode out of sight.

\*\*\*

EYVO-ILLE'S EYELIDS SLOWLY PULLED apart, but as soon as they did, they snapped shut again. The sun's brightness overwhelmed her. She lay still and groaned. "What—What happened?" she said to no one in particular.

When no response came, she cracked her eyes open enough to allow her to acclimate to the sun's rays. Through thin slits, she stared at the surrounding scene; Navo-Ille laying limp on the ground, covered in blood while tended to her. He forced water into her mouth and pressed cloth to her cuts.

For a moment, the view confused Eyvo-Ille. Then, in an instant, she remembered it all. The battle, the woman in white, Navo-Ille covered in arrows, and her own existence being choked away. And with the memories came panic.

Quickly she fumbled her fingers under her clothes, felt the familiar shape of a box, and breathed a sigh of relief.

"Savique!" she said, her voice hoarse. "Is Navo alive?"

"You're awake! I thought I may have been too late," he said, a look of relief on his face. "And yes, she is alive, but her breath is shallow."

Eyvo-Ille rose slowly and walked a few quick steps to her horse. She collapsed against her partner's side, patted its back, rubbed its mane, and said, "Not yet, friend. Thank you for watching over me."

"What are we going to do?" Savique said, gesturing at Navo-Ille. "I cannot help her."

Eyvo-Ille closed her eyes and rubbed her shoulder and neck as she grimaced. "Nevant is our closest camp. It may take a night, but the healers there will help her."

"How? She cannot ride like this. She won't make it. Her horse may not make it." Savique pointed emphatically at the horse standing nearby, arrows still littering its back.

"The horse will make it. Look," she said, smiling at the animal. "It stands—it has suffered no great injury. And Navo...will ride with you."

Savique shook his head. "It is not possible, she can't—"

"If she breathes, she can ride. You will help."

Despite his protests, Savique mounted Navo-Ille's horse, helped Eyvo-Ille load the woman behind him, and then sat still as Eyvo-Ille strapped her to him with rope. He felt the weight of the large woman pressed against his back, a mix of hard flesh and warm dampness. He shuddered at the feeling.

After securing Navo-Ille, Eyvo-Ille mounted her horse and beckoned to Savique. "The horse will follow me. It knows where to go; you need not guide it. Only watch for trouble. And do not worry. Navo is Noye. She cannot die atop her horse."

Eyvo-Ille's horse broke into a gallop as Savique and Navo-Ille followed close behind.

# CHAPTER 16

"MOVE IT!" A SHOUT came from behind Ajeau. "Out of the way."

Ajeau turned and saw a boy carrying what appeared to be bags of straw over his shoulder. He stared at her and, when she did not move, stuck out his chin and released a frustrated sigh. As he walked past her, he kicked dirt at her and said, "Trash."

"S-Sorry."

Nouv'eau was a confusing place. It was full of towers, buildings, and huts larger than Ajeau imagined possible. There was stone and metal as far as the eye could see. Paths seemed to lead in every direction and they were always full of people moving. So many people.

Ajeau had assumed a considerable number of people lived in Nouv'eau, but this was more people than she thought existed anywhere. It made the city feel constricting, like she was tied in ropes. Her breathing sped and her vision blurred. She had been inside the walls for a minute, or maybe ten, and was already disoriented.

And now she was the target of insults.

"What are you doing here, anyway? There's nothing for you." The boy had put down his sacks of straw and approached Ajeau. "Don't you know we don't want you around?" He stopped only inches from her face and peered into her eyes. It unnerved her.

"I-I'm not an outsider. I'm V'eauvian. My name is Ajeau." She tried to speak formally, as if the child would accept her as someone who belonged there if she spoke correctly.

"I've never heard of any Ajeau. You say you're V'eauvian? Where are you from? What family?"

"I don't know where I'm from or who my fam—"

"No family?" The boy raised his eyebrows. "You're right, you're not an outsider, you're a stray. Even worse." Chuckles turned into full-throated laughter.

It took all her restraint, but Ajeau did not insult the boy back. Nor did she smack him on his head. She remembered why she was in Nouv'eau. "I'm here to look for someone," Ajeau said. "Do you know Aube?"

The boy's eyes lit up. "Aube? The Aube? Of course, I know her."

Ajeau grinned at her good fortune. "Do you know where I can find her?"

"Sure do. But that information will cost you."

"I don't have much to offer."

"Yeah, looks like it, but..." The boy eyed her over. "What's in the bag?"

"Nothing." The word rushed out of her mouth too quickly. Then she tried to cover her lie by talking more. "It was food and water, but it's all gone now. I could work or help you—"

The boy lunged at the bag. He gripped it but underestimated Ajeau's strength. She shook him free with her forearm and yelled, "Thief!"

A few heads turned in their direction, but no one made any movements. Most people just continued to march along, ignoring the outsider and her antics.

"Where are you going?" Ajeau called to the moving crowd. "This boy is a thief!"

She pointed to where the boy had been, but he was gone. She shook her head and sighed. He was a lost lead but was likely to have caused more problems than solved. If nothing else, she was free of his endless irritations.

Then she heard the faint sound of footsteps coming closer. The familiar slap of soles on dirt. Such small strides, such quick feet.

As the footsteps came closer, Ajeau turned to see who was coming, but only saw the mass of people moving along the paths. No one running. Except—

By the time she saw the boy, he was nearly on top of her. He moved swiftly, and she had no chance to avoid him. Or the brick he held in his outstretched arm.

The boy slammed the brick into the side of Ajeau's head, causing a cloud of dust and debris to form in the air. A low grunt escaped Ajeau's lips as her eyes closed and her head rocked sideways. She lost her balance and started to fall. Her arms tingled and did not respond to a request to brace herself. Her vision spiraled then went dark as she landed on the ground.

The ground was hard but warm and it invited her to rest. Yes, rest was a pleasant idea.

Ajeau couldn't see, but she felt the boy grab her small bag and take it from her. Then he said, "I told you, there is nothing for you here. No matter your business, you shouldn't have come."

***

A CROWD FORMED AROUND Ajeau as she lay on the ground. She heard the whispers and felt their kicks. But what concerned her most was the numbers growing around her. The thought of guards finding her and exiling her from the city ran through her head.

She forced her eyes open and willed herself to stand. The world spun around her and as soon as she made it to her feet, she lost her balance. She reached out and caught the arm of a woman nearby and used it to steady herself. Ajeau locked eyes with the woman and gave her an appreciative smile.

The woman shrieked as though Ajeau was a monster and yanked her arm away. Ajeau wobbled, but before falling over, she stared at the ground and planted her feet. She regained her balance, raised her head to find the woman, and readied a fist to strike her.

Before she could, she heard a booming voice say, "All right, all right. What's all the commotion?"

"An outsider, causing trouble again! And look at the state this one is in. Bleeding, can't even stand—"

"I will deal with the situation," the voice said dully, "All of you, back to work."

No one moved.

"Back to work now! I will not say it again."

A well-groomed man with a short beard and shorter hair walked towards Ajeau. He wore a clean white robe that glided in the breeze as he moved. Ajeau met his gaze, then saw the dagger sheathed at his waist. Her breath caught in her throat.

But the man made no movements towards his blade. Instead, he extended his arms towards her with his palms open and lowered his head in a sign of peace. When he arrived beside her, he spoke softly. "What is your name, visitor?"

Ajeau said nothing.

"Do you understand me? I do not mean to harm you." He held his hands out again, showing there was nothing in them. Then he placed one on his chest. "My name is Puy, and I am a merchant here. I bring goods from across Bas to our great city. I have met people from all over and I help them find work in our city. Where are—"

"I am not here to work," Ajeau said. "I am here for a purpose."

Puy chuckled. "Good. No work for you then. Perhaps I can help you with your purpose?"

Again, Ajeau responded with silence. If the man truly was a merchant, perhaps he could be helpful. He might even know Aube. But she had no intention of allowing him to know anything about her before she knew his goals. She wouldn't make the same mistake she had just made with the boy.

"Perhaps your purpose has to do with that bag Gogorain ran off with? Hmm?"

Ajeau's eyes grew. She needed her satchel back, or at least the stone from Seule and the blue arrow which were inside.

Puy stared at her a moment, then held up a finger. "Yes. I think so. The bag is important? Most bags I come across are." He chuckled to himself. "How about a deal? I will bring your bag back to you by the end of the day. You can have it. All I ask in return is your name."

She knew the deal sounded too good to be true—deals with powerful people were never what they seemed—but she could not refuse. She had nothing else to offer. "I am Ajeau."

"Well, Ajeau. It is nice to meet you. I am sorry your time in our city has been so..." the man hesitated and waved his arm, "turbulent. Now, where are you meant to rest?"

Ajeau looked at Puy, confused. She understood the question, but had no answer. That much should have been clear to him.

"My apologies. I meant to say, where should I bring your bag when I find it?"

"I have no place," she said and threw her hand to the ground. "I will rest along the path here."

Puy scoffed. "Nonsense! You would not survive on the roads here. A child almost ended your life in the daylight. How would you survive the darkness?" He stroked his chin and shook his head. "No, you will rest at my cottage, under my protection. The rats of this city will not bite you if you stay in an owl's nest."

She could not refuse such terms. Alone in a city larger than she could comprehend, without shelter, food, and friends, his offer was her best chance of survival. Though very much skeptical of the man, she closed her eyes tight and resigned herself to his offer.

***

AJEAU SAT IN THE small courtyard of Puy's cottage as the sun set. Puy had left, saying he would return with her bag and she should avail herself of his amenities. So, she sat there for a while—uninterrupted except for a man who brought her water and food—and recovered from the day's events.

She watched as men and women worked throughout the cottage, cleaning, cooking, forging bricks, and making repairs. It was as if the entire cottage were a small estate unto itself. There were even places for small gardens, trees, and a pasture for grazing. Not much grew, but that it existed at all stunned her. The man was so wealthy he had small storehouses for food and a well for water.

The cottage was as disorienting to Ajeau as the city, but for very different reasons. She could not reconcile Puy's extravagance with the barren world she knew. While fields and crops failed and people hungered, one man had more than he could ever use or consume. His personal supply outlasted Foreman Crevir's by years.

But as the sun descended below the horizon, Ajeau appreciated the security Puy's cottage provided for her. She realized how right he had been in judging her, unable to survive a night without shelter. It was then she remembered Seule's warning; the city was dangerous. It was a warning she wished she had heeded earlier.

The sounds that rang throughout the night were chaotic and barbaric. Screams, commands, metal and stones clashing, even music, rose like the city's wall, a barrier to harmony.

Around the perimeter of the cottage, Puy's men roamed with weapons driving off would-be thieves, vagrants, or just the starving. And Ajeau realized that even the cottage, a place of wild luxury and affluence, was not safe from the chaos of the world.

Puy returned to his home a while after nightfall, carrying Ajeau's bag in hand. He appeared more disheveled than when she first met him, and his clothes were now tinged with dirt and sand. He laid the bag on the table and said to Ajeau, "Your bag, yes?"

She opened it and looked inside. "Yes."

"Great!" He turned his head and nodded in confirmation at a woman. She returned the nod, then left. Soon after, servants brought a cup of wine and some bread to Puy. He ate a few bites, drank a sip of his wine, and glanced at Ajeau. "I must admit, your bag carries interesting items. An item even I have not seen before."

"You looked," Ajeau said, unsurprised.

"I apologize. It was too enticing, and I am a curious man. I had to look, but I did not take anything." He grinned, then continued, "Are these items related to your...purpose, as you said?"

Ajeau stared at the man and considered her options. If she lied to him, she would lose the help of a powerful and wealthy individual. He may know Aube. But if she told him the truth, she risked what he did with it. She rubbed her forehead with her hand and decided there was only one way to find Vaten.

So Ajeau told Puy of herself and her friend, of the men who took him, of Seule, and of his advice to find Aube. Throughout the telling, Puy sat attentively and did not interrupt, save for a few exclamations of surprise.

When she finished, he said, "I am sorry you had to wait until now to see the great city of your people."

Ajeau smiled. It was the first time anyone told her she was part of a people. Joy swelled in her chest, an ache of pride.

He continued, "But the city is different now. The drought has changed much. The nights are tumultuous, full of lawlessness and violence. In the days, good men and women of this city still work. But the days are becoming shorter and shorter. Night will displace the day soon enough."

"Now that you know why I'm here, are you willing to help?" Ajeau asked.

"Yes, I will do what I can to help. Ajeau, there are many things you do not know about your people. You would not be here if you did." He scratched his beard, then stroked it. "What I mean to say is, I will help you find answers to your questions. But you may not like what you find."

***

THE EYES SCOWLED AT Puy. He had always been a thorn, even on his first journey. Perhaps he had forgotten who sent him on that day and what riches they sought. No, he was no fool. But the man had grown too large for his plot. She now recognized that.

But that did not answer the question of why he took in some girl from beyond the wall. The man—a merchant—consumed by value and purchase and coin, housed one who provided him with no worth. One who only took from him. Did he know?

No! That was impossible. Unless he saw the scars, too. And heard the whispers from the wind like she had. Was Puy clever? The Eyes shook her head. Not clever, greedy perhaps.

"Remember what I told you on that journey, Puy?" the Eyes said to no one. "Know whose tree you fell."

Today, it was her tree. And she would forbid it. His interference would have to cease immediately. Only the Eyes knew the visions of the Arboricole. The Hijeuse was hers.

# CHAPTER 17

SOCCIA WAS NOT A city. It was barely larger than a village and Vaten thought it similar in size to Crevir's Estate, though even that may have been an overestimation.

Vaten had heard stories of cities, the vast rows of huts, walls, and towers, and that is what he expected to see. Instead, he was met with a plot of land without a wall, dozens of huts, and not even a handful of small buildings.

Though the city was unremarkable, the surrounding area was exceptional. Immense amber fields extended in nearly every direction. Even when the estate was at its most productive, it never looked like this.

"Have you seen anything like these?" Vaten asked Levitien, pointing to bushes and trees full of fruits he had never seen before.

"Oh sure, kid," Levitien said with a smile. "I think those are lychees, sweet and tart. Delicious though. And those might be mangoes!"

"You've tasted them?"

Levitien shrugged. "Once or twice, they were rare even for us. But they are sweeter than anything. Juicy too."

Vaten laughed eagerly and imagined the moist fruit breaking apart in his mouth, the juices dripping from his beard.

As the two men passed from fields to the village itself, Levitien regaled Vaten with tales of fruits and foods common for people of means, but far out of reach for workers like him. Here, however, in Soccia, they seemed within Vaten's grasp.

He was again daydreaming of the delicacies that awaited him on the island when a girl approached him. "Sirs," she said, her voice accented but loud and confident. "Zejela will see you at her hut. Follow the path here and take a left at the large rock. You will see her hut adorned by blue paint at the very end of the row."

Levitien stared at the girl through narrow eyes. "How do we know what you tell us is the truth? How did Zejela know we would come?"

The girl shrugged her shoulders and said, "You will only know if you follow." Then, with a glint in her eye, she said, "Beat you there!" The next moment, she was in a full sprint away from them.

Vaten laughed at the audacity of the girl and then glanced at Levitien, who eyed the fleeing child. Eventually, he turned to Vaten, and without speaking, they agreed to follow her.

Zejela lived in a small cottage with a courtyard in front. Along the sides of the building were lush gardens with small trees, shrubs, and an assortment of colorful flowers. It appeared no crops grew there though, and the tending of the garden was done for leisure, rather than work. Behind the cottage was a stable, a pit for fire, a kitchen, granaries, and stairs running to a cellar. Vaten thought the features were simple, more practical than luxurious.

Several people strolled about the courtyard, entering and exiting the hut or the cellar at will. They ate and drank and wore smiles of joy and delight. They spoke to each other with animated gestures, laughed, shook each other playfully, and embraced each other as though deep friends. Both men took hesitant steps forward.

But before he entered Zejela's land, Levitien grabbed Vaten's arm and stopped him. "What is this?" he said, staring at the people ahead of him through narrow eyes.

Vaten shrugged. "It would appear to be a gathering. Maybe a celebration of some sorts?"

"Yes, I know that—" Levitien said sharply. "But why? Why are we here? Why did Zejela invite *us* to a celebration?" He shook his head and said quietly, "She knew we would come."

"I don't know. Perhaps we truly are equals, as she said."

Levitien closed his eyes and sighed in mild annoyance. "No, she has a purpose in mind for us." He grabbed Vaten's shoulder and stared into his eyes. "Stay alert and do not forget our aim. The boxes. We are the wolves come for the sheep, no matter under what pretense."

\*\*\*

ZEJELA MOVED THROUGH THE gathering with ease. Like the robe that hung from her shoulders and obscured her feet, she glided through her courtyard as though floating, meeting her guests with hugs and soft smiles. It was the familiar and elegant Zejela they so adored.

And she indulged. She was home, finally, and the dirt that touched her feet was soft and comforting. The people she spoke with were warm. It had been too long in the harsh dry weather of the large continent and the stringent rules of the Sentries. Here she could be unburdened, even in the presence of her fellow elders.

It helped that she had been so successful on their trip. And though their discovery was the reason for the celebration, no one seemed interested in talking about it that evening.

"Elder Zejela." An old man approached her, his back hunched over his shuffling feet. His hands were folded flat in front of his chest, palms pressed together, and his white beard rested upon them. He bowed. "Welcome home."

"Thank you, Elder Diros," she said, matching his demeanor and pose. But after she bowed, her faced cracked into a grin and then a soft chuckle.

Diros grinned back at her. He grabbed her gently by the shoulders, stared at her a moment, then embraced her. "I am very proud of you," he whispered in her ear.

"I know," she said as they separated. "But you were before I left, right?"

He chuckled. "Of course, of course. But now...you are like the left hand of Castres!"

Zejela rolled her eyes and shook her head. "Flattery is often unsuccessful for a man so unknowing. It is his right hand that moved the moons."

"Well, you are not moving moons." He shrugged playfully. "But you are a success, nonetheless."

She tugged at the blue headband resting above her ears and blushed. "I suppose that will do. Now, enough about me. Tell me what has happened on our glorious land since I have been away. It was not a brief trip."

"No," he said. "But our work was mundane this year. The harvests were plentiful, the workshops outside of Brevais were completed, and we initiated a new class of Sentries." He plucked a bug from his beard and flicked it away. "Oh, a new fishing route was discovered thanks to Liffel."

"You make our work sound so dull. That could not be all!"

"Well, there was the matter of the—"

"You should know better, Diros," a round man with deep eyes said. "Elder business should not be in the open." The man turned to Zejela. "Welcome home. Your presence buoys my spirits."

Zejela bowed. "Thank you, Elder Uluard."

Though she wore a warm smile when her head rose, it masked the dislike she felt for the man. He was everything she was not: rigid, uncompromising, and ardently traditional. He argued his ideas with such passion and repetition he earned himself the nickname Tide; it was never said to his face.

Diros folded his arms in front of him and scowled at Uluard. "No quorums set here, Uluard. No votes. No discussion. Simple conversation. You need not lecture me on the policies."

"Right," Zejela said, attempting to smooth over any disagreement between the two men. She disliked Uluard, but did not want to antagonize him. "No need for an Assembly. It was my question that began his storytelling."

Uluard placated Zejela with a nod, then turned to face Diros. "And what was it you were about to say?"

"The matter of Larza's—"

"Zejela!" a woman called and waved to her. Then she rushed to Zejela's side and hugged her. "Oh, it is so good to see you!"

Zejela greeted the woman warmly and said, "And you as well, Marsan." She smiled at the two elders next to her. "I cannot wait to hear what new teas you have concocted, but for now, duty takes precedence."

"Duty?" Marsan glanced at Uluard and Diros and bit her lip in embarrassment. "My apologies Elders." She turned to Zejela. "Tonight, after the moons rise, I will tell you all about it!"

"Do," Zejela said. When Marsan had left, she glanced at Uluard, then Diros. "What is this about Larza? What happened to him?"

"Yes, well..." Diros glanced around at the growing gathering. "I think perhaps Uluard is correct. I should not share details of a confidential matter so flippantly. If any of Larza's friends were to hear—"

"I barely know the man," Zejela said. But when she saw the stern looks on Diros and Uluard's face, she knew her protests would fail. Instead, she tried a new tact. "We can convene in the cellar. I will have Digna watch it and ensure no one interrupts us."

147

Diros and Uluard shared a glance, then Uluard said, "All five must attend an Assembly. There are rules."

"Of course there are," Diros said. "Find Wehlat and Ryiera and meet us below ground soon."

Uluard sighed. "In the cellar?" He shot Diros an exasperated glance. "What are we, mice?"

"It is not so bad. There is plenty to drink," Zejela said with a flick of her eyebrows.

Diros nodded. "And a little time out of the sun will not hurt."

"Fine," Uluard said and pointed at each of them. "No business is to be spoken of until all five are present. The procedures are clear." He stared at them a moment, then stomped away.

Zejela glanced at Diros. "Don't start. I know," he said, holding up a hand. Then he smiled. "What of the newcomers?"

"Interesting," she said. "One is fit for this place. He will adapt well. The other...we will need to keep an eye on." She turned and saw the empty road leading from her cottage. She nodded, then turned back to Diros. "Now, follow me. I will procure us some tea for our Assembly." She patted him on the shoulder. "It is good to be home."

***

THE FIVE ELDERS SAT on creaky wooden stools around a table covered with dirt and dust. On top of the table, Zejela set a pitcher of tea and five cups. She glanced around the table at each person and gestured to a cup, asking if they would drink. Each one nodded. She poured the brown liquid into the cups, passed them around, took one for herself, and then sat.

"So what is this business with Larza?" Zejela asked and took a sip of tea. She winced at its heat.

Ryiera, a lanky woman who showed no signs of her true age, bowed her head and said, "Welcome home, Elder Zejela."

"Yes," Wehlat said. He was tall and broad like a bull and glared intensely at Ryiera. "It is wonderful to see you have returned. The time away has not dulled your shine at all. Like the sun—"

"More than the sun," Ryiera said, speaking over her fellow elder. "The time on Bas has rejuvenated you. You appear stronger and more confident than when you left." She raised her cup.

"Are you saying she should still be there? That you wish her gone from this place?"

"Of course not!" Ryiera said, standing. "Such nonsense. I am glad to bask in the glow of—"

Wehlat stood. "You are unable to show respect—"

"Enough bickering," Diros said with a gentle slam of his hand on the table. It was not his first time doing so. "All have welcomed her aptly." He smiled at Zejela.

"Yes, Elder Diros," both Wehlat and Ryiera said and sat down.

"Now, about Larza," Diros said. "Those sitting at this table, except you," he pointed at Zejela, "will remember during the previous moons he failed to make payment on the sheep provided by our land. He was short the grain and the livestock because of the injury to his arm from a fall the season prior." Diros waved his hand. "Unimportant."

"Quite," Uluard said. "The failed payment was deferred to the next harvest—the harvest now passed."

Zejela shrugged and said, "And the regionals could not handle such business? Hardly worth our time."

"True," Uluard said. "It came to us because of what happened next."

Diros nodded. "That's right. The regionals sorted the initial delinquency. But recently, they have found others under their jurisdiction refusing to pay for less obvious reasons."

"Less obvious reasons?" Zejela said, looking around the table. "Like what."

"One man said his feet would no longer follow his orders," Ryiera said.

"They were in revolt, were his exact words," Wehlat added. "Another said his hair had become too unruly."

Diros rubbed his head as if annoyed by the very thought of the excuses. "Others said their eyes blinked too quickly or their teeth were too close together. Others simply did not answer the regionals' questions."

"Nonsense," Zejela said, shaking her head. "What was the response?"

"The regionals were dumbstruck," Uluard said. "They tried idle threats but found that only exacerbated the problems."

Zejela took a sip of her tea. "So Larza and others in the Lower Brush refuse their levies?"

"Exactly," Ryiera and Wehlat said at the same time, then glared at one another.

"And this council has done what?" Zejela asked.

"We have put the regionals on notice and provided elder support for collections," Uluard said. "As of this evening, we have been unsuccessful."

"Have we tried the Sentries?"

Diros stood and poured himself more tea. "It had been suggested but dismissed. We do not believe violence, or the threat of it, will resolve this conflict suitably."

"There is concern that Larza may see this as a chance to disrupt the share of yield that flows from Lower to Upper," Ryiera said. "Which could lead to retribution."

Wehlat nodded. "The Upper would not take such insults lightly."

Uluard stared at Zejela, annoyed. "Besides, many Sentries had traveled with you."

"Many, but not all," Zejela said, annoyed by the accusation.

"Yes, yes," Diros said. "It remains a poor idea for several reasons. That brings us to now. There has been no payment and no suggestion that the situation is improving."

Zejela sat back in her chair and drank the rest of her tea. She and the other elders silently thought of how they could induce payment from those in the Lower Brush. But unlike the others, she could not stop her thoughts from wandering. There were far more prominent issues to work through in the coming days. Her discovery on Bas would necessitate many changes for the people here.

And at that moment, two men's faces appeared in her mind; the captives they had taken from Bas. Yes, she had forced them at one time, but now they were free. And they would need a reason to survive. No, it was not just about survival; it was about pride.

"We need to give them a reason to pay," Zejela said. "Something beyond the policies that require it."

"What do you have in mind?" Diros said.

"What about a...a Great Sycore?" Zejela said, as though the suggestion surprised herself. The other elders initially met it with silence.

But eventually Uluard, after he scratched his head and closed his eyes, said. "You want to reward their defiance? They'd never pay their levies again!"

"They will because it attaches them to the land," Zejela said. "And to us. Do you not see? They will want to pay because they will be proud to live on the land that holds the great tree."

Uluard said nothing and only shook his head.

"Elder Zejela," Diros said. "The Great Sycores are rare for a reason—"

"A testament to Aul's greatness!"

"Hush," Diros said. "Only a few of them remain, and they are under the authority of special caretakers. How would such a plan even work?"

"Surely, one can be planted in the middle of our most fertile region. A sapling that the caretakers could nurture."

"It will make others upset," Ryiera said. "What is to stop them from refusing to pay for the same treatment?"

Wehlat nodded. "Envy can be disastrous."

"I cannot solve jealousy," Zejela responded. "But if we want their yields, we must offer something *they*—the people—find valuable. What is more valuable than the Great Sycores?"

Diros planted his hands on the table and stood, sending the chair falling over behind him. "You are right. Not only about the people, but the trees themselves." He smiled at Zejela. "You are wrong about one thing, though. We can solve jealousy."

"What do you mean?" Zejela said.

"No, no. I don't know magic to steal the emotions of our countrymen." He chuckled. "But we can calm the resentment the way we always have. We invite the concerns of our fellow Zevacese. We listen and respond as elders have since they came to this island."

"You don't mean..." Uluard said.

Diros pointed at Uluard, his grin growing. "I knew someone would remember. A Hearing!" He clapped his hands together in excitement.

Uluard laughed heartily. It was the first time Zejela remembered seeing him laugh. "It has not been done for some time."

"Then we are due!" Diros said.

"I suppose we are," Uluard said. "Like the elders of old." He nodded at Diros, then said, "I call for a vote. A Great Sycore to the Lower Brush and a Hearing for the island. I am in favor."

There was no dissent. Not even Ryiera or Wehlat would argue with the other over some minute detail. And it appeased all because it was for all. A part for the old, the traditional, the devout, the reformist, and the pragmatic. The five elders exchanged gracious bows and excited pats on the back before they left.

When Zejela walked from her cellar back to the courtyard where her party continued, she grinned. Not because her plan had taken the day or from the pleasure she found in arguing. No, she smiled because she saw who rode down the path and knew she was right. It was about pride. And she knew just how they would earn it.

***

VATEN DID NOT BELIEVE his eyes. As he stood watching Zejela from just outside her cottage, he could not reconcile her with the person he had known on Bas and the ship. The features were the same, but the air around her had changed. She was graceful and sincere. Home had nurtured her warmth like loam nurtured crops. Vaten was captivated.

He remained staring at her even as she saw them standing beside the courtyard and began walking in their direction. It took a Levitien slap to his arm, to shake his gaze.

"Remember kid," Levitien whispered. "We are here for the boxes. That is all. Don't go giving the pigs away for nothing."

Vaten nodded. "Right, the boxes. You think they're here?"

"Not a chance. No one is defending the place," he said. "Wherever those boxes are, they're going to be well-guarded."

Zejela arrived in front of the two men and greeted them formally with a slight nod of her head, her arms bent at the elbow, palms facing upwards.

"Zejela, it feels good to be equals." Levitien grinned as wide as a river.

She put her hand on her chest and chuckled softly. "Levitien, we could never be equals for your wit so far exceeds mine, I am forever hopeless in matching it."

As an awkward silence descended on them, Vaten tensed. He felt heat growing in his hands and through his back. He forced out the first question he thought of to relieve his anxiety. "Where are the Sentries?"

"Why? Are you thinking of raiding us?" She locked eyes with him and her face grew serious. Then she patted his arm and laughed.

Vaten could not stop a smile from crossing his lips. "N-no, no. I'm just...curious where the Sentries are? Why is no one here? I mean, no Sentries." Vaten glanced down at the ground to avoid seeing anyone's face.

"It's all right," Zejela said. "There are Shere, though not many. We do not have much need for them. The Seat of Elders is a sacred and respected place. And the fields that surround us are the heart of this land. One who does harm here harms themselves most."

"You have no people like that here?" Vaten said. "People who seek to destroy even despite themselves."

"We do, but they do not last long." Zejela stared at him to emphasize the point.

In her stare, Vaten saw the intensity and severity within her. It seemed incompatible with the warmth she had presented moments before, but it intrigued him as much as it unnerved him. Still, he dropped his gaze to the ground.

Zejela continued, "Anyway, I have other engagements, so let us get to the point. Why have you come? For help? For work? What can I do?"

"We are here to—"

"For work," Levitien interrupted. "We have skills but can't speak the language and don't know where to go. We thought you could help us."

"Yes, I have work for you," Zejela said. "Something that will help you grow and tether you to the people here. I once traveled a similar path." Zejela paused, as though recounting those times in her head. After a moment, she continued, "Tomorrow, at dawn, you will follow me to the Outer Ridge, where our Sentries train."

"Sentries?" Levitien's eyes darted to Vaten.

Vaten stared at Zejela, his mouth open. He expected to be put to work as a farmer or a craftsman, not a Sentry. Not one of the people who killed his fellow prisoners on Bas. And for a moment, he saw the arrows from their journey—from Crevir's guards as well—and abhorred the idea.

But as the initial shock subsided, the prospect fascinated him more and more. The Sentries were not simply guards, and these people were not Crevir. The Sentries had shown him unwavering discipline and strength in the face of demanding challenges. He had sought such strength some time ago. Perhaps this would be his way of gaining it.

"Does that sound agreeable?" Zejela asked.

Vaten stared at the woman, lost in her dark eyes. A warmth encased him. "Y-Yes."

Levitien grinned widely. The man could hardly control his joy. "Yes. Of course. It is perfect."

Zejela nodded at each man and said, "Then until tomorrow."

As Zejela walked away, she appeared to sail over the grass courtyard. Vaten could not take his eyes from her. His heart pounded with excitement and apprehension, and he wondered whether this would be his chance to banish his weakness for good.

But as soon as the thought passed, he realized he did not care what the answer was. All he cared about was that Zejela would be joining him.

\*\*\*

THAT NIGHT VATEN SLEPT fitfully. The ground was too cold, the dreams were too real, and Levitien, with his wine-stained breath, was too noisy. Vaten thought it would never come, but morning arrived and, despite the lack of sleep, imbued him with a renewed spirit. For the first time since being captured, he experienced something like hope.

Before the others woke, he retrieved his horse, fed it barley and straw, and readied it for the journey. He asked the horse how long it would take them and what they would see when they arrived. There was no answer, of course, but Vaten found solace in the silence. Either the horse knew the journey and was ready or was ignorant of what lay ahead and shared such a bond with him.

"I never knew you had the power to commune with animals." Zejela said, interrupting his one-sided conversation with the horse.

Vaten's voice caught in his throat. He coughed. "No. I-I was just—"

"A joke." Zejela chuckled and rested her hand on his shoulder. "I do not believe you speak with animals."

Vaten forced a small laugh but said nothing while they both tended to their horses. It left an awkward void in the conversation.

Zejela finally broke the silence, speaking earnestly, "I am impressed that you woke early to care for your animal and ensure it is fit to journey. That is admirable, and I am sure it will be rewarded." She turned to the horse and said, "We have a long journey today. But there is no need for you to worry, you ride with a *lami*."

"Thank you, I think?"

She nodded at him. "Yes, it is a good thing." Then, to the horse, she asked, "Right?"

The horse neighed softly and nosed Vaten. He smiled and rubbed the bridge of its nose. "Good," he said. "I was told once by my captain that horses are more divine than us. Eau themself rode one. He used to say, when we are atop them, we..."

"Yes?"

He shook his head and shrugged. "I don't remember the rest. It was some time ago." He turned to face her and swallowed loudly. "Why did you choose the Sentries for us?"

"Oh, there are many reasons. It will bring you and Levitien respect and understanding and it will soothe my fears about you. But most of all, it will allow you to see yourself as a member of our nation. It did the same for me when I came here. I know your start with us has been difficult, but the start is not important. It is where you end up that matters. The tree is not the seed."

"And if we don't see ourselves as one of you, what then?"

"Nothing," Zejela said with a casual shrug of her shoulders. "You can continue or end your training. You can find other work at your pleasure. Remember, you are free here."

Vaten breathed in deeply, summoned all the courage he could, and said, "If we were truly free, we would choose to return home. Like you did."

Zejela's lips tensed, but that was all. If the comment surprised her, she did not let it show. "Vaten, I returned to Bas because I am Zevacese, not because I am V'eauvian, even if that is where the moons pulled me into the world. I say this with goodwill. You should not dwell on returning home. It is as likely as the sun failing to rise. Instead, you should think of this land and its people."

"And that is to be the purpose of our training with the Sentries?"

"Yes," Zejela said. "You will learn who we are and why we are. It will not be easy, but it will leave you stronger." She stared at Vaten, as though she wanted him to understand she knew what the words meant to him.

Vaten dropped his head and looked at the ground. The optimism with which he started the day dimmed and a harsh reality set in; even in this world, where he had much, he was still too weak to control his fate.

"A stronger Vaten? Impossible!" Levitien said, a wry smile on his face.

Zejela glanced at him, ignored the comment, and, upon taking stock of the situation, said, "Well, it appears all are here. Ready your horses. We leave for the Outer Ridge immediately."

She pulled her horse from the stable, mounted it, and trotted towards the path from the city. As she did, Vaten turned to Levitien and whispered, "I am glad to have you on this journey with me. It steadies my nerves."

Levitien nodded, "Me too, kid. Whatever lies before us at the Outer Ridge and with the Sentries, we face together."

The two men met Zejela on the path. She said nothing, only broke the horse into a sprint leading away from Soccia. Vaten and Levitien followed.

# Chapter 18

"Get the healer! Hurry!" Eyvo-Ille shouted to a group of Noye warriors as she broached a wall no taller than her legs. The horse easily jumped it, then came to a rest.

Savique, riding behind her, set eyes on a Noye camp for the first time and was amazed. Not by the size, it was a small settlement of tightly packed tents and huts huddled against a rock outcrop, but by everything else.

Whoever settled the camp, knew and used the land well. The tor, along with the makeshift barrier of rocks and bones, provided simple and effective protection. An army may have overwhelmed it, but the Noye could eliminate any unwelcome guests before they approached.

If that did not work, it appeared they would abandon the place without hesitation. Noye mobility and resourcefulness were rumors, Savique now knew to be true. They made huts out of found materials—mud, sticks, and leaves—and stored valuable goods in bags or bundles they could easily load onto a horse or mule for transport.

Yet, it was the life of the camp's inhabitants that surprised him most. He saw young children running and playing games and learning to ride horses. He saw men and women sharing stories and laughing while they worked. There was a leisure to their life that was unfamiliar to Savique. He had always worked to survive, and that weight fell heavily on his shoulders. Here, it was as if the weight were a pebble, carried easily in a pocket.

An old man rushed towards Savique's horse and said, "By Eau, what happened?"

"Ambush by the Lord's Guard." Eyvo-Ille rushed the words out without breathing. "She got hit with arrows but lives. She still draws breath. Are you the healer?"

The man shook his head. "I am the Chief of the *Pou*." He turned and waved towards the camp. "Haguen! Over here!"

Haguen-Pou raced to the chief's side. When he arrived, he said, "Cut her down. I want to see her."

Eyvo-Ille and several other Noye helped cut the rope that bound Navo-Ille to Savique, then gently placed her on the ground for the healer.

He moved around Navo-Ille, inspecting her, poking her, sniffing her wounds, and mumbling to himself. When he finished his performance, he turned to a young woman standing nearby and whispered to her. The next moment, the young woman ran off quickly.

"Can you save her?" Eyvo-Ille asked.

The man hesitated, though it was not clear whether he did not know the answer or he did not want to deliver bad news. After apparently reaching his conclusion, he spoke. "I do not know. Not all her wounds are deep. That is good. But some are, and that is troubling. Her skin is losing color and some wounds begin to fester. I've sent my associate to bring some rameuse leaves and water to help. It will be many suns before we know whether she is saved."

Eyvo-Ille exploded at the healer. "That is not an answer! Will she live or die? I am Eyvo of the Ille and I will not wait suns passively for my sister's fate to be decided."

Haguen-Pou closed his eyes and slowly bowed his head. "Eyvo of the Ille, welcome to Nevant. I am sorry it is under these terms. Rest. I will care for your sister as my family. I will wrestle fate itself for her life."

Eyvo-Ille turned and stormed off. After she did, Haguen-Pou walked towards Savique with a suspicious look on his face. "And who might you be? Riding with Elders, but not a Noye. Skin of an Islander." His eyes narrowed, and he stuck out his chin.

"I am Savique," he said. "I was with Eyvo and Navo before the fight. We rode together. Then I was there when they were ambushed."

"Yes, I see. But why? Why were you with them?" The healer stared at him, unblinking. "Why are you here now?"

"I—I don't know."

The answer was as frustrating for Savique as it was for the healer.

***

158

A CALM EYVO-ILLE SAT on a wooden stool near where Navo-Ille rested. She watched over her fellow elder like a new mother might watch a resting baby. Any movement or noise Navo-Ille made, she would jump out of her seat and see if her sister awoke. When she saw that Navo-Ille did not, she would sit back down slowly without averting her eyes.

Despite her concern, Eyvo-Ille did not interfere with Haguen-Pou or his associate. When they asked, she helped them steady Navo-Ille's horse while they tended to its wounds.

"Was the horse ever in danger?" Savique asked her after they finished.

"Of course not," she said. "It rode for its companion, its spirit. As long as Navo lived, the horse would not break stride." It was as if she described her faith in the sun rising.

Eyvo-Ille returned to Navo-Ille's side while Savique stroked the horse's muzzle. Then he caught sight of the suspicious glances of his hosts, their eyes inspecting him as though he were an intruder, and walked to the outskirts of the camp where he had made a crude shelter of sticks and leaves. Even if he rode with an elder, he felt unwelcome.

He did his best to ignore the Noye's wariness and scrutinizing glares, but then they began to throw objects—scraps of unused materials, sticks, one woman even threw a broken basket—in his direction. They rarely hit him, but they were an obvious attempt to disturb him and scare him into leaving.

On one such occasion, Savique watched as a small boy picked up a pebble, cocked his arm awkwardly, and threw it at Savique's chest. The throw was weak and the small rock caused Savique no physical harm, but it produced much anguish.

After days of this treatment, he finally moved farther away from the camp to prevent altercations. It mostly worked. The assaults did not stop completely, but he no longer felt he had to be alert at every moment. And he finally got some rest.

Then one night, as he tended to a small fire he made to keep warm, Eyvo-Ille approached him. Her presence surprised him. She had not left her post watching over Navo-Ille for weeks. He wondered what made this night different.

"Do you bring news of Navo?" He asked her.

"No," Eyvo-Ille said. "I am here for you."

Savique shook his head. "What do you—"

"I have seen the treatment you have received here. I know what they say about you. Tonight, you should enter the camp with me."

"I..." Savique glanced at the small village and saw its denizens gathering around the fire. "I do not think that would be wise."

Eyvo-Ille glared at him. "It is the night of the Star Circle. We will share a meal and many stories. You should listen to them. You should listen to my story."

"I do not want to intrude on a special occasion. It would be a distraction. I think I will—"

Eyvo-Ille grabbed Savique by the arm and began dragging him towards the camp. He was reminded then that Eyvo-Ille had often won many of the arguments with Navo-Ille. Now he knew why. She was persistent beyond reason, the very definition of stubborn.

Savique eventually picked up his feet, swung free of her grip, and walked on his own. If he was to attend their celebration, it would at least appear to be on his own terms.

As soon as he entered the gathering and saw the residents glaring at him, he immediately regretted his decision. His feet stopped, but Eyvo-Ille prodded him on and then gestured to a place on the ground next to the stool where she would sit. Savique sat there watching the Noye as they watched him. His chest fluttered, his heart uneasy.

The next thing he knew, food and drink were in front of him. He had been so focused on the villagers, he did not notice Eyvo-Ille had placed it there. Turning his head as if to question her, he met Eyvo-Ille's eyes and received a single nod in response. They ate.

Before he could finish his first bite, a woman stood and told a strange tale of giant creatures in the woods who fed on the flesh and bones of humans and animals alike. It was only through a pact with the smartest of the beasts, the horse, that they both survived and defeated the monsters.

Then a man rose and told a story of greed. One who stole from his tribesman, who tried to take everything he could carry and more. When he loaded his animals with everything he accumulated, it broke their backs, leaving the man stranded, alone, and dying.

A different man told a fable of twins separated soon after their birth. They would both grow to become powerful elders of their tribes. But one was poisoned with a lust for power. To find it, he went from tribe to tribe, stealing children and extracting their blood. Until he met his twin, who defeated him and ended his vile search.

Then Eyvo-Ille stood and told her story. A story of daring raids, found treasures, near escapes, a strange foreigner, an ambush, grave injuries suffered, and a woman nearly dead at the hands of her enemies. They only survived because of a timid protector.

She concluded by saying, "The story I told is the one that brought me here. Those injuries were suffered by our Elder." She gestured to where Navo-Ille rested. "I nearly died, a bowstring around my neck. And the savior? That is the man who sits next to me." She pointed at Savique.

"The man you shame, revile, and even assail saved our lives—the lives of your elders. You dishonor yourself and all Noye with such treatment. May the spirits of the dirt forgive your transgressions."

Silence followed. Savique heard no one chew, sip their drink, or even breathe loudly enough to make a noise. The camp stared at him, but not with suspicion or revulsion; instead, they looked on with wonder and regret.

The chief stood and said, "Savique, on behalf of the people of Nevant, I apologize. You are always welcome with us, to share in what we have. Long live your triumphs in the name of the noble beast!"

Savique, unsure of what to do, met the eyes of the chief and bowed his head slowly in acknowledgement. Then took a bite of his bread, hoping the stares would stop. The old man sat back down and, eventually, the Noye dropped their gaze and went back to their meal.

The night wound down with more tales, more food, and more drink. With his place among the camp secure, Savique reveled in the entertainment. He laughed loudly at their jokes, sang songs with enthusiasm despite not knowing the words, and drank as though it sustained him. It reminded him of the best times on Crevir's Estate when he would find rare moments of freedom with his fellow workers. Here, unlike then, no Foreman waited to drive them back to work the next day.

Before the fire light dwindled and the camp retired to their huts for the night, Eyvo-Ille turned to Savique and shook him awake. Something about the way she looked at him worried him, even despite his drink.

"Savique, do not rest yet." She paused and glance at Navo-Ille, still convalescing. Then she turned back to Savique and said, "It has dawned on me that there are things you need to know, things I intentionally withheld from you. That was...a mistake on my part. I regret it."

Savique nodded as though he understood. But between the drink and his fatigue, he had trouble following her words. And the more she spoke, the more lost he became.

"Navo tried to convince me of this. It was important for you to know. She wanted me to tell you the full history of our people, why our find excites us so, but also why we must keep it such a secret. I dismissed her, thought you too green. I thought her foolish. But you were not, she was not, and now she may never recover. I should've listened..."

She is rambling, Savique thought. He had not known her to be unsure or indirect, but her words wound in circles, crossed each other as though they were trying to lose a tracker. Perhaps it was her tiredness, or his. Either way, she made his eyelids heavy. They shut involuntarily. He pried them open with whatever energy remained.

"When I told that story tonight, I thought about our time together and I now fully believe Navo. He and Vrai were right all along. You can help us. You did help us. Proved yourself worthy. But if you are to restore the Noye to our place, our rightful place, if you are to save us all, as the Ascetics said, we will need more. I remember my words though, we will not only take, but we will also give in return and someday you can return..."

His eyelids fell shut again, sleep approaching, descending like a fog in the night. Before it could take hold, he jolted his eyes open once more, shook his head, and tried desperately to follow her speech.

But by the time he had done so, she was no longer talking. He had missed some important point. No bother, he told himself, he would ask her about it tomorrow.

In the last moments of wakefulness, before Savique's eyes shut for the last time that night, in a haze that could have been mistaken for a dream, he saw Eyvo-Ille reach into her robe, and grab a bag attached to her body. From it, she pulled out a wooden box with ornate metal trimmings. She opened it. *Was that a seed?*

\*\*\*

SAVIQUE AWOKE STARTLED AND sat up in a quick, erratic jerk of his torso. He glanced around the village to find what disrupted his sleep. It was still dark, but with light from the moons and the dying fire next to him, he could see he was not the only one who stirred.

A call for support came from the lookout. Savique stood and joined the others, who moved to find the reason for the yell. It did not take them long to see a woman who had approached the wall of the camp. She wore none of the green cloth of the Noye.

Sitting atop her horse, the woman raised her arms and smiled at the guards holding spears pointed in her direction. "I mean no harm. I am a friend."

The chief stepped forward. "What business do you have here, friend?"

"Careful," Eyvo-Ille said to him. "We do not know whether we can trust her."

"I have spied for your kind for a man named Huvat-Ac, in the lowlands outside Malo. He has returned to the earth now and I have urgent information for your elders." She lowered her arms but was met by advancing spears.

"Make no movements," the chief said. "Or you will find yourself impaled. Friend or not."

The woman nodded and put her hands back above her head.

Eyvo-Ille turned to the chief. "Do you know a Huvat? I have met few of the Ac."

The old man shook his head. "I know many Ac but no Huvat. Not surprising if he was in Malo."

"This is how you meet a friend?" the intruding woman said with a slight shrug of her shoulders. "I have—"

"You are no friend of mine," Eyvo-Ille said, walking towards the trespasser. "I see the V'eauvian blades you carry, the common horse you ride. Do you think us blind? We are not so easily tricked."

"I wear these blades and I ride this horse because I am V'eauvian. I do not deny that," the woman said. "But your people enlisted me, and I am here to make good on their wishes." She lowered her hands again, then stopped and sighed. "Allow me to show to you something."

The chief nodded.

"You touch those daggers, and it will be the last move you make," Eyvo-Ille said.

The woman nodded and reached into a small bag at her side. She took out a piece of wood no larger than her hand and threw it at the chief and Eyvo-Ille.

Both Noye flinched back as though it was a weapon of some kind. But after it fell to the ground harmlessly, they leaned forward and inspected it. Eyvo-Ille sighed, then picked it up and handed it to the chief.

"The mark of the *Ac*," he whispered. "So she tells the truth."

"I am unconvinced. Marks can be stolen." Eyvo-Ille said to him and then turned back to the woman. "What is this meant to be?"

"Proof. I told you, I am a friend," the woman said. "Why else would I ride into your village? How would I even know your location? If I meant to harm you, this would be a poor plan."

"She has a point," the chief said to Eyvo-Ille.

Eyvo-Ille glared at the woman. "A poor plan, indeed," she said softly to the chief.

"What?" he replied, but she had already begun advancing towards the woman.

"I do not know of your agreement," Eyvo-Ille said as she gestured to the guards to lower their weapons and let her pass. "But you may speak to me alone. If I find your information adequate, we will give you refuge. Otherwise, you will be turned away. If you do not leave, you will be returned to the earth."

"Agreed," the woman said as she dismounted her horse. "I will wait here. Hands aloft."

Eyvo-Ille grabbed a spear from a guard and continued towards the woman.

Savique watched from afar as Eyvo-Ille and the woman met. He could not hear what they said, but tried to infer the words based on their faces.

At first, they were stern and suspicious. Then the other woman smiled and laughed. Eyvo-Ille frowned, unamused. The other woman shrugged and nodded, with her hands still above her head. Eyvo-Ille stared at her a moment, then turned her head to look at the camp. The woman's hands dropped.

In a heartbeat, she had unsheathed her blades and struck at Eyvo-Ille's back. The Noye sensed the attack. She leaned forward and swept her foot back, knocking the other woman off balance. The woman swung her daggers wildly to regain her balance. But before she could, Eyvo-Ille stuck the spear into her side.

The woman fell to the ground, still slashing at the Noye elder as she did. Eyvo-Ille easily avoided her flails and spit on the ground next to her as the woman writhed.

Eyvo-Ille strode her way back to the camp. As she walked, she pointed to Savique and said, "The V'eauvians know."

"Know what?" Savique called back. There was no answer.

He moved past the chief and guards to meet Eyvo-Ille, but she did not stop. She continued past him as though he was a stranger. Before he turned around to follow her, he locked eyes with the woman struggling for her breath on the ground. The fury in her eyes surprised him.

He approached her, all the while staring at her as though she was a puzzle he could not solve. He stopped safely out of reach of her daggers and said, "Why? What are you after?"

The rider twitched on top of red puddles that dampened the ground like a fish out of water. Anything to get one more sip of air, one more moment of life.

"What is worth your life?" he asked.

The rider coughed, a river of red pouring from her mouth. Then said, "The mark...you fool...she has the mark."

"What mark?" But as soon as he asked it, he saw her eyes glaze over and fix on a single point. She stopped moving. It was over. Only questions remained.

# CHAPTER 19

NO ONE KNEW AUBE. At least, that's how it seemed to Ajeau and Puy. They had spent days looking for the woman and then for anyone who might know where she lived. At their most desperate, they simply asked if anyone had heard her name. But all they received were blank stares and shrugs.

It was not all bad news for Ajeau, though. She quite enjoyed her walks through the city and what Puy revealed to her during them. There were vast markets full of clothes, pottery, food, and metal objects she had never seen before. A busy port where she watched an endless number of hands unload, store, and then re-load cargo like bees in a hive. It was a stunning sight, though she could never stay there long; the port was as windy as it was busy.

Puy also took her past statues of great heroes and buildings that were decorated in grand fashion or gleamed with white paint. Some even had names, though Ajeau never remembered them. The names didn't matter to her. No, what mattered was that the city celebrated itself, its history, and its peoples. It was a place where one could find their purpose and be among their own. And she relished it.

After one walk, Ajeau sat down to eat with Puy, as they had done for the past several evenings. The flames of candles and torches illuminated a table full of bread, wine, cucumbers, and even a melon. The sounds of chaos echoed outside the merchant's walls, but the two diners paid it no attention.

"Still nothing," Ajeau said. "I am beginning to wonder whether Aube exists at all. Maybe she died long ago."

Puy nodded and said nothing.

"Or maybe Seule got mixed up. Maybe she is in some other city—I don't know."

Puy nodded again and took a bite of his bread.

"He wouldn't have lied to me, I don't think," Ajeau said. "Do you think she might be hiding?"

Puy swallowed his food and drink. "Ajeau."

"Seems unlikely. But we must keep—"

"Ajeau, stop." Puy held his hand up to get her attention.

"What?" Ajeau said, annoyed by the interruption. "What is it?"

Puy's smile grew wide. "I found her."

Ajeau slapped the table with both her hands. "What? When? Where?" She rose out of her seat and leaned towards him.

"Well, no. I haven't found her yet. But I know where she will be tomorrow. I had a friend look through the logs of the runners. I thought—"

"Where?"

Puy chuckled. "She comes in on a boat."

"She runs boats?" She smiled, relieved, and sat back down.

"Yes, but Ajeau." Puy's smile disappeared. "She runs boats for the Vizier. We will have to be careful. Even I hold little power over the Vizier."

Ajeau exhaled a long breath. The Vizier. No, it didn't matter. If Aube knew anything that could help her find Vaten and his captors, she would risk her life for it. "Yes. I will be careful. But I must speak with her. Vizier or not."

***

The following day, Ajeau and Puy left the cottage early. Before they could head towards the port and wait for Aube, Puy insisted they stop at the market and buy Ajeau a traditional V'eauvian robe and a leather sheath for a dagger. The two items would work in unison with a third that Puy had secured for her earlier. The robe shielded her arms from view. Fixed to her arms was a sheath. A sheath that held a dagger.

"Do I need this?" Ajeau said, putting on the robe.

Puy handed her the sheath. "Of course. When meeting with others, you take precautions. Even if you know the person, you do not always know their motives. And with Aube, you do not even know her."

"What if she sees it and thinks me the aggressor? What if she becomes defensive? Stops talking and leaves. This will have all been for nothing. I don't want to risk that."

"Put it on." Puy pointed to the sheath. "If you bring the dagger, you risk failure. If you don't, you risk death. The choice is obvious. Do not be irrational."

"Here, failure is death," Ajeau said, as if it was some grand philosophy.

"No, Ajeau. Death is death," Puy said with half a smile. "Do not mix words. Failure may alter your journey; death will end it."

Ajeau pondered a response, but none came. Puy was right. She picked up the weapon and secured it to the inside of her arm. It was invisible behind the recently purchased robe.

"See, you look strong." Puy made a fist with his hand. "Powerful."

"Maybe you are right." She knew the power a dagger could bring. "Maybe if she won't give the information willingly, I can take it."

Puy nodded, then began walking. "Let's go. We don't want to miss her."

The two separated when they arrived at the path to the port. The plan was for Ajeau to go alone. Puy was known to too many and his presence would draw the attention of others, possibly even the Vizier. "Too many eyes, close mouths," Puy had said when they finalized their plans.

Ajeau kept walking towards the port as Puy stopped and watched her. Before he turned down the path that would return him to his cottage, he called to her, "Good luck and careful of the winds."

She waved a hand to acknowledge hearing his words but continued on her way.

It did not take long for the winds to howl. Puy was no prophet, the winds near the port gusted every day, a product of the city's geography, its wall, and the drought. But today, unlike her other trips, the wind did not subside.

No, it grew and eventually became so fierce that it threatened to knock Ajeau over. It shook the buildings she walked next to and, when Ajeau looked up at one of the city's towers, she was sure it would topple over onto her.

But that was not the worst of it. Soon, all manner of debris—cloth, leaves, chaff, dirt—flew at Ajeau. The wind even picked up droplets of water from the river, carried them on its back, and released them all around. If Ajeau had not known otherwise, she would have been sure it was raining.

Still, the wind did not stop. Now, it gusted with such savagery that rocks and pebbles pelted everything in their paths. Ajeau heard screams for help from around her but could not open her eyes, the air too filled with dust.

Then, a piece of brick connected with her leg, and she fell to the ground. She wrapped her head in her arms, using the new robe to shield her face, and pleaded for nothing to fall on her. She lay there helplessly until the gale departed.

As suddenly as they came, the winds disappeared. The rushing noise stopped, only to be replaced by cries and coughs. Ajeau unfurled her arms, removed the cape from her face, and saw people strewn everywhere. Some crawled along the ground, trying to collect their belongings or console a loved one. She saw one man near her with his arm outstretched, asking for water. She shook her head; she had none to give.

In the next moment, pain from her wound burst into consciousness. It felt like a hammer had smashed her leg. When she tried to stand on it, she collapsed.

But she would not be deterred. She had to get to Aube and time sitting on the ground was time she did not have. The woman may be leaving the ports right now. So Ajeau grit her teeth, stood through the pain, and hobbled towards the water.

Once there, Ajeau set to work finding Aube. Puy's informants told him Aube would arrive on the fourth or fifth boat of the day, ferrying wheat and barley with two men. There were no other distinguishing characteristics. Ajeau didn't need any.

In the port was a boat full of wheat and barley with three people aboard. Two men and a woman. And there were already three boats docked and unloading their hauls. It had to be Aube.

The boat crept through the port to the dock, moored there, and the sailors disembarked. They got to work moving the crop off their boat. When they were done, the two men walked towards the overseer, leaving Aube alone. Ajeau pounced.

"Aube?"

The woman stared at Ajeau. "What?"

"Aube. I am Ajeau. I know a man named Seule. He's from the coast. He told me you would help—"

"Seule? Ha!" She spit on the deck beside her. "That bastard is still alive? Where is he? I'll cut him up and take my payment from his insides."

Ajeau's eyes darted to men and women working at the port or walking near her. Aube's voice was loud enough for them all to hear. But none stopped to inquire.

"He's...living in the woods," she said. "Somewhere to the south. The Tentir. But I'm—"

Aube cackled. "Doesn't surprise me and it serves him right. What'd he do, cheat the wrong person? He never could settle his debts."

"He..." Ajeau said, then shook her head. "I'm not here to talk about Seule. I need help. I need some information about—" She reached into her bag. But as she did, Aube grabbed her arm.

"What do you think you're doing?" Aube said.

"I—" Ajeau struggled with the woman's firm grip. "I want to show you—"

"A knife? You a friend of Seule's come to make sure I never call on his debt."

The two women wrestled, a flurry of hands grasping and releasing. "No...Let me..." Ajeau nearly broke free for a moment, but in doing so, she showed Aube the dagger sheathed on her arm.

"I knew it. A blade." Aube backed away from Ajeau and continued, "I ferry for the Vizier. She protects me. Even if you cut me, you'll never survive." Aube's voice shook.

"Shh—No. I'm not going to stab you. Wait." Ajeau held up her arms, displaying the dagger openly, and that she did not intend to use it. Then she reached inside her robe, pulled out a small bag, and removed a small stone from it. "Seule wanted you to have this."

Ajeau tossed the stone to Aube, who juggled it, then secured it in her hand. Aube stared at it for a while, as though it was the face of someone she had not seen in some time.

"A *patinoie*?" Aube whispered, then let out a small exhalation through her nose, amused.

In identifying the object, Aube's disposition changed. She seemed calmer, lighter, and more poised. Gone was the leery, fearful woman of a moment ago. Ajeau thought if the woman knew how to smile, she would've done so then.

Aube clasped the rock in her palm. "Seule used to bring me these from his village. There was a man here who traded for such stones. Made some jewelry with them, I think. But he's long dead and now I run boats. Half because of Seule's debts. What am I supposed to do with this?"

Aube turned and walked a few steps towards the water. She opened her hand, rotated it, and dropped the stone into the river, watching it disappear into the darkness. Without speaking, she glanced once more at Ajeau, then walked in the opposite direction.

Ajeau quickly followed, dragging her injured leg as she tried to keep up with the woman. "Wait. Please wait!"

The words had little effect on Aube. But Ajeau did not stop. She grunted as she willed her legs to keep pace. She stopped only long enough to catch her breath and send pleas in Aube's direction. Then more grunting, teeth gnashing, as she set off again.

This pattern repeated several times until it drew inquisitive eyes from those around them. Aube noticed this, turned to her pursuer, and said in a hushed tone, "Stop. You are drawing attention. Attention I do not need. Leave me alone."

"Please," Ajeau said, panting. "Listen."

Aube glanced at the wound on Ajeau's leg for the first time. She pointed and asked, "What happened there?"

"A rock hit me during the windstorm." She winced as if talking about it made it hurt. "Nearly took off my foot."

Aube nodded. "Almost lost my arm to a storm not long ago." She bent her arm and showed Ajeau a not-yet-fully-healed laceration on her elbow. "They're a menace. Like you."

Ajeau detected a hint of teasing in the woman's voice that had not been there earlier. This was her opportunity.

She reached into her bag, pulled out the blue arrowhead, and said, "What do you know about this?"

Aube stopped moving. Her eyes widened. She closed her mouth and swallowed audibly. Then, hurriedly, she covered the object with her hands, angled her body to block any onlookers, and looked Ajeau in the eyes. "Are you a fool? Do not show such wares openly here. People have been killed for far less."

"So you know what it is?" Ajeau smiled. "Do you know where it comes from? *Who* it comes from?"

"No." Aube shook her head. "But I have seen something like this before. Once."

Aube then stopped and glanced around her. Seeing nothing of concern, she continued in a soft voice, "When I first started working the boats, we traveled to an estate outside Lac'eau—village up north, on the sea. One man I was with found a stone in the grasses. It was so blue, so bright that he couldn't not see it.

He showed it to me and I told him to keep it. Could be worth something in a trade, right?" She shrugged casually. "Well, when we got back, the Vizier found it in his belongings and seized it. It was the end for him, but I'll never forget the way she acted, like the stone was a weapon or a warning...or something. It scared her. I saw it on her face, fear. And I've never seen it since."

"So the villagers of Lac'eau make these?"

"No, no. That's just it," she said. "When we found it, we asked some villagers for more. They had seen nothing like it. One woman even told me it must be left over from the great battles of the past. People of the sea that rode the wind fighting those of the earth that were taller than trees. Each band on the rock was a clash of these titans."

Ajeau looked at the rock, then back at Aube. "But you do not know where the rock is from?"

"I don't." Aube paused. Then, with a sigh, she said, "But I know someone who might."

"The Vizier?"

"No, not the Vizier, you fool. She wouldn't help me if I was lit aflame." Aube chuckled and shook her head. "No. An old friend from before I ran boats. She knows all there is to know about Bas and its people."

Ajeau leaned towards Aube with anticipation. "And she will help?"

Aube shrugged. "Who knows these days? But for a glimpse of something so rare, the temptation would be hard for her to resist." Aube folded her arms and looked to the sky. She remained there, quiet for some time. Then said, "I will bring her here the next day I am due at the ports, in a fortnight, and we will see what she has to tell us."

A smile that wrinkled her eyes burst onto Ajeau's face. She had found a trace that would lead her closer to Vaten. Finally, she would have him back soon.

"Don't go showing that to anyone," Aube said, pointing at Ajeau's hand with her head. "You hear me? You'll get us both killed if you do."

"Yes. Of course." Ajeau nodded excitedly.

"Remember. Here in a fortnight...And take care of your leg. It will rot off if you don't."

As Aube walked off, the smile still beamed from Ajeau's face as though it were a permanent fixture of the world.

She returned the arrowhead to her bag, secured it to her body, and then turned to leave. The elation continued to rush through, pushing everything else aside like a flooded river that topples trees.

Her leg throbbed and bled, but it was an afterthought. Her mouth was dry, sand from the windstorm in between her teeth, but she did not think of water. She thought only of Vaten, his release, and their impending reunion.

A fortnight. She would have her answer in a fortnight.

***

THE EYES SLID HER tongue over her lips as she descended a long stairway to a chamber underground. She opened the door and found a woman sitting in front of her. It was no surprise; it was exactly who she had demanded to see.

She walked to the woman in the room, grabbed her hair, and wrenched her head so she could stare the woman in her eyes. "You met one today. Talked with her. Of what matters did you speak?"

"I speak with lots of folks. Who?"

"Do not trifle with me!" The Eyes pulled the woman's hair to expose her neck, then brought a dagger to it. "The young woman who sits with the merchant Puy, who entered the ports broken, who followed you. I see you! Of what did you speak?"

Aube swallowed loudly. "It was a rock, a patinoie," she said. Her eyes blinked erratically. "From an old friend. It sits at—"

"Your next lie will be your last. Tell me now." The dagger drew a drop of blood.

Aube panicked. Her heart raced and her hands shook. "Her name is Ajeau. We spoke about a strange banded blue stone. Shaped into an arrowhead. Like the one from Lac'eau. She wanted to know where hers was from."

"And what did you tell her?"

"Nothing." Aube shook her head quickly. "I don't know anything about it. Or her."

The Eyes pressed the dagger further into her neck. The blood was running now. "What did you tell her?"

"I-I would ask a friend. M-Meet her at the ports in a fortnight."

The Eyes inhaled furiously, then held her breath. But when she exhaled, she had calmed her growing rage. There was a path forward. Yes, she told herself, a vine must climb on others to reach new heights.

"Good." A wicked smile crossed the Eyes' lips. "You will meet her then. Now leave me. And do not forget, Aube, our deal." Laughter echoed in the small room as Aube grabbed her neck and hurried through the door.

The Eyes licked her lips, then blew out the single flame lighting the room. She stared into the darkness.

The drought, the stone of Zevaco, the return of the Hijeuse; she had seen it all. *Now is the time to believe, Syais. Or else...make it so.*

# Chapter 20

As graceful as she had been in her cottage, Zejela was like an owl in flight atop her horse. She glided through the grasslands and forest, her focus never wavering. She spoke little and stopped to rest even less. While she steered the horse with her arms and absorbed each gallop with her legs, her body remained fixed, as steady as her gaze. It intoxicated Vaten.

It did not help that when he crossed behind her, he would catch hints of her scent, spice and honey that he drank as eagerly as he had water when he was a prisoner. It sustained him and solidified his resolve. He was going to become a Sentry, someone Zejela would respect. Someone *he* would respect. And then he would return home and find his loved ones.

As they exited a small grove, he spotted a mountain in the distance. Entirely gray, it seemed to lack any of the pigment of the surrounding area, like the color had washed down the slopes in a rainstorm. And unlike the other mountains Vaten had seen, it did not rise to a peak. Instead, its top was uneven, with what appeared to be clouds forming out of its summit. Somehow, he knew it was their destination.

A moment later, Zejela confirmed it. "There. That is the Outer Ridge. That is where you will train."

They arrived not long thereafter and, as they entered, Vaten gazed at an amazing sight: an entire village of Sentries. Hundreds, perhaps thousands, of them all engaged in labor of some kind. Some crafted weapons from a stone brighter than the sky. Others trained in combat and practiced sparring in small groups. Still others listened to scholars and recited from scrolls.

Everywhere he looked, their actions reminded him of the confidence and efficiency he saw from them on Bas.

As they trotted through camp, a colossus of a man approached them on horseback. Vaten stared in disbelief, not only at the man's size—his shoulders seemed wider than the horse's—but at his smile. Evey Sentry Vaten had seen wore an expression of seriousness on their face, but this man wore a grin that shined like the moons on a dark night.

"Zejela," the man called to her with a salute of his right arm. Then he glanced at Vaten and Levitien. "I, Aloc," he said, moving his right arm to his chest.

Vaten knew immediately where he had heard the name before. The Sentries had used it as a threat on Bas. Vaten now understood why.

Aloc continued to introduce himself in heavily accented Bassian. It was clear the language was not his first, though he spoke it confidently. "I tall...big...heavy—*Oviette*—of Sentries," he said.

"Chief," Zejela corrected him. She waved her hands. "Like a commander."

He nodded once at Zejela, then glanced back at Vaten and Levitien. "Command!" he said, throwing up a finger to the sky.

Vaten glanced at Levitien, unsure of their fate with the strange, giant man.

Aloc waited as though he expected a reply. When none came, he clapped his hands and said, "Welcome to Outer Ridge, *jezunes*—Sorry...littles!"

"He speaks of your rank," Zejela corrected him. "You will be trainees here. Apprentices. You will learn."

Aloc grinned. "Yes, learn!"

With their induction into the Sentries assured, Zejela turned her horse from the three men. "My work brings me to the Lower Brush. And though I would relish the opportunity to stay and study under these masters, I must leave. I am confident your time here will not be in vain." She glanced at Vaten. "Remember, you are Zevacese now. If you wish to discover yourself, discover what that means."

"You're leaving?" Vaten said. His face fell.

She nodded, and without saying another word, darted down the path and out of sight.

Vaten watched her leave with a familiar sense of rejection. He had been a fool to have thought of her in any other way than his captor. Whatever optimism he began the trek to the Outer Ridge with had fully evaporated, leaving only cynicism in its wake.

"Walk," Aloc said, clapping both men on the shoulders at the same time.

The force of the hit shook Vaten from his thoughts. He glanced at the man's giant paw on his shoulder, then to his face. He grimaced as the man squeezed and then pushed him and Levitien forward.

Vaten and Levitien marched alongside Aloc and soon arrived at a ring made of stones where small groups of twenty or thirty Sentries practiced graceful poses and efficient movements. Aloc shouted a word Vaten did not understand, and the groups stopped instantly. A man walked towards them.

Aloc faced Vaten and Levitien and said, "You here now and time is for your start. This is Besan. Both you will make conflict with him until rest on ground." He paused, searching for a word. Eventually he said, "Hands and feet only."

Before Vaten or Levitien could respond, Besan pointed at Levitien and said, "You first! Come."

Levitien smirked and nodded. He walked towards Besan, whose hands rested on his opposite shoulders, arms crossed in front of his chest. At first, Levitien stood in front of Besan and waited. Then, realizing that the pose was intended as a starting position, a sign of readiness for their contest, matched it.

Besan bested Levitien within three blows. Levitien dodged the first blow, a hand at his face, but fell to the next two blows, a foot to his leg and a second hand to his chest before he could react. His arms barely moved from his shoulders, and he never even attempted a strike on the man opposite him.

Vaten's jaw dropped. He wouldn't stand a chance against the man. The exercise would only bear his weakness for all.

After Levitien fell, Aloc yelled, "Slow! You join Osani. Here." And pointed to the small group at the southeast end of the circle.

Besan still stood in the circle and beckoned Vaten to join him. As Vaten walked into the stone ring, thoughts raced through his mind, as though he listened to many conversations at once. But they only left him terrified and unprepared.

Vaten felt the impact of the blow—a kick to his chest—and was reminded of a fight he had as a boy when an older child stole his food. It wasn't a kick then; it was a punch. But the strength of it, as with the kick from Besan, removed something vital from his body. His will. His spirit. And there was nothing he could do but watch the world blur around him as he crashed to the ground.

As soon as he landed, he heard Aloc yell, "No focus! You join Omessa." And when he looked for reassurance from Levitien, he could not find him anywhere. Deserted again. Weakling.

\*\*\*

THE RAIN PELTED VATEN mercilessly. It fell in heaps from the sky, hammering him and the ground like the footfalls of an unbridled horse. He could not open his eyes. He could barely inhale without taking water with his breath. But still Vaten stood, a pillar amongst the torrents.

It had only been a week since he had arrived at the Outer Ridge to train, but Vaten already knew the poses well. Rain or shine, wind or calm, sunup to sundown, he practiced them. They all did.

The Omessa did everything together. They started their day together, ate their porridge and drank their water, then collected their belongings and journeyed to the ring where they practiced. And when they practiced, each one made the same move at the same time. No matter the interference. It was a lesson Vaten would have missed if Aloc had not provided explicit instruction.

A day after his arrival, as Vaten struggled to adjust to the routine, Aloc walked towards a man following the progression of poses and shoved him. It was not a gentle tap either. The man he pushed bent, his top half nearly perpendicular to his lower half, then toppled to the ground. The rest of the class fell in the same manner.

Vaten, alone, remained standing.

He looked at the people lying on the ground and smiled, thinking the sight was ridiculous. If one man fell, why should all, he asked himself. Then they are all as weak as the one who falls. The weakest should not hold the strongest back.

Eventually, the first man returned to his feet, followed quickly by the rest of the class, and they all began their poses once more. Vaten too continued his practice.

But then, as he had done before, Aloc walked up to another trainee and tripped her. She made no attempt to stop him or keep her balance. It was as though Aloc was a stiff wind she tried to ignore. Even mid-fall, Vaten watched her continue to pose.

Like the man before her, she fell to the ground. Then the rest of the class, save Vaten, followed. Again, he stood alone. This time, Aloc stared at him, locking eyes with a fierceness Vaten had not seen before.

The ground seemed to shake with each stride Aloc took in Vaten's direction. Once his chin nearly touched Vaten's nose, he stopped. He did not say a word, but Vaten understood and gingerly lowered himself to the ground to match the position of his fellow Sentries.

Then, as the class stood, Vaten stood too. But Aloc did not move. Vaten remained close enough to the man to inhale the dampness from his mouth.

The group began their poses, but Aloc's presence disoriented Vaten. He fell. Then started again. Then fell again. Over and over the pattern repeated, with the rest of the Omessa falling around him each time, until Vaten's frustration boiled over.

"Why?" he screamed at Aloc.

Aloc said nothing, remained motionless in front of Vaten.

"What are you doing? You're making me fall!"

Aloc blinked but continued to say nothing.

"Get out of my way!"

But the large man did not move. Vaten felt heat radiating through his body, his muscles tensed, his vision focused only on Aloc's face. He balled his hands into fists and swung them at Aloc in a frantic attack.

Aloc dodged him without moving his feet, and, as he missed, Vaten lost his balance and tumbled to the ground.

He slammed the ground. He was too weak and should have foreseen his failure. As he lay on the ground, the rage slowly being replaced by shame, he noticed his fellow Sentries there with him.

"Why?" Vaten gazed at Aloc like an uncertain child. "Why do they fall with me?"

Aloc lowered himself to the ground beside Vaten and said, "Focus. Not you. Not them." He gestured towards the other Sentries. "On one, on all."

"But I am making them—"

"Not I. Not them. We are same." He held his hands out like a balanced scale.

"Then we are all weak!"

Aloc chuckled; his voice lightened. "Why we train." He offered his hand.

Vaten stared at the giant outstretched paw, wondering if he could ever banish his weakness or if he was fated to remain forever powerless.

When Vaten did not take his hand, Aloc said, "Listen, fall is not weak. Fall because no think, no focus. That is the weak. So, stop worry on strength. Focus on one, on all." Then he grabbed Vaten's shirt and hauled him to his feet.

"Poses," Aloc said to Vaten, then turned to the rest of the group and said something in Zevacese.

Aloc's words did not penetrate Vaten on that day. But he continued to practice. And the more he did, the more his focus sharpened, the more his awareness grew, and he understood how the Sentries worked and why they all fell. Zejela had been wrong. He was not an equal here; he was the same. One. All.

So, when the rains fell relentlessly one day, he remained calm and focused, like the rest of the Sentries. And if one fell, he would fall, too. He was a Sentry, after all.

***

WEEKS PASSED UNINTERRUPTED, EACH day a blur of motion with his fellow Omessa. And while the training refined his attention and strengthened his body, it stole his sense of time and purpose.

He awoke with the sun and rested in its absence as though they were reflexes. There was no more hunger or thirst. He ate when there was food and drank when there was water. And he no longer thought about how many days it had been since he left Bas. He existed on Zevaco. Everything before seemed as though it had happened to someone else.

Then one day, the practice stopped. Aloc arrived at the training ring with hundreds of Sentries accompanying him. Vaten saw the others and immediately scoured the crowd for a familiar face.

There were so many faces, all of whom were unfamiliar to him. Though they all practiced in the Outer Ridge, Vaten never once crossed paths with the other classes. But there was one who he recognized, regardless.

Vaten saw Levitien towards the middle of the crowd, a little stockier than when Vaten left him, but looking otherwise the same. After Aloc ordered the Omessa to join the rest of the Sentries and follow him, Vaten walked to Levitien.

"Kid, how are you? You look good. Strong," Levitien said.

"I'm well, thank you." The words were stiff and artificial, as though Vaten spoke to a superior. "How're you?"

"Good. Yeah, I think good. It has been, what, nearly an entire season of hard training. But I—we survived." He patted Vaten on the shoulder, then leaned towards him. His voice grew quiet. "Have you found anything?"

Vaten nodded. "I think I found a…" he paused and looked at the ground. "A focus. That's what Aloc says—"

"No. I didn't mean—Not that Sentry horseshit. Have you found anything about the boxes? You know, the ones they took back from Bas." Levitien stared him in the eyes. "Do you know what's in them? Or a way back to Bas?"

Vaten stared back blankly. It had been so long since he thought about the boxes and what might be inside, he had almost forgotten they existed. And Bas seemed like a fantasy, some place existing only in his dreams. "No, I haven't found out anything about the boxes or a way to return to Bas. Why would I? I'm a Sentry now. We all are."

"What did they do to you, kid?" Levitien grabbed Vaten's shoulders and gave him a little shake. "Have you forgotten? They forced us here. They stole us and brought us here as prisoners."

"But we aren't that anymore," Vaten said.

"What about your father? Your friend? Have you given up on them? Don't you want to see them again?"

"I've not forgotten them." Vaten removed Levitien's hands from his shoulders. "If I see them, then I will be joyous at our reunion. But I cannot hope for a return that will never happen."

Levitien shook his head. "Listen, a few of the Osani speak Bassian and they've heard talk of more excursions to Bas. Something about the drought there. We can go back!" Though his voice remained muted, Levitien's eyes widened, and he shook Vaten again, this time with excitement. "We can go back!"

The words stirred Vaten like cold water on his neck. "Even if that were true—" No, he would not allow himself to believe it. "—but it's not. You know what Zejela said, we're not going back. Besides, we're Sentries now. We are equals, no matter what you said. You were wrong. We have everything we need here."

Levitien glared at Vaten as though Vaten had cursed him. He spit on the ground. "Then you stay. Stay here forever. I will go back to my home and my *family*." The last word an aimed stab at Vaten's heart.

The mob of Sentries pushed the two men along as they continued their parade through the Outer Ridge. Eventually, the entire camp joined in the procession. And when they arrived at a building built into the mountainside—the Blue Hold, he was told—they stopped and fanned around it. Aloc walked towards the open doorway, but before he entered, he turned to the people who had followed him.

He spoke dramatically, his voice rising and falling. He struck powerful gestures as though he performed some magnificent scene. And though Vaten and Levitien could tell the speech held some great importance, they did not know what he said. It was entirely in Zevacese.

After Aloc finished, Sentries walked towards the building. Vaten stepped tentatively forward, then glanced back at Levitien. The man had not budged. It didn't matter. A moment later, Aloc approached them both, grabbed each man by the shoulder, and said, "Follow!"

Vaten and Levitien walked silently inside the building and gazed upon an ornate hall filled with paintings and sculptures and names carved into its walls. They were lit by rows of torches as bright as the sun.

"What is this? Are we fighting in here?" Vaten asked Aloc.

"No," Aloc said, chuckling. "This is ritual for end and beginning Sentry. A...ceremony. For littles."

"I thought we were already Sentries," Levitien said.

Aloc shook his head. "Yes, but only begin. You not complete yet. You be full after tonight."

"Does that mean after tonight we are done training?" Vaten asked.

"No," Aloc said, as if it were a rebuke. "Training never stop. Not for me too. But you be real—like us." He pointed at others around him. "Sentry."

Vaten nodded. "So, this is an initiation?"

"Yes! Initiation." Aloc clapped Vaten on the back.

"If this is only for us," Vaten said. "Why is everyone here?"

"Tonight, special ceremony." Aloc gestured at the adorned room. "In special place. It for all."

Aloc nodded, then left Vaten and Levitien and walked to the center of the room. He stood next to a tall blue sculpture of a man running with a tree growing from between his shoulder blades. Aloc placed one hand on the man's foot, his other high in the air, and shouted a word in Zevacese.

The sentries let out a thunderous roar that seemed to shake the mountain. Vaten wished he could have understood Aloc's shout or the reason for the resulting roar. But he remembered his teachings—when one falls, all fall. And he joined the cheer of his fellow Sentries.

There were more speeches, songs, chants, cheers, and a growing rapturous energy. Vaten joined where he could and the zeal flowed through all, save Levitien, who seemed intent on resisting it.

Eventually, Aloc moved towards the back of the room and unveiled a table, on which lay a small knife, a bowl with some black liquid inside, and a brush. The Sentries may have known what was coming, perhaps Aloc explained it to them, but Vaten had no clue. And the knife made him nervous.

The Sentries formed a line leading to the table. Although Vaten was hesitant, the other Omessa would not allow him to remain an observer. They pushed him towards the table and forced him to join with the rest.

Then the line moved. A man stepped to the table and removed his shirt. A woman, who along with several Outer Ridge inhabitants stood behind the table, picked up the knife and carved something into the man's back. The man tensed his muscles and gritted his teeth but stood proudly. If he was injured, he did not show it.

Next, the woman took the brush and dipped it into the bowl of black liquid. She removed it and then made strokes on his back like a painting. The man did not flinch. But his reaction after the woman set the brush and bowl down startled Vaten.

The man roared as if possessed by some great intensity, picked up the knife from the table and threw it at the statue of the man with a tree on his back. The blade of the knife hit the tree and carved a small branch into it.

Aloc patted the man who threw the knife on his back, then pushed him towards the statue. The man who threw the knife walked to it and retrieved the blade. As he did, Vaten saw the design carved on his back, a vertical line with a triangle resting near its peak. It was a crude tree.

As soon as the knife returned to the table, another Sentry stepped forward. She received a carving on her back, had the carving painted, and threw the knife at the statue. To Vaten's surprise, the knife landed in nearly the same spot, the tree on the man's back. Again, a small branch formed where the blade cut the statue.

The pattern continued until it was Vaten's turn. He stepped to the table, still unsure of his exact direction, and glanced at Aloc. He caught the man's eye and when he did, Aloc held up his hand to stop the woman.

"You Sentry," Aloc said. "Focus." He grabbed Vaten's shirt and pulled it upwards. "No shirt. She cut you, then paint you. Then throw at tree." He pointed at the knife on the table, then the statue.

Vaten said nothing as he continued to remove his shirt. He did not know what was about to happen to him. But the other Sentries had survived and appeared uninjured. But they had also all hit the statue in the same spot. He had not thrown a knife since his time on the estate. He considered of all the consequences—death, remediation, expulsion—of missing the tree.

The sharp sting of the knife's blade cutting his skin jolted him from his thoughts. It was not agony, but he felt it. He winced as the cool tingle of the balm seeped into his skin. At least it did not make the pain worse. Then he picked up the knife and his world changed.

Standing at the table, his arm outstretched, a strange feeling enveloped Vaten. It steadied his mind while it excited his body. It invigorated his senses. He could see clearer and deeper, as though the world somehow constricted around him. He looked at his hand, saw the ridges on his fingertips, and felt them individually for the first time.

The knife he had picked up from the table was as light as a feather. He could move it quicker than any other blade he had ever held, as though the air provided no resistance. No, the air assisted him. It carried the blade as the tide might a ship. His hand was only a passenger.

Vaten turned and looked towards the statue. It now became clear how the others hit it so perfectly; the statue seemed only an arm's length away, like he could reach out and touch it.

So, he tried. He threw his arm out, hand still holding the knife, toward the tree on the statue of the man. When the knife seemed to arrive there, like it would make contact regardless of his movements, Vaten let it go, and saw it stick deeply in plaster. Another branch made.

The effect of the balm wore off quickly. And once it did, his normal perception returned. Vaten walked to the statue and retrieved the knife as he had watched others do. Then he placed it on the table and walked towards the back of the building, waiting for the rest of the Sentries to take their turn and make their branches.

But as he sat puzzling over the odd sensations he had experienced, the sounds of footsteps from the doorway of the Blue Hold drew his gaze. A person in a blue robe called out for Aloc. Before Vaten could see her face, joy ran through his body. He recognized the voice immediately, even if he did not know what she said. Zejela had returned.

# CHAPTER 21

EYVO-ILLE BERATED NEVANT'S CHIEF. "How do the V'eauvians know? Tell me!"

Savique had never seen Eyvo-Ille this angry before. Even amid battle with the Lord's Guard, she had seemed restrained and poised. Even when receiving a stranger that proved to be an assassin, she was controlled and dispassionate. In all her arguments with Navo-Ille, she had never been angry.

But now Eyvo-Ille was furious. Small droplets of spit accompanied the words she spoke, her face tensing with each one. She pointed at the Chief with an open hand as though it would compel him to answer her question.

"I don't know," the Chief said calmly. "Certainly you don't think it was anyone in this camp. We are loyal and support your...pursuits." He bowed his head.

Eyvo-Ille put her hand on his chin and lifted his head. "Look at me. I have been here less than a moon's crossing and no Lord's Guard have followed. But a V'eauvian assassin arrives asking to speak with an Elder? It is no coincidence. They knew what I possess and where to find me. How?"

"Perhaps the Lord's Guard put her on to your location. Or perhaps the V'eauvians scouted your position long ago. Or perhaps—" The Chief waved his hand. "There are many explanations, Elder. Do not blame your friends for your ill results. The entire camp is now at risk. We must move again soon."

Men and women bemoaned both Eyvo-Ille and the Chief. The leaders were not beyond reproach for their failings and for the impact those failings had on the people of the camp. But instead of seeking to reassure those people, they simply tried to convince everyone the other was truly at fault.

Savique listened as the two Noye traded barbs and accusations, convincing no one of either's blame or coming any closer to the truth. But as they spoke, he watched Haguen-Pou make his way to where the V'eauvian assassin lay dead.

The healer scrutinized every part of her body. He took his time as he examined each limb, the torso, and turned the body over to check its back like it was some unique and exciting find. Savique thought the man uncouth—let the land reclaim what is its due—until he heard the healer speak.

"Stop your quarrelling a moment!" Haguen-Pou called to the two arguing Noye. "I have some troubling news."

Eyvo-Ille looked at the healer as the Chief continued talking. She put up her hand in front of his mouth, as though saying she had enough, and nodded her head at the healer to continue.

"Look at this." Haguen-Pou pointed at the V'eauvian's arms and legs.

"The scars?" Eyvo-Ille said. "Likely wounds from battles. Assassins are not innocent creatures, they are born in combat, forged through—"

"Yes, yes." He waved away Eyvo-Ille's explanations. "Some of these scars are likely battle wounds. You can tell by how they have healed." He drew his fingers across scars on the woman's shoulder and legs. They were jagged, asymmetrical, mountainous.

"But others, like those here," he continued to talk as he slid his fingers from the V'eauvian's legs to her arm and then to her neck, "are not from battle. They are too, even and smooth. Too well-healed."

Eyvo-Ille grew impatient. "So, what of it? What is your point?"

"My point is, I believe these wounds are from some intentional cutting." He stared at her as he delivered the words.

She glanced at the body, then at the man staring at her. "An intentional cut? Like a ritual for assassins? What does that matter?"

"Yes, a ritual. But what if it were not only for assassins? Think on it," he said, widening his eyes. "A V'eauvian ritual cutting. Does that trouble you?"

As soon as he said it, Eyvo-Ille's face dropped. She drew her breath in sharply, audibly, and held it. Then, as she released it, said, "No. You do not think they brought back such sin?"

"I do," Haguen-Pou said.

The Chief glanced at Eyvo-Ille and then Haguen-Pou and shook his head, confused. "What sin? What is this about?"

Eyvo-Ille ignored the Chief and said nothing. After realizing she would not tell the man anything, Haguen-Pou said, "They search for the blood of the One Tribe."

The Chief shook his head. "The One Tribe exist? I thought it was a legend. A tale woven from imaginations."

"I don't know if they exist." Haguen-Pou shook his head. "Or if they ever existed. I only know that the V'eauvians once searched the blood of their kin for them. Many healers know to use merage leaves to slow the bleeding from wounds because of it." He pointed towards where Navo-Ille recuperated.

While they spoke, Eyvo-Ille paced. She glanced around at the camp and mumbled unheard words to herself. Then she brought her head to face Savique and locked eyes with him. He knew immediately she had an idea.

She strode towards him, an unshakable purpose in her eyes. When she arrived by his side, she put her hand on his shoulder. "Ready yourself to ride. We will gather the tribes to bring an end to the V'eauvian offenses. They strike at me, they seek what is ours, and they offend us all with their rituals. No more! We will bring an end to their depravity."

"But Navo is—" Savique began.

"Do not worry, Haguen will see to her," she said without looking at the healer. "We will collect her when our battle has ended."

"Battle? You aim to bring war against the V'eauvians?" Savique could not believe what he heard. It was like suggesting war against the sun and moons.

She nodded. "Yes. It is the only way."

"Why? What does any of it mean?" he said, shaking his head in disbelief. "The One Tribe? Some ritual? And a mark. What mark?"

"Stories for another time," she said. "Not here. There may be foreign ears listening. For now, we ride."

Savique recalled the stories he had heard weeks ago at the Star Circle celebration and grew resentful. They were fables, not real. And they would pull him into battle against the mightiest of foes.

He stepped back out of reach of Eyvo-Ille's arm. "Do you ride into battle over some fiction? Do you chase ghosts for your own glory?"

Eyvo-Ille leaned in, filling the space Savique vacated. With eyebrows falling over her green eyes, she said, "Glory comes to those who take it. I will defeat the V'eauvians, and you will join me. Perhaps it is there you will save us."

Savique saw the rope back to his son and his home being yanked away. The Noye had wrapped him in their innumerable vines so that he could never escape.

"No. I will not ride with you. I agreed to help you so I could return home. I do not belong in a battle against a foe for a crime I know nothing about."

A silence fell as Eyvo-Ille scowled at him sharper than her spear. But slowly, her glare turned into a smile. "I will ignore your brashness," she said. "And instead, I will be practical. If you choose to stay here, I will tell the Chief about your past." She glanced at the man and continued, "Do you trust him?"

He followed her gaze to the Chief, wondering if she would punish him so harshly. These people owed him nothing. Not more than a day ago, they had threatened him, assaulted him. He knew he could not stay. And Eyvo-Ille knew it too.

"If you think him unreliable," she said. "I suggest you ride with me. You will meet our people and learn our ways. And you may even come to help us. I have not forgotten our deal and I will honor it when it has been executed. No sooner."

Savique's stomach dropped. It was an ultimatum phrased as a choice. If he did not ride with her, he would never return home or see his son. Both options were perilous, but one gave him a glimmer of hope.

He sighed and relented. "Fine. But our deal is complete after this raid."

Eyvo-Ille nodded, equal parts agreeing to and ignoring Savique's demand. She then spoke to Haguen-Pou, leaving instructions with him, rather than the Chief, on when they would arrive to check on Navo-Ille again.

She gathered her weapons and supplies and readied her horse for travel. "We leave now," she yelled at Savique. "Until she is well again, you ride Navo's horse."

The horse brayed at him. He thought it sounded like an introduction.

***

THE RIDING WAS UNBEARABLE. Savique had expected the leisurely pace and frequent stops of his earlier journey with the Noye. But neither materialized now. In complete silence, Savique and Eyvo-Ille spent their entire first day riding without interruption.

When nightfall finally descended upon them and Eyvo-Ille gave the signal to stop, Savique could not feel his legs. He dismounted and fell to the ground. Lying there, his back ached and his hands burned from their ride. It was misery.

As Savique sat and tried to massage feeling back into his legs, he watched Eyvo-Ille work feverishly to collect rocks and sticks and leaves for a fire. To his surprise, she appeared entirely unaffected by the ride, moving with the same speed and strength she had in Nevant.

He wondered where her energy came from. But that was not the only question running through his mind. "Where are we going?" he asked her.

She ignored the question and threw sticks in the growing pile of timber surrounded by rocks. Then she bent beside it, took a handful of leaves, and lit them with the drill. She placed the lit kindling next to the sticks and blew softly.

"I asked where—"

"I heard you," she said without looking at him. "And I told you. We are gathering the rest of the tribes."

"And that is..." He waited for her to complete his sentence. But she sat with her back towards him, tending the fire. "To the east? I can determine that from the moons, but how far east do we go?"

She blew on the fire once more than leaned away, pulled a waterskin from her hip, and drank from it. Then she threw it to Savique. "Drink then rest. We ride before the sun rises."

Savique sniffed at the bag, then swigged the water greedily. When he was done, he said, "But what about—"

"The tribes are north and south and east and west of here." She finally turned and stared at him. "Do not concern yourself with it. Instead, worry about your condition. You appear incapacitated by a single day's journey. There are seasons of this ahead. You cannot break now." She spoke the words as a command.

Savique opened his mouth as if to say something, then closed it and tossed the bag back to her. He lay on the ground and stared up at the moons as they traversed each other, wondering how long he would survive. If not for Eyvo-Ille's stubbornness, he would have been far more concerned. But she had ordered him to endure, and so it would be. He chuckled to himself before his eyes closed for the night, thinking perhaps that was the luck the moons offered him on their crossing.

He woke to Eyvo-Ille's boot on his back. "Up," she said with a gentle push. When he glanced at her with slits for eyes, she smiled and threw a chunk of bread at him. "Eat quickly. We are already late."

Savique blinked and sat up. He fumbled for the bread, found it, and devoured it. The food in his belly, though not much, pacified his growing annoyance and revived him. At least enough to stand when he wished to.

Before he mounted his horse, Eyvo-Ille approached him, holding a long strip of gray bark. "Rub this with your hands," she said.

He glanced at the bark, then at Eyvo-Ille, then at his raw and broken hands. "Why?"

"If you wish your hands to blister and swell, then continue riding as you have. Your pain is not my concern. But if you wish your hands to recover, then take it."

Savique did not hesitate, the pain still fresh in his mind. He grabbed the bark and ran his hands over it, coating them in a dry sap that tingled and soothed them. And when he mounted the horse and held its mane, he found them sticky enough to grip it without strain.

The day's ride progressed in much the same fashion as the previous day's, except when they stopped at its conclusion, his hands did not ache. His legs were weak, and his back stiffened, but his hands were comfortable.

After Eyvo-Ille made the fire, Savique sat beside her as they drank water and thanked her. At first, she did not move nor recognize his gratitude. She stared at the fire, lost in thought.

After a moment of listening to the fire crack and pop, she said, "I told you, you must not fall."

"I assure you, I have no intentions of returning to the earth. Not until..."

She poked the fire with a stick. "My sister would have said the same thing. But she rests on the ground, closer to it than life." She sighed. "One well-placed swing severs the flower from the stalk."

"Navo will recover," he said. "She is—"

"I do not need platitudes. Your concern was shown on the day you saved us. That is worth more than words." She threw some dry leaves on the fire and watched them burst into flames. "And it does not change my warning to you. You must remain."

"Why?" Savique said. "What am I to you?"

"To me?" She turned slowly to face him, then stared deep into his eyes. "It is not me. It is us. You are the hope of our people." She drew her hand to her chest. "You and the mark."

Savique immediately recognized it as the same word the V'eauvian assassin used in Nevant. "What mark? What does that mean?"

"I showed you that night." She shook her head. "Perhaps I should not have. There was too much joy in our hearts for such a serious matter."

"I...I..." He remembered the night she spoke of, remembered he saw something, but could not remember what. His tone lightened. "You're right, I could not see it properly in Nevant. But perhaps I can identify it now and we can avert this battle before it happens. That may be why I'm here."

"We do not need you to identify it. I can do that. And it will not change our course. Not now." Eyvo-Ille sighed. "But what I carry is a clue to—have you ever heard of the City of Z'eau?"

Savique shook his head. "No."

"It was a great and ancient city, now lost to time." She glanced at the moons and stars above her. "It is said our people once lived there before the split of the One Tribe and that it holds a power to reshape the land. Whoever wields it can destroy entire armies in a matter of moments. If it were us, we could gain vengeance over the traitors with ease, no matter their strength."

"What power? What traitors?"

"I do not know the nature of it. All I know is this," she touched her hand to her bag, "is a clue to understanding it. If we find the city, then perhaps it will allow us to know its power. The traitors, you know them better as V'eauvians."

"What did they do?" Savique asked.

"The list of offenses is long and ongoing. I cannot detail them all, but they have hunted our kind for as long as we can remember. They destroy our land. They steal children and bleed them to gain Eau's favor." She spit on the ground. "Perverse."

"That is the ritual you spoke of in Nevant?"

"Yes." She stood and shook her head. "It is an evil thing for an evil purpose."

Savique stared at her. "And what is that purpose? Why wound your own people?"

"Dominion and extinction. They seek control over every blade of grass." Eyvo-Ille gestured to the surrounding fields, then tapped her chest. "And to end us."

Savique brought his hand to his chin. He felt his straggly beard as he shook his head. "I know nothing of it. Rituals and ancient grudges are beyond me. But the mark, let me see it. I will tell you what I know. For good or ill."

Eyvo-Ille glanced up to the moons and stars as if trying to find guidance in them. When she lowered her gaze back to Savique, he saw relief wash over her face. She reached into her bag, pulled out the box, and revealed the object inside. Savique did not fall asleep this time, but he was no closer to understanding what was in front of him.

He knew it was a stone—not a seed, as he once thought—and it was a strange one at that. It was rounded but angular, full of spikes and points, as though to prevent someone from holding it comfortably. If it had been shaped, only the most careful of hands could have done so. But it did not appear created intentionally. It appeared natural, which was even more unusual.

After inspecting it for a moment, Savique shook his head. "I've never seen anything like it." He tapped one spear of the stone gently. "Nor do I have any idea how it is to be used. It appears more a weapon than a clue."

"But it is no weapon," she said. "At least not a worthwhile one." She chuckled softly.

He let a quiet smile cross his lips. "I suppose not." He ended his inspection and leaned away from the object. Eyvo-Ille closed the box and returned it to her bag. "I'm sorry I'm unable to help. The Ascetics were wrong."

"I do not believe that yet, Savique," she said, resting a hand on his shoulder. "There are many days to come where a man such as you can be helpful. You may not even know how yet."

Savique shrugged and warmed himself by the fire. He stared at the brands gracing the back of his hands as a smirk fell across his face. How far he had come from that a moment; a humble mason to the trusted confidante of a Noye Elder.

If only he could tell his son of it.

***

THE FIRST NOYE CAMP Savique and Eyvo-Ille arrived at, Blieux, appeared no different from Nevant. Yes, the camp was in an open plain, rather than a forest, and it was at least three times the size, but the stone wall and the huts and the guards with spears and the communal circle were the same. Even the air surrounding the camp smelled the same, a combination of horse, earth, and smoke.

Eyvo-Ille hollered as she rode towards the camp. It sounded like nonsense to Savique, but the spears lowered and the guards parted. The two rode past workers and children playing in the center of the village. When they reached an unassuming hut, they dismounted as a woman approached them.

"Eyvo of the Ille," the woman said, then bowed. "The *Eme* are blessed by your presence."

"Brehan, thank you for receiving us." Eyvo-Ille grabbed her by the shoulders, raising her head to her, and then embraced her. "It is wonderful to again be among friends. But our time is short. You are ready to discuss my proposal?"

"I've spoken with my brothers and sisters, but...it is not a simple matter. We will require assurances."

"Yes, of course," Eyvo-Ille said, then waved for her to follow. "Let us talk in private and discuss these oaths."

Savique stared at the two women and observed how similar they were. Not only in stature and strength—both were tall and muscular—but in confidence. Both women appeared as though they were a boat that could not be tipped. They commanded the waves; they did not bow to them. Not even the chief in Nevant moved with such certainty.

It was strange the woman knew why they had come. Savique had not seen Eyvo-Ille send word to anyone on their ride. It was like the wind and the trees carried the message for her.

Brehan-Eme returned Savique's gaze and nodded once. "You may sit with the teachers and learners and rest." She gestured to a group of nearly thirty elderly and young children. "They will be interested to hear from you. As perhaps you will be of them." A warm smile fell across her lips. "And do not worry, you will not find harsh treatment here. We appreciate those who help our tribe, even if they find themselves born under a foreign sun."

"Foreign sun?" Savique said softly as his eyes narrowed. But the two Noye were already walking from him towards the woman's hut.

Savique watched them exit, then turned and stared at faces who mirrored his own, some mix of interest and acceptance. He strolled towards them, hoping the faces would not turn hostile. Yes, Brehan-Eme gave her word, but he knew he was an outsider there. And he remembered the treatment in Nevant.

He sat far from the group of Noye, still eyeing them until a young boy wandered over, drew a circle in the dirt in front of him, and then handed him the stick. Savique stared at the boy, then at the group behind him, who was anxiously staring back at him. He shrugged.

"Make your mark," the boy said with a grin. "One mark per turn and no false moves. No cheating either."

Savique chuckled. He had no clue what game he was playing, but from the boy's instructions and his tone, at least he knew it was a game. Likely a game he should know how to play.

"Alright," Savique said. He made a cross on the ground next to the circle. Then he leaned back and glanced at the boy, who stared at him as though he spoke an unfamiliar language.

"What're you doing?" the boy said. "Marks go inside the circle. Have you never played ussel before?"

"I never learned. Besides, I prefer kantir. Do you know how to play?"

The boy shook his head.

"It's easy. You move stones through…" Savique glanced up to see the boy had already returned to his group and appeared to be sulking. Savique got up to return the stick but then thought better of it and sat back down. He didn't want to make any trouble.

After a moment, an old woman rose and approached him. "Don't worry about Elue. He fancies himself an ussel master even if he hasn't discovered how to block an end run." She picked up the stick and threw it towards Elue-Eme. "He thought you would be easy."

Savique stared at the ground but smiled. "Thank you. I suppose it was too easy a win for him."

The woman patted him on the shoulder. "Now, you are no Noye, stranger, so tell us. Where are you from?" She lifted the backs of his hands. "Where did you get these?"

When he looked up from the ground, Savique saw the group had moved closer to him. They spread around as if he was a teller readying a story. "I…I worked in Ortolan on an estate. That is where I met Navo and Eyvo. And was mistakenly called a thief."

"Yes, we heard…" the woman said.

"That is a weak story," someone from the crowd called out. "No spirit! The cochon does not even know how to speak."

Savique ducked, as if expecting to be hit by a rock. Then he turned to the woman. "Cochon. Navo called me that when I first met her. But I did not hear it in Nevant. There is a strange—you do not speak like them at all."

"Of course not. We are the Eme, not the Pou," she said. "We all have our accents, but we all know how to tell stories." She laughed heartily, as if she had told some great joke. Savique stared at her, confused.

"Which tongue do you speak formally?" he asked. "How would you speak to your Elders or the Lord?"

The woman glared at him, her laughter fading quickly. "You know so little about the Noye, cochon. There are no formal discussions and no Lords. We speak to the Elders as we are," she said. "But of course ours is the original dialect."

A loud crack came from Savique's left and he sprung to his feet, his head spinning with him. The children and their caretakers jumped as well. They all stared at Eyvo-Ille striding angrily from a hut, a broken log in her hand and another piece on the ground.

Eyvo-Ille turned back to Brehan-Eme. "They are our enemies from the time before the sun. And we are the great Warriors of Eau. What more reason do you need? I will lead it. I will win it. And when I return to the ground, I will curse the earth the Eme ride upon. Crops will wilt in your path. Trees will fall to avoid shading your horses. Rivers will disappear rather than quenching your thirst. And all to save a people who seek Z'eau to end it—and us!"

The woman leaned towards Savique and said, "The V'eauvians." Savique nodded. "That is how you tell a story." She chuckled softly.

"Eyvo!" Brehan-Eme yelled back. "This matter is not settled."

"It is!" She turned and looked through the camp. Seeing Savique, she pointed to him and said, "Let us go!"

Savique took a step, but felt a tug on his arm from the woman. He glanced at her.

"You're not going yet," she whispered to him. "Just wait."

"Eyvo, you cannot win without us. We have the most spears, the strongest arms. We do not break. We are the Eme. If you wish to die by their hands, do so alone." Brehan-Eme glanced at Savique. "Leave the cochon with us. But if you wish to destroy our enemies, the child-bleeders, Eau's corruption, then provide me what I need. The Ille are not lacking!"

Eyvo-Ille stopped walking. She inhaled deeply, then spun. "All of them. Every last arm holding every last iron follows me. Bring the sickles, the scythes, the spears, the daggers. And you will have your horses."

"We will have no defense. Even raiders—"

"Fine." Eyvo-Ille spit out the word as though it were rotten fruit. "One capable hand to help raise the next generation. Then you will have all you need."

"Eyvo..."

"Yes, Chief?" Her presence seemed to loom over the camp. "Are we to be even like the old days? Can I call you friend once more?"

"So be it," Brehan-Eme said. "The Eme follow in your mighty footsteps." She turned to the camp and held her arms out wide. "Warriors, ready yourselves for glory. We will not be raiding fields or driving off thieves. No, on this day, you ride to save your spirits from those that would see them salted. You ride for the ground to quake in honor of your step. You ride for your Elder against the only foe worthy of your strength. Destroy the traitors. Destroy the V'eauvians!"

A cheer ran through the camp. Even young boys and girls, far too small to fight, joined in the shouting. Horses stomped on the ground as if they too understood the immense task being asked of them. The only two unaffected by the speech were Savique and the old woman standing next to him.

She stared at him, sadness in her eyes. "It tears mother and father and brother and sister and son and daughter from their home. Will they see it again? Will you?" Her hands shook. "We are warriors, yes. But all glory fades in the shadow of the tree."

\*\*\*

THEIR RIDING NEVER STOPPED. They rode across hills, grasses, forests, streams, and rivers. They rode around lakes, farms, mountains, deserts, and cities. They rode through rain, heat, ice, wind, and sand. On one path, off another. Up one coast and down the other. All of Bas, it seemed, they rode.

Harvests arrived and departed. Plants grew dense, bloomed, then dropped, withered, and shrunk back into the land from which they came.

When they stopped by lakes or large pools of water, Savique began not to recognize himself. His hair grew in wild directions, in endless tangles that were covered in dirt. His eyes appeared lower—the result of a hanging lower eyelid—and were red from dust.

The only breaks were when they reached a Noye settlement. Each time they arrived, the routine was the same as it had been in Blieux. Eyvo-Ille would meet with the chief while Savique and the rest of the horde that followed would rest with others from whatever tribe they intruded upon. Even the arguments seemed to be similar, with shouting and threats and ultimatums common.

Savique used the time to talk to the Noye, though he mostly listened. As he now knew, all was a story to them, and it should be told with the required flair. And it was. He grew fond of their wild exaggerations, but he realized he learned something in each one. Sometimes it was their naming conventions, other times their faith in the ground, and still others their proud unbending nature.

But once Eyvo-Ille had spoken with the chief and received her warriors, they would ride off again, following her to their next destination. Savique lost count of the camps, but the mass of horsemen behind him grew ever larger.

More days, weeks, months, and years passed—Savique did not know how many—and as they did, he noticed troubling signs. Supply houses were in disrepair. Towers to store crops were abandoned, empty, and ruined. Where there was once moist clay, the ground had turned to dry dust. Lakes and rivers that were once difficult for horses to cross because of their depth were now easily walked. Green and yellow grasses turned brown, then disappeared entirely.

But they kept riding. The earth shook under the hooves of the hundreds of Noye. Until one day, their riding stopped.

Eyvo-Ille pointed to the horizon and the great imposing wall that appeared there. Savique trembled at its sight and the slow realization it was the target of their raid.

Sensing his hesitation, she leaned her mouth to his ear and said, "Do not worry about the wall. We do not need to ascend it to destroy the V'eauvians. A tree is best felled from the bottom."

Savique looked at her. "What is your plan?"

"You, Savique. You are my plan." She grasped his hands, turned them over, displaying his brands. "You are a thief, after all."

He chuckled and shook his head. "I am no thief. You know as well as I how I came to be branded."

"Oh yes, I know very well how you came to have these brands. But the V'eau-vians do not." She gestured at the wall. "I'm sure they will be all too happy to imprison a thief and a raider like yourself."

Savique's breath caught in his throat; his chest tightened. The world swirled around him as though his belly were full of wine. He stumbled and would have fallen over if he had not grabbed on to Eyvo-Ille's shoulder for support. He looked her in the eye but could not speak.

She patted the hand that rested on her shoulder and laughed. "Oh, do not worry. We will come to your rescue."

He found no reassurance in her words.

# CHAPTER 22

AJEAU SUFFERED THROUGH THE days leading up to her meeting with Aube. Time crawled by as if the sun and moons conspired to prevent her meeting. Even when she occupied her time tending to her injured leg or engaged in games of ussel or accompanying Puy when he conducted business, the day passed no quicker. All it did was make her more frustrated.

So she stopped doing much of anything. For long stretches of time, Ajeau laid about the cottage, absent of any motivation. If time would not move, then neither would she. It seemed fair.

But in giving up the desire for days to pass quickly, and accepting their unending stagnation, she found time sped up. Or if it did not speed up, at least she was not tormented by its tedious pace.

On the thirteenth night since she first saw Aube at the port, she spoke with Puy about her excitement. Words raced out of her mouth with no pause or breaks for breaths. Had she been more aware of Puy, less focused on her own emotions, she would have noticed the man was distant, unresponsive, and distracted.

But Ajeau drank wine, heaved words into the night, and enjoyed herself. She fell asleep mid drink, her head on the table, still trying to speak about the time she saved Vaten from falling into a bucket of piss.

Her dreams that night were chaotic and surreal. Strange shapes assaulted her, then flames burned away her flesh. Fierce winds blew her around the world before they placed her atop a horse, bounding towards a cliff. Before she fell over it, she grabbed an arm and pulled herself to safety. Then she sliced the arm with a knife.

She awoke the next morning groggy but excited. Even though her head throbbed and her eyes burned in the light of day, she could not contain her smile. Until she discovered the bag that held the blue arrow was nowhere to be seen.

Ajeau frantically searched the room, looking everywhere she may have put it. But she knew she never took off her bag; it stayed strung around her torso night and day, wake and sleep. Its disappearance was no accident. Someone else had it. But who would take it?

There was only one person who would know the answer. Puy. He knew everything that happened in his cottage. Either Puy would find the stolen her bag, and the arrow it contained. Or it was not stolen by a person, but by a phantom.

Ajeau knew exactly where to find Puy. He sat where he did every morning, the same chair he had occupied the night before, this time eating figs, grapes, and all manner of delicacies rather than drinking wine. His expression was also different. Now he looked satisfied. No, not only satisfied. There was an arrogance and smugness about him that Ajeau had never noticed before.

"Puy," Ajeau said, rushing to the table where he sat, "someone has taken my bag!"

Puy leaned back in his chair and smiled. He sent his servants away with a flick of his hand.

"Did you hear me? I said my bag has been taken. It has the arrow!"

"I heard you." Puy stared at her, unconcerned. "But perhaps you should have a seat first."

His demeanor puzzled Ajeau. She could not understand why he reacted to such shocking news with complacency. Unless it was not shocking news, and he already knew.

She took a seat sitting opposite Puy, as she had countless times before. "What do you know?"

"Ah, Ajeau, you know me well." He reached under his chair and held her bag in his hand as if it were a trophy.

Ajeau breathed deeply, her fears calmed. But as she reached to grab the bag, Puy moved it away from her.

Ajeau smiled. "Great joke. Now give it to me."

Again, she reached out to take the bag and again he rebuffed her advances. She watched as a grin crawled onto his face and she lost her sense of humor.

Ajeau looked him in the eye and, without reaching out, said, "Give it to me."

"I suppose I do owe you an explanation," Puy said. "Ever since you stepped foot in this city, people have been after you. You have seen some, Gogorain and his bunch are not a subtle crew, but others you know nothing about. You were warned this city was unsafe and yet you plowed ahead without—"

"Give me the bag, Puy!" She slammed the table.

He held up his hand. "Do not interrupt. It is unbecoming. Now where was I? Yes, this city is unsafe, and many people are—"

"What does this have to do with my bag? Are you a common thief like the rest?"

"A thief? No, I would not call myself that. But I am curious." A half-grin slithered over his lips. "Yes, I'm a seeker of many things. And the rarer the thing, the more curious I am. This," he held up the banded blue arrowhead, "is a most rare thing. I cannot help but be captivated."

"You can be whatever you want, but if you are not a thief, you will return what is mine." Ajeau held out her hand.

"Well, I also cannot do that," he said. "We need the arrow, don't we, to find out about its origin. The only thing rarer than this arrow may be who created it. I cannot imagine what we will discover."

Ajeau glared at him through thin eyes. Her shoulders raised. "So, you have gone through all this trouble, feeding me, sheltering me, showing me Nouv'eau—all of it to take the arrow now. Why? You could have killed me at any time and taken it."

"Make no mistake," he said, dismissing her idea with a wave of his hand. "I have no dispute with you. In fact, I've even grown to like your...intrepid nature. And bloodshed is too common these days as it is. But," his face grew darker, "I must know what this arrow is."

"You may not like bloodshed, but I don't mind it. I will do what I must to take that back." As she spoke, Ajeau stood, then leaned towards Puy and swung her fist at him. Before it came anywhere near Puy's face, guards grabbed and restrained her.

They carried her off when Puy said, "Wait, wait. I need her for the meeting. Aube is expecting her, not me. I do not want to alarm her and her friend. Simply restrain her here for now."

Ajeau struggled, but the guards overpowered her and tied her to the chair. They remained next to her in case she thought about escaping.

Puy stood to leave, but before he exited, he turned to Ajeau and said, "We will both get what we want. You can find out where Vaten is and run off to rescue him, or whatever you plan to do. And I will know what this blue arrow is. You may not know it, but knowledge is worth more than coin in this city. And I am nothing if not a merchant."

Ajeau said nothing in response, only admonished herself for trusting him. She fell prey to a scam a fool would have seen coming. Conveniences and luxuries from a wealthy man? She knew better. She shook her head and bit her lip. *Stupid.*

\*\*\*

AJEAU WALKED TOWARDS THE port ahead of Puy and a cohort of his personal guard flanking him on either side. The sun beat down on her, but the air was still and musty; dust and dirt floated on the bursts of wind created by the workers passing her. They paid her no mind as they shuttled barrels and carried bags and, for some, wandered aimlessly. But she stared at each one as they passed, at first pleading for help with her eyes, then wondering which would betray her next.

Puy grabbed her arm. "Approach the port naturally," he said. "We do not want her to think there is something amiss."

Ajeau glared at him but said nothing.

"Are we clear?" He leaned towards her, still grasping her arm, and showed her the blue arrow, which remained securely fastened behind his cloak. "Need I remind you of the stakes here? For you especially."

"Yes," she said flatly. "We are clear."

"Good." He grinned. "When Aube and her friend appear, I will approach and tell you, you left the arrow behind. You must ask for the information then."

"I will."

"You will have to be adamant."

"Yes."

Puy squeezed her arm tightly. "I mean it," he spit the words with a fury Ajeau had not seen before. "Do not play, if you wish to continue living."

"I won't."

Puy finally released her arm, then shoved her forward. "Walk."

Ajeau did so, knowing she could have ignored his plan, planted her feet, and refused his scheme. But he may have killed her right then. Even if he didn't, she would lose the chance to learn where Vaten was. Puy had not lied when he said she could get what she wanted, but the price left a bitter taste in her mouth.

As she continued to make her way to the port, troubling thoughts surfaced in Ajeau's mind. Aube and her reclusive friend would surely notice something was amiss. There was nothing ordinary about a rich merchant like Puy appearing out of nowhere, even if he claimed to help. No, it was too obvious.

And Aube had explicitly told her not to tell anyone. Aube would be vigilant for any irregularities, and Puy's presence was certainly that. She felt disaster looming, like the dark clouds gathering before a storm.

Ajeau stopped and took a deep breath, trying to steady her nerves. She caught the faint odor of earth, wood, citrus, leather, and food. The port was near. If she was going to withdraw, now was the time. But she did not. She continued to march forward like a soldier into battle, aware that it might be her last.

Ajeau spied Aube immediately, though she looked nothing like the brazen and presumptuous woman she had met earlier. No, she was tense and restrained, as though she could not move her arms and legs naturally. But Ajeau was just as rigid and could only muster an awkward nod to the woman before she approached.

Ajeau arrived beside Aube but said nothing. They both stared at each other in silence for some time until, as though forcing words, Aube said, "Your leg looks healed. I'm glad for you." It sounded as stiff as she was.

Ajeau nodded, then said, "Thank you." She looked around. "Where is your friend?"

"She will be here in a moment." Aube said. Then she leaned in close and whispered in a tone barely audible, "I'm sorry, there was nothing I could do. Nothing I can do now. But I am sorry."

Ajeau's eyes flashed. *What?*

Before Ajeau could speak, Puy arrived beside her, received by two shocked faces: Aube shocked by his presence and Ajeau shocked by Aube's words. Puy glanced at them curiously, then launched into his ploy.

"Ajeau, you left your arrow at my cottage," he said with a smile. "But do not worry, I have it so that your meeting can go on."

Ajeau said nothing in response. Her throat became dry and even though she remembered what she was to say, the words refused to exit her mouth. All she could think of was why Aube apologized and none of the options were good.

There was a loud whistle. It was not to alert Puy's guard, Ajeau could tell by the confused look on the merchant's face. She wondered whose call it was.

Before another breath escaped Ajeau's lips, chaos erupted at the port. Armed guards descended on Ajeau, Puy, and Aube, who each promptly scattered. Puy hollered something to his guards as he ran for cover. Ajeau found a place to hide beside bushels of hay and mud. And Aube fled right into the arms of the person who arranged the trap.

From her hiding position, Ajeau saw the turmoil turn violent. Guards, some she recognized as Puy's and others who were unfamiliar to her, clashed with swords and spears. Loud clangs and occasional screams rang out as workers ran for cover. Blades eventually found veins and emptied them. Red covered the port, spilled into the river.

Ajeau thought about trying to use the confusion to escape or steal back the arrow from Puy, but both options seemed too risky. There were still too many guards about and no clear access to the exits. She stayed hidden, hoping it would save her.

Then Ajeau spied a slender woman in the melee, who did not appear to be a guard. She did not wear their clothes nor hold their weapons. The only blade she carried, a dagger that sparkled in the sunshine, remained sheathed on her belt. Her purposeful walk and peering eyes let Ajeau know the woman was not at the port to fight, she was there to search.

As the woman hunted her prey, she moved through the fighters as though she knew where each strike would land and avoided it. Ajeau could not believe it; the woman stood amid the battle without a speck of blood or dirt on her pristine white robe. She was like a wraith until she arrived at her destination.

It was there Ajeau discovered why Aube was sorry and for what the hunter sought.

The woman grabbed Puy's arm, then held it high in the air as though it were a trophy. But the real prize was what he held in his hand. Ajeau's arrow. Puy struggled to free himself from her grip, but failed. He swung his dagger with his free hand but hit only air. The woman laughed at him, then pulled him up by his arm, stretching him like a plant about to be plucked from the ground.

In a flash, the woman drew her dagger, severed his hand with her blade, and then snatched the arrow from the disembodied flesh. Puy collapsed to the ground, screaming in agony. The woman stared down at him and said something Ajeau could not hear. Then she plunged her dagger deep into his chest.

Ajeau felt no sorrow for the man gone. He had died by his own greed, and she spit on the wood beside her and cursed his name. "Even the rich and powerful return to earth, Puy," she said to him without speaking. "None of your wealth could save you from that fate."

The woman who held Ajeau's arrow called to her guards to finish their business quickly. Their work was done. As Ajeau heard the words, she hoped the next ones would confirm the woman's departure. But before any more orders came and before any of the guards withdrew, a familiar roar descended on the port.

The wind surged across the port, knocking over Ajeau and covering her with spray from the river. She closed her eyes. Her vision was useless with the dust flying, anyway. She covered her face, wrapped herself in a ball, and hoped she would survive this storm better than the last.

***

THE WINDS DID NOT stop the Eyes. Such storms did not bother her; the deafening, turbulent air was her home. She rode the gusts as some rode horses. Guards fell to the ground next to her, their final screams stolen by the wind. But it would not steal hers, nor would it prevent her from her ultimate ambition.

The Eyes searched the port until she found what she sought once more. As she set off to take her prize, a noise, not the wind, came from beside her.

"Who's there?" She gripped her dagger, still dripping with Puy's blood.

"Master, did you get what you needed?" A man screamed the words over the sound of the wind.

"Yes, Warden," the Eyes said. "I have found what I was looking for, what this merchant stole from us."

"It is my honor, Vizier." The Warden bowed his head.

"Make sure all know what happened here. Puy is to be an example. His name is to be ruined."

"Of course, Vizier. The merchants knew of Puy's betrayal long before this day."

"Well done. I am most pleased."

"Thank you, Vizier. I—"

"Go. Now." The Eyes raised her arm, pointing towards the center of the city. "I have one last piece of business here. And then I will see to you."

When the Eyes turned from her Warden, she saw something amidst the gusts. The other reason she had come to the dock that day. And though she was pleased to hold the arrow, her plan would not have been a success if she left the girl behind. And there she was, curled in a ball, fighting against the air. It was almost too easy.

The Eyes smiled, deep and rich. She cast off her doubts. It was all as the seers had foretold. Yes, the visions of the Arboricole were real. They were the truth. She was the Hijeuse and that meant the Eyes nearly had what she long desired. The world.

She walked the port, then stopped beside barrels covered with mud. She reached out an arm draped in white cloth. It fell on Ajeau's shoulder. Ajeau opened her eyes and stared back at the woman in horror.

# CHAPTER 23

VATEN APPRECIATED THE OUTER Ridge most after sunset. Not only was the village filled with stillness during those hours but, with few animals stirring, Vaten could hear the magnificent rumbling of the land. Parts constant humming and loud bursts, hisses and roars, the ground at the Outer Ridge sounded alive.

And whenever Vaten heard a bang or a whistle emanating from below ground, it brought to mind a story Aloc told him during his training.

One night, after their evening meal, Aloc put his arm around Vaten and walked with him towards his hut. As they moved, a loud roar came from under their feet. Vaten stopped and looked down. He saw nothing but the dirt path they had been walking on.

When he looked up, he found Aloc smiling at him. "The spirits welcome us."

Vaten shook his head, confused.

"This where first Zevacese live," Aloc said as he stomped his foot on the ground. "They came in from sea. The sowers believed mountain and peak were like great fracture from Istor."

"What is that?"

Aloc frowned and said, "Not know? It is break in earth where first spirits enter land. Give birth to all living."

Vaten shook his head. "I hadn't heard that story."

"No matter. Not point," Aloc said dismissively. "The first Zevacese live here many year. But then mountain exploded. Rock, flame went all over. Fell on some people. People learn quickly, they not safe here and move. Stay on island but away from that." Aloc pointed at the mountain.

"Why—Why train the Sentries here if it is not safe?"

Aloc laughed and clapped Vaten on the back. "Sentries train because not safe. Must conquer fear. All who live in Outer Ridge must do. Fear in sowers not allowed to spread."

Vaten looked at the top of the mountain at the sparks that danced there like flying candles. "What fear do I have to conquer?"

"Same as all." Aloc pressed his hand on Vaten's chest. "Returning."

***

ON THE NIGHT FOLLOWING his induction into the Sentries, Vaten did not stare at the mountain nor think of the rumblings below. Instead, he stared at an equally enthralling and mystifying sight. The woman who sent him there.

"Vaten, you look well!" Zejela embraced him. "Training suits you as I thought it might. Did you participate in today's ritual?"

A smile erupted onto his face. It could not be contained. "Thank you. And yes. Did you not know? Did you not orchestrate it?"

Zejela shook her head. "No, I had no part in it. Aloc is a friend, but he controls the Sentries as he desires. My involvement in it stopped after you enrolled."

"Oh, I—" Vaten eyes darted to the ground, ashamed she had not planned the night's events, had not come to see him. "Never mind. What was that ritual, anyway? What happened to me?"

One corner of Zejela's mouth peeled upwards in a coy smile. Then she burst into a small laugh. Vaten did not know what was funny and didn't care. He brought his eyes to hers and savored her laugh like it was a fig he had stolen; sweet and, despite a hope that the taste would never go away, fleeting.

"There is still much for you to learn, much training to be completed..." Zejela glanced to her left and right, then looked at Vaten again. "But I suppose this one bit of knowledge won't disrupt things too much. The liquid is made from the root of the oirn plant. When applied to wounds, it enhances your concentration and motivation. It helps bring things into focus. For a brief time."

"Is that how I was able to..."

Zejela nodded.

"Amazing," Vaten said, stunned. He couldn't think of anything else to say about it. If her description had not been so perfect, he would not have believed her. Sure, a plant could satiate or calm you, but help strengthen your perception and sharpen your skills. It seemed unthinkable. And yet, it was exactly what happened.

"Yes, the Sentries have used it in their ritual for quite some time. As preparation for—well, another time." She turned her head back and forth, scanning the camp. "Where is Levitien? I never thought I would see you apart."

"I don't know" Vaten sighed. He paused and scratched his beard, weighing his next words. "He's stuck and can't...move forward. He lives only for the past."

"The training is difficult, but like those who carve stone must lop off large pieces for their work, the Sentries here transform us through large slashes."

"Yes," Vaten said, then glanced at the ground. "And in that transformation, I found a...a way of being." He shook his head. "I don't know how else to describe it."

Zejela nodded with understanding.

"But Levitien hasn't changed. He...he doesn't seem willing. And he will not accept mine. Because of that, we are at odds."

"Yes, that is difficult." She rested her arm on his shoulder and gazed into his eyes. "But paths cross and divide. Perhaps you two are ready to separate."

"But he is a friend," Vaten said as though he was convincing himself. "He is my connection to Bas and the ordeal that brought us here. Even if those things lose meaning for me, it is hard to let go of the bond we share because of them."

"You speak wise words, heartfelt and true. I wish I had a simple answer for you, but I do not. I would offer to help and speak to him on your behalf, though I am sure my involvement would only cause more problems."

"Yes," Vaten nodded. "I think it would. I wish he could see beyond himself. For his sake as well as mine. I've lost many and I do not want to add him to the list."

Zejela pursed her lips and brought her hands together in front of her. She glanced at them and then back at Vaten. "I know. Listen—" A gust of wind swallowed the words Zejela spoke.

Vaten watched as Zejela's hair rode the breeze, streaks of white and black dancing before her face. Before it settled, Vaten spotted something he had seen before but forgotten. His eyes darted to it, then quickly away, to hide his glance. Zejela noticed the twitch but stood proudly, displaying her scar.

She found Vaten's eyes with hers and drew them upwards. They stared at each other, having an unheard conversation for what felt like days but lasted no longer than the time between blinks. Or a gust of wind.

Zejela continued, "I too know the pain of losing loved ones and the toll it takes on us. It is difficult."

She grasped his hand and drew it to her scar. He stopped breathing and worried that his breath may never return. But, after an alarmingly long pause, the air finally rushed out of him in an audible huff.

"What happened?" Vaten whispered past dry lips.

"It is from a long time ago—who I was, not who I am." She removed his hand from her neck but held it for a moment before letting it go.

"But I want to know that, too."

Zejela smiled, tucked her hair behind her ear, leaned close to Vaten, and kissed him. Vaten's eyes widened for a moment, then closed as he surrendered to the warmth.

An energy pulsed through his body in rhythm with his heartbeat. He would burst, he was sure of it. The force within him was too strong to be contained. It was a fire that found a fresh forest to consume.

And then Zejela straightened. Their lips separated, and Vaten opened his eyes. His heart steadied as the world rushed back in.

After a pause, Zejela said, "Hmm. Right. I was talking about my scar. When I was young, I lived with my mother in a small village outside Gencourt. One day, a man of Lord Ourve approached our village and told us they were looking for children to assist them in finding the blood of the Elders." She smirked and exhaled a breath through her nose. "I remember thinking: don't they have their own blood?"

Vaten shrugged, but she did not wait for a response.

"My mother initially resisted but then became convinced. This was a chance to help our people and our land. It was a *responsibility*. So, whatever the Lord needed from me, my mother offered."

"And you went with him? And what, he tried to kill you? How would that help?"

"No, he didn't try to kill me. What he did was far more systematic and intentional, like it was a ritual he had long been trained for. He tied me to a tree and slashed my neck apart with his knife." Her fingers rose to her neck as though some phantom pain remained.

"I remember screaming in agony and as I watched my mother retch. The pain was intolerable, not like the small incisions here," she gestured to her back and the Zevacese ritual. "It burned and stung and stabbed throughout my being."

A sight flashed before Vaten's eyes. It was another's scars. Different, though very much the same. Arms, not a neck. He had not seen or thought of those arms in a long time, but they were once a daily presence in his life. Had Ajeau gone through the same ritual?

Vaten blinked away the image of Ajeau, then asked, "How did you survive?"

"Strangely, the man who cut me wrapped my neck in leaves and animal skins after collecting my blood in a flask. He did not try very hard to dress my wound." Zejela pointed to a rough portion of her scar. "But he did enough to keep me alive. Then he left."

"He only wanted your blood? What for?"

"Perhaps they believed it would help them. Perhaps they used it in some strange way." She shrugged. "There are many rites of the V'eauvians I know nothing about."

Vaten started to ask her more about the ritual and whether she knew if others had gone through a similar ordeal, but he closed his mouth before speaking a word. He thought it impolite to disrupt her story for his.

"And that is how I came to have this scar. Now, it is simply a reminder of a mother's naivety, of her indifference towards her daughter and her suffering."

"You blame your mother?"

"I do—I did. But that is because..." She hesitated. And shook her head. "It does not matter. I am here because of her. And I am thankful for that. Remember what I told you, it is where you are."

Vaten gazed into her eyes and smiled. "And we are here."

"Yes. We are. It has been sometime since I told that story. Thank you for listening." Zejela placed both her hands on his shoulders and returned his gaze.

In the dark, Vaten could not perceive the fire that had ignited in Zejela's eyes, nor the passion that raged within her. But it was there all the same.

She ran her tongue across her lips, drew herself close to Vaten's ear and whispered, "Follow me."

Under the night sky, a flower bloomed.

***

VATEN AWOKE TO A brightly lit sky and the sounds of talking. He stretched his arms and legs and, for a moment, wondered where he was. This was not his hut. But he soon remembered the previous night, felt the scars on his back, and repeated the bliss in his mind.

He stood, gathered his clothes, and walked out of the room and into a hallway that led to a small vestibule. There, he glimpsed Zejela and another woman near the entrance to the hut, speaking urgently in Zevacese. He froze.

Zejela, upon noticing Vaten, introduced him to her advisor Harlae and vice versa. To his surprise, Harlae greeted him in Bassian. He tried to greet her in Zevacese but ruined it.

Zejela and Harlae spoke for a short time longer, then ended their conversation in a last flurry of gestures. Afterwards, Zejela walked towards Vaten while her advisor rushed through the doorway, saying nothing.

Zejela embraced Vaten and gave him a small kiss on his cheek. "Something has happened—"

"Yes, I would say so." Vaten smiled, trying to be funny. It did not work.

"It is no joke," she said with an admonishing shake of her head. "Something grave is afoot here. The boxes we returned with from Bas are empty. What we brought back has been taken."

The boxes. Levitien had asked about them only the day before. And though he wanted to believe his friend to be innocent, he knew it could not be a coincidence; the timing was too perfect.

He recalled what Levitien had told him on Bas. The man had traveled north in search of something. On that night, Vaten did not ask for specifics. But now he wished he had. Had Levitien been searching for the same thing the Zevacese sought? The same thing now missing from those boxes.

"Do you think it was—"

"I do not know." Zejela presumed his question. "It seems unlikely Levitien could have been involved. But I would have said this whole business was unlikely. Something strange is afoot, anything is possible."

"I'll find out what he knows." Vaten spoke the words more as a pledge to himself than to inform her.

Zejela nodded, and before Vaten could turn to leave, she grasped his forearm. "We know very little now and what I have told you is known only by a few. If word were to leak, it could destabilize things further." She stared into his eyes, all the warmth there a moment ago, now gone. "If those who plot find out, they may seek to do us harm. Take heed."

"Yes, of course. I'll be cautious."

After relishing her touch for a moment more, Vaten slipped from her grip and walked towards the doorway of the hut. Before he stepped through it, Zejela called his name as though she remembered some important point.

"In the time ahead, things may not always be as they seem. It may be difficult to know who to trust and who to doubt. Know that you can trust me. Indeed, your survival may depend on it."

\*\*\*

VATEN EXITED THE HUT and emerged into quiet desolation. It was a wholly unrecognizable place from the night before. Where paths were once full of chants, songs, food, and drink, there was now only stillness. It was as though the previous night was a dream; the Sentries were specters who had returned to their world without a trace.

But not everyone had disappeared. Present were the cooks, cart runners, and skilled tradespeople who ran the Outer Ridge during the day. The only ones who were missing were the Sentries. No Aloc, no Besan, not even a familiar Omessa face.

Vaten wondered if maybe he missed part of the ceremony during his time with Zejela. A nighttime climb up the mountain or a sparring session under the moonlight were genuine possibilities. But there were no walking sticks missing or early risers to spread the word. There was simply no trace of them at all.

He thought of Levitien. If the man had left too, Vaten would discover nothing. Perhaps that was the man's plan all along: to steal from their hosts and then leave. Vaten shook his head to clear his thoughts. Such conjecture was not helpful. He needed something tangible to tell him where Levitien, or any of the other Sentries, had gone. But there was nothing amiss. Everything appeared as it should be.

Then he heard voices coming from the distant end of the camp. The low baritone of one speaker sounded remarkably like Aloc. Though he could understand none of the words, Vaten broke into a sprint and ran towards them.

He made it nearly halfway there when he thought he heard his name. He stopped and looked around, at the trees ahead of him, at huts beside him, even at the path behind him. Upon seeing nothing, he started running again.

But this time he was certain. Someone called his name. As he turned again to place the sound's origin, he saw a hand sticking horizontally out of a bush beside a wall.

"Vaten! Over here, kid," Levitien said.

"Levitien?" Vaten walked slowly towards the bush. "What are you doing? Where is everyone? What is going on?"

Levitien brought a hand to his mouth, then whispered, "Keep your voice down, kid. I've got no idea what's going on, but something's happening. There're people here to round up the Sentries and take them somewhere."

"What? I think I heard Aloc talking with someone over on the far side of the village." Vaten pointed in that direction. "I was headed there—"

"Aloc is in on it...I think. And Zejela. I saw them talking earlier before they started sending the Sentries away."

Vaten shook his head in disagreement. "Impossible. I was with Zejela all night. At her hut outside of the camp."

Levitien's eyes narrowed, full of suspicion. "I wondered how you didn't get caught up in this mess. Never mind. I told you what I saw, and I meant it. The two of them talked. About what I don't know, but soon after, we get this." He spread out his hands to show the circumstances they were in. "I've been trying to get out of here since the first sign of trouble. Some of us are still trying to get home."

Vaten heard the slight but ignored it. Instead, he stared at the ground in front of his feet and remembered what Zejela had said to him earlier that day. *Anything is possible.*

"Kid... Hey kid!" Levitien's words broke Vaten's thoughts.

"What?"

"Last chance here. I am getting as far from this place as I can. I'll figure out some other way home, but I'm not getting in the middle of some power struggle in some miserable place. Need to be alive to get home. I'll work on the latter after I secure the former, you know?" He chuckled to himself. "So, what do you say, you coming with me?" He stuck out his hand for Vaten to shake.

Vaten thought for a long moment. Then remembered why he sought Levitien in the first place.

"Wait." Vaten slapped Levitien's hand down and pointed a finger at his friend. "The boxes. The ones from Bas. They're empty, their contents stolen."

Levitien stared at Vaten, trying to understand what his point was. Not finding it, he asked, "All right. And?"

"What do you know about it? Did you do it?"

Levitien expelled a short laugh through his nostrils. "I don't know anything about that, kid. But it explains what's going on here. Something big is happening. We best stay out of the way."

"Are you not interested in the boxes' contents now? Or that they have been taken? The very theft you wanted—"

"Oh, I am interested. And given the chance, I would take them. Whatever they are, they're valuable. But I didn't take them now. How would I?" Levitien paused and rubbed his beard. "Now you've got me thinking that maybe there's a way to use this disturbance to dig up some more information about the boxes. But that'll have to wait until we're safe. So what do you say?" He rose from out of the bush. "You—"

"Stop!" a shout. The words were in perfect Bassian. Levitien instinctively ducked back down behind the bush. "We saw you behind the bush. Do not try to run, Levitien."

Vaten stood, looked at who spoke, and smiled. It was Zejela. She stood in front of a crowd of armed men. They did not look like Sentries—they looked like soldiers—and they approached the two men until they were within a couple paces of them.

"He didn't do it, Zejela. It wasn't him. I—"

Zejela said something in Zevacese and, nonchalantly, a soldier spun his spear over and rammed the shaft into Vaten's stomach. He spit, nearly vomited, doubled over in pain, and searched everywhere for his breath. Falling to his knees, he found it, but it remained shallow and weak.

Vaten tried to look up at Zejela but couldn't. Instead, he stared at the ground and whispered between pained breaths, "Why?"

"You know why. Thieves!" Zejela exclaimed and pointed at Vaten and Levitien. "We gave you freedom in our land, allowed you to join the ranks of our Sentries, and you returned our favors with thievery. All will know your treachery, but your fate has already been decided. Death!"

"No...You know—It wasn't...No," Vaten pleaded through labored breath.

Another word in Zevacese and the spear shaft came down upon his back. Vaten fell to his side and stared at Levitien. "What did you do?" He closed his eyes without waiting for a response.

Levitien remained silent, his eyes flickering between Zejela and the armed men, searching for an escape route. Finding none, he remained still.

Vaten struggled against the pain. He coughed and spit and pushed himself to his knees. When he opened his eyes, he saw an ominous image staring back: a half-smile creeping onto Zejela's face.

The words, now harsh and cruel, stabbed at him from inside his mind. Anything is possible.

# PART III

Letters Twelve through Seventeen
Collected Letters from the rule of Oeillet by Grand Observer Ralmatien

*Dearest Aumille,*

*I apologize for the lack of correspondence recently. Do not understand this to reflect my feelings or of my desire for you. The lack of letters is solely the result of the lack of time in my days. But I do not complain about this, because it has led to a most wondrous stroke of luck. Oeillet, Second Queen of the Balafre, Glorious One among All, has sought my council and promises me work in finding a resolution to our changing world.*

*It has been nearly three harvests, more than twenty moons since I left you and Naum, and journeyed into the unknown to find something better. And finally, we are rewarded. If there were any doubts left, we now know we made the correct decision. The pains of the past will remain there. Only glory is in our future.*

*I am not callous and unaware of the great hardships others suffer through. I have walked and searched the plains with these people. In my time here, I have spoken with them, shared their fatigue, impatience, and anxieties. I am brought high by events that bring others low. I know this. And though it is a painful and bittersweet turn, it is a welcome one.*

*Oh, how I wish you were here to celebrate this amazing fortune. You would have no doubt produced such an opportunity long before I did, but I am appreciative it came at all. You should have seen my lack of grace when approached. My tongue remained stuck in my teeth, as you know it does often, and I could barely manage coherent words. And then, all the words came at once in a jumbled mess. Afterwards, to soothe my confidence, I imagined your laughter at my rambling and laughed along with you. If only I could have heard such sweet tones in the world, rather than in my mind.*

*But I remain in good health and good spirits. I am fortunate enough to have food on most days and sleep under cover. I hope the same for you.*

*It is nearly time for me to go. My last comment is this: I know when I left you and young Naum, we feared we may never see each other again. But that will not be so. We will be reunited. We will see each other again. My work for the Queen all but assures it. I look forward with great anticipation to the day that my concern for when I will see you both again is no longer relevant.*

*Do not despair. The winds are with us!*

*Devotedly,*
*Balomont*

✳✳✳

*Darling Aumille,*

*It has been more than a month since I have last taken a letter from you. I thank you for writing when you are able and am saddened by the trials at home. I hope when this reaches you, Naum has recovered, and you find protection amongst your people. Please return a letter as soon as you are able. I await your words desperately.*

*My days continue to be filled with work. I will not bore you with the exact details of it, but I believe I know what may help us. It is an inclination I have had ever since my study of the plants in our fields. Do you remember when I observed the differences there? Where and why the plants grew. Such information helped us back then, and I believe it can help us now.*

*As to whether I have spoken to Oeillet, Second Queen of the Balafre, Glorious One among All, or not, I have not. But I am assured that if I work hard, if my discoveries are important enough, that it is only a matter of time. And time seems to hurry here. That is one benefit of good and righteous work.*

*I do not know if all see my work in that light, though. I continue to instruct the Queen's advisors on how they may assist me, on the stakes of getting this right, but I do not believe they understand me. I worry they dismiss me or think me a fool. But this could change our very understanding of the world. Would there be no matter more fit for the Queen's attention?*

*Perhaps I am being too worrisome or overzealous. Do not fault me for that. The sooner I am able to speak with our Queen, the sooner we will be reunited. Of that, I am sure. I glimpsed her form moving about the castle several nights past. A bright light shocked my eyes, like a bolt of lightning through the darkness. She is virtuous and purity in our form.*

*I remain in good health. I long to see your face again soon. May the luck that has found us continue.*

*Devotedly,*
*Balomont*

\*\*\*

*Dearest Aumille,*

*I am glad you are safe, and Naum is well. One night, not more than a week before your letter arrived, I saw the moons disappear and feared the worst. It gives me great relief to receive your letter. I treasure your words as the merchant does gold.*

*Are you able to sustain yourself with the rations your people give you? Are they able to train Naum? I want to see him learn the ways of the earth, even if those ways are likely to change. He should know what his father knows, even though I am far away. I know your people are generous and helpful, but they are also suspicious. As am I. I do not trust them to act in his interests unless they are told explicitly. You must do this so he can become an honorable man.*

*I have wondrous news. I met with Oeillet, Second Queen of the Balafre, Glorious One among All this past day. It was as though I spoke with the sun. I am radiating with joy from the goodness and beauty that she infuses into the world. I am forever grateful she watches over us. I am as sure of that now as I have ever been.*

*Because the audience I was allowed with her was brief, we did not speak about your arrival in the city. Matters of work took precedence. I am sorry for this. I know this news disappoints you, but I promise that my work will require far more audiences with the Queen and far more opportunities to arrange your travel here. Do not despair. We will be reunited soon.*

*I must cease writing this letter because of my endless engagements. The pace of my efforts is increasing and causing great stress. Days race. My head hurts from reading, writing, thinking, and talking about all I do. I am in good health, though my spirits are frayed. But the work is imperative, and I must endure.*

*With Affection,*
*Balomont*

\*\*\*

*My Honest Aumille,*

*Are you safe? Are you healthy? Are you still among your people? How is Naum? I have had no word from you in ages. Please return a letter. I cannot bear not knowing.*

*Today, I write with only good news. My work has been a rousing success, and I believe that we no longer need to be worried about the days ahead. The world has given us, and our magnificent Queen, a glorious gift. We accept it with smiles, arms open, ready to embrace it.*

*I will tell you some of my findings, though most are too sensitive for such letters. That is why I must stay here. What I work on so diligently beside our great and lovely Queen are matters of the utmost importance.*

*Many moons ago, I discovered a plant that only grew during our drought. I thought it may grow with other plants, but nothing planted next to it succeeded. I thought it may defend other plants against harsh conditions. That appeared to fail as well. At an impasse and with a desire to understand the plant, I tried many ways to infuse it into the body—my body. It was foolish, I admit, but it worked too. I learned something important about it. That fact, which I cannot reveal here, may save us all.*

*That may sound unbelievable to you, but I believe it. And though there remains much to be known, it is a grand discovery. I am forever grateful for our Queen's gifts and the bountiful fortune she bestows on us.*

*It may not need saying, but you should not share this information with anyone. I worry enough about your safety as it is. That is why I have resisted bringing you to the city. It is a dangerous place, and my work will make both of us, and even young Naum, a target. Please, keep this to yourself or you risk danger.*

*Last, any rumors you hear of me are false. Many here try to ruin me, and the kingdom with it, by fabricating stories of immorality and debauchery. They are lies spread by hateful individuals. Do not believe any who speak of me. I alone will provide you the truth.*

*Faithfully,*
*Balomont*

***

*Aumille,*

*This letter will be short, and I do not know whether it will reach you. I have been naïve. My trust has been misplaced. The advisors work against me. They have perverted my work for their own goals. They even seek to distort the Queen's opinions of me. What desecration! Sinners! But there will be a penance. They will not know the price they have paid until it is too late. The plant gives, but it takes in return. I know this now.*

*I remain without word from you. I live not knowing your fate. Have any of my letters reached you? Do the liars who seek to ruin me tamper with our communication? Do they intercept these letters? If so, a curse on them! They would rather destroy our world than unify it. That is not the purpose of my discovery. That is not the gift of our wonderful Queen.*

*Be well. Do not come here.*

*Balomont*

\*\*\*

*Aumille,*

*If this reaches you know I am besieged by dangers. I scrawl this letter as fast as I can while hidden away. The child is not mine! I will return to you and Naum. I promise.*

*Balomont*

# CHAPTER 24

ALONGSIDE THE VILLAGE OF Savique's youth was a crater, forbidden to all but the Elders. It was a place bordered by cliffs and filled with sand. The sun and rain seemed powerless to create there, as though it was cursed to be desolate for all time. But like any place restricted to them, it drew the village children, Savique among them, like flies to honey.

They would tell stories about the tiny beasts living at its base who ate rocks to survive and spread rumors of birds falling from the sky as they flew over it. The children even named it the Ferran after the mace-wielding giant who drove the great serpents underground. No one else could have created such a cavity in the world. The name, like the place, inspired equal amounts of fear and curiosity in the children.

And they stayed away from it until their curiosity outweighed their fear. Or until their pride would not let them turn down a challenge. So, when one of his friends goaded him, Savique—not yet a hair found on his chin—climbed into the Ferran.

He climbed slowly down the cliffs, twisting and jumping from rock to rock as he descended the steep slope. Each time he landed, he sent a rush of dust and pebbles down towards the bottom. But he took his time and ensured he did not fall, worried if he did, his tumbling would not stop until the bottom.

When he started, the sun was above him. By the time he reached its floor, it was nearly dark.

"Did it!" He yelled at his friends looking down at him. "I told you!"

Savique did not hear any of their responses but basked in the glory all the same. Then he looked around him and glimpsed things he never saw before. Stones spotted like an oncilla or painted with colors more vibrant than the sky.

"Savique!" His friend yelled. "Sun is going down. Get out of there before Ferran comes back." The boy laughed.

But Savique had already noticed the darkness growing inside the crater, and the chill it brought, and made his way back up. He crested the wall faster than he descended it, but night had still arrived once he arrived on fertile ground once again.

The next day, and for many days after, Savique ventured down into the crater. The fear that had held him back was gone, and now he was free to enjoy the wonders he found there. He even convinced a few friends to join him. And though they were skeptical at first, they too were astounded by their findings there.

"Hey Savique, look at this." One of his friends held up a dark rock. There were no imperfections. It was black like a starless night but also shined as if one polished it.

Savique inspected it. "What is that? It doesn't even look like a rock."

"But it is, here see." The boy passed the rock to Savique.

He rubbed it between his fingers, then felt its edges carefully. "Yeah, you're right. But how could it even get this black and shiny? Doesn't seem possible."

"I know." The boy's eyebrows jumped. He smiled. "Think it's valuable?"

"I doubt it, look." He held the stone in both hands, then pulled. It broke the rock in two. "It's too fragile."

"What did you do that for?" his friend said, trying to grab the pieces of rock from Savique's hand. "I could have traded it for something."

"I don't think so," Savique said, still gripping the larger piece of rock. "Even if it looks amazing, no one is going to want it if it breaks—"

"Wait. Look."

Savique noticed it too. The rocks stirred. "It's moving?"

"Yeah, I think—Hold it like this." He held the rock flat in his palm.

"It's turning in my hand," Savique said, excited and incredulous. "How is it—"

"So is mine!" his friend exclaimed.

They both stood looking at each other and the rocks, wide grins affixed to their faces. It was like witnessing Eau appear before them.

But as Savique stared, he had a realization. The rocks were not moving randomly or floating in the air. They turned so that one side faced towards the other like they were trying to reconnect. "They are pointing at each other!"

"You're right! But..." His friend shook his head. "Why would they do that? It is...alive?"

Savique scoffed. "No...no. It's only a trick. But still a neat one. Maybe we can find more."

"Does it work with this?" His friend picked up a different rock and held it in his other hand. When the broken rock did not stir, he frowned. "I guess not."

"It must only work with the same rock. Like it's drawn to something within in. And *only* within that rock." He shrugged. Then his eyes grew wide. "But that means I'll always know where you are."

His friend laughed. "And I can find you whenever you got lost on the garden path. And do you know what?"

"What?"

"The Keepers will all want one. Now do you think it's worth something?"

"Maybe!" Savique said, laughing along. "If we find more, we can make—"

"Savique!" a yell came from above. His mother. "Get up here now! You know you are not supposed to be down there. If anyone else catches you..." She did not need to finish the sentence.

"Sorry," he called back as he put the rock in his pouch and began running up the slope. A few paces up, he turned to his friend and said, "Don't lose it. We'll find more. We can see what—"

"Now, Savique! You are late for your training as it is!"

Savique raced up the wall of the crater. He held true to his word and kept the piece of rock for as long as he could. But the other piece disappeared, along with his friend not more than a week later. And when it was Savique's turn to disappear, he threw it back into the crater and forgot about it. Whatever it was, it had only brought bad luck.

***

Eyvo-Ille rode ferociously through the forest, spurring her horse forward at every opportunity. There was little time before she had to deliver Savique to the V'eauvians and she had work to do before then.

She followed the signs carved in the trees, traversed the plains, and finally arrived at a familiar location. At one time, she had called the land home. Then, it had been a bustling village full of work and trade and joy. Now it was deserted—empty not only of people but of their marks and paths; their life—and without her sister or her tribe, it felt as foreign as any other place.

But it no longer mattered now. She was out of time. It had taken her more than a day to ride there, and it would take as long to return to Nouv'eau. If she left now, it would not leave much time before their raid, and she had not yet finished what she came there to do.

She sighed, then found a small piece of land below a rock outcropping. She dug at the ground as though some great treasure lay beneath. There wasn't, Eyvo-Ille found only soil, a mix of browns that grew colder as she dug deeper, but it did not trouble her. No, the deeper the better.

She removed the box from under her cloth and gently placed it in the hole. She waited there a moment, with her hand on top of the box, considering whether she made the correct decision. Then she piled dirt on top of it, filling in the hole as quickly as she dug it.

After she filled the hole completely, she stood up and stared at the burial. It was not obvious she had dug there at all, but still she found it unsatisfactory. She wandered the abandoned clearing, finding twigs and leaves, and other debris to camouflage the site. Then it was done.

Eyvo-Ille walked to her horse and mounted it. Before she rode away, she stared at the site of her birth and gesticulated as though conversing with someone. But no one else was there. Her head dropped.

So many of her sister's words had gone ignored over the years, about Savique and countless other topics. But she had let Navo-Ille down, hadn't covered her when her sister needed her most. If she had listened—if she had anticipated, seen what was to happen—perhaps she would be with Eyvo-Ille now. It was a mistake she would never forget. Or allow to happen again.

She straightened her back and picked up her head. The horse beneath her pawed at the ground and nickered loudly. She could not change the past, but if it mattered, she would heed her sister's words now. And end the V'eauvians for what they had done to her.

Eyvo-Ille's legs gripped the horse tightly. It broke into a gallop back towards the hills outside Nouv'eau.

***

SAVIQUE PACED THE NOYE camp. It had been more than two days since Eyvo-Ille rode off without telling him where she was going. Or that she was leaving at all. As much as their plan troubled him, her absence unnerved him more. How could an Elder abandon her soldiers, her people, *him*, on the edge of battle?

But as he walked, he realized no other Noye appeared concerned with her absence. It was quite the opposite. The hills were alive with the sounds of conversation and games and stories. If he had not known otherwise, he would have assumed he attended a celebration. The drink flowed in such quantities; he questioned how they had carried it.

He posed that question to one woman who responded with a laugh and said, "Wine and weapons, that's all one needs." Then she thrust a cup into his hand and tipped the bottom, nearly spilling its contents on him.

Savique drank the wine and relished in the warmth as it spread throughout his body. He moved on from the woman and her drink to a group of a dozen people crowded around two men on the ground. At first, he thought it was some dispute or fight among different tribes. But when he pushed himself to the front, he saw they were playing a game with sticks and stones.

It was unfamiliar to him, nor did it appear to be the game the boy in Blieux had attempted to play with him. There were no marks made here. He watched intently, trying to understand the rules from the men's play, but there was no pattern he could understand. He sighed and turned to leave when a hand fell on his shoulder.

"It's called dolvi," an unfamiliar woman said. "They try to pass the rocks through the different points on the stick." She pointed at one of the men. "There."

Savique peered through the crowd, but eventually sighed and shrugged his shoulders. "I don't understand it. What—"

"Wait," she said. "When one misses, the stone goes to the other. They can set their stick to block or strike. You need three passes to win."

A cheer went up from the onlookers. Savique glanced at them, then at the woman. She threw her hands up and said to him, "That's two for Warce." When she saw his blank face, she dropped her hands. "It's not that complicated."

Savique shook his head. "It's not the game. Well, I still don't understand it, but I don't see how you can play games and drink and relax when we sit in the shadow of that," he gestured to Nouv'eau's wall, "without your elder."

The woman turned from him, her eyes big as she rose, then sighed and dropped her shoulders. "Close," she said, then glanced at him. "It is what we do. You should know that by now, cochon."

"Yes," he said. "But here, and now? So near to..."

"To glory?" She nodded. "Yes, we are close." Then she grabbed his shoulder and shook it. "Do not lament the barrier in front of you. Celebrate the challenge you will overcome. The bigger the obstacle, the greater your success. No one remembers one who climbs a single step."

He met her eyes and wondered if it was that simple: the Noye would risk their lives for glory, no matter the opposition. It was the V'eauvians, though, and she had to know what that meant. As soon as he thought it, he realized, perhaps that would make the conquest all the sweeter.

Another loud cheer broke out, as he heard someone say, "Great strike, Warce." This time the cheering did not quiet quickly. He figured Warce had earned his third pass and won the game.

The woman turned from him and shouted into the crowd. "That's the Ono's finest! Great job Warce. You've made us proud." She put her hand on the man's head and rubbed it with a playful zest. Then she returned to Savique's side and clapped him on the back. "Great game! If you knew what to look for."

Savique said nothing in response.

The woman gestured with her head and said, "Follow me."

He did and soon found himself sitting around a fire eating some nuts and seeds while listening to others speak. It was quite like the Star Circle in Nevant, but instead of stories, he heard about different trades. There was talk of how to plant certain crops, techniques to cut stone, and ways to keep pests—both big and small—away from camps.

He leaned towards the woman beside him and said quietly, "What are they doing? Why are speaking of this now?"

"Because," she said. "The tribes rarely come together. And when we do, we share our knowledge. We may all be warriors here, but at home we make pots, build shelters, cook, and do many things. And after this, we will take what we have learned home and improve our world."

"But you will have to—"

"Shh," she said and admonished him with a quick slap on his leg. "Listen."

Savique did and heard more advice in the short time there than he had in the years before it. But eventually, the circle emptied as men and women were called to other duties or games or refused to listen any longer. Even the woman beside him rose and said goodnight.

He would have joined her, but when he glanced at the sky, he saw stars blink and run between moons slowly fading. So he stayed a while longer, staring at the entrancing sight. It so captivated him, he did not notice when someone sat next to him.

When he finally glimpsed the person beside him from the corner of his eye, he jumped. Eyvo-Ille had returned. He exhaled and stared at her, thinking she appeared drained, like she was the ashes of a fire that once raged.

"Savique," she said, gazing at him and past him at the same time. "Tell me about your family. What brought you to them, to Ortolan?"

The question stunned him. Savique had accompanied her on a ride of inde-scribable distance. They had witnessed seasons pass and raided farms together. He had saved her life. And through it all, Eyvo-Ille had never once asked him about his history.

He did not believe it was rudeness. No, she only cared about what was useful, only wanted to know the past in case it would influence the future. She was an ox with blinders ploughing the fields; she saw what was in front of her and moved in that direction. It had served her well.

But the question so surprised him, that Savique's response was not to answer the question, as perhaps he would have done if others had spoken the same words. Instead, he asked, "Why?"

Eyvo-Ille smiled softly, knowingly. "Because tomorrow we will walk to the gates of Nouv'eau and into an unknown world. Who knows when we will speak again and under what circumstances? So, tell me."

"Tomorrow?" Savique's eyes grew large. "We go tomorrow?"

Eyvo-Ille nodded. "Now, tell me."

Savique swallowed his fear and said, "I came to Ortolan after leaving home and a few stops where—"

"No." Eyvo-Ille shook her head, embarrassed for him. "You're speaking in bland tones, with no excitement or spectacle. Your time with us should have taught you better. We make stories, we tell dramas for our kin. We honor our loved ones by giving emotion to the words, by making their accomplishments memorable for all. Now, try again."

At first, Savique said nothing. But as he sat there, mind spinning, he gazed again at the stars and moons. The same ones shone over the estate. And then, like a flash, he recalled running through the fields under a dark sky—absent the very light he now looked at—his heart leaping against his chest, not from the running but from the fear and the excitement. And it all flowed from there, like the river that begins as a trickle and ends in the sea.

He told the story as well as he could. Of a man who wandered and then found a home in a foreign land. The man worked and built a place of endless bounty. He found a family to replace one left behind. But then the world fell apart, his family disappeared, and the man was driven from the place he made.

When he was done, a soft sheen covered his eyes, and he remembered why he was there. It was not for the Noye, despite any bond he shared with them. It was not for some mysterious power in some fabled city. It was not Eyvo-Ille, despite their friendship. No, it was for his son. To see him again. And he would suffer any fate for it.

***

THE SUN CRACKED THE horizon and sent rays of warmth scattering across the hills that housed the Noye. It woke flowers, releasing the scent of pollen into the air. It pulled animals from their slumber and the trees became alive with birdsong. The next morning had arrived.

Before they marched to the wall, Savique stood next to his horse—Navo-Ille's horse—and thanked it for its service to him and stroked its neck. "You rode steady, strong, and swift all this time. I could not have asked for a better partner." The horse whinnied back.

With his horse at his back, he walked to Eyvo-Ille's tent, had his arms bound by a man he had never seen before, then waited until he was ordered to move. It did not take long for him to hear her voice behind him prodding him along.

They arrived at the gates as the sun crested high in the sky. Before the guards approached, Eyvo-Ille turned to Savique and whispered something in his ear. Savique's mouth dropped open, his eyes darted towards her while his head remained forward toward the guards. "You did what?" An urgent whisper burst from his mouth.

Eyvo-Ille said nothing more, turned her spear so that the dull end faced Savique, and nudged him forward. A moment later, they were surrounded.

# Chapter 25

Ajeau shivered. She leaned against the rock walls of her cell and peered through a small window in the door, preventing her escape. The torch outside was still lit and, though it provided a modicum of light, none of its warmth reached her. Her teeth chattered.

She felt a tap on her shoulder and glanced up at a small crack in the rocks above her. As she watched, a drop of water traveled along the stone until it reached the crack. It hung there for a moment, then fell on her shoulder once more. She crawled to her left and listened as the water smacked the ground.

On any other day, in almost any other place, a glimpse of water would have delighted her. But in her cell it only made the air heavy and damp and suffocating. And when she put her face next to the rock, she could smell its foulness. She recoiled from it and sat at the far end of the cell.

No matter how far she moved, she could not get away from its incessant tapping. And it slowly gnawed at her sanity. She tried to pass the time, thinking of where she was. *Drip.* She wondered who the person in the white outfit was. *Drip.* She took a deep breath to calm herself. *Drip.*

The isolation, confinement, and boredom were unpleasant, but the constant dripping was unbearable. She stood and pounded on the doors. She screamed; not words or a name, but guttural noises. Anything to drive the dripping from her mind and give her a moment of peace.

But the dripping continued.

Ajeau spun from the door and kicked the walls. She laughed wildly and tried clapping her hands in time with the drips as though it were a song. But they were irregular, and she could never quite match their rhythm. After a few mistakes, she no longer cared and clapped with abandon, as if surrounded by singers. Such lovely hymns, she thought.

"Ajeau."

The voice stopped her clapping. That voice.

"Ajeau. I'm sorry..."

Ajeau stood up and looked around frantically. "Who's there? What do you want?"

"Ajeau. I'm sorry, there was nothing I could do."

She remembered whose voice it was. "Aube? You wretched bitch! You traitor! I'll never forget what you did to me!"

Silence. Ajeau stopped looking for the woman. There was no one there.

"Aube!" Ajeau screamed until her voice cracked.

Then there was nothing but the sound of water falling on rocks. Ajeau questioned whether that was real, too.

"Wait, I almost forgot." Another voice echoed through the room. But this time, Ajeau placed it immediately.

"Seule! You're as much to blame as anyone—" She pointed a finger at the wall in front of her as if the man was there. Then she sighed and hung her head. "No, that's not true."

"And be careful. Nouv'eau can be dangerous..."

"I realized that too late, Seule. It's not your fault, but your friend didn't help much." Then she thought for a moment. She shook her head. "You never said she was your friend, did you? Why did you send me to her, Seule? You knew more than you told."

There was no answer.

"Got it!" Another voice, one she knew as well as her own.

"Not you too, Vaten." She held her head in her hands.

"How do you figure? I found it..."

"I'm sorry for so many things. I wish you were here now. Even wish we could be back at the estate reaping whatever harvest remains there." Her heart stopped. "Are you alive? Tell me you are alive."

"I can't argue with that."

Ajeau smiled. The pain relented. She knew the words were nothing more than a memory. But it was his voice. He was alive, she knew it, and that meant she could still find him.

"Where are you?" She asked.

She heard only drips.

\*\*\*

"ROUSE YOURSELF!" AN UNFAMILIAR voice called and began opening the door to Ajeau's cell.

At first, Ajeau thought it was another hallucination. But hallucinations could not open the door. The person was real; there was both relief and fear at that realization.

The torch outside her room flickered with the movement of bodies. Ajeau knew nothing of them other than their footsteps and whispers, but they told her all she needed to know. Someone significant approached.

When the footsteps stopped and the flame steadied, she glimpsed a woman wearing white. Even though a veil obscured the woman's face, Ajeau knew where she had seen her before. The docks. The Vizier had come. But instead of bringing blades and terror, she brought provisions.

"Hijeuse, here." The Vizier passed a tray of bread and water to Ajeau. "Eat and drink. You look unwell."

Ajeau hesitated and leaned away from the food. But she quickly realized the woman did not need to poison her. If she wanted Ajeau dead, she could do it at any time in any number of ways. Her kindness was suspicious, but it was also food. And Ajeau was hungry.

She grabbed the bread, took a large bite, then grabbed the pitcher of water and drank it in an entire swig. Ajeau placed it on the ground and pushed it towards the woman. "More."

The Vizier nodded.

In between bites, Ajeau said, "I'm not Hijeuse, my name is Ajeau. You must have me confused with someone else."

"No. I do not confuse you with anyone," she said. "A name is not what you are. I know both. You seem to know only the one."

Ajeau stared at the woman in silence, confused. The words were nonsense. But at least she had food and water.

"Allow us to start again." The Vizier waved her hand in front of her as though clearing some imaginary slate. "I am Syais."

"The Vizier..." Ajeau took the pitcher from the guard and drank again.

"I am known by many names here. You do not need to know them all. Syais will serve you best." The woman took a piece of bread and a full pitcher of water and placed them on the tray. She passed it back to Ajeau.

"All right, Syais. Thank you for this." Ajeau nodded at the food and drink. "But what do you want? Why am I here?"

Syais remained still, staring at Ajeau. "You are here so that you will not escape. What I want is you."

Ajeau said, with a mouth half-full of bread. "Me?"

"That will become clear soon. For now, you need only answer my questions."

"And if I do?"

Syais turned to her guard and gestured for him to leave the cell. He bowed, then quickly left the room. "I believe I have something of yours," she said, removing the blue arrow from her bag and holding it in front of her. "Perhaps you wish to—"

"Give it back!"

Syais held up her other hand. "What if I told you who the weapon belonged to? Or who creates such objects? Would that interest you?"

"Yes," she said slowly, wary of the woman in front of her. "But what do you want in return?"

"Good." Syais returned the arrow to her bag and brought her hands together in front of her. "I will start with a straightforward question: where did you find it?"

"I found it on the ground."

Syais chuckled. "Ah, yes. Of course. But where—what ground did you find it on?"

"Somewhere off the paths south of here, in Ortolan. I was in the Tentir."

"And you saw no people there? No one amongst the woods? You found only the arrow?"

"Yup, when I found it, no one else was there."

"Hijeuse," Syais said, her voice growing stern. "Do not lie to me. Who was there?"

Ajeau said nothing.

"Look around you. You are in no place to bargain. If I can trust you, you can learn much. You can be free of these confines. They are ill-fitting for someone so...essential." Syais leaned close to Ajeau and whispered harshly, "But do not lie to me."

The words sent a shiver through Ajeau. There was something vicious behind them. But Ajeau ignored the warning. "What do you mean, essential? Can't you release me now?"

Syais shook her head. "Trust, Hijeuse, that comes first. Let us try another question then. Why did you bring it here?"

"I needed to know where it is from. This seemed like the place to find that out."

"I have no patience for your games. Our conversation is over." Syais stood, spun from Ajeau, and began exiting the cell.

"Wait! I answered your questions. What do you know about it? Where does it come from?" Her voice sounded more desperate than she intended.

Syais stopped and turned back to Ajeau. "Tell me, why do you care so much about this arrow? You know nothing about it. What would a location do?"

"It's a powerful charm. I found it near our—"

"Liar." The Vizier's hands clenched.

Ajeau caught her breath and flinched at the prospect the woman might hit her. She glanced at the ground and the rock walls, at the door and the lantern beyond it. The woman was right; she had no leverage. Even if she was important, as the woman said, she was beholden to her will. If she wanted to leave, she could not be vague with the Vizier any longer. She sighed. "It is a clue to where a friend might be held."

"A friend?"

"Yes, a friend who was captured. Who I must save." Her voice faded as she spoke, as though she did not want to admit the fact to herself.

Syais nodded and walked back to Ajeau. "Captured? By whom? And saved from what?"

"I don't know. That was where the arrow came in."

Syais nodded slowly. "There were people with the arrow? A lie."

"No. There were no people when I found it...But yes, there were people before then."

"Hmm." Syais shuffled her hands and arms under her robe. The answer appeared to agitate her. "And what were these people like?"

"They were...lithe and moved through the forest as though they knew the lay of every branch and every root. They had blue paint—"

"On their blades." Syais finished Ajeau's thought. "Yes. I know these people. The Zevacese, evil savages from another world."

"Who? Where?" Ajeau sat up, interested. "Where are they from?"

"Zevaco." Syais said the word softly, more to herself than to Ajeau, and paced the cell.

"Zevaco? I've never heard of it."

"A far-off place, not one that is reached easily. But if they are already here—"

"What does that mean?" Her voice cracked. "I can't get there? There must be some way. You must know a way."

Syais shook her head. Ajeau was unsure if it was in response to her question or some inner dialogue. Then she turned and stared at Ajeau. "Your friend—taken by these people? You are sure?"

Ajeau nodded.

There was a pause as both Ajeau and Syais reflected on the information they had gained from the other. Both absorbed by Zevaco, but for entirely different reasons.

Eventually, Syais walked towards the entrance of the cell. Before she exited, she turned and said to Ajeau, "That is all for now. We will speak again soon. And you will remain here until then, as much for your protection as ours. But I have not forgotten your assistance today. Stay well."

"No, please."

But Syais had already exited the room. Her guards followed, locking the door behind them.

Ajeau, alone again but far more confused than before, sat reflecting on the Vizier's words. Zevaco—Vaten—was out of her reach. No, she would not accept it. They had to be somewhere and she would find them. She only needed a longer reach.

\*\*\*

SYAIS PACED HER CHAMBERS, full of agitation, glaring at the white walls surrounding her. Unlike her attire, they were scuffed and blemished from years of use. The place was a travesty, a poor reflection of a person running the great city, leading her people. Her servants should clean them right away before stains covered every inch of the room.

But as she passed a painting of the first Arboricole, she stopped. The portrait was a lie, no doubt, but the woman holding plants and scribbling on parchment was there as a reminder of her story; miraculous things can be found if someone searches for them.

As Syais stared at the painting, the woman in it appeared to smile and said, "A blessed day."

"Have you seen these walls?" Syais said with disdain. "I live in filth! The purity of this place has been tainted. It is no wonder Eau rejects us and withholds our water."

"The walls do not trouble you," the woman in the painting said. "Neither does Eau. You fight yourself—"

"I know what troubles me, vision," Syais said. "They are here. Or they were here? Either way, it is a troubling development."

"But this time you have been fortunate." The woman grinned. "They are always so careful to erase any trace of their excursions into your land. And this little creature, one who knows nothing of herself, hands you proof they come."

"Fortunate? You call this fortune?" Syais's voice rose with fury. "They come now, during the drought. The two are not a mere coincidence," she yelled.

"Remember the visions. The drought, the return, the wind, the Hijeuse. It is real. You are fortunate!" The woman in the painting pointed to a red dot on her cloak. "Trust us."

Syais shook her head and slammed the wall beside the painting with her fist. "No! If they know of the drought, then we are in a most precarious situation. There are too many who would welcome their arrival and my departure."

"Perhaps, but with the Hijeuse, you need not worry. Do you forget what she brings? Do you forget what you gain? You will remake the world!"

"If it is so. But what of this other, the friend they captured? Who is he? Does he know anything? Is he foreseen?"

"No. Impossible! He is nothing!" the woman shouted.

"Then why? Why do they come if not for the blood? What is their plan? Tell me!"

There was no response. The woman in the painting did not move nor smile; she sat writing as she always did.

"Tell me!" Syais screamed. "Do they know more than me? Do they know more than you? Do they know all? Are they at our doorstep? Is our time finally—"

A knock on the door broke her thoughts. "Vizier?"

Syais breathed heavily for a moment, then composed herself and said, "Come." She walked from the painting as Warden Passil entered. "Yes, Warden. What is it? Do you have news of the samples?"

"Thank you, Vizier. I do." He bowed. "But you will not be pleased. There is no record of her having completed the ritual. Not only that, but the samples are missing. The workshop has long been abandoned. Nothing remains."

Syais's muscles tensed. She ground her teeth together. Her face flushed. "It is all gone? How is that possible?"

"I do not know, Vizier. I started an inquiry, but they knew I was coming. Many fled long before this day."

"Was this their doing?" She pointed at Passil. "Have they turned on me?"

"No. I am certain those who remain are loyal and—"

"Eau damn it! Are we to learn nothing?" She slammed her fist against her open hand. But then she glanced once more at the woman in the painting and smiled. "No. There is a way to know. Bring me an Arboricole."

"What do you have planned?" he asked.

"Don't you see?" she said, grinning madly. "We will take a new sample! The Hijeuse is here and the Arboricole will know what I need and where to find it."

"You do not mean—"

"Yes! I will know whether she is of the blood. If I must, I will risk all to find their ancestors." She held up her arms triumphantly. "There is hope for us! Ajeau, there is hope for us yet!"

# CHAPTER 26

VATEN STOOD NEXT TO Levitien with his hands and feet bound and thought he had done this all before. He had been a free man, captured, free again, and then captured again. Both times he stood next to the same man, Levitien, and wondered whether he would die a prisoner.

There was a growing commotion in front of the two accused thieves. Soldiers surrounded, shouting or pointing indignant fingers in their faces. Some even hurled small rocks in their direction, though that stopped after the Elders arrived.

The Elders, Zejela included, spoke in a huddle between the prisoners and the soldiers. Occasionally, a soldier would wander towards the group and attempt to say something, only to be quickly dismissed with a shake of a hand, or even a stern glance.

A bead of sweat rolled down Vaten's cheek and fell to the ground. He stared at the damp imprint it left in the dirt. But then a pair of sandals appeared in his line of sight. And though the sandals were not unique, he knew who stood in front of him.

"Vaten. Levitien." Zejela spoke calmly and gestured at each prisoner like she was introducing two strangers to each other. Or introducing two strangers to a crowd.

She continued, "You know why you are imprisoned here. You stole items of great worth to our people. You are Zevacese and, like the rest of us," she gestured at the soldiers behind her, "you are subject to our rules. We showed mercy once, but there is no mercy for thieves here."

"We don't even know—" The words brought the blade of Zejela's dagger to Vaten's throat. Any movement—talking, swallowing, even a turn of his head—would draw blood.

"Do not be foolish. We are not conversing here. I am speaking to you as a courtesy. A last chance." Zejela withdrew her dagger. "We do not believe you could have done this alone. You had help. Tell us who helped you. Tell us where the items we speak of are now. Tell us everything you know."

Vaten swallowed, stared at Zejela but said nothing. He knew nothing, except that protesting was futile. Levitien too remained quiet, seemingly unbothered by her threats.

"Silence is not your friend," she said. "This is your last opportunity to tell me what you know. It may not save your life, but you won't die as a pariah in your own community. You will help your people. Your path to the earth will be secure."

Laughter erupted from Levitien. Vaten jerked his head to glare at the man as though he'd lost his mind. Zejela did not flinch, unimpressed by the man's outburst. She raised her hand to quiet the shouting from the soldiers behind her.

"Do I have this correct?" Levitien said, as his laughter faded. "You want us to confess, tell you all we know about the theft of some *things* in a box you stole—along with us, I'll add—and in return, you will make sure our spirits have a safe journey."

Zejela nodded. "That is correct. A spirit unburdened will flourish with the earth."

Levitien chuckled again, then said, "Do we look dumb? How about you tell us what was in those boxes?"

It was Zejela's turn to be quiet.

"Can't even tell us that?" Levitien smiled at Vaten. "Then I don't think we have anything to say to you."

"Then the choice is yours. You die unabsolved."

"We die as innocent men!" Vaten yelled.

Zejela walked away from the two men and returned to the circle of Elders. When she arrived, they launched into a vigorous discussion. Neither Vaten nor Levitien could hear of what they spoke, but neither seemed to mind. Vaten was not even looking at them. Instead, he continued to glare at his fellow prisoner.

"So, you finally decide to speak," Vaten said.

The smile slowly faded from Levitien's face. "What else is there to do?"

"You don't have a plan? No ideas on how to escape?"

Levitien cocked his head to the side. "Nope, no plan. No schemes. I don't know how we escape this, short of a miracle. But, you know what, if I die here on this Sol damned ground, I'm doing it with a smile on my face."

Vaten noticed, despite what he said, there was no smile on Levitien's face. The words seemed to be only words, as though they were something Levitien once heard and thought sounded good.

But a question lingered in Vaten's mind. And this close to death, with no chance of escape, there was no reason for lies. "Do you know who did it? Who took the boxes or whatever was inside them?" Vaten asked.

"No. Not a clue. I told you—"

"Levitien." Vaten's voice was stern. "Did you do this? Were you a part of it, even in the smallest way?"

"You're getting suspicious, kid. Not that I blame you. But the answer is still no. I'm not a part of this. I had nothing to do with it. But I have a guess who did."

"Who?"

"I told you. Zejela and Aloc spoke before all this. And now she's leading the accusations against us. Seems odd, no?"

Vaten frowned at the thought. "I don't know. I was there when Zejela found out about the missing items. She appeared genuinely shocked and concerned. And where is Aloc?"

"I hate to tell you this, kid. But she played you. Played us. You—we—were a convenient pawn in whatever this is. And who knows about Aloc? Maybe he's hid away with whatever they stole."

Vaten glanced at Zejela speaking with the Elders. She certainly looked involved. He turned back to Levitien. "Maybe, but I still don't really believe it. I guess it doesn't matter now anyway, right?"

"That's right, kid." Levitien shook his head and sighed. "I'll tell you this though I would have loved to die knowing what was in those boxes. You know? Solving that mystery. My father would be proud of that. I bet yours would be too."

Vaten stared back at Levitien. It was the first time he had heard Levitien mention his father in their time together. He knew of Levitien's mother, his sister, and countless other insignificant details of the man's life, but he never even heard a reference to his father.

Perhaps, under different circumstances, Vaten would have inquired further about it. But in that moment, it seemed inconsequential. So he shrugged his shoulders and said, "I don't know. I won't ever know."

The Elders nodded their heads in unison and separated. Ryiera strode from the circle and spoke with a soldier. She grasped the woman's hands, smiled, and nodded her head vigorously.

The others in the crowd shifted and now encircled the woman who had spoken to Ryiera. She whispered as if her words were a secret. Vaten chuckled. Who were they keeping a secret from? He couldn't understand them even if he heard the word. But once she was done, the crowd broke into boisterous cheers. It was a celebration.

As the soldiers continued to roar in delight, the Elders departed. They walked towards a long stone building Vaten knew as the Forgotten Rest, the meeting place of the Sentry masters.

All but one Elder entered. Even from a distance, Vaten could tell the lone exception was Zejela. She made her way down a path, in the direction of the hut Vaten and she had shared a short time ago, and was quickly out of sight.

With the Elders away, the crowd of soldiers became unruly. They shouted and hurled rocks at Vaten and Levitien once more. A few soldiers ran up to the prisoners and kicked them. One yelled something with a giant smile on his face, thrust his fists in the air, and walked back to the other soldiers to a loud ovation.

For some time, Vaten wondered whether the soldiers would deliver their sentence now. Perhaps the Elders, and Zejela, did not want to see such bloodshed. But the soldiers' enthusiasm for taunting the prisoners eventually waned and, not long after, Zejela returned. She carried a pouch over her shoulder as she entered the Forgotten Rest.

Moments later, the Elders returned to the group of soldiers, announced something to them, and then led them back to the building they had emerged from. When they had cleared the area, Zejela and three soldiers remained.

She approached the two prisoners and said, "Your fate has been long known, but your punishment has only now been decided. It is known here as 'selmal' and reserved only for the most severe of crimes. I do not if there is a word for it in Bassian, so I will describe it."

Vaten's eyes darted to and from Zejela as his heart raced. A punishment that had to be described, without a similar Bassian word; it instilled only terror.

"You will be buried in the ground for four suns. The earth you forsake will slowly steal every breath from you until it departs your body for good. After the land has administered its justice, you will be plucked from the ground and thrown into the sea. The salt will burn your spirit and the great sea serpent, Bourzon, will consume your body. You will never again return to the earth and your spirit will be forever lost. You will nurture nothing."

Vaten felt his stomach rise in his throat, the bile exploding into the back of his mouth. He tried to swallow to prevent vomiting. It did not work. He turned his head and retched.

Zejela continued, "There is no changing your punishment, but I will grant you the opportunity to say a last word if you wish."

Levitien closed his eyes and looked down. He said nothing.

Vaten coughed and spit. He could barely get the words out, his lungs had no air left in them and his throat burned from the vomit, but quietly he said, "Zejela...Please."

Zejela glanced at both men quickly, nodded, then turned to the soldiers standing behind her. She said a few words, then watched as they grabbed the prisoners, hoisted them onto their feet, and dragged them along the path towards the Forgotten Rest.

It was Vaten's first time inside the building and if panic had not been surging through him, its modesty would have surprised him. It was nothing like the Blue Hold. But it didn't matter, they did not remain inside for long.

They exited the structure at the back and arrived in a field with two freshly dug holes. They were deep, thin, and dark. The colors of the dirt and clay changed at different levels, but the bottom was so black it appeared to steal the light. It was fitting, Vaten thought, the darkness of death here in the earth.

After the soldiers positioned Vaten and Levitien in front of their respective pits, Zejela approached one final time with a small bag in hand. She said something in Zevacese, which strengthened the grip of the soldiers on Vaten and Levitien. Then she drew her dagger and made cuts on the prisoner's shoulders.

The cuts were not deep. They hurt and drew blood, but they barely drew a reaction from Vaten and Levitien. A reaction other than confusion.

Zejela sheathed the dagger, then reached into her bag. She pulled out a pink powder and rubbed it into each man's cut. It burned for a moment and then nothing. There were no discernible effects.

Vaten wondered what it was for. They were going to die, and the Zevacese were going to salt their spirits. What more could the Zevacese do? He quickly realized he didn't want to know the answer. But, unfortunately for him, it came anyway.

"This is to ensure you do not fall asleep," Zejela said without remorse. "You will be awake for every agonizing breath, every cry for help, every claw at the dirt that surrounds you. You will live your death until the earth is done with you. Then we will come for your spirit."

Vaten's panic turned aggressive. He struggled against the soldiers, gripping his arms. He tried to step on their toes. When he thought one was behind him, he threw his head back to headbutt them but missed.

Finally fed up, one soldier struck him in the stomach, causing Vaten to lose his breath and stop resisting.

Zejela grabbed him by the hair, leaned close to his face, and stared into his eyes. "Remember. Anything is possible." It was a snake's hiss.

Shoves from the guards forced him to march down the stairs into his tomb. He stood wide-eyed as spear-point and watched as the dirt piled in front and on top of him until he could no longer keep his eyes open. Light to dark, life to death. And through it all, he could only think of the words Zejela spoke.

*Anything is possible.* What does that mean? What—

Despite the promise that he would stay awake, Vaten fell asleep.

*** 

WITH THE RITUAL PERFORMED, Zejela patted the reed under her robe and breathed a sigh of relief. The final pile of dirt poured on top of the two interlopers' graves meant she had accomplished the first part of her plan. Vaten and Levitien were no longer a problem. And that meant she could execute the rest of her plan without interference.

Best of all, no one suspected a thing. How could they? Most wanted the outsiders gone. It wasn't hard to get them to agree with her accusations.

Yes, that was the simple part of the plan. Now came the hard part. She would have to start with the Elders. Thankfully, and because of her, they were here. It would require a delicate touch. Finesse. Warmth and strength in equal amounts. She had that, though she had little time.

As she walked back towards the Elders, she said to herself, *four days*. She had four days to finish her plan. Four days to make sense of her world. Four days to save them. It was time to get to work.

# CHAPTER 27

"AND WHAT DO WE have here?" A guard wearing a white shirt stained with dirt, blood, and sweat grabbed Savique's forearm and dragged him forward.

He stumbled but said nothing, as Eyvo-Ille had told him to do.

The six guards who encircled Savique and Eyvo-Ille did not appear to be formidable warriors. Despite their weapons, they were thin and clumsy. They approached with feet too close together and awkward and easily breakable grips on their spears. Savique thought Eyvo-Ille could dispatch them with one arm. Still, he paid them deference, as the plan required.

"Who are you two?" A guard behind Savique asked.

"I am a shoemaker from the north, not more than a day's walk. I found this thief," Eyvo-Ille spit on the ground by Savique's feet, "trying to steal the sandals I make—"

"A thief, you say?" Another guard said.

The guard who grabbed Savique looked him over, top to bottom. Then he leaned in and squinted his eyes to inspect Savique's face closely. Finding nothing interesting, he blinked a few times, leaned back, and stood at attention.

This caused Savique a bit of a problem. The guard should have discovered his brands. They were essential to the plan; corroboration of their story. But the man didn't even look at them.

And he knew Eyvo-Ille would not reveal them. It would be too suspicious, too forward. The guards were incompetent, but if she pushed his brands on them, they were likely to become more skeptical. They needed the guards less wary of them, not more. They needed the guards to find the brands on their own.

At first, Savique simply fidgeted with his hands. It felt natural and helped with his anxiety, too. But the guards paid it no mind. Too subtle.

Then he scratched his hands vigorously as though he were infested with bugs. He received a questioning glance from one guard, but no mention of his brands. Still too subtle.

"And what say you? Are you truly a thief, as the woman says?" He could feel the air of the words on the back of his head.

Time was now a factor. The guards would not accept his silence forever, even if it was deferential. He had to get them to find his brands, and soon. Then it would not matter what he said. Their minds would be made up.

With the pressure growing and the guards now staring at him, Savique produced his last attempt to bring a guard's attention to his hands. Regardless of if they notice or not, it would be his last try.

He charged at Eyvo-Ille. He tried to wrap his hands around her neck, but because they were still bound, he could only get his fingers to dig into her flesh. It served its purpose well enough.

Eyvo-Ille, stunned by the attack, recoiled, but then quickly pivoted and began reacting with histrionics. She coughed, gagged, and gasped for air. She tried to scream for help, but caught her own words in her throat. She flailed her arms wildly, trying meekly to disrupt his grip. It was a wonderful performance.

The guards lowered their spears, tips facing Savique.

"Release her now!" A guard said.

Savique did not and instead screamed, "I'll kill you for this!"

Eyvo-Ille faked a look of terror, her eyes nearly bulging out of her face.

It was the last thing Savique noticed before he felt wood crack across his back. He was thankful they choose to hit him and not to stab him.

As he lay on the ground with a guard's knee now firmly between his shoulder blades, Savique completed his plan. He stretched out his arms, palms facing down, and flailed them. A guard would have to further restrain them. And there was no way they would miss—

"Look at this...brands," a guard said.

"So the woman was telling the truth, huh?" replied another.

"Yeah, must be. Almost got herself killed, though." He chuckled.

The guard on Savique's back pushed his head into the ground and said, "Yeah, hublon. You almost killed her. Trying to become a murderer too?"

"Doesn't matter. He's going to die now, anyway." The guard mimed Savique's hanging.

"Who branded you? Whose property did you steal?"

"Who cares? Let's take him in," the guard on his back said. "The Captain will be pleased. We'll look good and she can show off in front of the Lord."

"Fine. But what about this one?" The guard pointed to Eyvo-Ille.

"Leave her, who cares?" another guard said with a wave of his hand.

"Wait," Eyvo-Ille protested. "What about my reward for his return?"

"What do you want?" The guard bent down and picked up some loose dirt and threw it in her face. "There you go. Your reward. Now leave."

Eyvo-Ille waved the dirt from her face. "No. I demand payment. If not from you, then from the man who branded him. Let me explain to him what I have done. I'm sure he would want to provide restitution."

Savique could not move and would not risk speaking, but he wanted to shout at Eyvo-Ille to stop. It was foolish to bring the Foreman upon them. He was a blight on the world; it would only lead to ruin.

A few guards laughed her off, but the one who had noticed Savique's hands responded with a growing smile on his face, "Oh yes. That sounds like a wonderful idea. You want to explain to him what you have done? Want to demand payment from him? Follow us." The words were spoken as a warning, more than an invitation.

There were a few curious glances shared between the guards and a few shoulder shrugs, but then they hoisted Savique onto his feet and dragged him towards the great wall of Nouv'eau. Eyvo-Ille followed.

***

Savique shivered. Nouv'eau felt a frigid place, far colder than he had expected. Perhaps it was the long shadow cast by the great wall or the cool breeze that whipped through the city at random intervals. Or maybe it was chills from the uncertainty that lay ahead. He brought his arms tight to his sides and tensed his muscles, trying to keep warm. But the shaking would not stop.

The guards dragged him through the gates and into an open space punctuated by a large white statue of a woman holding a spear in front of her. Eyvo-Ille followed closely behind Savique, walking freely but under the guards' constant vigilance as the group continued to move alongside the wall. They stopped when they reached a set of tents where guards ate and drank and rested beside racks of chipped and snapped weapons.

A guard pushed Savique to the ground. "Try nothing stupid, thief," the man said, looming over Savique with his spear point pressed against Savique's back.

As Savique lay there staring out at the buildings stretching endlessly into the city, he saw feet moving in the distance. At first, they passed in and out of his view quickly. But then more and more grew closer, larger, and more frequent. They were uncovered and unprotected, not the feet of soldiers or guards.

He squinted, trying to see who was approaching him when he received a kick of sand in his face. He jerked his head to the side and closed his eyes to avoid it, but was not quick enough. His eyes burned and tears ran down his face. The cloud of dust even found its way into his mouth and down his throat. He coughed loudly, deeply, each spasm forcing the guard's spear into his back.

The abuse did not stop there. Shouts and rocks came hurtling towards him. When he opened his eyes, he saw workers—men and women no different from him—admonishing him with fury in their eyes.

The crowd grew in size and Savique worried they might kill him long before Eyvo-Ille fulfilled her plan. "Please..." he said. "Stop." He tried to raise his voice but the shouting still drowned him out. "Stop!"

Then he felt as the spear's cold metal lifted from his back.

"Eau damn it! Knock it off!" the guard yelled at the mass of people. "You hit me in the eye. Next one to throw something and I'll take it out on you."

And though the sand flew less often, the insults and screaming only worsened.

Savique tried to find Eyvo-Ille near him for reassurance, but when he lifted his head to look for her, a clump of dirt, exploding on impact, struck him.

"I said stop it!" The guard turned his head and coughed. "What was that?"

"You! I saw that...You want a spear in your gut?"

"Take him to the Cave and be done with it. We'll go tell the Captain after."

The guard reached down and grabbed the rope binding Savique's hands. Soon, he was on his feet and being pushed forward. "Walk." As Savique moved past the crowd hurling insults, the guard pushed him again. "Faster. Unless you want to return here." Savique hobbled urgently.

Before exiting the tent, he swung his head, hoping to catch Eyvo-Ille's eye before they were separated. But it was no use. He didn't even glimpse her clothes prior to stepping into the open city. There would be no final confirmations, no signals; he would have to trust she would not abandon him.

Savique stood at the top of a staircase leading underground and finally understood how the Cave earned its name. His legs barely supported his weight as he descended into a deep blackness. There, he silently pleaded with Eyvo-Ille to save him. He did not want this to be the last time he saw the sun.

***

EYVO-ILLE PERCHED ON A stool under the tent as a few dozen guards rested and loitered around her. After Savique left and the crowd disbursed, there was something like a peace in the small shelter. It surprised her. She was a stranger to them, and she expected harassment, or at least mild provocation. Instead, they ignored her. They appeared far more interested in their own lives than in hers.

She decided it was for the best. Not only did it lessen the chance someone would discover her story a ruse—or worse, discover her a Noye—but it allowed her to plot how to overpower the guards, what routes to take to the wall, and what she could use as a beacon to signal her comrades.

And as she strategized, time raced. She looked up at the sky once and saw the sun peaked high overhead. The next time she looked, it was nearly below the wall. Then darkness fell upon the city, and she rested.

When she awoke the next morning, she saw little had changed. There were still guards present and some bread and water had been left for her, but otherwise the day seemed a copy of the previous one.

That changed quickly as the sun rose over the great walls. A crowd of people, far larger than those who arrived to abuse Savique a day before, began forming near the gates. They sang songs and chanted tributes Eyvo-Ille had never heard before. It was clear something was happening, but she did not know what.

An image flashed in her mind: the guards dragging Savique from his prison and him being hung up in front of the crowd. She knew a public execution of a thief was possible—the V'eauvians were vile people—but she did not expect it would be so soon.

But as the crowd kept growing, Eyvo-Ille found them to be peaceful and joyous. There was no bloodlust in these laborers. They were not calling for the head of some insignificant thief. They celebrated something virtuous.

Then the gates opened, and the crowd erupted in joy. The songs and chants were louder than cracks of thunder. People drummed feverishly. Eyvo-Ille tried desperately to see the reason for the uproar. She climbed on her stool, standing tall enough to touch the roof of the tent with her head, and saw it. The procession of Lord Balay.

A shiver of excitement coursed through her body—not unlike the V'eauvians, she thought, but for a very different reason. As she watched the man pass her by, she imagined grabbing a spear from a guard, rushing to the Lord's side, and driving it through his armor.

Eyvo-Ille smiled as she watched the Lord and his personal guard ride past. She felt her neck and remembered her battle with them. Mistakes aside, she and her sister had slayed them all. She would do it again, and when she did, she would be known as the Noye who reclaimed Bas. Glory would be hers.

The Lord's Guard did not slow for the crowd and he passed her before she even finished her thoughts. Her glory would have to wait for another day. She would make a fool of him yet. Her smile widened.

But as she watched the receding procession ride off into the city, she noticed something familiar. She couldn't place it and her guesses—the white armor or a horse she had seen before—did not satisfy her.

She continued to probe the depths of her mind, looking for what she recognized. But she brought back nothing helpful, only feelings of grief, fear, despair, and a color as golden as the sun.

Darkness once again fell over the city. With no answers, Eyvo-Ille slept. The second night passed uneventfully. Only one more to go.

*** 

SAVIQUE SPENT A LONG time in the dark. He did not know how long—there was no way to know—but it felt like an eternity.

He was chained to disheveled men and women and crammed in a small room with no fresh air or light. The smells—piss, shit, sweat, breath, iron—never dissipated. The screams of the beaten echoed incessantly off the walls of the cell and inside his own head. The ground was cold and hard on his bare feet. Even the light, once a source of joy, now only brought a burning sensation to his eyes whenever the door to the outside would open.

It was all abhorrent, worse than a nightmare. And all he could do was wait for a rescue that he did not know was coming.

He tried to pass the time talking to his fellow prisoners, but quickly gave up after a woman spit in his face and then screamed unintelligible words at him. He tried throwing and catching small clumps of dirt. But after hitting a fellow inmate and receiving a whipping from the guard, he stopped. He tried jumping, but that hurt his feet. He tried sitting, but that hurt his ass. He tried to lie down but was pulled in every direction by the others bound with him.

Though despair pulled at him from every angle, he refused to surrender hope. There was an end to his captivity, he repeated to himself. Eyvo-Ille would come, open the door, and free him. When she did and they were done with this raid, he could go home. He could see his son again.

When he thought of his son's face, he pictured the baby he knew back then, even though the boy would be grown by now. It didn't matter; he smiled all the same.

Then someone grabbed Savique. He couldn't see anyone in the dark pit, but when he tried to shake free of the person's grasp, he received the dull end of a spear to his gut. He doubled over in pain. It was a guard.

He didn't understand why a guard had grabbed him, but he did not say a word. Not even when he found his hands and feet free of their binds and hands propelling him forward.

Though he should have been relieved by his release, panic surged through him. This wasn't the plan. He was not supposed to be taken by a guard; Eyvo-Ille was meant to rescue him. Unless she had already failed. Savique's legs buckled.

It didn't stop the guard from dragging Savique to the surface. Once there, his eyes burned as they tried to adjust to the light. But the words he heard next burned far worse. They seared his very soul.

"Well, if it isn't my old friend, Savique. You look so much better than I expected." A vile chuckle slithered from the man's mouth. "I don't suppose that will last, though."

Savique recognized the voice. He squinted his eyes and saw a pair of immaculate white gloves shining in the sunlight. He knew who wore them even before he caught sight of the man's wild grin. It had been a long time, but he could never forget that face. The face of evil.

"Foreman Crevir."

# CHAPTER 28

AJEAU NEVER KNEW A time before her scar. It had always been there, on her left arm, like the mole on her stomach and the spot on her knee. It was as much a part of her as anything else, and she accepted it as such.

Of course, there were days she wondered how she came to have it. Maybe it was from a hard birth or a terrible fall. She even imagined herself blessed by Eau, who left a trail through her skin like they left a river through a forest. She used that line once with Vaten when he asked about it.

But most of the time, it was air; something she knew was there, but never thought much about.

That was true until she met Seule and chewed on the buscade root. There was no proof that what she had seen was a memory, and not a hallucination or a nightmare, but it felt real. And Ajeau accepted it as such. She had felt that pain, lost that blood. But what it meant, who she was back before the estate and Vaten, she did not know.

Ajeau had nearly finished tracing the length of her scar with her finger when she was interrupted by three guards in her cell.

"On your feet, Hijeuse." The last word spoken mockingly.

Ajeau said nothing, made no movements except a small raise of her head to look at the guard who spoke.

"Fine," he said. Then to the other guards, "Grab her."

The two guards who hadn't spoken leaned down, grasped her arms, and hoisted her onto her feet.

"Let's go."

The guards dragged her out of her cell, though she put up no resistance. If they were taking her out, they would encounter no opposition from her. She would've run if they let her.

The door to the outside world opened, and she saw the sunlight for the first time in nearly a week. The colors, movement, and sounds overwhelmed her, but she welcomed them. She basked in the light as though it were a friend's embrace. Even the air, dry and warm as ever, was refreshing.

They took her across a dirt path, then down a road. It did not take long before they stopped in front of a large brick building painted white. The Beacon, Ajeau heard one of them say. And until she saw it, she didn't know why.

It nearly blinded her. The white paint shined like the morning sun. She could barely look at it. And when she did, she thought it was a most remarkable feat, to keep such a large building so white. Had she seen the back, she would've discovered how they did so; a plethora of workers cleaned and painted the building regularly.

The guards dragged her into a massive foyer as white as the outside. Running alongside the wall were statues of men, women, beasts, and plants. She wondered if she ever knew any of their names or had ever been told any of their stories.

Even if she had known them, the guards did not stop long enough for her to inspect any of the statues more closely. They continued to pull her through the only open door at the far end of the room and up a flight of stairs to a landing, where they waited outside a closed door.

While they waited, a woman walked past Ajeau and the guards, opened the door, and entered the room. She wore a white cloak with two red circles on her chest, just below her shoulders. The door slammed shut behind her as though it was a warning not to pry on the activities conducted inside.

It was only after the door closed Ajeau realized she had seen the woman's outfit before. But not recently. The memory of those red dots was hazy. Even if white was common amongst the high born of Nouv'eau, those red dots were not. Wherever she had seen them before, it was not in the city.

She told herself there were countless reasons they might be familiar. Most of them were innocuous. Perhaps they were envoys from a nearby community who she had seen on Crevir's Estate or the red dots adorned some trader's cart she had passed while wandering with Vaten. Whatever it was, she shouldn't waste her time on it.

The moment she stopped thinking about it, she remembered. All at once, the images came back to her. Her heart raced. Her chest tightened. She shook as though she were freezing.

It was the man, the one she saw in the vision at Seule's hut. He cut her open. The red dots on his shoulders, they were the same. She was sure of it.

A door opened, and the guards hoisted her back on her feet. This time, she resisted. She twisted and flailed. She screamed. It echoed through the building as the guards pushed her through the doorway. The door closed behind her as her voice cracked and gave out.

***

"STOP, PLEASE. STOP." A woman spoke garbled words through a mouthful of blood. It dripped down her chin and on to a white robe next to two circles of the same color. If she had looked down, she would have had difficulty telling which stains were blood and which were the designs sewn into the clothes.

"Will you tell me what I need to know?" Syais asked. There was no red on her flawless white garb.

"I don't...know. There is nothing...Please...Stop...Let me—"

"Then you are useless to me." Syais drove her dagger into the woman's chest, forcing it through the resistance of her ribs. She heard a crack and a pop, then grabbed the woman's hair and forced her head up, meeting the woman's eyes. Syais stared into them as the woman's mouth fell open and she coughed her final breaths. Blood pooled on the floor.

"Filth," Syais said as she turned and gestured to Passil. "Bring me one who will talk."

"There are only a few left."

Syais waved him out of the room, then sighed. She tired of their resistance. They did not need to die; it was their choice. If they only told her the truth, they would live and she could save the V'eauvians from extinction. Save the land too. It was a noble and righteous goal. But to do it, she needed the leaves.

"Can't you see how selfish your being?" She yelled at the man Passil escorted into the room. Like the others, he wore a cloak of white marked with two red circles.

"Selfish? Never," the man said. He looked around at the grisly scene, then bowed his head. "Vizier, I serve you. I do as you ask. Please, ask of me."

Syais smiled. Finally. "Can you perform the ritual?"

The man did not look up. "No, Vizier. We have not conducted the ritual in many years. We have no supplies. And we believe the rumors to be false. The bloodline is pure."

"You do not believe the words of Ormyphant? You do not believe the drought has birthed another?"

He straightened and met Syais's gaze. "No, Vizier. The ravings of a lunatic, surely." He waved his hand in front of his face as if a fly bothered him. "And the rest, simple speculation. It would be quite amazing if it were true, but do not—"

"Never mind!" She threw up her arms in frustration. "I do not care for your thoughts. You are not here for a conversation. Tell me where the remeur leaves are."

"I don't know. I've never collected them, Vizier." Then he narrowed his eyes and cocked his head to the side. The edges of his mouth twitched into a smile that disappeared as quickly as it appeared. "You intend to bring back the ritual?"

Syais glanced at the dagger still stuck in the woman on the chair. The man followed her eyes. "You do not ask questions of me," she said. "Do not forget your place."

"Yes, Vizier. My apologies." The man bowed his head and averted his gaze once again. "The only source I know for the leaves is..." As he stared at the ground, he rocked slowly, as though he knew he could not leave his sentence without an end but had no conclusion for it. But a moment later, his eyes widened, and he threw up his finger and shook it. "Yes, the old charts. We have old charts that the first Arboricole used to keep records of their travels. They might—I mean, they lead to where the remeur grows."

"Charts? You hold records you do not share with me?"

The man held up his hands. "The charts are not mine to oversee. But I know where they are. Under the tree in the workshop's courtyard. There is a chest with the old documents. It is there in case some calamity befell us, we would always have the records of the first." He smiled.

"Yes. Prudent," Syais said, nodding her head. She walked to the man and put her hand on his shoulder. She stared into his eyes. "This is such a catastrophic time. I need those charts and I will do my best not to disturb your place of labor. Thank you for your help. You have given hope to all V'eauvians."

"Yes, Vizier. It is my pleasure."

Syais turned from the man and walked to Passil. She leaned next to his ear and whispered, "The man lives. But he tells no one else about the charts. Take his tongue."

Passil drew his knife and smiled at the man.

***

"Welcome Hijeuse," Syais said and gestured to the chair across from her. Guards dragged Ajeau to the chair, threw her into it, and left the room. "I told you we would talk again, and here we are."

Syais's cheerfulness unnerved Ajeau. "What is this place? What are you going to do with me?" Ajeau said.

"You have no reason to worry. Today we have received a gift."

Ajeau stood up to leave, but Passil pushed her back down into the chair. Though the guards had left her unbound, there was no escape.

"You cannot leave yet, we haven't even begun our discussion." Syais grinned as she sat down across from Ajeau. "Did my guards not treat you with respect?"

Unable to tell whether the woman was taunting her or being sincere, Ajeau said nothing.

"They were under strict orders not to hurt you. If you are injured, I will reprimand them."

"No," Ajeau said as she glanced up at Passil, who loomed over her and then back at Syais. "I am unharmed, though I would like to leave."

"Yes, I understand that impulse," Syais said, nodding. "This is all new for you and that must be...overwhelming. But you must stay and hear what I have to say."

"And what about those with the red dots?"

Syais shook her head. "The Arboricole? What about them?" Then her eyes lit up. "Oh, you remember? Well, I can assure you no harm will come to you today. They were here on my behalf, not yours."

"I don't..."

"It may be difficult to trust that, I know. But I am not lying. Didn't I honor my word the last time we spoke?" Syais eyed her with large, inviting eyes.

Ajeau hesitated, then relented. "Yes." It was the truth, even though it did Ajeau little good. Zevaco may as well have been the sun. No, the sun would have been better. At least she had heard of the sun.

"Then trust me now as well," Syais said. "And I will trust you. If I have your word that you will stay and not try to escape, I can dismiss the Warden and we can talk freely."

Ajeau said nothing.

"I assure you I have plenty more gifts for you."

There was no choice. She glanced once more at the man looming above her and said, "Fine."

"Wonderful." Syais clapped, then nodded once to Passil, who promptly left the room. "I am glad we can trust each other. You are so unlike the others—they didn't even remember. Well, that is inconsequential now."

"There are others? Who?"

"Ah," Syais sighed and shook her head, "so you don't remember everything. Yes, there were others. But I already know about them. I know so little about you."

Ajeau folded her arms in front of her chest. "I thought you knew what I was, the Hijeuse."

"Of course," Syais laughed loudly. "I know what you are and what you will be. But the title is only that, it does not reveal all."

"I don't understand," Ajeau said. "You speak in contradictions."

"Perhaps I do. These things are difficult to explain, especially to someone who does not know their history, but—"

"Then tell me. Or let me go."

Syais held up a hand. "In time, you will know everything. But that is not why I brought you here today. Today, I need to talk to you about your friend."

"My friend? Who? Vaten? What about him?" The name slipped out as though it was a rock covered in moss.

"Vaten? Is that his name?" Syais rubbed her chin. "Not familiar. But the Zevacese took him, is that correct?"

"Yes." Ajeau sat forward in her chair. "What about him?"

"And you are trying to save him?"

"Yes, I told you that last time."

Syais smiled and nodded. "Of course, I was simply confirming it."

"Then, what?" Ajeau said, frustrated. "What about Vaten do we need to talk about?"

"Well…" Syais folded her hands in front and leaned back in her chair. "I need to know what you are willing to do to find him."

Ajeau stared at Syais through thin slits. "Why?"

"Because I am offering you a chance at what you want. Though I do not know if you are ready."

"I…How? What do you mean?"

"The people that took your friend—the Zevacese—are pests, a disease on this world. They are wicked beyond comprehension. I have no doubt that they took Vaten for some wicked purpose. Though if he is alive—"

"He is." Ajeau said as she pounded the chair. "And I will find him. I will do whatever it takes."

Syais smiled and nodded once at Ajeau. "Good. But you must know, we will deliver swift and harsh justice to this blight. It must be eradicated or it will spread."

"Eradicated…?" Ajeau said, as if unsure of the word's meaning. "People will die?"

"Yes, the Zevacese will not release him willingly. It is a hard truth, but, as I said, they are wicked."

"But why? Why Vaten? Why won't they—"

"I do not know their plans for your friend. It could be so many things." Syais paused, then leaned forward. "But I will ask you again, will you do what you must? Return who you must to the earth?"

Ajeau thought for a moment. "If they are as evil as you say, then—"

"They must be as I say," Syais grinned. "No honorable people would steal someone. Your friend, above all. There can be no reason other than wickedness."

They were convincing words. Ajeau nodded. "I will do whatever it takes. If they will not give him to me peacefully—"

Syais shook her head. "I can assure you they will do no such thing."

"Then they reap what they sow."

"Exactly." Syais pointed at Ajeau. "It is reassuring to know we agree. Because I can help you find your friend and wipe the Zevacese from this world."

"If that's what it takes. Then I accept."

Syais reclined, satisfied only for a moment. As soon as she hit the back of the chair, she shifted forward, clasped her hands together, and rubbed them as though applying a salve. She stared at Ajeau, her visage eventually turning sour. Something agitated the woman. "If I may ask, what will you do once you find Vaten? What do you want?"

Ajeau stared at her hands and shrugged. "I don't know," she said. "I suppose we will wander as we did before."

"You want to wander?" Syais said it as though she bit into a rotten piece of fruit. "How small. You want nothing else?"

"I don't know." Ajeau thought for a moment, still looking at her hands. Then she saw her arm and remembered. "Maybe I'd destroy those people with the red circles and save the kids they torture."

Syais shook her head. "Pay them no mind," she said. She stood and pointed at drawings that hung on the walls of the room. "Look at these people. Men and women who created the world, the systems and order we need to survive. Some fought off chaos, others saw the future, and yet others *created* it. This one here. She journeyed out of the desert to escape a massacre and laid the first bricks of this great city. Do you think they were driven by the inconsequential?"

"I don't..." Ajeau shook her head. "No, but I am not some great—"

"You are. And you must think like one." Syais lingered by the painting, then moved beside Ajeau. "This is the help I am offering. Greatness. Hijeuse, what you want—Vaten, the eradication of the Zevacese—they will be yours. But after that...Think, what do you desire?"

It took Ajeau some time to answer. And when she did, her voice came out as faint as a rustle of leaves. "To belong somewhere, to be part of something. A family. A people."

"Yes," Syais threw her hands up in a display of genuine excitement. "A people. *Your* people. Now that is a desire worthy of a Hijeuse. But you must ask yourself, what are they worth?

"Worth?"

"Yes. Vaten. The Zevacese. Your place among your people. What would you risk to make them real?"

"Real? They can be—"

"Oh yes. If you will do what you must, they, and everything else, will be yours. So will you? Will you risk it all?"

Ajeau's eyes glimmered. Her smile wrinkled the corner of her eyes. "Yes, I will risk it all."

***

PASSIL LISTENED FROM OUTSIDE the door and smiled. It was exactly as Syais had told him. The Hijeuse would learn, she would see her potential, and then they would remake the world. Yes, their plans were coming to fruition. Praise Eau!

He left his post beside the room, descended the stairs, and walked towards the exit of the building. In the middle of the empty hall, he heard a voice. "She will replace you."

"Who said that?" He turned but found no one near him.

"Yes, you are the fool. The deceived. How can you not see it?"

"No, no." Passil shook his head. "Shut up! You know nothing of her. Nothing has been decided yet."

"If she is there, you are no longer needed. If she isn't, you have failed. You are finished either way."

"I said shut up!"

"Oh, poor Passil. He ignores the blade sinking into his back."

"It's not true!" Passil shut his eyes and grabbed his head. "There is no blade!"

"We will see, won't we?" The voice laughed.

# CHAPTER 29

SOUNDS FROM INSIDE HER hut jolted Zejela awake. She slid out of bed, giving a quick glance at the man who rested there unclothed. She had not intended to spend the night with him, but she did not regret it. He had been kind and inviting in some irresistible way. So she did not resist.

But there was no time to linger on him, not while danger lurked inside her own hut. She dressed, stepped out into the hallway, and crept toward the disturbance.

Zejela had no weapons. No one who followed the Sentries' code in the Outer Ridge did. It was aggression in a place of tranquility. At least, that is what they told everyone. More likely, it was to prevent training accidents or brawls from turning deadly. Regardless, she followed the rules.

But she did not know whether whatever made the noises followed them, too. They had no qualms about entering huts unannounced. And if they skirted one rule, they'd likely ignore others. She planned for violence.

She walked to the end of the hallway and tapped on the wall loudly enough to be heard, but softly enough to feign a misstep. After a moment in silence, she huffed so the intruder could hear it was her. Then she made the sounds of footsteps retreating down the hallway, quieter and quieter until they were gone.

Instead of moving down the hallway, as her steps would have suggested, she swung behind the curtain that hid access to her well. It was a cramped space with stairs leading downwards, though she did not descend. She remained right behind the curtain, waiting and hoping they took the bait.

Zejela could not see the intruder pass her with the curtain blocking her view, but she heard their footsteps. As they moved past her, she took a step to follow, then stopped. It sounded as if the intruder had whispered her name. It was faint and too hard to hear clearly, but the person had made a noise. She froze. Zejela had assumed only a single intruder, but what if there was more than one?

She held her breath and listened. For a moment, there was silence. Then she heard the same delicate footsteps as before. When they stopped, all noise ceased. Zejela finally exhaled; there was only one intruder. It was time to spring the trap.

Zejela burst from behind the curtain and rushed down the hall towards her intruder. She did not disguise her approach and went only for speed. Within five steps, she was upon the trespasser. She grabbed their arms and swept their legs out from under them. As the intruder fell to the ground, they made a small squeal, then grunted as Zejela landed a knee on their back.

They were pinned; if they had a weapon, there was no way for them to use it now.

Then, for the first time, Zejela stopped and looked at the back of the intruder. In that moment, she realized the mistake she had made. She removed her knee and turned the woman over.

"Harlae?" She spoke the name in between heavy breaths. "What are you doing?"

Harlae coughed and winced. "I came to find you."

Zejela helped pick her up, but the woman doubled over in pain as soon as she was upright. "It was reckless to come here without warning and in the darkness of night."

"I know, but—" Harlae winced again.

"Come, sit down and rest," Zejela said and put her arm around her advisor. "I am sorry about the attack, but you are lucky I was unarmed. You would be in much worse shape if I had a weapon." She chuckled softly and walked Harlae to the vestibule, then placed her on a bench.

After Harlae sat a moment and gained her composure, she said, "I am sorry too, for my intrusion, but it is truly urgent. It could not wait."

"Well, then speak. What is so urgent?"

"Are you alone here?"

"The young Bassian, Vaten, is here." She gestured down the hall. "Asleep in my room. Though even if he awoke and heard us, I do not think he knows our language. No one else will hear what you say. Now tell me, what is the matter?"

"The boxes are empty." The words rushed out of Harlae's mouth.

"What?" Zejela shook her head. "That can't be true. Who would—"

"It's true. I have checked them myself. The seed, the flowers, the leaves, everything, gone. They are empty like there was never anything in them at all. And—"

"And what?" Zejela interrupted Harlae with a flash of anger. Not at her advisor, but at the notion that all her hard work, her years of planning, her long trip to Bas, it was all for nothing.

"Something else is happening. Something—"

"What could be more important than this thievery?" Zejela's anger ruined her patience.

"The Sentries are being evicted from the Outer Ridge. There are only a few left here, and they are being forced out as we speak."

"What?" Zejela looked as though Harlae told her the rain fell upwards. Theft of rare items could happen. But the Sentries' eviction from the Outer Ridge was unfathomable. Their home was as respected as anything in Zevaco.

One rare event, as upsetting as it was, was a coincidence. Two such events, occurring simultaneously, was a plot. Zejela recognized it as soon as the disbelief evaporated. Harlae was right. Something was happening.

"Yes. Aloc informed me as I was coming here. He is concerned, he thinks..." Harlae's eyes darted from side to side as if scanning for a threat.

"What does the man think?" Zejela said. "Time is a consideration here; the sun rises soon."

"A coup," Harlae whispered as though the words were forbidden.

"Hmm." Zejela pursed her lips together and stared at her advisor. She would not have believed such an act could happen. But Aloc was insightful and hardly an alarmist. Like a dog finding plants below the ground, he had sniffed out a revolution before it came into view.

"Did he say who?" she asked.

Harlae shook her head. "We had little time to speak. He was attempting to warn his people."

"Yes," she said as her mind already began to wonder. Whoever orchestrated the coup had sought to weaken Zevaco by weakening the Sentries. It would ensure their reach for power was unimpeded. They took the seeds, flowers, and roots brought from Bas to help keep that power forever.

And though it was a cunning plan, it also gave them away. The usurpers knew about the boxes, knew what was in them, and knew why they were important. Only a few people could have designed such a scheme.

An idea formed in her mind instantly. There were no doubts about whether it was the right strategy, only whether it would work. But in this new era, she figured anything was possible.

It was then Vaten walked into the room.

After Zejela made brief introductions to ensure no suspicions were raised, she turned back to speak with Harlae. Their conversation had not concluded.

And though she trusted her advisor, she could not let Harlae know her plans. Her advisor was her own woman, as beholden to her as the birds that flew overhead. No, she would have to dismiss Harlae in an appropriate fashion.

She spoke to her advisor while Vaten looked on. "Aloc may be right, but we know nothing for certain. I am more concerned with the boxes. We must find and return the items taken. That is our priority now."

"Do you have a plan?" Harlae asked.

"Yes. I want you to ride to Soccia, to the Elders, and tell them I have found those who stole from us. Tell them I will administer our justice and I invite them here to see for themselves."

"But who—You know who stole the items?"

"Do as I say. Tell the Elders what I told you. Make sure they come. And hurry." Zejela pushed Harlae towards the door.

Harlae nodded and left.

Zejela did not stop for a moment. She walked towards Vaten and gave him a hug and a light kiss. She was in a rush, but first things first. She had to take care of Vaten.

***

WHEN VATEN OPENED HIS eyes—at least that's what he thought he did—he saw nothing. Not darkness, not light, nothing. But he knew what he was not looking at, and that was dirt. He was thankful for that.

He stood up and spun around. He walked forwards, backwards, jumped, and even punched the air or whatever was in front of him. Nothing happened.

He screamed. Still, nothing happened.

Then, he asked, "Is this death?"

He half expected to hear Levitien next to him saying, "Yup, kid. We're dead." But there was only silence.

He closed his eyes and took a deep breath. When he opened them, he was back on Foreman Crevir's Estate.

He was small, a child still, and worked in the fields with the rest of the children. The rain still fell occasionally then, and crops still grew. There were still yields to be harvested. And that is what Vaten did.

While he worked, he noticed a nut on the ground near his feet and bent down to pick it up. He should have put it back in the basket, that was his job, but as he lifted the small kernel, he locked eyes with a girl who had only recently arrived on the estate. Another stray, like him.

He wondered if he knew her name. If he did, he couldn't remember it, though he would come to know it well in time.

Bent over and staring at her, he saw the girl make a gesture to him; the tips of her fingers came together and her hand bounced in front of her mouth. "Eat it," she seemed to say.

He knew he should not. You were not supposed to eat the crops. That was theft and it broke perhaps the most important rule of working the estate. Even so, she beckoned him. And her smile was persuasive.

Vaten grinned as though he had heard a delightful secret and glanced around him. Seeing no one, he nodded and threw the nut into his mouth. His smile grew and he mimed delight.

"Hey! I saw that young one. I saw you eat your stock!"

His smile vanished in a blink. He knew immediately from who the voice came. The guard who oversaw them. And he was angry.

Vaten stood up, his shoulders raised, trying desperately to hide his head. He had seen the punishments before, adults abused until tears, or worse, silence. There was no hope for him.

"You will pay for that." The guard slapped his cane against his hand, making a clapping noise in rhythm with the words he spoke. "You know the rules. You pick the crops, you don't eat them. If you do, well, you're about to find out what happens."

Vaten imagined the same sound being made as the cane fell against his back.

Tears welled in his eyes. And as he turned to look away from the approaching guard, he glimpsed the girl whose appeal had gotten him into this mess. He saw her bend down, pick up something small, and hurl it at the guard.

It hit the man's left shoulder, and he flinched as though a fly bit him. He stopped his approach and scanned the fields with mild annoyance and confusion. By the time he looked in her direction, the girl had gone back to work.

The guard pursed his lips, shook his head slowly, and then continued walking towards Vaten. Another projectile flew and hit him. Vaten did not see who threw this one, but he knew. It had the same trajectory as the previous projectile.

This time, the guard erupted. "Stop it! If I find out who is throwing those rocks, you'll never throw anything again. You hear me?"

The shouting brought some attention. A few other guards wandered over and workers stopped their work and looked on. Among them was Vaten's Keeper, Tille, who spent her days supervising the children in the fields.

She was initially unfazed by the yelling until she saw the guard marching toward one of her children. She did not know what happened, what infraction one of her children had committed, but she also did not care. Vaten and the others were her responsibility. And if they broke a rule, it would reflect poorly on her.

But she was not selfish. Her concern was not only about herself. The kids were a blessing and brought her the happiness Eau had taken when she discovered she could not bear her own. Yes, she handled them, but she wanted to. Because that meant their joy was hers, too.

So Tille ran to intercept the guard. And she arrived next to him before he reached Vaten.

Vaten pretended to work as he listened to the conversation on the wind. His fate was far more important than that day's quota.

"Tille," the guard said while shaking his head. "I saw him eat it. He—"

"What? One nut? You'll ruin him over a single nut."

"He must learn. No one steals."

"He's a child. Barely taller than your legs." Tille put her hand on her chest. "I will discipline him, let me—"

The guard shook his head. "You know that cannot be. I cannot let it go. He must be punished."

"Why not? I will ensure you an extra ration for a week."

271

"My rations are fair. And you know why." He pointed at Tille. And then to himself. "What will happen to me if he sees me let the boy go?"

"That is it?" Tille scoffed. "You are too scared of the Foreman? How about wine? I'll have the vintners give you an extra pitcher."

"Do not insult me and bribe me in the same breath. It gets you nowhere." The guard pushed Tille out of the way. "Now, I have had enough talk. The boy comes with me."

The guard walked forward again. But before he could move past Tille, she stepped in front of him once more.

"Wait. What about—" Tille grabbed at something in a small pouch she wore around her waist. She held out her hand for the guard to see a silver stone shining like the moon.

There was a long silence as the guard looked at it and then back at Tille as though he did not know whether she was serious.

"Take it and forget you saw anything," she said.

The guard looked around, then said, "Fine. But if it comes back to me, I am telling him you took responsibility for it. You are the thief."

The guard snatched the stone from Tille's hand and put it in his bag. Then he stared at Vaten for a moment. There was something in that look, but Vaten could not be sure of what it was. A warning? Confusion? Disdain?

Finally, the guard turned and walked back to his post.

Tille had saved him again. She was some fabled protector, though at this moment, she looked more like she was going to thrash Vaten than save him. But Vaten knew, behind it all, she was someone he could rely on. She always had been and always would be.

As for that girl that got him in trouble in the first place, Vaten glimpsed her smiling at him while Tille chastised him. He didn't know what to make of it. Was she happy he was in trouble or happy he escaped the guard's punishment? Regardless, she was new and exciting. He liked it.

Then, he was his older self again, back in the nothingness. He coughed and tasted something awful. Dirt. His eyes closed and he fell asleep.

\*\*\*

TIME TO GET TO work, Zejela told herself as soldiers poured the last grains of dirt on top of Vaten and Levitien. She acknowledged their work, then walked towards the other Elders.

When she arrived there, she was quick to exchange words of congratulations with them. Though she had led the pursuit of the thieves, it was a win for all of them. And she was happy to share the accolades. Nothing made people's guard drop lower than compliments, earned or not.

And as the compliments flew and defenses dropped, Zejela peered at each one of the four other Elders as though she could determine the traitors on sight alone. Though she knew it was at least one of them—Diros, Wehlat, Ryiera, or Uluard—which one was a more difficult problem to deduce.

It had not been more than a month since they had worked together to solve the crises in the Lower Brush. And then they had sat through the Hearing together. She smiled through grit teeth as she admonished herself for sitting so close to one who sought to ruin their nation.

But there was nothing irregular about their meeting at her cottage or the Hearing. Even the disagreements were handled with respect. But the planning must have been ongoing during it. Zejela coughed and turned from the group to hide her frustration.

The conversation ended soon after and the Elders dispersed to their dwellings prior to the celebrations occurring that evening. "I will see you there," she said and waved her hand. But when it came time to move her feet, she found herself staring instead, as Diros, Wehlat, and Ryiera departed together.

She closed her eyes and rubbed her head. On any other day, it would have been as normal as the sun's appearance. Today, though, everything was a clue. She opened her eyes and watched intently as they disappeared behind a row of huts.

Was it a meeting of conspirators or a simple discussion among friends? But Diros seemed least likely to be involved. He was the eldest of them and, in many ways, their leader. If he initiated the coup, it would have been against many of the rules and regulations he instituted and oversaw. It would have been to overthrow himself.

And Wehlat and Ryiera were hardly better choices. They were more likely to bicker about the proper decorum during a coup than actually initiate one. And it was no surprise they would follow Diros; they would want to hear the man's opinion on the situation. It was the only way they could parrot it back later.

Zejela spun and caught Uluard meandering down the path, scribbling notes in a small book. Perhaps then, she thought, it was the man walking alone who is most suspicious. His writing was likely the machinations of his rebellion. Yes, he was a fine suspect, one she could loathe.

But even her aversion to the man was unconvincing on its own. She knew he would never displace his beloved Sentries nor seek old world herbs. She remembered keenly his strong objections to the trip to Bas.

Most convincing, though, was that the coup required supporters. The man had few allies and fewer friends. He would not have been able to muster a force to build a hut, never mind removing the sentries.

Everything she knew about the elders led her nowhere. Not one of them seemed a likely usurper. But she knew that before. She kicked the dirt, realizing she was back where she started. But she took solace from the knowledge that her plan had only begun. She knew nothing, but that would change.

She walked to her hut and waited out the remaining hours of daylight. The festivities would be there soon and she would be present for all of them. Not to celebrate, but to find who sought to hold her nation as a trophy. Time was running out.

# CHAPTER 30

FOREMAN CREVIR LOOMED OVER Savique, a dagger clenched in his hand. He brought it above his shoulder, ready to strike downwards. Savique tried to look at the man who was going to return him to the earth, but the sunlight burned his eyes.

Before Crevir made his final move, a commotion arose nearby. Savique heard it too. A cacophony of yells, hooves, whistles, and horns moved swiftly towards them. His heart leapt with images of the Noye charging through the city. They had begun their raid at the most fortunate of times. But who cared? They would come and rescue him. He was saved.

"Sir. He is coming this way now," a man standing behind Savique said. Savique thought the voice familiar, but could not place it. "We shouldn't do this here, not in front of him."

Crevir sighed, frowned, and then nodded at the man who spoke. He dropped his hand and put his dagger in its sheath. He glared at Savique and said, "A momentary reprieve. Your end will come soon enough." Then to the man beside him, "Keep him here while I deal with this. And this time, he does not escape."

Before walking forward to meet the approaching riders, Crevir straightened his back and neck and tilted his chin upwards. Though he would show them all due respect, he would not grovel in front of them. Workers groveled. He would honor them as an equal.

As Crevir walked away from him, Savique glanced at the man behind him whose voice he had recognized. He could not help but smile. Despite the toll time took on the man's features, Savique knew immediately who he was. Vrai.

***

275

EYVO-ILLE HEARD THE SAME noises Savique had, though she remained on her stool under the tent, planning. There was still more than a day before the raid, and she had not yet completed her preparations. Even if she had, the uproar some ways away would not have concerned her. Especially when she knew who caused it.

Earlier that day, as she sat under the tent, a man approached her. As soon as she could see his face, she knew him. She had not expected him to be there, though she understood why he was. And though she wanted to, she could not embrace him as one of her own. It was best if no one knew they had met before.

"You are the one to see Foreman Crevir?" Vrai said through thin disapproving eyes, as though she were some insignificant peasant. "Stand and await his presence."

Eyvo-Ille said nothing, only waited for the Foreman to appear. When he did, she was unimpressed. She had heard tales of his wickedness, but in person, he appeared small both in statue—his head didn't even reach her chest—and presence. She scoffed quietly.

"You are the one who found the thief?" Crevir glanced at Vrai, looking for confirmation. He received none but continued, regardless. "Thank you for his return."

"Yes. I returned him and—" Before she could finish her statement, Crevir had turned his back and began walking away. "Wait! Where is my payment?"

Crevir turned only his head. "No payment. You may leave now."

Eyvo-Ille threw up her arms in outrage. She did not truly care about any recompense, but she did not want the guards to know that. They still had to believe she was genuine and wanted her payment or else they would cast her out.

"No, wait!" She rushed after Crevir. "I demand a reward!"

He stopped and stared at her. A dark smile slithered onto his face. "You...You demand of me?" His eyes narrowed, full of loathing. "What are you?"

The fake outrage was gone, replaced by a flash of fear. "What? I-I am a simple shoemaker. But I..." She chose her next words carefully. "I would like fair compensation for the return of the thief. It is only right."

"A shoemaker? No. I do not need shoes." Crevir stuck a foot out to the side and displayed his sandals from underneath his cloak. "Look closely."

Eyvo-Ille leaned in and gazed at his sandals. Nothing remarkable about them. But she realized too late, it wasn't about the sandals.

Two hands on her back pushed her forward. She stumbled into Crevir, who grabbed her hair with one hand and pulled her head up. By the time she knew what was happening, cold metal was resting against her neck.

"I said look, flea." Crevir spit in her face. "Do you think I need sandals?"

Eyvo-Ille closed her eyes and resisted the urge to retaliate. She figured she could dislodge his blade with one of her arms before it cut too deeply. But if she did so, it would get her exiled from Nouv'eau, if not thrown in prison. Their raid and Savique's life would be lost.

She continued to play docile as a shoemaker would. "N-No," she said meekly.

"Sir," Crevir said. "I am your Foreman, and you will address me as such."

"Yes. Sir."

Crevir smiled. "Good, now, do you have demands of me?"

"No, sir. No demands."

"That is what I thought. Remember, I say what is fair. I make the demands. You make shoes." Crevir laughed and threw her to the ground. "If I see you again, I will squash you like the bug you are."

Eyvo-Ille nodded. "Yes, sir."

Crevir delicately sheathed his dagger and walked from the tent with Vrai next to him. Neither man looked back at her nor said another word.

A few moments after Crevir left, with Eyvo-Ille still on the ground, a guard approached her and said, "You heard the Foreman, get out of here."

She could not leave. She was too close to fail now. Her heart raced. "But I have no place to go and I will not make it back to the village before nightfall."

"I don't care. We aren't an inn. Find somewhere else to sleep."

"Please," she begged. "I have nowhere else. Let me sleep here tonight. Please!"

The guard thought about it for a moment, then shrugged his shoulders. "Fine. Sleep here tonight and in the morning get out. But we're not giving you any more food or drink. We're off to see the Lord, anyway."

Eyvo-Ille watched the guards leave. Then, from that same direction, several moments later, came a commotion.

***

Foreman Crevir would have preferred to meet Lord Balay in a more formal setting, rather than on the streets of Nouv'eau beside a prisoner. It was unbecoming of a man of his importance. And it also meant the Lord would be on horseback, while he dirtied himself like a commoner.

Even on flat ground Balay towered above him, but while the Lord was riding a horse, Crevir had to crane his neck almost entirely upwards to look at his superior. The Lord made Crevir look like a mouse trying to glimpse the crown of a tree.

It irritated him incessantly. He shuffled his feet and brought his hands behind his back, then back out in front of his stomach. His nostrils flared from his heavy breathing. He even smudged one of his white gloves on his belt, a most embarrassing mistake.

"Ah, Crevir. What are you doing here?" Balay spoke the words dully, as though the conversation already bore him.

"My Lord." Crevir bent his neck in reverence. "I am here to deal with an estate matter. I assure you it does not concern you. It is a matter—"

Balay eyed him. "Does not concern me? All are my concerns."

"Yes. Yes, of course. I meant nothing by it, of course, only that I had the matter handled." Crevir spoke as though he was trying to get all the words out at once.

"And that matter would be?"

Crevir swallowed. With his neck still craned, he had to stretch his head to the side in an unnatural move to get the saliva down.

"This man is a thief." Crevir gestured to Savique. Then to Vrai, he said, "Show him the brands."

"I see," Balay said. "He is one who has been caught before."

"Yes, he is a—we are ensuring he does not steal again," Crevir said.

"Right. Good." Balay nodded once at Crevir. "It is a shame that many good hands turn to theft during this disaster. A disaster that has broken your land too, yes?"

"Yes, my Lord."

"Well, do what you must to keep your workers in line." Balay trotted forward, then stopped. "And Crevir. You have men to take care of these nuisances. Use them. Do not dirty your hands with such work." He grinned. "Though it seems you already have."

Crevir winced at the insult but said, "You are correct, as always, my Lord."

Before he departed, another horse arrived beside Balay. Something about its rider was familiar to Savique. Their gait on the horse and that golden hair on white armor. He had seen those images before. But he could not place them.

The rider whispered something in the Lord's ear and he nodded in return. The woman dismounted her horse, walked to Savique, and dragged him to his feet.

He could almost see under her hood, but it still covered most of her nose and eyes. He was not sure, but he thought he saw her smiling. And for a moment, he had no idea why.

As if reading his thoughts, she screamed in a voice no louder than a whisper, "You may not remember me, but I remember you. And I will pay back everything you did to me one-thousand-fold. You will end up like your Noye friend, punctured by a thousand cuts."

Savique's eyes danced, his breathing sped. Who was this woman?

Balay pointed at Crevir. "My Warden wants control of the prisoner. Bring him to her quarters, alive, by nightfall."

"But my Lord, he is my—"

"I will not repeat myself, Crevir." Balay said. "If the prisoner is not brought to her quarters, she will have her fun with you instead."

Crevir nodded his head quickly, "Yes, my Lord."

The Lord turned his head from Crevir, patted his horse and said, "Let's go."

The woman mounted her horse and followed. As Savique watched her, he finally remembered who she was. Panic spiraled through his body.

***

NEARLY THERE, EYVO-ILLE THOUGHT to herself. The sun had begun its descent behind the massive wall, sending shadows to swallow the city. And though darkness was creeping forward, night had not yet fallen. If it had, Eyvo-Ille would not have been sitting on the ground.

In her nearly three days of waiting, Eyvo-Ille had devised a plan she was sure would work. She had studied the guards around the gate, knew their movements, when they chatted, when officers arrived, and, most importantly, she knew when everyone tired. That was the moment she would lift a weapon, slay the guards, and open the gate.

But that was only the beginning. She still had to signal the Noye waiting outside the city. For that idea, she had a merchant to thank. When the woman deposited a cache of oil next to the gate to keep their torches lit throughout the night, her plan was set. Once the gate was open, she needed only to light the oil with the torches, then wait for her reinforcements and the battle to begin.

The sun dipped lower. Twilight had come to the city of Nouv'eau. But that was not nightfall, Eyvo-Ille told herself. Be patient, follow the plan. But it was what to do after the plan that stirred her mind.

As the faint smell of burned meat wafted over her, she stood and stretched. There was much to do once the Noye rode as conquerors through the city; rescue Savique, end an abhorrent ritual, kill the Lord, and salt the city. It would be difficult to accomplish one on its own, but to achieve all of them would be near impossible. She grinned at the thought. It would make the glory all the greater.

Yes, she would be the Noye who brought the wicked V'eauvians to their knees in their own city. And then, with the mark and Savique, she would deliver her people to Z'eau. There she could rest happily, in the land of her elders. She only wished her sister was by her side.

Twilight gave way to nightfall. The third night had come at last. The moons hung low in the sky, a slice of its light shining over the top of the wall. It brought darkness to most of the city, leaving only the obsidian outline of buildings. Eyvo-Ille, however, remained in a sliver of light, as though she were a white flower in a dark thicket.

She did not look up to glimpse the bright moons and motionless stars; she did not believe in Istori nonsense. Instead, she rose slowly from her seat and smiled. Her soul was quiet. But her mouth whispered a prayer she and Navo-Ille once learned together:

*You are the horse. The speed. You are the ox. The strength. You are the bear. The resilient. You are the wolf. The pack. You are the Noye.*

# CHAPTER 31

SYAIS PASSED THROUGH CRUMBLING pillars and entered the grounds of the old Arboricole workshop. The buildings there were dilapidated. A granary that once would have provided for the Arboricole was empty and its barrels broken. The small temple had collapsed on itself, preventing anyone from entering. A verandah for sitting no longer provided any shade, its roof long ago destroyed. All that remained of the stables were stakes in the ground.

Debris was everywhere. Remnants of old clay pots and cups lay in pieces on the ground. Slivers of broken wood jutted from the dirt as though they were grass. Syais nearly impaled her foot on a bronze nail from some object that no longer existed.

The winds that swept through Nouv'eau had deposited sand and dust in piles along the walls of various buildings. They were once adorned in red and white, but now appeared only a hazy beige. On windows and doors, where fine curtains once hung, only tatters remained, if anything at all.

Syais didn't know what had caused such destruction, only that it was clear the place had been neglected for some time. Perhaps it had never been rebuilt after the Night of the Silent Hoof, so long ago. Either way, Passil had not lied when he said nothing was there, no remnants of the Arboricole's work to be found. They had worked hard to ensure that no one would find their secrets.

But Syais always discovered secrets. And now she would have theirs.

Guards began zealously digging under an old tree in the corner of the workshop's courtyard. Syais did not know exactly where to dig, but she had plenty of people at her disposal and plenty of time. When one hole was dug deep enough, the guards would climb out and dig another. Again and again, this pattern repeated until the holes ran together and piles of dirt and clay littered the courtyard.

Syais paced the grounds, wondering whether the Arboricole she interrogated had lied to her. She had wanted to believe the documents existed and believed the man implicitly. Had he recognized his only way out and fed her falsehoods?

The very thought of it enraged her. She had been too naïve, the Arboricole only sought to obstruct her. Idiot! And in a fit of rage directed only at herself, she struck the tree with her hand.

It made a dull sound. No, it hadn't come from her hand. Odd. Syais heard the sound again, the thump of metal on wood.

"Something hard down here, Vizier," a guard yelled.

"Is it the chest?" Syais asked.

There was a moment's pause. It seemed to last an entire night.

"Yes!" It was a cry of delight. "Yes, it is a chest. Small, suitable for documents. We will have to open—"

"Bring it here!" Syais was not about to have the documents she so coveted exposed to every guard on the dig. No, these were for discerning eyes only. They were her secrets now. "Do not open it there or I will open your head."

The courtyard became silent under the moonlight. Even the wind seemed to have ceased in reverence to Syais's words. Then, in a flurry of activity, shovels pounded the dirt and footsteps echoed as guards ran up the stairs out of the hole. A trio of guards stood before her, though only one was needed to hold the chest, waiting for their reward.

Syais stepped forward and snatched the chest out of their hands. "Well done. Excellent work. Talk to the Warden and he will sort you out."

The trio of guards smiled, nodded, then wandered away, leaving Syais staring at the chest, eyes as big and bright as the moons.

It took some effort to break the lock, but when she did, a wondrous sight stared back at Syais. Charts, papers, scrolls, and documents of all sorts. The works of the first Arboricole. The location of the leaves and who knew what else. They were hers. And so was the Hijeuse. All was together as she had intended.

But when she removed a scroll and unfurled it, she shook her head. She turned it around and then looked at others in the chest. She put the papers down and gazed out into the night as if it would hold some answers. They were like nothing she had seen before. The words on the page were indecipherable. They were foreign. Some kind of meaningless scribbles.

No, she told herself, the Arboricole would not seal and hide meaninglessness. Think. There had to be a reason, an explanation.

Syais stared at more pages, scrutinizing each one for something she could recognize. The guards and Passil stared at her, unnerved by her obvious dismay.

Then, finally, she saw it and nearly laughed with delight. On one page was a word she knew. She had seen it before. A word that told her everything. *Balafre.*

Yes, of course, she should have assumed it earlier. They were written in the script of the High Elders. And that meant they were real. It was a triumph of the highest order. Yet, there was still one problem: she needed someone who could read the language.

No one came to mind.

***

AJEAU WALKED THE STREETS of Nouv'eau, free of the foul confines of her cell. And though guards supervised her every step—for her protection—the chance to walk and breathe fresh air again was a blessing, and she cherished it as such. Sitting in the shade of the palms, she appreciated the towers and statues lining the paths she strolled, and stared at the craftspeople making the finest pots and pitchers she had ever seen.

Though none of it was new to her, she had seen much of the sights with Puy, the beauty of the place took on a new importance; she was among her own. Whether or not they knew it, her place was with them. And she smiled, imagining her and Vaten's reunion in the shadows of the great wall, among her great people.

But every night, as the sounds of chaos broke through the veil of order and restraint, the guards would usher her back to a hut not far from the Beacon where they could watch and protect her. It was a reminder that not only was she not yet free, but her place in the world was not yet assured. Syais was about to change that.

One evening, as Ajeau walked through the doorway of her hut, followed by a cadre of guards, she saw Syais waiting for her.

"Eau has smiled upon us," Syais said without waiting for Ajeau to greet her. She waved the guards back out of the building. "We have made a grand discovery and must hasten our preparations."

"What? What preparations?" Ajeau asked.

"The ones we make for the world ahead." Syais moved closer to Ajeau as a greedy smile graced her lips. "Your world."

"I still don't understand. What do your preparations have to do with me?"

"They have everything to do with you. The sun itself rises because you ask it."

Ajeau stared back blankly.

Syais exhaled and her smile vanished. She bit her lip and shook her head, as if frustrated by Ajeau's response. She sighed then said, "You must know, all I have told you—the path I have offered—it was no lie.

"Yes, but—"

"No." Syais held up a single finger. "Let me finish. It is imperative you hear me now."

Ajeau nodded.

"Good," Syais said. "The path you must walk is one that countless before you have started. But you will be the first to finish it. You have what is necessary to cross the boundary. The blood of the High Elders runs through you. You are our Hijeuse."

Ajeau opened her mouth as if to speak, but said nothing. There was nothing to say to such nonsense. The High Elders—the Balafre—were characters in tales. They were not real.

Syais continued, "I understand this must come as a shock, but we have—will have—confirmation. The Arboricole envisioned such a day long ago. And now it is here."

Finally, Ajeau found her voice. "You believe in such superstitions?"

"Oh, they are far from superstitions." Syais snatched Ajeau's arm and turned it towards her. "Do you see this?" Syais displayed Ajeau's scar.

Ajeau nodded.

"These are how we search for those with true blood. There is no superstition there."

"My scar?" Ajeau stared at it, puzzled by how it had withheld that secret from her all these years.

"Yes, your scar. The High Elders are real," Syais said. "And you are of them. That is why the world is yours."

Ajeau did not know what to believe. The scar was real, so was the ritual that gave it to her. She had seen that. And Syais had not lied to her before. Then perhaps it was possible. And in that moment, she dreamed of her world.

"So you see now." Syais leaned back and smiled as if she saw the fantasies of Ajeau's mind. "Good. If you have questions, ask them. We will waste not a moment once the script has been deciphered."

"I—I don't know where to start," Ajeau said. "I was cut, drained of my blood because I was a High Elder?" Ajeau shook her head. "It doesn't make sense. I was a stray. I was traded."

"Someone identified you as a candidate in your youth. I do not know why. It was before I—" She shrugged. "You may have been lost once, but now," Syais licked her lips with anticipation, "I have found you at last."

"Does this mean I will be able to rescue Vaten?"

Syais nodded. "Yes. And so much more. You wanted a place—how about leading the V'eauvian people? Don't you see? They would be at your command, and with them, no obstacle would be too great. Your friend, your family, whatever you want."

"No," Ajeau said. It was too unbelievable.

"Yes." Syais grabbed her by the shoulders. "This is who you are."

Ajeau could not help but stare into Syais's eyes. And when she did, she lost all reservations. The woman spoke the truth. She was sure of it, and it meant she could have everything she wanted. Vaten, her family, a place. It was hers.

"What do I need to do?" Ajeau asked as she shook with anticipation.

"I will return soon with our plans. Until then, ready yourself. There is not long now."

Ajeau smiled. "I can do that."

Syais nodded and exited the hut.

As Syais stepped into the darkness, she smiled too. Ajeau was not the only one seeing their dream become a reality.

***

AFTER THEIR MEETING, AJEAU took to roaming Nouv'eau once more. It was there she spied a familiar face. One of the few in the city she knew. Aube.

Yes, there was no question; it was her. Ajeau would never forget her face, no matter how much it changed. The woman who betrayed her, stole her arrow, and got her imprisoned occupied a permanent spot in her mind. Ajeau was out of her cell now, but Aube had no role in it. She would have let Ajeau be executed to spare herself.

Her thoughts raced. Perhaps the woman was meant to be quartered but had escaped. Or worse, perhaps the guards had failed to act on Syais's orders. They were idiots; she glanced at the two distracted guards tasked with following her.

Yes, that was it. Aube was not supposed to be here. Someone had botched Syais's orders, and the Vizier was unaware of it. Only Ajeau knew. And only she could fix it.

A plan formed in her mind as though it were always there.

She sprinted at Aube. Though Ajeau was not quick, she ran fast enough that when the guards following her turned and saw her, she was already a few hundred paces away from them.

Aube had little chance to react. She heard footsteps approaching her quickly and turned in time to notice someone racing at her at full speed. It was only in the last moment before Ajeau tackled her that Aube saw the face of her attacker.

Ajeau knocked Aube to the ground but quickly lost any leverage on the woman. Aube was bigger than Ajeau and had little trouble wrestling the smaller, weaker woman off her. Had Ajeau planned for it, the fight may have been fairer and lasted longer. As it was now, the fight was over nearly as soon as it started.

"Shit!" Ajeau struggled under Aube's grips.

Aube wrestled her way on top of Ajeau and sat on her, holding her arms down. Ajeau bucked like an unbroken horse trying to dislodge the larger woman. But no matter how she moved, Aube would not budge. Soon after, much sooner than Ajeau would have liked, she gave up and screamed.

"Ajeau stop. Stop!" Aube said. There was no anger in her words. "Listen to me."

"You! You tried to have me killed—"

"Stop! Listen! Before the guards get here. Listen to me." Aube was shaking Ajeau as much as holding her. "I'm sorry. I had to do it. Syais breaks people until they do her bidding. You cannot trust her. She will break you—"

"Liar! I could not trust you! You betrayed—"

"All right. Break it off, you two." The guard grabbed Aube and pulled her from Ajeau, then turned to her and said, "And don't go running off again."

Whatever truth Aube tried to convey to Ajeau was lost to the breeze. Ajeau raged at Aube for lying to her, at herself for failing to maim and capture the woman who betrayed her, and at the guards for being too stupid to help her destroy an enemy. When she had her world, they would all be disposed of.

"Heed my words, Ajeau. Do not trust in her deceit or you will be as broken as I," Aube yelled as she walked away.

Ajeau heeded nothing.

# CHAPTER 32

"To a fine hunt!" a voice from behind Zejela shouted. "And our leader in justice!"

Zejela recognized the voice immediately as belonging to Uluard. And it surprised her. Not the words of the toast, they were awkward, but so was Uluard. No, what surprised her was that he had come to the celebration at all. He was not one to indulge in festivities of any sort.

But like the rest of the Elders, he was there, and she could ask them all about recovering the seeds, flowers, and leaves they had taken from Bas. Whoever didn't pledge themselves to that aim was at least a suspect, if not the leader of the coup.

She was not naïve. She expected resistance and dismissal from those she could not force into a response, and ignorance from those she could. A conspirator wouldn't give themselves up easily. But if you weren't a conspirator, you would want the stolen items retrieved and truth and honor—the very things Zevaco stood for—restored.

Zejela turned to recognize the toast with a humble nod of her head. "We were all victorious today. We all rooted out the evil in our midst and we all benefited from it. Thank you to everyone for your hard work. But our work is not done..." She let her voice trail off suggestively.

After a moment's pause, Zejela said, "And thank you, Uluard, for your stirring toast." She let a small smile break across her lips, a subtle jab at her fellow Elder, appropriate for the situation.

A light laugh broke out under the evening sky where elders, soldiers, advisors, and even some Outer Ridge workers drank, sang, told wild stories, and danced.

As Zejela moved through the crowd, a group of young soldiers approached her. Though she recognized their blue sashes and common clothes, it was their endless chattering that truly gave their rank away. But as soon as they arrived beside her, they froze.

They shared some nervous glances, then one pushed another forward. "Elder Zejela," the man pushed in front of her said, then stopped to catch his breath. "C-Con-Congratulations on your successes."

Zejela did not belittle his compliment nor ridicule his nervousness. She smiled at him as if he was a longtime friend and bowed, lowering herself to his level. Then she reached out her hand and gently clasped his arm. "Thank you."

To all who heard it, it sounded heartfelt, but to Zejela it was a means to an end; a path to what they knew. Though weapons still hung at their side, she disarmed them all the same.

"Yes." Another one stepped forward, now brimming with confidence. "It was brilliant of you to determine the Bassians' guilt. Few others see beyond their noses. You see beyond the sky! And to think there were rumors you were sympathizing with the outsiders."

"Shut up," one soldier whispered. Then to Zejela she said, "He didn't—"

Zejela laughed. An infectious chuckle, both alluring and dismissive, as though what was said was so preposterous it had to have been a joke. One they could all enjoy together. As friends.

And they laughed until one intrepid soldier stepped forward. "Yes, Elder. We would follow you to the ends of the world or our return to it."

She smiled and gave the man a nod. "You are brave and loyal and for that I thank you, but I hope I will not lead you to your end. That is no way for an Elder to treat the future."

They nodded enthusiastically at her. She knew it now. She had them. They would tell her anything they knew, maybe even help her if they were not involved. "Well, who—" Zejela began before a hand on her shoulder interrupted her. The soldiers' faces dropped as Zejela spun around to face an irritated Diros.

"A popular person tonight, are we?" He waved the young soldiers away, and they receded into the party. "No surprise, it was your great—what did Uluard call it—a hunt? Yes, a hunt. A great hunt. True, true. But it is curious, is it not? A man you just laid with, a thief. Now dead. How interesting!"

Zejela's eyes narrowed, and her mind raced. How had he known who she slept with? Was it Vaten or Harlae or, worse, someone unknown? She shook the questions from her mind. She still had a goal to achieve. Besides, she needed no pretense with Diros. "I laid with him before I knew his deeds. That is all."

"Yes, and what of these deeds? Where are the stolen items? The ones you—yes, you—convinced us necessitated a trip to Bas. You leave, return with two men who you put to death as thieves and we still have nothing." He shrugged his shoulders suggestively.

"The trip was supported unanimously, including by you," Zejela said. "Do not pretend as if you were against it. And as for the two Bassians, that too was a unanimous decision. Thieves die, that is our way."

Diros leaned close, his voice barely audible. "Where are the seeds, Zejela? Where are the leaves? Few know better than you their importance."

She met his eyes and matched his tone and said, "Exactly what I would like to know."

The two elders stared at each other as though the other spoke an incomprehensible language.

Zejela leaned away from him and straightened her back. She spoke forcefully, without care for who heard her. "And I pledge to find them, no matter what. Bring everyone—man, woman, child, Sentry, farmer, builder, potter, teacher—I don't care who they are. Have them all search this land until we have secured the stolen items."

Diros shook his head, his voice still a whisper. "You want them back—You did not—Where are the..." Zejela could tell something she said troubled the man.

"What is it?" Zejela asked.

Diros said nothing, only looked at the ground and scratched his beard. His head shook one final time and then he walked slowly from Zejela.

"Diros. Wait!" Zejela said quietly, hiding the urgency in her heart. "What do you know?"

He stopped and turned to look at her as though her question was some great insult. "What do I know? What do *you* know?" His shoulders fell. "I am too old for these games, Zejela. Did you move the Sentries to the bay?"

"Of course not. They should be here."

"Yes, they should. But they are not. Uluard told me you ordered their movement, but I've not heard of their arrival. They should have made it by now." He stared her in the eye. "Where are they? Why did you remove them?"

Zejela's jaw clenched and her nose twitched. She forced her hands together and rubbed them as though she was trying to extract juice from a piece of fruit. Her eyes blinked too often. Rage coursed through her veins.

She should have known. *Uluard.*

\*\*\*

A SINGLE GUARD STOOD over the plot of land under which Vaten and Levitien lay. She peered at black piles of dirt, the flaxen grass beyond it, and at the building behind her. She spun around to ensure no one had seen her approach. When she was certain she was alone, she pulled down her pants and pissed on the earth. "*Va cazz!*" she said and spit beside her. Then she composed herself, secured her pants, and slunk away. She never once saw the reeds sticking out of the ground.

Somewhere under it all, Vaten thought he opened his eyes.

When he did, he was again a child but this time older, his limbs gangly and his face peppered with the sprouts of a beard. He sat on the ground in the middle of the camp with a smile on his face and a jug of beer in his hand. He passed it to the person next to him.

"There's barely any left," Ajeau said. "You didn't have to drink it all."

"What? There's plenty left for you. Besides, I deserve it. It was a good day today."

"Oh yeah, and why is that? They promote you to captain of the harvesters?" Ajeau laughed.

Vaten did not laugh. "Funny, but no. We did, however, make our quota. It's not even the end of the harvest and we'll have—"

Ajeau put a hand in front of Vaten's face. "Don't start with it."

"With what?"

"You've done this the last few harvests. 'There'll be plenty of food for everyone. The Foreman will raise our rations. We will eat until our bellies are full.'" Ajeau emulated Vaten's voice. "It's never true."

"This year, it will be. Just wait." Vaten pointed to the sky and shook his finger. "We'll have enough to put in the storehouses, and then we'll see our own shares improve."

"You don't get it, it doesn't—"

"Vaten!" A call came from a few tables down. "You're up next in ussel, but it's against Cournon. Good luck!"

Vaten stood and called back, "I'm not scared of him. Today, fortune is with me."

Whether it was or it wasn't, Cournon defeated Vaten easily. But it did not sour his mood, and he returned to Ajeau's side with a smile fixed on his face.

"That was quick," Ajeau said.

"Cournon got lucky and blocked me early. There was nothing to do." Vaten shrugged his shoulders. "I couldn't—"

"I have some good news for you," Tille said as she sat down next to the pair.

Vaten smirked at Ajeau. "See? A good day!" Then to Tille, he said, "Is it about the yields?"

"No, not that. Will you ever give it a rest?" Tille laughed. Ajeau laughed too. "I spoke with Vrai today. He thinks he may find you a spot soon."

"What?" Ajeau turned to Vaten. "You're joining the guard?"

"Hopefully soon," Tille said.

Vaten tried to hide his face in his shirt. He knew Ajeau would oppose it, which is why he had told Tille in secret. But she had moved quicker than he expected. If only he could have told Ajeau first, perhaps things would have gone better than they did.

"Tell me it's not true. You can't be that dumb." Ajeau glared at Vaten as if he was a disobedient child.

"I'm—It...It is true," Vaten said, looking at the ground. "I thought it would help me learn—"

"Help you? How? So you could bully some workers or ensure your rations?" Ajeau's eyes narrowed. "Are you that weak?"

"That's not fair, Ajeau..." Tille said.

The two argued, but Vaten heard none of it. Like a butcher, Ajeau always knew exactly where to cut. And the words she spoke sliced Vaten deeper than perhaps any before. He stared at the ground, envious of the ants.

Tille and Ajeau's discussion ended, but Ajeau would not be convinced nor calmed. Instead, she stood up to leave. As she did, she glanced once more at Vaten, who did not turn his head to meet her gaze. She kicked at the dirt and then left.

Vaten felt Tille's hand on his back. "You know she will get over it. It just takes her time. She's a little more stubborn than us."

Though he continued to stare at the ground, he knew Tille would always support him, and it brought a smile to his face. He nodded.

"Here." Tille handed him a pitcher of wine. "Have something a little stronger. It'll help take some of the sting off tonight. Plus, it's good news. You'll be a guard soon."

Vaten took the pitcher and drank a swig. He didn't like wine, especially not the dizzy feeling it gave him, but it dulled the burn of Ajeau's insult. It did not, however, return any of his enthusiasm for the games and stories and events of the night. So he returned to his hut to rest.

Vaten held the pitcher of wine in one hand and a lamp in the other. More than once on his walk back, he nearly drank the oil from the lamp. But each time, he caught himself and chuckled. And once the pitcher was empty, he tossed it and listened to it shatter.

"Hey," a voice yelled, "you trying to hit me?"

Vaten didn't recognize the voice, but he could see the metal of the man's sickle reflecting the light of the lamp.

"I ask you a question. Answer me!" The words were both rushed and slurred with heavy breaths between them. "That you with the light?"

Vaten's eyes grew wide, and he placed the lamp down next to him. He would not wait to find out whether the drunk was a friend. Vaten turned and ran to his hut, never looking back.

From the nothingness under the ground, Vaten called out, "The lamp, you idiot! Move it. You left it in the wrong spot. Move it. Please." But he knew his younger self would not.

***

Zejela strode away from the celebrations. She had remained there briefly in search of a man who drew her ire like few had ever done before, but Uluard was nowhere to be seen.

That conniving little liar. But at least she knew now. It was he who had started this coup. And he had pointed his finger at her to prevent suspicion from falling on himself. It could have gotten her killed had Diros not been so brash.

It was all she thought about as she continued her march to his hut.

The dark night gave her some cover as she approached. Despite her anger, she had taken care to not draw attention to herself, but she did not know if the man had lookouts or spies—maybe even traps—outside his hut. She would not underestimate him again.

She crept to a side wall and listened. There was silence. In the window above her, she saw no flames flickering. Perhaps Uluard was asleep. It would have been an early night for him. Or maybe he was not in the hut at all. Laying with one of his new acolytes, Zejela thought and shuddered.

But if he was not there, it was a perfect opportunity to search his hut for evidence. The seeds, leaves, and roots from Bas may even be hidden somewhere within.

It took her a few tries to jump and grab the open window. Once she did, she pulled herself up and twisted her way through the opening. She thought herself quite spry even as she landed on the floor of the hut with a loud thud.

She stood completely motionless, even held her breath, as she listened for any other sounds. It was still silent. Perfect, she thought. No one had heard her. Still, it was no time to be complacent. Someone could still lurk within.

Zejela did her best to move quickly and quietly through the hut as she searched for evidence of Uluard's coup and theft. She looked in the various rooms, under pieces of furniture, and in holes in the clay bricks. She shook jugs to see if anything rattled inside. Though she didn't know what she was looking for, she assumed she would know it when she saw it. But she found nothing suspicious.

She sighed and wondered if she should continue. She realized Uluard had been too smart to leave any evidence of his plot lying around his hut. Before she turned to go, she noticed a cluster of rooms down a hallway yet to be explored. And though she expected nothing to come from them, she could not leave them be.

As she crept down the corridor, she heard a noise emanating from one of the rooms. She froze and listened. It was a faint scratching, clawing noise. And there was a rhythm to it. The scratching sound would repeat for a few moments, then stop, then more scratching.

She turned as if to leave. She should ignore whatever was in the room and strategize a new plan. But like a plant growing towards the sunlight, Zejela could only move towards the room. She had to know what was in it.

She approached the door, ensuring each footfall and breath made no sound. When she leaned against the door, the noise stopped. Whatever made the sounds had heard her or sensed her somehow.

Then, from inside the room came the sound of small feet pattering away from her, and she breathed a sigh of relief. Zejela knew immediately what had made the noise. A rat. With a smile on her lips, she chuckled to herself and apologized for disturbing the small animal's snack.

But when she opened the door and peered into the room, her smile vanished. In its place was a look of shock and horror. The animal had been gnawing on a corpse. The man, freshly dead, lay on the ground, blood still pouring from his wounds. Small red prints led away from the body through a hole in the wall.

Even though he was badly butchered, Zejela did not need long to determine who it was. She had seen him toast her earlier that night and she was in his hut now. It was Uluard.

But that was all she knew. The questions swirled in her mind, but there was no time to think about them; she had to leave quickly. She could not be caught with a murdered Elder, that was for sure.

She retraced her steps from the room, exited out a side window, and scurried off into the dark, not unlike the rat—though she left no footprints behind—and did not stop running until she made it to her hut.

As the sun's first rays broached the horizon, Zejela stood in her entranceway and breathed deeply. The shock still had not subsided, but the agitation and arousal finally waned and she realized how tired she was. She needed rest. But there wasn't enough time. She had to know more. Her eyelids closed. And the last thing she saw before falling asleep was the mutilated Uluard whisper to her, "Only two days left."

# Chapter 33

A LIGHT SPARKED IN the dark night. A woman, waiting patiently for such a signal, saw it and turned towards the hundreds of her brethren standing behind her. She roared at them. It was time.

The ground shook as if a giant was trying to split open the world with a hammer. Though the night was dark enough to obscure the vision of the horde, the sound reverberated across the land. It was a rolling thunder that never ceased.

Hooves rose and fell as one. They sent dust flying upwards, backwards into the legs and chest of the horses behind them. But it did not bother horse nor rider. Their heads floated above the debris and they rode through the clouds like cranes through the sky.

They were upon Nouv'eau before the guards could organize.

It was not only the speed of their approach; it was the guile of it. The front horses of the horde rode through the city without riders, stunning and disorienting anyone on watch. And as the V'eauvians' attention was drawn to the first pack of horses, a second group followed. On these horses there were two riders. And they were not there to stun and disorient. They were there to kill.

Spears pierced flesh as shields shattered bones. Horses trampled those too slow to move. Chaos engulfed Nouv'eau. Yet, two people in the city waited for such chaos. It was their horses who bolted through the city. It was their weapons that drew blood. It was their kin who came.

\*\*\*

EYVO-ILLE EXHALED LONG AND slow. It was time for her to act. And though her plan was simple, it would not be easy. It required patience, careful attention, and a willingness to improvise. She would need to be at her best.

Her first task—finding a weapon—was straightforward enough, though. She did not have to walk far or look for long before she found a sizeable rock, one that she could barely hold in one hand, and thought it would work.

She picked up the rock, made a few practice smashes with it against the air to ensure she could wield it properly, then returned to the shadows to observe activity at the gate. Once there, she could ready the next step in her plan: kill the guards.

From her position, she saw four guards, in groups of two, patrolling either side of the gate. One group stood next to the roping mechanism of the gate's lock and the other next to a ladder leading up to a small platform that opened to the other side of the wall. Three other guards stood atop that platform, though they focused their attention outside the city.

To light the torches outside the wall, she had to eliminate all of them. If one saw her, they would no doubt alert the rest. And though she was a formidable warrior, she was still only one against many. A swarm of bees could bring down a hog.

Eyvo-Ille crept in the shadows until she was close enough to the first set of guards to get their attention by tapping her rock against the wall. She hoped the noise would bring both the guards, even all four, if she was lucky. But after a brief discussion between the two guards, only one moved towards her. She quickly laid down and hid the rock under her hand.

Not even the guard's tentative steps could prevent him from tripping over Eyvo-Ille's torso. As he stumbled, a leg fell on Eyvo-Ille's chest. She did not move or speak. The only sound was a loud grunt from the falling guard.

"What happened over there?" the guard's partner hollered, but stood in his position.

"Nothing. I think it's another dead one."

"Here?" the guard groaned in disgust. "We'll leave it for the morning duty. It'll give those new recruits something to do."

The guard who had tripped shoved Eyvo-Ille twice. She moved back and forth in response like a doll. But the third time he reached to push her, Eyvo-Ille grabbed his arm and, before the man could make a sound, she smashed the rock up into his face, breaking his jaw and nose.

Blood splattered everywhere. Eyvo-Ille did not relent and smashed the rock against the side of his head twice in quick succession, sending him to the ground, motionless.

Eyvo-Ille glanced at the dead guard's partner and saw him remain at his post. The attack had been so swift not even the dull thud of rock on bone drew extra attention. But the man would get suspicious eventually, so she had to move fast.

She wiped the blood off her hands and then pulled a small javelin from the dead guard. It was his only weapon, but it was sharp. She only needed a momentary distraction.

Eyvo-Ille's rock sailed through the air, past the two guards on the far side of the gate, and crashed into the wall. It made a loud clang as it contacted the wall and then a thump as it fell to the ground. The guards, all three of them, stared confused at the rock that had seemingly appeared out of nowhere.

Their brief loss of focus was all Eyvo-Ille needed.

She bolted towards the near guard, who had her back turned to Eyvo-Ille. Before the guard realized anyone else was there, Eyvo-Ille slashed the woman's neck with the javelin and eased her down to the ground.

Like her partner, the woman barely made a sound. But now, Eyvo-Ille was exposed under the gate. If the two guards opposite her had turned at that moment, they would have seen Eyvo-Ille standing over a dead guard, soaked in blood. They would've yelled and ruined the plan, or worse.

But they did not turn.

Eyvo-Ille grabbed a spear from the guard whose throat she slit and dashed to the other set of guards. When she arrived, she rammed the spear through the neck of one guard. He lurched forward, legs buckled, head thrown to the sky, and fell. Eyvo-Ille dropped the spear.

The last guard, who stood next to the now impaled man, did not react. She had heard nothing strange coming beside her. But when she saw her partner's body fling forward with a spear in his neck, she turned slowly, with eyes bulging from her sockets, and stared at Eyvo-Ille.

She tried to yell, but no sound came out. She drew her hand to her neck and felt a warm moistness. Blood. Eyvo-Ille had slit her throat.

The guard blinked, then collapsed to the dirt, questions written in her eyes.

The night around Eyvo-Ille was quiet, though she could hear small drips, like a light rain falling on a lake. Blood covered her face and clothes, while it rolled down her arms and fell from her blade, dripping steadily onto the ground.

She inhaled deeply, then exhaled and crept towards the ladder leading to the platform above. She knew there were three guards there, but could no longer see them. They could have been preparing for her arrival at that very moment.

But there was only the single ladder. One way up and the same way down. If they knew she was coming, she wouldn't stand a chance. But if she climbed the ladder before anyone saw her, she could block the guards' exit. It would mean that no one could get help. It also meant fighting three guards at once in a small area, while trying to block access to their escape.

She placed a foot on the first step of the ladder. If she was to be a hero, if the glory was to be hers, she would have to earn it.

In the end, it required little tact or cleverness. The guards were clumsy and inexperienced, and Eyvo-Ille dispatched them with ease.

When the last guard dropped, Eyvo-Ille climbed down the ladder and began sawing at the ropes that locked the gate's doors. It was arduous work, but the ropes finally snapped and the gates opened. A moment later, she lit the oil. When she did, it took no time at all before the earth shook.

Now she had to find Savique.

\*\*\*

SAVIQUE SAT TIED TO a chair in the woman in white's room. She stood with her back towards him, staring at a table of tools. It was the same profile he had glimpsed when she had her bowstring around Eyvo-Ille's neck so long ago. But now it was he who needed saving.

Her head turned slowly toward Savique, her eyes narrowing as she did. She appeared confused but about what, Savique did not know. Then he felt it. The floor underneath his chair vibrated.

Though he did not intend it, his reaction betrayed an understanding. His jaws unclenched, his breathing slowed, his entire demeanor lightened. There was even a hint of a smile on his lips. And the woman in white saw it all and knew.

But before she could speak, before she could move, there was a knock on the door.

"What?" she yelled.

"Sorry for the interruption, Warden," a man's voice said. "The city has come under assault and the Lord requests your presence."

She opened the door enough to poke her head through and said, "Where is he?"

Savique could not see the guard's actions, but the woman in white straightened her back and smoothed her clothing. Then she said, "My Lord. An assault?" and closed the door behind her. Her footsteps clicked faintly until they were gone.

It was true, the Noye raid had begun. Savique relaxed for the first time since Eyvo-Ille first put him in ropes and walked him to the wall. It had been more than three days of horror and dread and depression, but he would be saved, finally. If Eyvo-Ille could find him.

And then he had a horrible realization. Eyvo-Ille would not know where he was. He was not in the Cave, where Eyvo-Ille saw him taken. He was in some nondescript room in a building currently occupied by the Lord. It would be the most well-defended place in the city.

The only way to ensure his rescue was to free himself from the woman in white's room. If he could make it to the street, his chances of survival were far greater. He could hunt for Eyvo-Ille or other Noye in the chaos. Otherwise, the chair he sat in would be his last.

Savique searched the room for something that might assist him. And though he once feared what they were to be used for, the woman in white's tools now were his best chance to cut himself free. He only had to get to them.

First, he tried to hop the chair forward. When that didn't work and nearly caused him to fall, he tried to drag the chair with him. That too, failed. He finally found some success by leaning his body, and thus the chair, to one side almost enough to tip over then dragging the opposite side forward. Then repeating the motion with the other side.

It was excruciatingly slow, but it worked and each small step brought him closer to the table the tools rested upon and freedom.

***

OUTSIDE THE ROOM WHERE Savique remained imprisoned, the woman in white and the Lord discussed their plans for the raid.

"Yes, it appears the Noye lay siege to our great city," the Lord said. "We must prepare to escape this place until the battle has completed."

"You wish to escape?" The woman in white seethed. "Our guard will drive them from the city, perhaps the world."

"Eyes, do you see?" The Lord stared at her. "This is not one Noye, nor even a tribe. This is a legion. Someone has united the Noye. Such a force may destroy this place for good."

"I do not care. I—"

"You should," the Lord said, as though they would be the final words on the matter. But they were not.

"If you do not wish your guard to fight, then let me. I will join the V'eauvians in battle and lay waste to our enemies."

The Lord sighed. "Such bravery, or perhaps it is arrogance, I don't know. I admire your commitment, but I cannot allow it. You are too valuable to me."

"Then trust me, sir." She would not beg, but she came close. "I will return to you washed in the blood of a thousand Noye. You will—"

"No." The Lord shook his head once. There would be no more discussion. "Let the recruits fight and die. We will find safer ground and return when we are able."

The woman in white fell silent, but she raged under the surface. To defer to those monsters, it was weakness, subservience to a people who deserved extinction. And she could be the one to deliver it. With a well-timed charge or a well-placed trap, she would destroy them as she nearly had done in the woods years ago. Perhaps this time she would even recover the mark.

But the Lord had made his intentions clear and there was nothing she could do about it. Not yet, at least.

"Retrieve your weapons, gather the Guard, and meet me beside the stables," the Lord said to her, then turned and walked down the hall.

She nodded to his receding figure, then hurried back towards her chambers where she could take out her rage on the man trapped there. That would calm her lust for blood. But when she entered, she saw no one, only her tools and pieces of broken wood strewn about. She slammed her fist on the table and screamed curses into the night.

\*\*\*

SAVIQUE, AFTER WRENCHING HIMSELF free of the chair—most of it, a piece of wood remained tied to him—exited out the woman in white's window and fell hard on the ground. He dragged himself quickly to his feet and limped off to find a hiding place in the neighboring garden.

He rested for a moment and tried to decide which direction to head. Nothing looked familiar. But then he glimpsed an old man wearing a white robe with two red dots scurrying down the path. A guard followed, clearly exasperated by the situation. The man in the white robe turned every few steps and waved at the guard to hurry.

The two seemed to be undisturbed by the clashes happening around them. Savique supposed they strode with a purpose, but otherwise they could have been two friends on a nighttime walk.

As they passed him, Savique heard the old man say. "Come along, come along. I am so glad a man like you has shown interest in our samples. I have made a wonderful discovery! Yes, the child is gone, but if I am right there will..." The old man's voice faded into the chaos of the night.

The guard never once looked at the man and made no sign he heard or even listened to the old man. Savique then saw the third person in the group. He knew the stride immediately and grinned. Tonight he would see justice delivered and vengeance had.

Savique followed the group from a distance as they walked towards a workshop. When they arrived, the men stopped and discussed something for a moment, then entered. Savique wasted no time and rushed toward the building as fast as his battered legs could take him. He pressed himself against the workshop wall and listened.

"A pureblood, you are sure?" the third man said.

"Certainty is difficult. The leaves are not precise, but they work." The old man pointed to a jar of foliage. "I am more confident than I ever have been. The Hij—"

The third man grabbed the old man's arm. "You cut her, yourself? No one has tampered with the blood? I am not a man you wish to deceive."

"Easy, sir," the guard said. "The Arboricole is fragile."

"Yes, I did it," the old man said. "Quite a while ago, I remember little about the sacrament, but the vial is one of mine. And no one tampers with such things. I can assure you of that."

The third man dropped the old man's arm. "Yes. Good. Then I will avail myself of it."

Savique leaned away from the wall and scratched his chin. The conversation had made little sense at first, but the more the men spoke of blood and cutting and sacraments, the more Savique understood. It was the ritual Eyvo-Ille had spoken of in Nevant and on their ride.

"With this," the third man said. "I will gain enough favor to exceed Thouars and Escor, the idiots. Maybe I'll even be next in line for Vizier." A sharp laugh followed.

The ritual—an evil thing, Savique supposed—was not what brought him to that workshop. And the laugh reminded him; he was there for the third man. The man who had taken him from his son, branded him a thief, killed his friends, and tried to kill him. Savique resolved to make him rue his failure.

He swung around the outside of the workshop until he found a door. It was open, and it exposed him, but he moved through it quickly enough not to be seen. His first step on the dirt floor, however, echoed through the silent room. The men turned and glared at him.

As soon as eyes fell upon him, Savique rushed at the guard, knocking him down and preventing him from drawing any weapons. He battered the guard mercilessly, landing blows to the man's nose and throat, and then gouging his eyes. They were not moves borne of hate but out of survival. If the guard lived, Savique would not.

"What—What are you doing? This is a place of learning and scholarship! Stop this madness at once!" the old man exclaimed.

But Savique did not stop. He picked up the guard's head and slammed it against the dirt floor. And again. And once more, to be sure. The guard went limp in his hands. But before he could drop the guard's head, Savique found a dagger against his neck. He did not need to see the white gloves of the Foreman to know who held it.

"Savique." An ominous smile crept over Crevir's face. "How convenient. I owed you your death."

\*\*\*

MADNESS ENGULFED NOUV'EAU. FLAMES lit the black sky with bursts of orange and red. Screams, cries, and shouts were heard throughout the city. The clashing of weapons echoed, reverberating far from their origin. Hooves beat the ground and those who had fallen on it all the same.

Eyvo-Ille witnessed it all as she rode her horse furiously through the city, looking for Savique, dispatching every V'eauvian she met on the way.

She ran through buildings protected by guards and those empty of people altogether. She freed the prisoners from the Cave—they seemed so surprised by their freedom it took them several moments before they ran off into the night—but he was not among them. She called the man's name at every turn. Again and again, she did not find him.

She would not quit on him, though. She continued down the darkest corridors in Nouv'eau, those not lit up by fires and—though Eyvo-Ille did not know this—those used by informed men and women to escape the city.

In one of those corridors, Eyvo-Ille saw a group of V'eauvians sitting atop their horses. Even from a distance, she recognized the group. She had seen them ride before and knew their silhouettes. She knew their horses better. And the moment she spied the Lord's Guard, she committed herself to violence, to assassinating their leader.

Fate must have been on her side to present such an opportunity, she told herself as she raised up on her horse, cocked her arm, and aimed her javelin. It was a clean shot to the man, no horse or guard in her way.

She did not delay. Once aimed, she hurled the javelin at the Lord. It was a motion she had perfected over time, through repeated practice since she was a child. And like those times, she threw her weapon true. It would hit its target; it only had to reach it.

One of the Lord's Guard, sitting atop her horse alongside her leader, heard the subtle sound of a weapon darting towards them, drew her sword, and knocked it off course. It landed harmlessly to the side as shouts erupted from the group.

Eyvo-Ille cursed the woman. But with her glory so near, she drew blades and rushed forward with abandon.

There was momentary turmoil as the group organized itself around the Lord and in opposition to their onrushing foe. But Eyvo-Ille crashed into them before their defenses could be set and before they could protect themselves from her.

She calculated with brutal efficiency the best route, the easiest targets, the most devastating blows. And though she lacked a spear and the reach it provided, she moved nimbly atop her horse, bringing her into range of an enemy for a strike and back out of range before they could return one of their own.

Guards dropped to the ground as she moved past them and tried to gain access to the Lord. But each time she disposed of one, another seemed to appear. Then another. She was fast, but they had the numbers. Try as she did, she did not make any progress.

And soon, the Lord's Guard organized around her and displayed their might. They repelled her attacks; she rushed at them furiously and they simply dodged the charge. It was a stunning sight; the Lord's Guard moved together as a group like they were performing a well-choreographed dance to exhaust their enemy.

Eyvo-Ille did not tire easily, but her attacks became more frantic and desperate the more time she took. She knew once she lost the element of surprise and fear, she likely lost the battle. And now that the Lord's Guard was organized, she would never have her glory.

Though the reality of the situation set in, she gave no thought to retreat. She launched charges as best she could. She swung her blades at anyone nearby but only cut the air. She remained proud atop of her horse until the guards closed in around her and knocked her to the ground. Even then she stood swinging, peering up at the guards as they encircled her.

Then, a voice called out, "Stop! She's mine!"

It took Eyvo-Ille a moment to locate the voice. But even before she saw the woman dressed in white, golden hair hanging out from the bottom of her hood, she recognized the voice. It was the same one that screamed into her ear as life retreated from her.

She approached Eyvo-Ille. "How fortunate we should meet again. It has been a long time, has it not, Noye?"

Eyvo-Ille responded by slashing at the woman. But her arms were too badly injured from the fall for the strikes to be anything but minor annoyances. The woman in white avoided them easily and knocked the dagger from Eyvo-Ille's hand.

"I have not forgotten what you possess," she said. "Do you still have it?"

Eyvo-Ille spit on the ground. "Yes, and I have stored it safely away from here and you. No matter your efforts, your people will never again possess it. It is—"

"Noye. You know how this ends. You have no friends with you this time." The woman in white drew her hand to her back and felt the scar Savique had given her. "And I have mine. But if you give me what I want, I will make your return painless."

Eyvo-Ille laughed. "I would rather suffer the most painful of deaths than ever help you, trespasser. We have the mark and one day we will rule over our lands again."

"Liar! No stone will help you or your kind." The woman in white breathed deeply. "I am out of patience. You ask for a painful death. Then so be it." She nodded her head, but not at Eyvo-Ille, at something beyond her.

Guards Eyvo-Ille did not know were behind her advanced on her. She turned quickly to fend off their attack, but it was useless. Her screams joined the chorus of others across the city. They were one of many. As she was.

***

FAR FROM THE BATTLES, a fire sparked outside of a building. Though it was lit by a Noye, she was unaware anyone was inside. She only did what she came to Nouv'eau to do, destroy the city.

At first, Savique did not see the fire outside of the workshop. It was too small to be more than a modest source of orange light. But soon it was unmistakable; soon it was an inferno.

Foreman Crevir kept his dagger pressed against Savique's throat as he moved him towards the wall of the workshop, all the while taunting him. "Do you even remember your son, Savique? Do you know what he looks like? I do! Do you know where he is? At home in my guard." A vicious laugh poured from his mouth. "Imagine the look on his face when he sees me again!" It was the last thing he said before the roof of the workshop caught ablaze and fell to the floor beside him.

Crevir jumped back, taking the dagger away from Savique's neck with him. Savique did not waste the opportunity. He grabbed Crevir's arm with one hand

and struck the man's wrist with his other. Crevir's hand opened reflexively, and the dagger dropped to the floor.

Savique struck the Foreman again, in the face, and again, in the stomach, and again, in the face, as the man tumbled backwards trying to gain his balance. But it was no use. Crevir, upon receiving a final blow from Savique, fell to the ground.

Savique picked up the Foreman's dagger and stood before the beaten man. He looked up at Savique with fear in his eyes, as though he knew his fate.

"As you stole my life, I will steal yours," Savique said.

"No, please. Wait! I can—"

Savique raised the dagger above his head, then stopped. He sighed, then stepped back as a burning beam fell from the ceiling. It pinned a screaming Crevir to the ground.

"Help!" Crevir shouted. "Help! It's burning! It's burning me! Get it off me!" He struggled to move the beam as the fire spread. "Help! Please...Help!"

Savique watched and listened as the flames engulfed the man, his words fading into screams, his screams fading into nothing. Soon, all Savique heard were the pops and crackles of the fire.

He walked towards the door. But before he exited, he turned and stared at the room. He saw vials filled with liquid, leaves and plants in jars, and some papers scrawled in strange scripts. None of it seemed important, yet they had ignited the Noye's hatred and Crevir's desires. Yes, even if he did not know at what he looked, he knew they were important.

He stepped back into the room and scoured the place. Grab something, anything, he told himself. At worst, he could use it to barter safe passage back to his son on the estate.

The fire spread quickly, and the smoke became nearly too thick to see through. In the haze, Savique grabbed the first vial he saw. He couldn't even read the label on it before he tucked it into his bag.

He ran from the workshop and towards the gate. Eyvo-Ille or not, he had to escape the city before he became trapped there. He sprinted as fast as his legs could take him until he heard a noise from the shadows.

"Savique?" The voice was familiar.

"Vrai, is that you?"

"Yes." Vrai ran to him. "We must leave this place now. I will explain everything once we are safely free of the city."

Savique nodded in agreement. "Are you coming with? Where is Eyvo?"

"Not now, we—"

"Crevir is dead! The Foreman—"

"Good," Vrai said flatly. "Now follow me." He took off running in the opposite direction of Nouv'eau's gate.

# CHAPTER 34

AJEAU SAT ON A stump under a leafless tree in a grand courtyard. All was brown and yellow there, but the towering structure that rose from the ground seemed impervious to the muted colors. It remained as white as ivory, as imposing as its master.

Syais and the guards who watched over Ajeau spoke briefly. Then Syais gestured to Ajeau and said, "Walk with me."

The two moved slowly through the yard towards the gleaming building. Ajeau had expected the air to be charged with Syais' rage but, like the winds, all was calm. When she glanced at Syais, she saw a deep thoughtfulness rather than fury.

"Your actions today were foolish," Syais said frankly, as if she was teaching a student. "They only drew more attention to us and put us at risk. The city is unstable enough, it does not need any further provocation. Do you understand?"

"Yes, I understand. I only tried to..." Ajeau let her voice trail off. In hindsight, she didn't know what she attempted to accomplish by assailing Aube.

"I will chide you no more on it, but do not act so impulsively again. Now here." Syais opened the door to her cottage and allowed Ajeau entry. "We have more important matters to discuss."

Ajeau and Syais moved through the cottage until they arrived in a room furnished only with several chairs surrounding a single table. On that table lay hundreds of scrolls and papers.

"What is all this?" Ajeau said, pointing to the documents.

"Our discovery. We uncovered these texts from—"

"These are what say I have the blood of a High Elder? That I am the Hijeuse?"

Syais shook her head. "It is not that simple. Indeed, that is one of the things I need to speak with you about before we leave."

"What do you mean? Where are we going?"

Syais placed a hand on her shoulder. "You must trust me on this point. You are the Hijeuse. But the only way to find your friend and your family and your place and your people is through blood. That is why we embark on this trip."

"Blood? I don't—Wait, do you mean?" Though Ajeau asked the question, she knew the answer. She wished she didn't.

"Yes." Syais stared into Ajeau's eyes. "But it is only through this act that I can offer you the things you want most."

Ajeau looked at her arm. The scene of a man grabbing her, slicing her open, and stealing her blood raced through her mind. She felt the same terror now as she did back then.

"You must harden yourself against fear," Syais said. "What awaits you on the other side is worth risking pain. It is worth risking anything, you once said that. Did you mean it?"

Ajeau remained quiet, her eyes locked on her feet.

"Wounds heal. See?" Syais pulled her shirt up and turned to show Ajeau her back. "They leave scars, but no pain. It is a small price to pay for a world."

Ajeau did not know whether Syais was correct. But, in that moment, it didn't matter. She would take all the pain in the world to have Vaten back with her. "All right. Yes. I will do it."

"You are braver than your years, truly." Syais patted Ajeau on her back. "But that is not all."

"What else?" Ajeau's eyes widened.

"There are many who are against us. These vermin would like to see us fail or harmed or worse, returned."

Ajeau smiled and exhaled a small laugh out of her nose. "Of course."

"It is not a thing to laugh at," Syais said. "These are formidable people—outsiders that seek to end our way of life. You have met some of them."

"You mean? The—"

"Yes. The Zevacese. But that is not all. You may know the Noye, those traitorous bastards. I have heard those from Rigolade have even begun their machinations. The world is fracturing once again, which makes our trip all the more important, but all the more dangerous, too."

Ajeau's heart sped. If the Zevacese were still on Bas, Vaten may never have left. She might be able to rescue him without venturing to, as Syais said, some faraway place. Hope surged through her.

Syais continued, "If they come across us, we must be ready. You must be ready. I am not the warrior I once was. It..."

Ajeau nodded again, but wasn't listening. She thought of Vaten, still on Bas with the blue-bladed marauders who had captured him. And now they came after her people and her place, too. She would not let them take any of it. Not again.

*** 

PASSIL'S PRESENCE INTERRUPTED AJEAU and Syais's conversation. He had entered the room stealthily but as he walked towards the Vizier, his sandals kicking up small clouds of dust as he did, his movement caught her eye and she glanced at him with displeasure. "You return so soon," she said.

"Yes, Vizier. I have reports from one of your fennecs. Regarding the..." The Warden glanced at Ajeau, then at Syais asking with his eyes whether he should reveal his information in front of her.

Syais waved her hand. He gave her a skeptical look, furrowed his brow, took a deep breath, and continued, "Yes. Regarding the papers. One of the fennecs thinks he may know someone who can solve your problem."

"And?"

"The fennec heard that a vizier from the Oyonnax region used to tell stories from old texts. He said the Vizier would read it right off the scroll."

"Were the texts written in Balafre?" Syais asked. "Did they know the language?"

Passil shook his head. "The fennec did not know. He only knew they were ancient and foreign texts, but he did not know the language."

"Intriguing." Syais paced the room with her hands clasped behind her back. "Balafre or otherwise, few foreign texts exist. And there are fewer people who can read them." Syais stopped walking and paused a moment. Then she turned to Passil and said, "It is a worthwhile lead. Look into it."

"Yes, Vizier. But there is another problem."

"Go on."

"The man left his community many years ago," Passil said. "The fennec's source hadn't seen him in many moons, said he ran off into the Tentir and no one has seen him since."

"Hmm" Syais chewed her lips. "I see."

Syais wondered if the man was deranged or defective. Running into the Tentir was madness and nothing else. But she had also heard rumors of viziers running into the sea to escape their underlings. Perhaps the same had happened there. And the Tentir was a better choice than the sea.

"Does this Vizier have a name?"

"Seule," Passil said.

Ajeau's entire body tensed as she heard the name of the man who rescued her long ago. She shifted in her seat. "What?"

Ajeau's outburst brought inquisitive glances from Syais and Passil.

"What was the man's name again? The Vizier," Ajeau asked.

Passil glanced at Syais. Hearing no objection, he reiterated, "Seule."

Ajeau smiled and shook her head. She could hardly contain her excitement. "I know the man."

"You know an old hermetic Vizier?" Passil glared at her. "One not seen even by our most trusted spies? It is..." He paused and broke into an incredulous grin. Then he laughed. "Absurdity of the highest sort."

"It is not," Ajeau said, meeting the man's eyes. "I met him in the Tentir."

"Of course!" Passil continued to laugh as he threw his back and his hands out wide beside him in a showy display of mockery.

Syais moved beside Ajeau and stared at her as though she were a strange bird. "Explain yourself," she said.

Ajeau did so, telling Syais about being saved by the man when she was lost wandering the forest and all he did to nurse her back to health. "What do you want with him?"

"You do not believe this story," Passil said. "I could invent one more compelling and less—"

Syais stopped Passil speaking with a raise of her hand. She still stared at Ajeau. "You know where this man is?"

"But..." Ajeau said. "What do we need him to do?"

Syais placed a hand on Ajeau's shoulder. "To help us—you—in becoming who you are meant to be. He will tell us where we need to go."

"And we can save him?" Ajeau said, smiling as she imagined raising Seule up out of the wretched conditions of his life, like he had done for her.

"It is your world, is it not?"

Ajeau nodded. "I know how to find him."

"Wonderful," Syais said with no hint of joy. It was all resignation. There were too many 'ifs'—*if* Ajeau knew the man, *if* she could find him, *if* he could decipher the charts—for her liking. But, like so many times before, she would have to make certainty from uncertainty and force it on the world.

She glanced at Passil, whose scowl had returned and now he scratched at the side of his head with an unpleasant vigor. "Ready us for travel," she said. Then to Ajeau. "Lead us to Seule."

*** 

PASSIL RAN FROM SYAIS'S cottage, down the dirt paths of the city, past guards, workers, and vagrants, without stopping. He raced towards his hut, hoping his pace and the safety of his home would protect him from the onslaught. He could not listen to another minute of their abuse.

When he arrived at his dwelling, he burst through his doorway and nearly fell over a bench in the small single room where he lived. He picked up a pitcher of water and poured it onto his face. It chilled him, and for a moment, relaxed him. The voices were gone. He exhaled loudly, then sat down.

But as soon as his breathing steadied, the voices returned. Their laugher echoed through his head, louder now than earlier. "That will be the last of your water for days!" they said, cackling.

"Stop it!" Passil yelled as he grabbed his head and squeezed.

"We are the only ones who see. What a fool poor Passil is! You are as blind as the man who stares at the sun all day."

"It is not true," he yelled and waved his arm in front of him as though pushing someone out of the way. No one was there. "The Vizier respects me. Keeps me close! I am trusted. I am the Warden of Nouv'eau. You are the perverse words of a tired mind. All will be—"

"And what after the trip? Where will you find yourself then? She will no longer listen to a pathetic worm such as you." More laughter. "No! No! The worm survives its brush with a knife. It separates and becomes new. You...you topple like an unsupported log."

"I will not! I will rule alongside our glorious leader until my return enriches the soil!" Passil slammed his fist against his leg. The pain hurt and it quieted the voices. But it did not silence them.

"Passil," they whispered. "You must see the path ahead of you is broken. If you fail, the plants do not grow. If you succeed, they are destroyed. No matter the course, you remain unfed."

Passil squeezed both legs, his fingernails beginning to break the skin. "I will feed. The rains will return. The Hijeuse is here. It is as they foretold!"

"Did they foretell your fates? No!" The voices were loud once more. Gone was their laughter, a venomous sting in their place. "The Arboricole speak only for those important enough. You are too insignificant for such visions."

He opened his mouth as wide as it would stretch and screamed. His head shook until his voice gave out.

"Shh, my boy," a single voice said. It was one familiar to him. "You must run now before it is too late to help her. If you are quick and smart, she will ride again, but if not..."

Passil, his voice weak, said, "Father...No. I have heard this story before. You will not win."

"Win or lose, you have already been replaced. Leaves fall." Wild laugher erupted. "He is not so graceful! He is the stalk, offering himself to the scythe."

A wind swept through his hut, sending the curtains into a frenzy. But when it ended, it was quiet. Passil slumped forward, his hands relaxed on his legs, tears rolling down his face.

"You will not win," he whimpered.

***

AJEAU SAT ATOP A horse next to Syais and whispered something in her ear. The Vizier nodded, pointed westward, yelled, and then rode off in that direction. Passil and a few trusted guards followed.

It had been more than a month—double Ajeau's initial estimate—since they set off from Nouv'eau and she recognized nothing familiar. Markers she thought she remembered were now gone. Trees, she was sure, stood, now lay on the ground, displaying their roots like a tangle of hair.

Still, she implored the group to continue riding even as their supplies dwindled and morale sank. They were close; she was sure. The land looked familiar, she told them, knowing she had never seen it before.

But when she said it about a boulder, however, she wasn't lying. At least, she wasn't sure it was a lie. She remembered seeing such a rock when foraging with Seule. The same thoughts about how it got there ran through her mind then as they did now.

"We are close now," Ajeau said.

"You've said that before." Passil turned to Syais and continued, "We should've never believed her. We should ride—"

"No," Ajeau said. "This time it's true."

They both looked to Syais for her decision. She ignored their glances and gazed at the forest. To turn back was to admit failure and start from nothing. They were too close to do that. The forest would reveal the man eventually. What did it matter if it took weeks, months, or years? The prize at the end was worth waiting for.

"Lead us, Hijeuse," Syais said.

She did and before the dark of night came, they had found Seule's hut. For Ajeau, it was as if she found her home again. She sprung off her horse and began running towards the hut. Before she got anywhere near it, Passil grabbed her.

"You will remain here," he said.

Ajeau struggled in his grip. "Let go of me."

Syais dismounted her horse and walked towards them. "Release her, Passil. She will accompany me to the man's—"

"What if it is a trap? You cannot let her—"

"Do not question me, Warden!" The words dropped Passil's head faster than a strike would have.

"Yes, Vizier. Of course," he said as his hands fell from Ajeau's arm.

To Ajeau, she said, "You will introduce me to this man. But I will explain why we are here and what we need from him. You are not to tell him anything we have discussed. I know you may trust him, but the information you know is dangerous. Do you understand?"

Ajeau nodded. "Yes. Fine. But you will see, he is kind and gentle. He will want to help us."

"I hope you are right."

The two walked together towards the hut. When they were close enough, Ajeau called out to Seule but received no response.

"Perhaps out foraging," she said to a suspicious Syais. "He spends many hours in the forest looking for food."

But when she peeked inside his hut, Ajeau knew something was wrong. His satchel was on the ground, his walking stick rested against the wall, and his supply was empty. But he was nowhere to be seen. Yes, something was very wrong.

Ajeau walked through the hut, then exited out the back. And that was where she found Seule, on the ground, gaunt and unkempt.

"Seule!" she cried out and ran to him. She bent beside him, and when he did not stir, she shook him. But he did not move. Ajeau stood and yelled, "Syais, he is here but unwell!"

"What?" Syais ran to the back of the hut. "Is he alive?"

"Yes. Alive. He's breathing, but he doesn't move!" Ajeau panted, out of breath. "How can we help him?"

"Run to Passil. Tell him to bring me the giseo root powder and a pot of water. I will—"

"What are you going to do?"

"Try to wake him." Syais pushed her away. "Now hurry!"

Ajeau ran as fast as she could back to Passil. She relayed the message and, a few minutes later, the two arrived beside Syais, holding what she requested. She poured the powder into the pot of water and stirred it with her finger. She inhaled and her head jerked back. "Perfect," she said with a cough.

Syais brought the tea near Seule's mouth, then stopped. She glanced up at Ajeau. "Are you sure you want to see this? It will not be pleasant and there are no assurances."

"Yes, I know, but he will wake up. He is strong."

"If that is your choice." Syais poured the tea down Seule's throat.

At first, nothing happened. Then, Seule twitched. A slight tremor to start, but soon his whole body shook as though he were shivering. He flailed and swung his arms and kicked his legs wildly. The three visitors backed away to avoid being struck.

Eventually, Seule stopped flailing. But when he did, he stopped doing anything. His body was as motionless as before the tea.

Syais turned to Ajeau. "Go get him food from the guards. If he wakes—"

"I should be here," Ajeau said.

"Do not worry. Passil and I can tend to him while you get the food. You will miss nothing."

Ajeau saw Seule's chest heaving up and down with each labored breath. "All right." Then to Seule said, "Don't wake until I come back, I don't want to miss it, friend." She ran off once again.

Passil waited until he couldn't see Ajeau and said, "You think he will awaken?"

A smile crept over Syais's lips. "Look."

And by the time Passil looked back at Seule, he saw the man's eyes open.

"Who—Who are you?" Seule brought his hands to his head and shook it as though trying to clear his hair dirt.

"Ah, Seule." Syais shook her head. "Is that your name? Do you not remember me? Perhaps you will remember this." She leaned close to the man's head, stuck out her tongue and ran it along the length of his cheek.

"You!" His hoarse voice tried to scream. His eyes darted around, looking for an escape. But he was far too weak to move anything but his head.

"Yes. Me. It is good to see you again," Syais said.

"Stay—Stay away from me. You will get nothing from me this time."

"You are far too weak for *that*." She grabbed his leg and chuckled at the thought. "But that does not mean you are not useful."

Still lying on the ground, Seule turned from Syais and said, "No. Leave me be. I said you will get nothing."

"But if I leave now, you won't see the present I brought. Does the name Ajeau mean anything to you?"

Seule rolled back and stared at Syais, eyes filled with dread. "No."

"Oh yes. She rides with me. For me. But you see, we need your help."

"No, I don't believe you." There were no tears in the man's eyes, but he was crying all the same. "I will never help you. I would rather die than give you a word."

Syais laughed. "Your life is already forfeit. It was the moment you ran into this dead forest. But you can still save her. Do not give up on her."

Seule's eyes closed and his head fell, defeated. "What do you want?"

"I have heard you read the words of the Balafre."

"What of it?"

"This." Syais took the charts from her cloak and thrust them in front of Seule's face. "What do they mean?"

He turned to look at the papers. "These—These are directions, signs for how to get to Z'eau, the city of the High Elders. Where—my Eau—Where did you get these?"

"That is not your concern. Tell me all you know."

Seule described the symbols and paths on the documents. And if she followed them, she would arrive in Z'eau. At least that is what the papers said.

"With that," Passil said quietly. "We will no longer need the leaves, no longer need..." He swallowed his voice when he caught Syais' glare.

Once Seule finished speaking, Syais took back the papers and returned them to her cloak. She stood to leave, but Seule grasped her leg.

"Please let me see Ajeau," Seule begged. "I have little time here and I would like to say—"

A hand around his throat ended Seule's plea. He gasped, surprised by the force choking the life out of him. He tried to speak, but the words were too quiet to be heard. Syais thought they sounded like, "I gave you what you wanted."

She smiled as his eyes bulged and his body shook. His lips grew a dark blue, as though they had been stained with the juice of berries. He slapped at her hands until they fell limp at his side. The rest of his body soon followed.

Syais left her hands on his throat a moment longer to be sure, but the man was gone. "You gave me nothing," she whispered in his ears. "I took it. And you will never see the Hijeuse again. You will warn her of nothing."

Ajeau did not return with the food for another several minutes. Before she did, Syais dropped a small blue stone near Seule's body in a place Ajeau would not miss. She would know who did this to her friend, who her real enemies were.

"He hasn't awoken?" Ajeau said as she saw Seule still motionless, her arms full of as much food as she could carry.

"No, Hijeuse. I am sorry," Syais said.

Ajeau glanced at Syais's face and the food fell from her arms. Tears burst from her eyes. She bent over Seule and shook him. There was no response, no movement. She brought him to her breast and yelled his name and then yelled a scream of anger and sadness in equal portions.

The only person, except Vaten, who she had called a friend in this life, was dead. And it shattered something deep inside her. She was alone again. Forever.

No family, no friends, no place. If the world saw fit to make it so, she allowed it. She surrendered.

*No. Fight it. You must always fight to control your destiny.*

Her eyes caught the glare of a blue stone, similar to the one she had brought into the hut so long ago. She knew from where it came. And in an instant, rage replaced the grief, like a fire to dry twigs.

Zevaco. First Vaten, now Seule. They would reap what they have sown. No matter where those monsters went, she would not stop until they were destroyed. Her wrath would know no bounds.

Syais smiled.

# CHAPTER 35

ZEJELA AWOKE AS THE sun cracked the horizon. She was calm only a moment before the images of Uluard's murdered body flashed in her mind and her heart began to pound. She sat up. There was no time to waste. She had less than two days to find the leader of the coup and retrieve the stolen goods, otherwise all would be lost.

But she had no leads. The celebrations had yielded nothing, except Diros thought her a murderer, a traitor, and if not the originator of the scheme, then certainly involved. Things could not have gone worse, and that was before she found Uluard dead in his hut.

She would never know why he lied to Diros, though the simplest explanation was that he suspected her and guessed. It was possible someone else started the rumor and then killed him to cover their tracks. Or worse, make it appear Zejela had murdered him.

Yes, maybe she arrived too early to the scene and escaped at the last moment. She had walked into a trap and not even realized it. But who would've done such a thing? Diros?

Zejela shuddered as she wondered if his words to her were lies made up so she would hunt Uluard down and confront him. Then she would be found holding the body of a dead elder. It was far more nefarious than she first realized.

But it was a lead. Even if Diros knew she was still alive, he didn't know she had deduced his plan. She paced her hut, wondering how to get the proof she needed. Her mind flooded with ideas good and bad, but she realized the time for caution had passed.

There was only one place where she would find any evidence of misdeeds. Yes, it would be dangerous, but she could no longer afford plans that yielded no results. She would walk into the thicket and bring back a berry, no matter how many thorns scratched her skin. It was not only Zevaco that relied on her.

She exited her hut and raced down the path.

\*\*\*

THE SCENE AT DIROS'S hut was unexpected. Men and women were either consoling each other or running about the compound, shouting for help. It was a scene of chaos and sadness. Though she had barely stepped inside the gate, concern washed over Zejela.

"What happened?" she called to anyone who listened. "What's going on?"

She received only skeptical and derisive glances like she was an uninvited guest at their party. Her concern slowly turned to dread.

She pushed her way through the crowd and into Diros's hut, where another mob of panicked faces met her. She continued past them and made her way into a foyer and then down a large hall. Any eyes she met returned only contempt.

When Zejela entered the sitting room, she knew why. Her worst fears were realized. Diros was dead. And there was no doubt his circle thought her the primary suspect. It was exactly what she thought she had avoided with Uluard. Her head spun.

"Zejela!" A call from Diros's partner shook her from her shock. The man was draped over Diros, but when he saw Zejela, he sat up and reached out an arm to call her over to his side. "He's gone!" Tears poured down his cheeks. "What will we do?"

Zejela rushed to the man's side and embraced him. He spoke out of grief but, intended or not, his question was sharp, and it cut its way into Zejela's mind. *What would they do?* She had no answer.

But she knew troubled times were ahead. No, they were here already. The theft, then the exiled sentries, and now the oldest and most respected man in all of Zevaco was dead, likely murdered. Their entire world threatened to crumble like a clump of dirt.

Eventually, Zejela released her hold on Diros's partner, stood, and turned to leave. There were others here to help the man bury his partner. She had to ensure whoever murdered him was held responsible. And did not end up ruling over them all.

She gathered her resolve and made her way back through the crowd of people. As she did, she realized there were only two elders left. One was a traitor, the other might be dead, but she did not know who was who. She had to find Wehlat and Ryiera. Unless—

Zejela began sprinting to her hut. But no matter how fast she moved her legs, she felt as if she was already out of time.

She burst through the door of her hut and saw items strewn about, pots and bowls smashed. That was not the worst of it. No, the worst of it was the red that dotted her previously clean walls. A gullible person may have thought it paint, but she knew better.

She followed a trail of drips and splatter through her dwelling, only to arrive at the body of Harlae in her bedroom.

Zejela's legs trembled as she stared at the scene in front of her. Then her whole body shook. No tears came to her eyes, her mind blunted any emotion, but her body reacted. It knew. And she fell to the ground as her legs gave way.

She lay there a moment, shattered. Her effort was spent and for nothing. Each time she tried to climb out of her hole, more dirt was poured on top of her. It was an appropriate image, given what she had done to Vaten and Levitien. Perhaps she deserved this. A penance for sins now and past.

The world spiraled in front of her. Faster and faster it went. She had no energy left to resist the vortex that pulled at her and dragged her into a world destroyed. After this, was there even a Zevaco to return to?

Zejela never answered that question because footsteps, soft but present, came from behind her and startled her from her malaise. It was not Harlae this time.

She stood and turned, in time to catch a glimmer of light reflecting off metal before someone rushed at her. They had finally come.

***

WHEN VATEN THOUGHT HE opened his eyes, there was a light in the distance. His heart leapt. Light! Something was there and that must have meant he was no longer under the earth.

But then the light grew and he recognized it. A fire. The fire from that night on the estate. He tried to run from it but could not escape the memories. They pulled him in to watch it happen once more.

The young Vaten had retired to his hut earlier that night but could not sleep. Not even the helping of wine could stop him from thinking of Ajeau's insult and reconsidering his decision to join the guard. Maybe his friend was right and it was a mistake. He should go tell Tille in the morning.

But long before morning came, Vaten heard what sounded like shouts from the camp. At first, he did not move, figuring it was only a disagreement over a game or someone who had drank too much. Maybe both.

When the shouts continued and seemed to grow in urgency, Vaten left his hut. That was when he saw the fire.

Several huts along the route Vaten had taken earlier that night were aflame. Around them, people worked to help contain the fire or move people to safety. Vaten hurried in their direction and then was promptly sent to fetch sand to help douse the flames.

It was only when he arrived back at the fire with a bucket of sand that he realized where he was, whose charred hut he stood in front of. It was Tille's.

"Throw the sand and get more!" a yell came from over Vaten's shoulder.

Vaten threw the sand, then asked, "Have you seen the woman who lives here?"

"I don't know. I haven't been here long. Now go get some more sand. We can't let the fields light."

Vaten nodded and ran off, thinking of Tille and all the times he had gone to her hut. It had been a home for him whenever he needed one. And now it was nearly burnt to the ground. He ran faster.

It took five buckets from him, and more from the rest of the workers, to calm the inferno. When the last flames died, they saw the destruction it had caused in the few moments it had been alive.

The fire had claimed twelve huts, and many more had damaged roofs or scorch marks on the outside. They stood but would need repairs. Thankfully, the winds had kept the flames from spreading to the fields.

While the workers went about cleaning the debris and rubble around the camp, Vaten searched for Tille. He asked around, and no one had seen her, but it did not trouble him. She always went for walks by herself along the grove or the western fields. Not usually at night, but maybe she did this night, Vaten told himself.

As Vaten searched, he found a familiar face, though not the one he was looking for.

He walked forward and embraced Ajeau. She hugged him back; their animosity turned to ash in the fire.

"What happened here?" Ajeau asked him.

"I don't know. I saw the fire and ran to help. I haven't been able to find Tille."

Ajeau could see the concern in his eyes. It bordered on desperation. "Hey!" she shouted at the men and women working around them. "Has anyone seen Tille?"

She received only blank stares and head shakes. One man said, "We're still cleaning up. We don't know who died."

Vaten grabbed Ajeau's arm. "Died?"

"Don't worry, he doesn't know anything," Ajeau said, looking into Vaten's eyes to reassure him. "Like he said, they're cleaning up."

But there was an uneasiness in Vaten's heart he could not shake. Something terrible was unfolding in front of him. And he could only watch.

"There's someone here," one man said.

"Are they alive?"

"Not sure, she's—she's not in good shape if she is. But I don't—" the first man said.

"Let me see here..." An old woman pushed her way to where they had discovered the body. When she arrived, she gasped and brought her hand to her face. "No. Tille."

Vaten heard the words and lost control of his body. His head dropped and his arms fell limp. His legs buckled as Ajeau put her arms around him to keep him from falling. But it was no use. She could not keep him upright. She helped him to the ground.

He stared up at her, tears pouring down his cheek, and said, "Tille?"

Ajeau brought her arms around his neck and rested her head on his. But he would not be consoled. He pushed her away, the sadness slowly turning into rage, and he screamed silently into the night.

"There was nothing you could do," Ajeau said, trying to console him.

Soon after, Foreman Crevir, Vrai, and several of his guards strode into the camp looking at the huts and the workers, first with curiosity, then with resentment. They were met with respect and bowed heads from those they walked past.

Crevir eventually stopped, folded his arms, and frowned. "Who started the fire?"

"I think it was an accident, sir," one worker replied. "Looks like someone left a lamp next to some chaff. It must have caught and—"

"For Eau's sake, a lamp?" Crevir said, his voice rising with frustration. "It looked like a raid. Who was playing with a lamp and nearly burnt our entire camp?"

"And the fields," Vrai added.

Crevir nodded at Vrai. "That's right, they could've—I can't even imagine it." He glared at the workers. "Who was it?"

The lamp. No. Vaten glanced at Crevir and then Vrai as though they were there to deliver a fatal blow to him.

No one said a word until Vaten, full of guilt and grief, opened his mouth and said, "I could've—I could've. It was my fault. I killed her. I started the fire." He had been too scared, too weak, and it killed the person who cared for him since he was a child. He deserved the same fate.

Vrai tapped Crevir's shoulder and said, "Savique's boy. He was going to join the guard in a few weeks."

Crevir smiled as if he had caught a rabbit in his snare. "Ah, yes. Well, I suppose it is time then. Grab him."

Vrai stepped forward and grabbed Vaten.

"Where are you taking him?" Ajeau said. "It was an accident and—"

"Quiet!" A guard stepped between Vrai and Ajeau.

"Don't worry, little girl," Crevir said, a devious smile on his face. "I am only going to tell him the truth about his father. And what the Noye did to him." He cackled.

"Don't, he didn't mean to. He..." Ajeau's voice faded as the guard dragged her from the scene.

Crevir glanced at Vaten and said, "Such a shame we lost Tille. She was the only one left for you. Well," he turned to Vrai, "let us leave these people to their rebuilding."

They carried Vaten down the path towards Crevir's residence. The same one his father helped rebuild before his exile. But Vaten would never know of it. No, Crevir would only tell Vaten of his father's thievery, his dishonor, his brands, and his horrific death at the hands of the vile Noye; lies meant to torture the boy more than a cane.

And that was when Vaten, the man under a pile of dirt, heard a slapping noise as if something was rhythmically hitting wood. He opened his eyes. This time, he was sure he did.

***

ZEJELA CAUGHT THE ARM of the assassin moments before they brought their blade down on her chest. She slid to the side and let the assassin's momentum take them forward, past her, as she pulled them down by their arm. They stumbled forward and out of striking distance.

The assassin recovered quickly, but Zejela was now ready for them. As they rushed towards her again, she moved forward into their path and bent at the knees, and using their momentum, threw them over and away from her.

This was not the first time someone had come to kill Zejela. And though she was no longer a young woman, she moved deftly and used the assassin's own strength to repel their attacks. She did not have to overpower them, she only had to outmaneuver them.

But the assassin was no novice either. After being thrown a second time, they stood, drew their second dagger, but did not advance. For a moment there was a strange pause, as the two fighters waited for the other to move first, for an opening that never materialized.

In the end, neither made another move. Before they could, a third person entered the room holding a makeshift truncheon. The noise from the struggle had concealed the man's approach. Though neither fighter heard him, Zejela glimpsed his face first. And as he raised his club to strike, she smiled.

Aloc landed a thunderous blow on the side of the assassin's head, sending them toppling over, unconscious before they hit the ground. Blood trickled from their ear. They may have been dead, but neither Zejela nor Aloc checked on them.

"What is this?" Aloc said, his arm extended towards the man lying on the floor.

Zejela caught her breath, then said, "Someone come to kill me, no doubt. There is much I need to tell you, friend."

Zejela spoke at length about the happenings of the past few days. From the stolen goods, to Vaten and Levitien, to the death of Uluard, Diros, and now Harlae; Zejela explained it all. Aloc had been right from the start. It was a coup.

When Zejela stopped explaining the situation, Aloc said only, "It's good I came back."

"Yes, and why did you come? You are supposed to be with the Sentries, no? Moving to the bay on someone's orders. Who ordered it?"

"The orders came with the Elders' sigil," Aloc said. "But it proved to be a trap. We marched a day without preparation and supplies. And when we were exhausted, hungry, and weak, soldiers, who clearly did not care for the rules of our world, attacked us."

"Oxalis?" Zejela said in disbelief. "In battle?"

Aloc nodded. "Yes, there was nothing we could do. The Sentries, I fear, are no more."

The news struck Zejela like a blow to the stomach. Again, she was too late.

"I am very glad you survived and are here." Tears welled in her eyes. "But it is too late to change the fate of our great nation. I have failed to protect so much."

Aloc smiled. He bent down and put his hand on her shoulder. "Even if it is just you and I, it is a thing worth fighting for, no?"

Zejela smiled through the tears. "You are right, as usual. Thank you." Zejela stood, her energy returning. "We must find Wehlat or Ryiera. One of them may be in grave danger. The other may be the leader of this uprising."

"They're not hiding. They're walking through the streets of this place, speaking with their circles and the circles of the other Elders. It is not—"

"They walk together?" Zejela's eyes narrowed.

"Yes."

And that is when Zejela finally saw the plot clearly. The two Elders had worked together to assemble a loyal base for such a time. Their bickering on the council allowed them to court people on both sides of every issue. Any individuals frustrated by a decision that did not match their own opinion would find a sympathetic ear in Wehlat or Ryiera, who no doubt filled their frustrated minds with ideas of a better world. Nothing fomented anger like grievance.

Then they only needed to sit and wait for a time of suitable disruption and confusion. The acquisition and return of the goods from Bas was the opportune moment.

And though it was not her decision alone—the Elders had all agreed they had to go—Zejela felt responsible. It was her initiative that spurred the trip to Bas. If she had not advocated for it, Zevaco may have been safe.

Aloc grabbed her, shaking her free of her thoughts. "Come. There is no more time to think. It is time to act."

\*\*\*

It did not take them long to find Wehlat and Ryiera. Aloc had been right, they were not hiding. If anything, they appeared to be flaunting their accomplishments as they sat atop their horses, smiling and talking joyously, as though it were a perfect day. To them, it likely was.

Zejela and Aloc approached the two elders outside the Forgotten Rest. When Wehlat first spied them, his smile vanished. He whispered something to Ryiera, who turned and looked at the approaching annoyances and sighed in frustration.

They quickly ushered those they were speaking with away—Zejela watched as they fled in fear borne of some lie, no doubt—and welcomed Zejela customarily.

"It is good to see you, Elder Zejela. I trust you have heard the terrible news. Diros and Uluard are..." Wehlat feigned sadness. It was not a convincing performance. "Dead!"

He turned to Ryiera and placed his face on her shoulder, hiding his fake tears from all.

"Tragic news," Ryiera said. "But we must move forward. We must calm the people and stabilize our nation. Don't you think, Zejela?"

She glared at them. "You! You want to murder your fellow Elders, you want to steal the samples taken from the tree, you want to destroy the Sentries, and then you tell me you want to 'stabilize our nation.' Turn yourselves in. Stop this coup. And then Zevaco will be stable again."

"But Zejela." Wehlat lifted his head off Ryiera's shoulder. There were no signs of tears anywhere. "Whatever do you mean?"

Wehlat and Ryiera's calm demeanor only infuriated Zejela more. She clenched her teeth together and balled her hands in a fist. "You know exactly of what I speak."

"Oh Zejela." Ryiera shook her head in false disappointment. "You tried, and that is admirable. But this is your doing. This is your fault. Isn't that right Wehlat?"

"Yes, of course. You, Zejela, brought all the Elders here, did you not? Who else could have killed them? You wanted the tree so badly you forced a trip to Bas. Who else to steal its leaves? You, and that man there," Wehlat pointed to Aloc, "sent the Sentries to some far-off city. And, as I hear it, they haven't been seen since. Who else would they listen to?"

"Nonsense! I would never," Aloc said.

"Oh, but you did. The two of you worked together to take over Zevaco!" Wehlat said.

"You see, Zejela." Ryiera's smile was full of arrogance. "You are not as clever as you think. You are like the elephant in the forest. You cannot hide your intentions; every movement is known."

No, it was not possible. They knew her plans and predicted her actions so perfectly. Was she that obvious? Was she that foolish?

"I think she is beginning to understand," Wehlat said to Ryiera. Then he turned to Zejela. "Of course, we didn't know you would blame and kill your lover. Ruthless as it was, it was not particularly clever." He turned back to Ryiera. "Did that confuse anyone?"

Ryiera simply shook her head no.

"No. And now you are here...to what? Stop us?" Wehlat laughed. "There is no stopping us. Not now. Not by you. Zejela, your coup is over." More laughter.

Zejela pointed an outstretch arm at Wehlat. "No! Lies. This rebellion flows from your tongue."

"It does not matter what you say. The people know who is responsible. They have seen your cruelty," Ryiera said. "The death of friends, of Elders! All for what? Your precious tree? To protect Bas? None will stand for that anymore. They will join us in ridding Zevaco of you and your acolytes."

Zejela shook her head. "You can try, but I will not rest until you—"

"Do you not see?" Ryiera held up a hand. "You are the face of deceit and treason. You may draw breath now, but it only delays the inevitable. Your end will come today, tomorrow, or sometime thereafter. But you will never again hold a shred of significance. Your life is already over."

Wehlat nodded. "Yes. And Zevaco will no longer be the spectator you want it to be. No longer a protector. We will attack. We will confront the Bassians. We will take back what is ours. And you will return to the earth." He spoke the words not as a threat, but as a fact.

Zejela was speechless. She had been beaten so thoroughly and underestimated her adversaries so greatly that she directed her anger only at herself. She was responsible for all of it.

After a brief exchange of glances and nods between Wehlat and Ryiera, they turned their horses and rode away without saying another word.

Zejela's mind raced, trying to repair the damage she caused. There had to be some way to restore Zevaco to where it was only a few days before. She thought of a thousand terrible ideas that would not work and dismissed them as quickly as they arose. She struggled and fought for one good idea. But none came.

And eventually, she resigned herself to the idea there was nothing she could do. No, that wasn't totally correct. There was one thing she could do. Something she could still save.

Zejela turned to Aloc and said, "We need to leave. Now."

"W-What? Where would we go? Soccia?"

"No, we need to leave Zevaco. It will not be safe for us here. Wehlat and Ryiera are correct. The people will believe we started this coup and that I killed Uluard and Diros. They will want retribution against me and anyone who would appear to be my friend. That would include you?"

Aloc nodded confidently.

"Then we must leave," Zejela said. "But there is one last thing we must do before we go."

She ran through the hall of the building and out into its back courtyard. It was quiet and peaceful, a lush landscape except for the patch of disturbed dirt with two reeds jutting out of the ground. She hoped she had counted her days correctly. And that they would all leave alive.

Aloc turned to Zejela and asked, "What are we doing here?"

"Digging."

# PART IV

Transcript of the final meeting of Istor Sotin III and Farseer Verbeuse

Farseer

*Thank you for calling on me, great Istor.*

Istor

*I am happy for your return to our shores, Farseer. Now sit and tell me of your excursions into the small continent. What did you see there?*

Farseer

*Many wondrous things, Istor. But many troubling things too. Endless waves of people stretching over the land, but all with different customs and different languages. Some are friends and some are enemies. Some wander and some remain fixed. Some fight for sport, some sing songs or tell stories, and others drink mightily. But I have seen them all and they are far more alike than different in their spirit. They all value the bounty of the land, and all fear its demise. They worship that which—*

Istor

*Yes, yes. I have heard far enough today about the people there. I call on you not for your opinion on them, but for your opinion on the land. So tell me, what are your impressions?*

Farseer

*My apologies, Istor. The land is...verdant. It is a thriving place full of rich soil and amber grasses that grow endlessly. Trees touch the sky. Storms powerful, but reviving, bring water in waves. Rivers and streams twist and wind throughout the countryside, bringing water to all. Even after they flood, the land restores itself and grows more fertile and more fruitful.*

Istor

*And? Is it suitable? Will it sustain our gift?*

Farseer

*Yes, Istor. I think it will be most suitable. There are many places where our gift would be most welcome.*

Istor

*That is excellent news, Farseer! Do you have a preferred location for its roots?*

Farseer

*Yes, I have thought much on it. A group in the north lives wholly in a system of caves built into mountains. There are those that live in the once flooded plains in the center of the continent. Even some of the coastal tribes have gained a knowledge of—*

Istor

*On with it, Farseer. I care not for your romantic descriptions. What is your preference?*

Farseer

*There is a clan that lives deep in the desert. They have lived there for as long as any of them could remember and they trace their lineage back to a time before even our records. They do not stray from this land. They bring in nothing from the outside. Everything they create starts and ends in this one place. It is truly a remarkable achievement for their kind.*

Istor

*And you think this makes them worthy? How specious! What would they do with our offering if they do not leave?*

Farseer

*I do not know what they will do with our gift, but they seem as worthy as any other. Their time in the desert has changed them. They shift with the sands. They wear white in deference to the sun. They worship water that arises as if out of nowhere. They destroy nothing for fear they will need it later. They know no bounds or restrictions. They are remarkable.*

Istor

*Oh, Farseer. I see you are enamored with them. But I care not for the people there and neither should you. I will make no decisions based on that. You know what our blessing is for.*

Farseer

*Of course, the judgment is yours, Istor. But know this, the continent is a fickle place, and the desert remains suitable. I can give no assurances of worth, or cultivation, or destruction. Those are not for me to see. But I have spoken with the people there—*

Istor

*You have done what? You outstep your place, Farseer!*

Farseer

*It is a hard thing to be without companionship.*

Istor

*Perhaps. But it is not your place to decide. You will be disciplined for such an offense.*

Farseer

*That may be, great Istor. But—*

Istor

*Enough! I have taken your council as much as I can, disgraced Farseer. I will heed your words despite your actions, but you do not escape judgment. I will return with my decision.*

***

*Hear my words. On advice of my assembly and this shamed former Farseer, I have decreed that the gift will take root in the desert city described. But I will not offer it whole. The blessing will be split and reconciliation will be left up to the great people of the desert. But worry not. Our gift will not travel alone. As punishment, the former Farseer Verbeuse will remain with the blessing. He will join the people he has become so fond of and no longer wear the title Farseer. Never again will he return to our land. None of his blood will. I am Sotin.*

# Chapter 36

"WHAT'RE THEY DOING?" SAVIQUE said through labored breath.

They had been running for so long. First, inside the city to a small door in the ground that, when opened, revealed a tunnel they used to escape. Then, after crawling through the tunnel and emerging on the other side of the wall, they ran more. In the darkness, they raced away from their only source of light: the fires that raged in Nouv'eau.

Far from the city, they stopped running. And when they did, Savique saw a sight most majestic and terrible. Against a black background were fluttering shades of orange and billowing gray clouds that blended into the night sky. His legs shook, though he was not sure whether it was from exhaustion or panic.

Vrai stared, then closed his eyes and sighed. "They are closing the gate. The battle is over."

"What do you mean?" Savique said. "Why would they close the gate?"

"Because it removes the possibility of escape." There was a slight tremor in Vrai's voice.

It took Savique a moment to understand what Vrai meant, but when he did, it stole whatever breath he had left. The Noye were lost. Those that had not already escaped the city were dead, dying, or captured.

"Is there nothing we can do?"

Vrai shook his head, said nothing.

The two men stayed there a while, staring at the burning city without speaking. As Savique looked on, he wondered who had made it out before the gate closed. He had met so many Noye during his travels, but the only one he thought of was Eyvo-Ille. She had not found him as she had promised. He had not found her either. Where was she?

Vrai interrupted Savique's thought with a slap to the back. "Come on, let us look at this sight no longer. We have much to discuss, anyway."

Savique nodded and followed Vrai to a fallen tree surrounded by dead leaves and bushes. It was far from a comfortable spot to rest, sticks poked and prodded them everywhere, but it was safe from any V'eauvian patrols that would come looking for escaped Noye.

As soon as they nestled into the brush, Vrai said, "It was strange to be called to Nouv'eau to pass judgment on an old thief. Even stranger to find that thief was you. But never did I expect...this." He shook his head. "What happened?"

Savique explained everything, from the assassin who came after Eyvo-Ille, to the recruitment of Noye all over Bas, to Eyvo-Ille's plan and their escape. Vrai listened intently but did not react. He remained silent and nodded occasionally, as if he knew what Savique was going to say.

When Savique finished the story, Vrai conveyed his true feelings. "Foolish," he said.

Savique's eyebrows jumped, but his mouth remained closed. He had lived Eyvo-Ille's plan for years and believed in its success for as long. To call it foolish was disrespectful. But he thought it best not to start a fight.

"Eyvo should've known better than to strike the V'eauvians here, under any condition," Vrai continued. "They built this entire place to prevent attacks. Within those walls, they hold all the power. If only she hadn't acted so rashly, then perhaps she would still be here."

"What do you mean?" Savique leaned towards him.

"Eyvo-Ille has returned to the earth."

At first, Savique did not register the meaning of the words. He had heard them, but they meant nothing like they were words in a foreign tongue. Then, slowly, he recognized them, but he found them incomprehensible. "What?" It was all he could choke out.

"Yes, I saw her myself. There is no doubting it. It was Eyvo and her body was mutilated. There were hundreds of cuts in areas designed to make death linger and make it as—" Vrai glanced at Savique, then stopped talking.

Savique felt as if he was falling. He had climbed a tree, and a branch broke; he had walked along the edge of the cliff and slipped. His stomach turned, his head swayed as if it was losing its tether to his neck. Everything was wrong.

Then the bile from his stomach crept up his throat and burst from his mouth. He spun his head away from Vrai and retched on the ground. Then he closed his eyes and shook his head to regain his equilibrium. His mind returned, but it did not bring any semblance of relief with it.

Instead, there was only anger. Not only at the V'eauvians, but at himself and Eyvo-Ille and the whole idea of the raid. Vrai was wrong. It had not been foolish; it had been senseless. She lost her life—and the life of many of her people—all to settle some ancient grudge. He knew what she would say, but that did not stem the rage or the grief in his heart.

Vrai stared at Savique and watched him cycle through emotions that he knew so well. "It is not your fault." Vrai grabbed Savique by both of his shoulders. "And though I am heartened by your sorrow—that you knew her well enough to feel for her return—it is misplaced. Eyvo knew what was at stake. She made her own choices on this day and every day before that. She wouldn't have listened to you had you tried to stop her."

Savique stared at the ground and, in a voice barely above a whisper, said, "But I could have helped her. I should've stayed and fought with her. I—She would still be here if I did."

"No." Vrai shook his head. "You couldn't. If she died in battle, I think it unlikely your presence would have mattered at all. Unless you simply wanted to join her in her return to the earth."

It was harsh, but Savique knew it to be the truth.

Vrai continued, "Take solace in knowing that she returned to the soil a warrior in battle—a bee in its hive. And even in that wretched place, she will nurture a new world. Let us hope it is a better one."

Savique sighed. His heart still ached, but the rage was fading. "Without her, what do we do now?"

"We will find your camp tomorrow, by the light of day, and wait for others there. Hopefully, some of our brothers and sisters escaped."

"And then what? What will those of us who survived do?"

"That is not for me to say. I imagine most will return to their tribes. Any of them would accept you or you can—"

"I can ride back home. To the estate." Savique's eyes grew wide and something like a smile appeared on his face. The darkness of Eyvo-Ille's death receded.

"Yes," Vrai said. "If you wish. But you should know, it is not how you left it."

"What? What do you mean?" Savique's chest tightened. He could not bear more bad news.

"The drought ruined the crop. There are no more supplies, nothing left with which to feed the workers. Most have left for any place with food. The estate is dying; it may already be dead by now. And your son is no longer there."

Savique's throat tightened, his mouth grew gritty and dry. "Where—Where is he?" He worried he was not ready to hear the answer.

Vrai shook his head. "I don't know. After he joined the guard, I watched over him as best I could. But he left the estate with a friend some time ago. I have not seen him since."

"He—he left?" Savique put his hands on his head and looked to the sky. He saw no moons there.

It was cruel. The Foreman was gone, banished from the world forever, and he finally had a way home. Only now, his reason to go home was gone, wandering a world that was not safe for warriors with armies by their side. What hope did the boy have of surviving? He knew the answer but would not allow himself to think it.

"Just because I have not seen him," Vrai said. "It does not mean we cannot find him. My duties with the Foreman kept me near the estate. We can search."

"Yes, search," he said, lost in the memories of his son's infant cries. They had once pulled him from a deep darkness and forced him to survive for something beyond himself. The boy would do so now, too. He would not give up, not until he saw Vaten again.

"We can start tomorrow," Vrai said. "We will gather with those who survived at the camp and plan for our journey. For now, try to rest."

Savique knew he would be unable to sleep, but he lay on the hard ground and closed his eyes, anyway. When he shifted in his spot, he felt something poke his side. For a moment, he thought it was a small rock or a stick. But then he remembered the vial he took from the workshop. He had not needed it after all. It was an important vial, though, at least to someone. Better hold on to it, he thought. It may prove useful yet.

\*\*\*

As HE EXPECTED, SAVIQUE did not rest for a moment that night. Not only was his head awash with grief and hope, pulling his mind in separate directions, but every noise jolted him out of any tranquility he found.

He imagined the woman in white coming after him to satisfy her vengeance. Or maybe it was the V'eauvians searching for their escaped prisoner. Maybe even the Foreman rising from his death to wrap his gloved hands around Savique's neck. In the blackness of night, all these horrors seemed possible.

But the sun rose soon enough, and with it, Savique's fears subsided. No one was around, as far as he could see, and the new day brought with it the beginning of his search for his son.

He walked alongside Vrai in the general direction of the Noye camp, keeping his eye on the city to help him recall its location. As they walked, he realized, in the emotions of the previous night, he had overlooked something Vrai had said. The man had given him the briefest glimpse of Vaten's life and Savique had inquired no further. He had slept next to a man who could fill his heart with tales of his son and had said nothing. He admonished his stupidity.

But the man was still next to him. Savique looked at Vrai. "Tell me about Vaten."

Vrai sighed and nodded as though he had been expecting the question, but had no answer for it. "What can I tell you?"

"Anything. Tell me anything of him."

Vrai scratched the back of his neck. "Well, when young, he used to tend the fields. Showed a real interest in the crops and plants there. He never—"

"Not unlike his father was at a young age!"

"Yes...well he was an energetic young one, and the fields allowed him room to stretch his legs. He worked hard, even if he did not always listen to authority. I had plenty of guards tell me of his incidents."

"Like what?"

Vrai opened his mouth, then paused and shook his head. "Oh nothing, minor offenses. The boy was young and mischievous and liked to talk. He learned quickly the way of the land and grew into an obedient, reserved man. I told you he made it into the Estate Guard."

Savique drank it up. It may only have been the smallest drop of water, but it refreshed him all the same. And he knew there was more. "What else?"

Vrai spent hours remembering everything he could about the boy. Like his attachment to his Keeper and how protective she was of him. Or his kindness at sharing rations against the Foreman's orders. Or how he beamed with joy whenever he was around that young girl.

He left out plenty of stories he remembered, too. There were parts of the boy's life he did not need to tell Savique now, perhaps ever.

Savique listened and dreamed. He pictured what Vaten would look like as a man—would he keep a cut beard or a long one—how he would act as a guard, and who his friends were. The images excited and soothed him at the same time.

But Vrai saved the best story for last. It was not some grand adventure or life defining moment. It was a simple meeting between Vrai and the boy after he had joined the guard. Under the guise of drunkenness, Vrai had passed him a message. One that bolstered the boy's fading spirit. Just as the story of that meeting bolstered the father.

Savique smiled widely even as he blinked away tears. Vaten knew his father was alive and wanted to see him again. Perhaps Vaten left to search for him. Perhaps Vaten would find him.

As these thoughts passed through his mind, Savique glimpsed a strange sight ahead of him. A cluster of horses. A handful of people. They had found the remaining Noye.

***

Upon arriving at the camp, the first thing Savique noticed was the horses outnumbered the people. Not by a small margin, either. There were nearly fifty horses. There were exactly twelve people—fourteen including Savique and Vrai.

The two men walked through the remnants of the horde once stationed there. Pots and pitchers lay empty but organized in groups. Sticks to secure tents remained stuck in the ground, some with their cover attached. Under heaps of dirt, they could see packs of food and drink. The Noye had intended to return to it all after the raid. But now, anything the remaining raiders could not carry would be left to crumble to dust, as their tribesman had.

When they reached a group of horses, Vrai stopped and stared. After a moment, he approached one, put his head against its muzzle, and whispered softly, "I'm sorry she didn't make it, friend. But I am glad you did. Will you accept me?"

The horse whinnied and raised and shook its head, sending Vrai stumbling backwards a few steps.

"I guess they have eyes for another," he said, while looking at Savique.

Savique stared back at him, confused, and said nothing.

"Do you not recognize them?" Vrai said with a smile. "You've known them as long as you've known Eyvo."

"It is..." Savique shook his head as he slowly approached the horse. "Eyvo's horse? How did you know? How did it know to return here?"

"A Noye does not forget their partner. And no one forgets this beauty." Vrai chuckled, but a hint of sadness tinged his voice. "They remember where to go, just as we do. Maybe even better."

Savique stood next to the horse and, like Vrai, placed his head against her muzzle. He didn't know what to do or say, so he simply told the horse how he felt. "I miss her too. But we will not forget her bravery. Her legacy will live on."

When the horse made no response, Savique turned and walked away. He had not taken more than two steps when the horse reared back on its hind legs, nickered loudly, and came crashing back to the earth. Savique froze and stared at Vrai with a concerned expression on his face.

Vrai smiled at him. "You are lucky to win their affection. They are one of the best."

Savique returned to the horse, gave it a light pat on its forehead, and let it run off on its own. It would come back, or it wouldn't. But it had chosen him, not the other way around. Savique accepted this and smiled back at Vrai.

They soon realized they were the only ones smiling in the camp. The mood there was appropriately dismal, as gray and gloomy as the sky was blue and radiant. The few people in the camp lay strewn about, mostly ignoring each other. Yes, they nodded and bowed as was appropriate, but no one spoke to anyone else.

The rest of the day passed slowly, with faces fixed on the ground or the horizon in seemingly perpetual sorrow. No one said a thing, not even Vrai and Savique. Several times, Savique thought he should speak—it is what Eyvo-Ille would have wanted him to do—but no words ever seemed appropriate. He could not offer them anything. Not joy, not inspiration, not even consolation. No, the silence was preferable to some forced speech.

And as nightfall fell, with their numbers never increasing, the Noye left. Some made gestures of parting and a few said, "Farewell," but all departed as sullen as Savique had seen them earlier that day. He hoped returning to their tribes—if indeed that was where they were going—would bring them some peace.

Savique already knew what would bring him peace. And now it was time to begin.

He sat next to Vrai and said, "There are no more Noye coming and the ones here are leaving. We should begin our search for Vaten immediately."

Vrai nodded. "And do you have a notion of where we should begin such a search?"

"Our home. Crevir's Estate."

# CHAPTER 37

"No. Leave me alone, you monster!" Ajeau screamed.

A spirit without form loomed over her. It eclipsed the entire field of her vision and prevented her escape. And though all was darkness, it was not black; instead, it was blue, a shade of which Ajeau had come to know all too well since Vaten's abduction.

She struggled against the shadow. Unable to run, she twisted her head and shoulders side to side and refused to look at it. It had no eyes, no face either, but she avoided its gaze all the same. Somehow, she knew if you looked at it, it had you. And once it had you...

The shadow loomed closer. It swayed over the contorting Ajeau like branches in the wind.

"Go away, demon!" Ajeau screamed again. "What else do you want? You've already taken so much!"

A thundering roar echoed throughout the world, followed by laughter. Ajeau opened her eyes and looked around, but saw no one laughing.

As she searched for the source of the laughter, Ajeau glimpsed the spirit in front of her. Strange images bombarded her. Trees gently swayed in the breeze. Men and women fled in all directions. The sun shined overhead. Thousands of shadows, like the one that stood before her now, screamed at her. Ajeau did not know if they screamed in anger, pain, or joy. All seemed possible.

Then she heard herself yell. It came not from the Ajeau in front of the shadow though, her mouth was shut. The yell was shrill, higher pitched; the yell of a child. But her ears were not mistaken, it was her voice. It was her yell. Only one she made long ago.

"Do not fear it. Embrace it." The spirit's words appeared in Ajeau's mind. "Remember your thoughts from that day. Remember what the girl showed you. Remember to—"

An unknown voice interrupted the spirit. "No!"

The azure haze that once covered everything lifted. The shadow in front of her shrunk to a size no bigger than her and it flickered as if it were a flame losing its fuel.

For the first time, Ajeau glimpsed the world around the shadow. She stared at it from afar like she was on a mountaintop, gazing at something below.

The place she saw was like none she had ever seen before. The ground looked as if it were ablaze. Not only was it a dusty brown, but it radiated heat that could be seen in hazy waves. And as wind whipped over the soil, it carried particles on it, like it might do to ash from a fire.

Ajeau would have thought it a land of fire if not for the vegetation. Trees, tall and nearly branchless, grew in a spotted formation over the land, their leaves long and green grew out of the top of their trunks. A small spot of blue sat near the trees.

She returned her attention to the small shadow in front of her. "I will banish you back to whatever world you belong to," she said.

"Do not forget..." it offered in response.

Ajeau bent down and picked up whatever she could find to hurl at the fading demon. She found a small object, rounded but angular, pointed. She wondered where she had seen it before.

As she cocked her arm to throw the object at the spirit, a peculiar feeling came over her. She could not part with what she had gathered. Despite not knowing what it was, she knew she needed it. And it stuck to her hand like a fly stuck to sap.

The word 'No' could still be heard on the wind.

Then, Ajeau's body lurched forward as if she had been pushed from behind and it nearly caused the object to become dislodged from her hand. But it stuck. When she turned around, there was no one behind her, nothing there at all.

She regripped the object as tight as she could. *I cannot lose this. I need it. I know I need it...*

The spirit with no face, no mouth, smiled.

***

"Wake up."

Ajeau knew the voice immediately. She opened her eyes and looked around. The spirit was gone, and so was the rest of the landscape. But quickly the light became too much for her and she squeezed her eyes shut to stop the light from searing them.

"Hijeuse. Wake."

This time, when Ajeau opened her eyes, she saw Syais's face in front of her, a candle between them. Syais had an arm on her shoulder and appeared to be in the middle of shaking her.

Like a fog lifting, the dream slowly faded from her mind. But she could not shake the feeling it left in her. She was sure there was a message in the vision she needed to know. As soon as she tried to think of it, the images left her mind and she was left grasping at a branch out of arm's reach.

"Good, you are awake," Syais said.

"What?" Ajeau shook her head and blinked her eyes to help them adjust to the light.

"We have found the answers we sought and will be leaving the city."

"What? Now? It's the middle of the night."

"Yes, we leave now." Syais grabbed her arm to help her up. "But we will return soon, once all the preparations for our larger trek have been completed. Are you ready?"

"I don't..." Ajeau said, confused.

"Good."

Though she still did not know what Syais wanted, Ajeau was more than ready to leave. Ever since returning to Nouv'eau from Seule's cabin, she had been restless. Images of Seule and Vaten dead haunted her day and night. The only reprieve from them came when she thought of the vengeance she would have on the Zevacese. It all led her to feel caged and crave release.

And so, when Syais came to tell her about their imminent departure, Ajeau was pleased even if she was confused. She didn't even know where they would go. But it meant they were getting closer to all the things she had been promised.

"What do I need?" Ajeau asked.

"For now, you need only follow me."

***

SYAIS AND PASSIL STOOD in her chambers, hovering over a table filled with papers, maps, and charts. The documents were intricately placed over the entire space as though they were strokes in a painting; individually they were meaningless, but together they created something wonderful.

What they created, the Vizier and her Warden did not yet know. They had stared at the table for days, trying desperately to match every step and point Seule had revealed to Syais with current maps of Bas. The work was painstaking, frustrating, and fruitless. It left a sour taste in each of their mouths.

"You should have taken notes," Passil said as he grabbed a scroll from the table. "Or written something down before you killed the man. You let your passions control you. You—"

"My passions are my own. You are not one to judge." Syais did not look up from the table. "The man would have revealed too much. Once he saw the papers, he could no longer be allowed to live. Not with the Hijeuse so near."

"Yes, but..." Passil put down one scroll, wrote furiously for a moment, then picked up another and shook his head. "...there is nothing here. If that is truly the location, how could the city be in such a barren place?"

Syais sighed. "I do not know. But it is what the man told me. That is the route the Balafre detail in their notes."

"Is it possible the man lied to you?"

"Deception is always a possibility. But he had reason to tell the truth. Not only for himself."

"Then perhaps he was wrong. He was old and emaciated." Passil stuck his finger in the air as though he had formed some great idea. "The lack of food starved his brain of reason."

"Nonsense. You were there and the rest of his notes are legitimate. The markers here and here," Syais gestured at two markings on the Balafre maps and their corresponding location on the V'eauvian maps, "are clearly the Tentir. The man was correct. Z'eau lies there." She emphatically pointed to where Passil had scrawled.

"And if you are wrong? If there is nothing there, like our maps suggest, then what? You would risk our lives on a guess?"

Syais grinned and nodded emphatically. "Yes. I would risk a million lives on this. We are going and that is the last word on the matter. Now, what I need is your help to arrange for such a journey."

"My apologies." Passil bowed his head. "Of course I will assist with the preparations. What would you have me do first?"

"First, we will need to gather the guard and soldiers. They will accompany us to Z'eau."

"Are you sure that is wise? The city—"

"Yes, yes," Syais said, annoyed. "The city will likely fall. Let the peasants riot and starve. We will return unburdened by their strife and unafraid of any insurgence."

Passil nodded.

"While you arrange for our travels, I will take the Hijeuse here." Syais pointed to a small, strange marking on one map.

It was not foreign to Passil; he had deduced its location and purpose. "Alone?" his eyes widened. "You will take her to the shrine alone?"

"Yes." Syais waved away Passil's concern. "She has become quite manageable these days. I think she is coming to understand her role and has given herself to it."

"How could she? She knows nothing of what awaits her, she only knows of her desires. Fantasies for a child."

"You doubt the Arboricole? You, of all people, should know better than that. Do I need to remind you of—"

"No, Vizier." Passil held up both his hands. "Of course not. I have no doubt in their visions. They are sacrosanct. But the girl is still...immature. She lives in her dreams, not in reality."

"Yes. That is true, but dreams are powerful. Our dreams drive us to remarkable ends. Do you recall your own dreams?" Syais walked behind Passil and ran her hands across his shoulders.

Passil shivered under her hands as though they were frozen. But he did not shirk from it. Instead, he embraced her touch, straightened his back and shoulders and leaned into her. A mumbled "Yes" floated from his parted lips.

"Good." Syais withdrew her arms slowly, letting her fingers rest on him a moment longer than necessary. There was no need for her to push further. She had made her point.

Passil, free of Syais's touch, looked towards the ceiling of the cottage and inhaled deeply. "If you must travel alone with the girl, be watchful. You may think you can control her. But she is more like you than you know."

"How do you mean?"

"She is calculated, ruthless, and, most of all, unpredictable." Passil lips spun upwards in a knowing smile.

Syais stared back, unamused, and said, "I will heed your advice. But we cannot linger here any longer. You have your charge, gather the guard and raise an army. Procure us supplies. I will return within a fortnight with our Hijeuse. Then we leave for Z'eau."

Passil nodded and walked out of Syais's chambers.

\*\*\*

THE GATES OF NOUV'EAU opened and allowed Ajeau and Syais to pass through the wall and into the world beyond without incident. Atop their horses, they rode swiftly back towards the Tentir Forest. And though she had traveled in the same direction only weeks earlier to find Seule, this trip felt different. She could not say why, but like the cool breeze that preceded a storm, she sensed something forthcoming.

For three days, the two riders advanced through the forest, mostly in silence. The more time they spent in the Tentir, the more Ajeau appreciated Syais's command over her horse. Where she took circuitous routes around tight passes, Syais rode through them, knowing the exact window her horse could fit through. She was nimble atop the horse, shifting her weight and positioning, so she was never off balance or thrown. It was graceful, Ajeau thought, so unlike all the riders who taught her.

And dressed in her customary white outfit with her hair flowing behind her, Syais appeared majestic atop her horse, like an egret mid-flight.

As they stopped to rest, Ajeau asked her, "How did you learn to ride like that?"

Syais swallowed her water and said, "I have been riding for a very long time. In places far more dangerous than this. You learn what you must to survive."

"I don't imagine survival was ever in doubt for you."

Syais chuckled lightly. As Ajeau stared at her, she realized it was the first time she heard the woman's laughter. No pretense, no anger, only her authentic laugh. It was soothing.

"One's survival is always in doubt. That is one of the first lessons I learned and it did not come easy." Syais turned and lifted her robe, revealing a scar near the middle of her back.

"You were wounded?" Ajeau said, eyes wide with wonder. It was like seeing the sun break in two.

"Yes, many times. But this wound was deep. It cost me much and nearly my life." Syais inhaled deeply, then released her robe. It covered Ajeau's hand for a moment before she withdrew it. "But it also taught me to do what I must to survive. To abandon the limitations others forced upon me. That is why I ride like the Noye and observe like the Rigoladers and contemplate like the Istori and fight like the V'eauvians."

Ajeau nodded as though she understood what Syais meant, even if she did not.

Syais continued, "The lessons we take from our scars are important. Whether they be gained on the field of battle or in our pastures. I learned what I must do to destroy those who aim to harm me." Syais grabbed Ajeau's forearms and turned them so that Ajeau could see her scars. "What have you learned?

Ajeau shook her head. "I-I don't know. That I am the Hijeuse?"

Syais tightened her grip on her arms. "No, *I* told you that. Think harder."

Ajeau could think of nothing. For so long, she had ignored her scars and intentionally not learned anything from them. But then an image of Vaten holding her arms and looking at the scars flashed in her mind. It took a moment, but she remembered what he said.

"The scars are meaningless," Ajeau said. "They are only scars, pieces of damaged skin. It's the person who bears them that matters."

Syais let go of Ajeau's arms but remained staring at her. After a moment in silent reflection, she nodded, stood, and walked to her horse. When she arrived, she said, "You may see how true that is soon enough."

She mounted her horse and waved for Ajeau to do the same. Their rest was over. It was time to continue their trek through the endless trees of the Tentir.

It took another two days until they reached a clearing in the forest. When they did, Syais stopped her horse and said, "We are here."

Ajeau dismounted her horse and milled around the small glade for some time. Something about it looked familiar, the rockface, the hill, and the abandoned camp protected within.

Then again, much of the Tentir looked the same and Ajeau had spent enough time there that she may have come across the site before. It was possible they had ridden by the place yesterday and she would not have remembered it.

Except she could not deny the place was unique. The discarded frames, the cart that lay to the side, the fire pits littering the place were all uncommon in the forest.

And then all at once, she knew. The rotting wood she assumed was detritus was not. It was wood arranged intentionally into a design. It was a sphere with sharp protrusions, somehow both round and angular.

She had seen such a thing only once before. When she and Vaten stumbled upon the clearing mere days before his abduction.

The clearing had undergone some change in the time since she and Vaten had been there. Much of the brush had simply disintegrated. The weeds and overgrowth, once hanging over the rocks near the campsite, had died off, leaving only brown and gray stems. Even the wooden designs, clearly intended to last ages, had dried, cracked, and become pale. But it was the same place.

Ajeau considered whether she should tell Syais the news. But before she could say anything, Syais caught her eye and said, "This is an old altar to Eau made by the Balafre—the High Elders. Wonderful, isn't it?"

Ajeau said nothing.

"Yes." Syais said, answering her own question. "And this is where you find out who you are. This is where—"

An arrow flew by Syais's head. She ducked long after it had passed. But even before the next one came, she knew what was happening. She rushed towards Ajeau and tackled her to the ground.

They crawled until they found sufficient cover. Neither of them knew who launched the attack or how many of them there were. But when Ajeau saw an arrow sticking out of a tree, its fletching was not blue but a golden yellow.

"Ajeau, look at me." Syais grabbed Ajeau by the shoulders. There was a strange glimmer in her eyes, as though she were excited. "You must trust me. We—You are going to fight. And save us both. But first...this is going to hurt."

Syais drew one of her daggers and drove it into Ajeau's arm. Red covered the white blades in an instant. Ajeau cried out in anguish.

The soldiers advancing on their position heard Ajeau's shriek. They knew exactly where she was. It would not help them at all.

# CHAPTER 38

VATEN'S EYELIDS BURST APART, but he saw only darkness. He could hear voices over the unfamiliar noises and felt hands shaking him, but he could not see a thing. He closed his eyes and opened them once more. Still, he saw only darkness.

The last thing he remembered was Zejela accusing Levitien and him of theft and calling for their execution. And then there were the dreams, the memories that arose like hallucinations invading his rest. But he could remember nothing else.

His mind raced, full of questions. Where was he? Was he alive? Why was it dark? Was this another dream? Why couldn't he see? What was that constant slapping sound? Is Levitien here? And on it went.

But before he could hazard a guess at any of them, a booming voice interrupted him and yelled, "Breathe!"

A pair of hands grabbed him, sat him upright, and clapped him on the back. Another "Breathe!" echoed through his skull.

The voice was familiar, but when he tried to picture the man in his mind, he was met with strict resistance. Thinking, he came to realize, required being alive. And being alive required breathing.

Vaten opened his mouth and inhaled as if it was his first breath. The air was warm and moist as it entered his lungs. It smelt of fish and tasted of salt. He had breathed this air once before, but like the man's voice, he could not place it.

Then he exhaled, a short irregular breath mixed with coughs. He tasted earth, and an alarm sounded in his mind. His eyes darted around, seeing nothing, as the panic raced through his body. The darkness was coming for him again.

"I...I don't want to go back." Though he tried to scream, his voice was hoarse and quiet.

A large hand rested on his shoulder. It covered the entire joint and when it squeezed to grip him, Vaten felt as though it might crush his bones to dust. Then he heard that same familiar bellowing voice say, "You alive!"

Vaten didn't know whether it was a question or a statement. So he breathed again and asked, "Am I alive?"

This time, he recognized the voice that answered him. But it only caused him dread.

"Yes," Zejela said. "You are alive. And I have much to explain to you."

***

"First, drink this," Zejela said. "If you sip it slowly, it will help soothe your stomach."

Someone placed a bowl in Vaten's hands and brought it to his mouth. It had been nearly five days since he last ingested anything. And when he took a taste of the drink, he found it as refreshing as anything he had ever put to his lips.

After he took a sip, he realized he should not have drunk it. It could have been some kind of poison. But he quickly disregarded the thought when he remembered they had cheered his breathing. And there were easier ways to kill him. Like leaving him in the ground.

And that is when his memory returned in full. He had been killed. Buried alive. Zejela had cut him, rubbed something into his arm, and then stood over him as dirt rained down on him. He shook his head and wondered how he survived.

"Vaten," Zejela said. "I once told you to trust me, and I meant it. Though I realize that may be hard given what you have experienced—"

"She must to do it!" The familiar bellowing voice interrupted her.

Zejela said something in Zevacese, then continued, "I am sorry for Aloc's interruptions. He is simply happy you have awoken. As I said..."

So the Sentry's leader survived and was with Zejela. A shiver ran down Vaten's spine. It was as Levitien had said. The two Zevacese conspired to blame them for the theft. He could only imagine why they wanted him alive. And none of the options comforted him.

"Whether or not you believe it," she said. "I am happy you are awake, too. But you must have many questions. Ask and I will answer as best I can."

Vaten shook his head. There were an infinite number of questions; he could spend the rest of his life asking them. But he started with the most important. "Why? Why did you accuse me?" Vaten's voice cracked. "You knew, and you had me killed. Or wanted to. And now you say you want me to trust you. Why should I? Why am I alive? What are you going to do with me?"

"One question at a time." Zejela smiled and patted his leg. "The accusations against you were part of an ill-fated plan, to protect you and to find out what was happening on Zevaco. By feigning a conflict between us, and your death, I could ensure no one else accused you. I could draw attention away from me and pass unseen amid the usurpers without suspicion."

Vaten stared blankly at her. "I don't understand any of it."

"I would not expect you to." Zejela disclosed the events of the past several days. Vaten had remembered about the thefts, but now heard about the coup, the deaths of the other Elders, the exile and entrapment of the Sentries, and how he had been used by Zejela.

"Yes, and for that, I am sorry." She reached out to grab Vaten's hand, but as soon as she touched it, he moved it. "But it was necessary. You were in more danger alive than you were buried. I—"

Vaten scoffed. "That cannot be true."

"It is. I made sure you would awake. The pink powder I rubbed into your wound comes from the theiodeux plant. It is an old remedy for sleeplessness. One that looks like it would do the opposite. And best of all, it slows your breathing and restricts your need for food and water." She smiled, proud of herself. "That, and well-placed reeds, would—and did—allow you to survive being buried alive."

"I—I don't know anything." Vaten sighed. "And I can't see an Eau damned thing. You may not have taken my life," he stretched out his arms in front of him, "but you've taken my sight. I'm as blind as the rain."

Aloc laughed heartily and said, "Rain don't see."

Zejela hushed him, then said to Vaten, "I do not think you are blind. Theiodeux takes time to leave your body but, let me look at your eyes." Zejela grabbed his face and held it in front of hers.

Not more than a week ago, she had held his face in a tender embrace. Now, his pupils were large and unfocused and the whites of his eyes were shaded with a slight pinkish hue. "Blink," she said. Vaten did so, but his eyes made no movement as though they were paralyzed.

Zejela dropped his head but continued to stare into his eyes. "The effects will linger, but your eyes look well. And you are awake and breathing. Those are good signs."

"Does that mean—" A horrible thought struck Vaten. "Is Levitien all right? Where is he?"

"He come too," Aloc said.

"Yes, Levitien is here. Against my better judgment, we brought him. But..." Zejela hesitated and put her hands on Vaten's shoulders. "Settle yourself. He is ill and resting below deck. He has, so far, been unable to expel the plant."

"He is alive though?"

"Yes," Zejela said.

Vaten sighed, this time relieved. For better or worse, he was connected with the man. And in that moment, he wished for Levitien's honest opinions about the situation. "Is he conscious? Can I speak to him?" he asked.

Zejela hesitated, then said, "Rest now. You too are recovering and it may—"

"No." Vaten's voice was sharp, forceful. "I wish to talk with him now."

"He will be here when you wake. You don't need to worry—"

"I said, I want to speak with him. If he is conscious, take me to where he rests."

Zejela relented. "All right. I will escort you to his side. Hold on."

She took Vaten's arm in hers and began walking slowly so the unseeing man could keep his balance. The warmth of her hand reminded Vaten of the night they spent together. Her grasp had steadied him that night, too.

But as he walked, swaying towards Zejela and then away from her, Vaten finally realized where he was and what made that rhythmic, striking sound. Water against a boat. He was on a ship. And the brackish air meant they were back at sea. No matter how long he spent on land, he would never forget the salted waters that took him from his home. He wondered where they were taking him now.

\*\*\*

BELOW DECK, LEVITIEN LAY on the floor of a small cabin lit only by the few rays of sunlight that passed through the wooden planks above him. Of course, Vaten could not see Levitien, but he knew he neared the man—or someone, at least—by the sounds of labored breathing. And the stench. The vicious mix of sweat, sick, and shit made Vaten heave as he entered.

Zejela lowered herself and Vaten to Levitien's side. Vaten stuck an arm out, hoping to make contact with the man and when he did, he flinched at the warmth radiating from him. Levitien was boiling.

Before Vaten could gain any distance between himself and Levitien, a hand clutched him. The hand was damp and warm and though the sweat should have made it more difficult for the hand to keep its grip; it did not slip. Vaten tried to shrug the man's hand off his arm but could not.

Levitien pulled him close to his mouth. "Who—Who is here?" His breath was stale and rotten and stunk nearly as bad as the room.

"It's—" Vaten gagged upon inhaling the smell. It took him a moment to compose himself, but he did so, then continued, "It's me. Vaten."

"Kid..." Levitien spoke the word slowly, as though it took great effort. "You alive too?"

"Alive but I can't see. They say it's temporary but—"

"Blind is better than whatever I got, kid. You..." Levitien groaned and shook as though a chill ran through the cabin. "You got any water?"

Vaten tapped Zejela's hand and turned in her direction. She spoke at the same time. "Yes, remain here and I will bring a brew for you both."

After Zejela left the cabin, Levitien said, "You remember what happened? My memories are blank."

Vaten relayed the story Zejela had told him to Levitien as best he could. Vaten was still unsure of all the characters and their roles, but he tried his best to remember correctly.

Levitien, in sudden jerky movements more like convulsions than gestures, nodded. "You believe her?"

"I do. I don't know why she'd lie, she—"

"There's always a million reasons to lie but, I agree with you." Levitien coughed. "And I'm not surprised."

"What? Why?" Vaten said.

"Because their society was cursed..." Levitien groaned as his body stiffened. Then he slammed the deck with his fist. "Sol damn it."

"What is it?"

"Nothing, shut up. They were cursed the moment they returned from Bas. Let me tell you, kid, what they came for, what they took—" Levitien swallowed his words as the door creaked open and Zejela returned.

She placed the pots beside the two men and took Vaten's hands in hers to show him where his drink was. He took a tentative sip.

"Is this caralluma?" Levitien said with more spirit than he had shown a moment before.

"Yes." Zejela responded with some surprise. "It will help—"

"I know what it does." Levitien said harshly. But then softened. "Thank you." He drank from the bowl greedily.

Vaten heard Levitien's gulps and followed his lead. After taking a swig, he said, "Zejela. I know we are on a boat on the sea. But where are we going? We deserve to know."

Levitien slapped the floorboards with his hand in support.

"You are correct," Zejela said. "We are at sea. I did not tell you of our escape from Zevaco because I did not want to worry you more."

Vaten had not been worried about leaving Zevaco until now. "What escape? What do you mean?"

"The traitors are in control of Zevaco and its people," Zejela said. "They will come after us, if they are not coming already. They have convinced the people there I am responsible for the death of our Elders and our nation's upheaval."

"And they probably don't like that you dug us up," Levitien added, straining through shivers to laugh.

"We didn't wait to find out," Zejela said. "We rescued you, gathered a few trustworthy friends, rode to the sea, took a ship, and left. But our crew is small, and if the traitors make haste, they will catch us soon enough. Certainly, before we arrive."

"Arrive?" Vaten said. "Arrive where? You haven't told us—"

The door to the cabin flew open. Vaten felt the wind from the door's movement pass him and then heard the door hit the other side of the frame, two planks of wood clapping.

"Bas!" the booming voice of Aloc said.

Zejela glanced at Aloc with disapproval. Aloc shrugged and replied, "What? He deserve knowing. It his home."

Bas. He was going home. Vaten had nearly forgotten about the place. "Is it true?" he asked. He paused a moment but not long enough for Zejela to answer and, betraying his excitement, said again, "Zejela. Is it true?"

"Yes," she said. "We are returning to Bas."

"I thought..." Levitien groaned again, though this time it was the sound of a man trying to break free from some restraint. "...it was impossible to get to Bas. That is what you told us when we landed."

There were the sounds of chuckles in the room. Vaten wondered how many people were listening to the conversation; how many people were with them on this journey.

"Yes, well, it was the truth for you. Crossing the sea is something we have perfected over many attempts. If you tried, it would have been an assured failure. We know the ways of the sea. We know its paths and trails, like those worn in the dirt." Zejela stood and walked to the door to close it. "And we will make it to Bas, as long as the traitors do not catch us first."

Vaten grinned with his mouth open wide. He saw visions of the land he knew and reunions with those he had left behind. And once back on his homeland, all would be like it had been before he left.

No doubt could sour his mood. Whether it was a land of famine or plenty, friend or foe, misery or delight; it was still his home. He could not wait to return to it.

***

SOMEWHERE IN LEVITIEN'S MIND, in a dark corner of a room with no windows and locked doors—no way for someone to see him—he smiled a fiendish grin. He only needed to survive the trip at sea, and he had done that before. Then his plan would be a success. Nearly, he reminded himself. Not yet. There was still one more thing to be done.

Despite all his troubles, the failure lurking under each step, he was so close to everything he worked for and everything his father had wanted from him. Salvation would be his.

# CHAPTER 39

SAVIQUE WAS THIRSTY. IT was the only consistent feeling he'd had since he and Vrai left Nouv'eau. He had been, in no particular order: anxious, sad, angry, morose, thoughtful, content, optimistic, excited, and then anxious again. The feelings came and went easily, some quickly, while others lingered.

But he was always thirsty.

Even after they found a nest of beetles—Vrai stepped in a ditch and found his leg covered in the crawling black bugs, but at least they weren't stinging grapplers—his hunger was satiated but his thirst never diminished. And it wore on him.

The horse Savique rode—it would forever be Eyvo-Ille's horse, he decided—seemed unbothered by the entire ordeal. Day after day it rose, ate a meal of desiccated grasses and shrubs, carried Savique until nightfall, then lay and rested alongside its rider. Even as he swayed on its back and his skin cracked and bled, the horse rode on.

But it should not have taken this long. They had been travelling for more than two weeks and Savique had not seen the rivers that descended the mountains to their east and flooded the land below. He had not glimpsed the familiar trees of the Tentir Forest. He had not traveled over the familiar wet clay from which beans flourished. He had seen none of the landmarks he expected.

And once the spit in his mouth dried for good and the sun no longer caused him to sweat, Savique snapped.

"Where are we?" He said to Vrai as though the man had insulted him. "None of this looks familiar and we should have arrived at the estate days ago."

Vrai glared at Savique. "Calm yourself already. I know the route! We are still several days out."

"You did not answer my question!" Savique yelled. "Where are we? Have you taken us on some convoluted diversion so that I may never return to the estate?"

"Why would I—Convoluted? You know nothing about—"

"I know how to get to the estate. And this is not it!" Savique threw his arms to the sky and shook them wildly.

Vrai waved a finger at him. "You are wrong! It is the way, but it avoids—"

"Avoids what? Ever arriving?"

"No, you fool. It avoids lands no longer safe for us."

The answer surprised Savique, calming some of his rage. "What do you mean, no longer safe?"

"Many of the lands in Oyonnax and Ortolan—maybe all of Bas—have become dangerous. You may have been safe riding with the Noye horde, but as two travelers, we would be carved like the pigs that once roamed here."

"You mean they..." Savique's eyes narrowed, his anger now gone, replaced by a growing confusion and disgust. "They eat...people?"

Vrai nodded. "The world and its people have been transformed since you left."

"I have seen the changes, but I never thought..."

"I know," Vrai said. "Many horrors awaited the Lord's laborers. You may have seen the change in the land, yes, but not the change in the people who relied on it."

"Enough to force them to such savagery?" Savique shook his head. "Such sacrilege?"

"Yes. I watched some of it, maybe even caused some of it. There was so little left towards the end and Crevir ensured he had enough. We had enough. The rest fought each other for nothing. But when you're starving, you believe the lies easily. Crevir knew that."

"You—You let this happen? Why did you not stop it?"

Vrai chuckled. "Stop what? The drought? What was I to do, force water from the sky? Grow food from dust? There was nothing to stop. Nothing to do. And I was hungry too."

Savique exhaled loudly but said nothing.

Vrai continued, "All throughout Ortolan, it was the same. Storehouses emptied and estates fell. When there is no food left, everything breaks down quite quickly. And now, even Nouv'eau falters, with its once significant supplies nearly empty. The city grows restless. Too many venture there for rescue, swelling the city and its animosities. It is only a matter of time."

"And this is why people destroy their spirits? Eat their own?"

"Yes, that is why. Like the rest of us, all they do now is try to survive."

Savique reached down and grabbed a handful of dirt. He sat for a spell watching small particles of dust be carried away on the breeze, then said, "So...nothing remains at Crevir's Estate?"

Vrai shrugged. "A few remain because they have nowhere else to go. They survive on what they find, perhaps a seed here or a nut there. But they will not last long. The place is dying. All places are."

"No." Savique shook his head. "We die. Places change, but they will remain forever."

"Then why do you—"

"Because...I must see it one more time before I go. It is the land of my family. A land..." He sighed. "It occupies a part of me."

"And to look for clues about Vaten's whereabouts?"

Savique stared at Vrai as he ran his dry tongue over his broken lips. He wondered if it mattered, but he didn't say it. Instead, he said, "Yes, that too."

***

Vrai had not been wrong about the estate, though it was still far worse than Savique's most dire visions. The camp had been abandoned, the storehouses toppled, even Crevir's residence looked beyond repair. And that said nothing of the land. The trees in the grove stood bare and gray. The fields no longer existed. In the place where they had once been, now was only dirt and dust.

They rode through the camp, then came to a stop beside Vaten's hut. It looked the same as Savique's hut, if not more dilapidated from its lack of recent use. And though Savique had assumed emotion would overcome him when he finally saw where his son lived, he felt little.

"What did you expect to find?" Vrai inquired.

"I don't know. I wanted to see the place for myself. I thought maybe I would recognize it and it would help me know him in some way." The words came out half as a question and half as a statement. Savique didn't know which it was. "But it is only an empty hut."

Vrai nodded.

\*\*\*

VRAI HAD WANTED TO say, "Of course it is," but swallowed the words.

He was not callous towards Savique and his plight, but he wished the man would have listened to him. If he had, it would have saved them time. But seeing the death of the place differed from hearing of it. And once Savique saw it, he would have no choice but to ride on with Vrai.

It was an idea that struck Vrai while the two men raced from Nouv'eau after the Noye raid. At that point, Vrai had no intention of going back to the estate. He was free of it, and Crevir, and was ready to be among his people again.

But he remembered the words the Istori Ascetics spoke to Savique long ago. *You will save them all, you will find the lost...*

Vrai believed them when they were spoken. Savique would help them discover the true purpose of the mark lifted from Crevir. And by doing so, he would help restore the glory of the Noye. Help save his people. And that is why, all those years ago, he had risked his own life to ensure Navo-Ille and Eyvo-Ille saved Savique.

Vrai then went back to work on the estate, until one day he found himself, a free man, running beside Savique who had discovered nothing, had restored no one's glory, and had saved no one's people. Worse, many of the Noye's best warriors were dead. Doubt bloomed in Vrai's mind.

He was angry. It was unjust. Vrai had waited patiently, in the employ of a barbarian, for his deliverance. And when it finally came, it did so with none of the expected gains. No, if anything, it came at an unbelievable cost.

He chided himself for believing in prophecies. The Ascetics' words were lies. The mark they stole from Crevir was as important as a plough to a frog. Prophecy? That is what fools believed in. The world worked in realities, not fantasies.

But no matter what he did, the words of the Istori Ascetics would not leave him. The belief would not leave him either, and it fought a war of attrition against his doubt. Unfair. Difficult. The Ascetics had said that too; he remembered. They urged Savique to forge ahead even in the face of indescribable darkness. Vrai should do the same.

And as he ran, belief eventually won. He decided he would still deliver Savique to the Noye, as he did all those years ago. He would do his best to ensure Savique discovered the purpose of the mark and save the Noye. It only required getting the man to follow him. At least he was already doing that while they ran.

But once they stopped running, he knew Savique would seek his home and his people. Vrai wanted the same. And trying to restrict Savique's freedom was bound to be met with resistance. He knew it because he would have resisted all the same.

However, there was an important difference between the two men. Vrai knew where his people were and knew some were still alive. Savique could not say the same about his son.

Vrai hoped that fact would lead Savique back to the Noye, the only friends he had left. If he wanted to find his son, he would need the Noye's help.

It hadn't exactly worked that way. No plans are without limitations, he laughed to himself, even those of the Ascetics. But now, standing in front of Vaten's empty hut, Savique saw almost exactly what Vrai thought he would see. And he said almost exactly what Vrai wanted him to say.

"What else is there to do?" Savique asked.

"Friend," Vrai said, reaching out and grabbing his shoulder. "There are still those who would help you in your pursuit. You overlook those who stand nearest, like the tree who misses the ferns at its base."

"Of who do you speak?" Savique said. "I run short of those who set in my shadow."

Vrai grinned. "Navo, of course."

\*\*\*

NAVO-ILLE STOOD AND BREATHED deeply. It was how she began each morning to stretch her sore bones and clear her mind for the day's duties. And though she was not as strong as she once was, she was not useless either. Most days she could clean the abattoir, organize the furriers, and instruct the children before her energy departed.

But on this day, there came an interruption to her morning routine. One of her students, Povie-Ose, ran to Navo-Ille's doorstep hollering about something. At first, she thought the sound may only have been him playing games with the other children. But the urgency in his voice made her realize something was amiss.

"Navo! Navo!" Povie-Ose said. "Strangers approach the camp. There are lots, but their weapons aren't raised. They wear a blue symbol upon their dark cloaks. Do you know them?"

Navo-Ille thought briefly, then said, "I do not. Prepare the defenses as best we can. Until we are sure of their intentions, we assume they are hostile."

"Yes. Good. I'll let the others..." He ran off before he could finish the sentence.

Navo-Ille knew he would get the attention of the guards in the camp. If there was one thing Povie-Ose was good at, it was getting attention. The only problem was there were a few guards left; most of the Ose had not returned from their ride with her sister.

Navo-Ille walked from her hut to her horse, mounted it and trotted slowly towards the barrier wall, a small scattering of stones and bricks, waving away concerned glances as she did. "Stay your worries," she said. "There will be no battles on this day." But even she was unsure whether they were the truth.

Soon after she arrived at the wall, a woman with black hair streaked with white, and a long scar on her neck, approached Navo-Ille. Their garb was as Povie-Ose had described it, but he missed an important detail; their blades, arrows, and shields all were painted blue.

Navo-Ille straightened her back and said, "Welcome I am Navo of the Ille, Elder of the Noye. What is your business here?"

"Greetings Navo," the woman said. "I am Zejela and I am here to speak to you of a tree. I hear you have a stone."

"Yes." Navo-Ille nodded as though it were a common request, but her mind spun with questions. "Let us speak in private. I trust blades are not needed." She pointed to the men behind Zejela.

"They will be no bother to you, as long as you are no bother to them." Zejela gestured at the handful of young men holding spears shakily atop their horses.

Navo-Ille waved them off, then dismounted her horse, turned, and walked toward her hut. Zejela followed.

Seated on a tree stump within the hut, Navo-Ille faced Zejela, who sat on the ground. From her vantage point, Navo-Ille could see through the front of the hut and out into the courtyard. If any trouble were to start, she would know before Zejela and draw the dagger hid in the far side of the stump. She may no longer have been a warrior, but Navo-Ille could still throw a dagger.

A tense silence hung over the hut before Navo-Ille said, "You wish to speak of a tree? Then speak."

"I come here peacefully, out of respect for you and your people," Zejela said. "The mark you stole cannot be used. You must return it to us."

"And where are you from, Zejela? That is not a Noye name. Not a V'eauvian name. Not Versudian either." Navo-Ille shook her head. "I have ridden Bas my whole life and have not heard such a name. Are you from the isles?"

"Where I am from is not important. You—"

"Not important to you, perhaps. Important to me." Navo-Ille put her hand on her chest. Then bowed her head slightly. "So tell me, where are you from?"

"I am not interested in answering your questions. I know you stole the mark and the stone it contains. It did not belong to the man you stole it from. It does not belong to you. It belongs to its creator. Me. Return it or you risk bringing ruin to your people and to all of Bas."

"I do not know of what—"

"It is important that you listen to me," Zejela said plainly, as if reciting a pledge she had spoken countless times before. "We will not allow the Faine and its fruit to be used again. We will not allow its power to be wielded. We know where the mark leads—we have been to the city before—and we will be back. You would be careful not to make enemies of us. Blades in tree stumps will not help you then."

Navo-Ille did not react. She was stunned, but she knew provocation when she heard it. Zejela wanted to make Navo-Ille angry, to elicit a response. Instead, she calmly said, "Zejela, from wherever you are from. We do not seek to make enemies of anyone. I assure you I do not have a stone, a mark, or anything. We use many trees, for fire, food, arrows, all sorts of—"

"If you do not have the mark, then I am sorry for you. You will not survive the year. The Lord and his V'eauvian army are on their way, exterminating Noye wherever they find them. We would have saved you to prevent you from using the mark. But now...I don't imagine I'll see you again." Zejela stood up and walked from the hut.

This time, Navo-Ille could not hide her horror. Her face dropped as she stared at Zejela's back. If it was true, if the Lord and the V'eauvians rode against them, it would not only be the end of her. It would be the end of the Noye.

*Where are you, Eyvo? Have you failed? And where is that Eau-forsaken mark? A curse more than a savior.*

Povie-Ose ran to Navo-Ille. "Are you all right?"

With tears in her eyes, Navo-Ille responded, "No, Povie. We are not all right."

# CHAPTER 40

SYAIS SAT ATOP HER horse and gazed at a break in the forest. They had ridden for days and had seen nothing but the same dead trees extending forever. Here, however, was something different. An absence, exactly what she sought. A grin burst onto her face.

The clearing was not only confirmation the map was real and Seule's translations were correct; it was confirmation her hard work was not in vain. It was a miracle. No, not a miracle. It was her will. She had finally contorted fate to her desires. She had finally won.

"We are here," she said to Ajeau.

While Ajeau wandered the site aimlessly, Syais strode towards a wall of rocks on the far side of the clearing. It was the location of the campsite, and it was Passil's best guess at where she should begin her search. It proved to be wise counsel.

The same symbol gracing her charts stared back at her from the center of the camp. It was a wooden replica of the design, but it was the same. And it sat atop a pattern of three interlocking rings with what appeared to be Balafre carvings on them. She didn't need to search at all.

A little obvious, she thought. Then again, without the charts, without knowing what it meant, it was just a pile of wood. Some design. Anyone passing by who saw it would have thought someone made ornate fire pits or models and ignored it.

But, to Syais, it was everything.

She stood in awe for a moment, then approached the wooden carving slowly and laid her hands on it as though to make sure it really existed. And as she drew her hands along the wood, feeling its brittleness and its cracks, she realized it should have been fragile, broken or even infested, but it was not. It was glorious in its resoluteness.

Now she simply had to acquire what she came for. Thanks to Seule, she knew where the seeds were. In his explanations, he had described how the markers worked—"the long points of the symbols always pointed in the direction of interest," he had told her. But here, the long point indicated down. She sighed in frustration, realizing what she sought lay buried under the wooden object.

Syais could not move the creation; it was too large and there were no places to grab that would allow her the leverage. She could not break the thing either. But a solution came to her quickly. It was onerous, but it would work.

She got down on her knees, took out her daggers, and began scraping the ground furiously. She resolved to dig beside the sculpture until she reached what was below it.

The daggers held up well to the digging and, despite a few nicks and cuts to her hands, the entire process was a great success. And it took far less time than she originally thought it would.

Kneeling over the hole she dug, Syais reached down and grabbed the bag she had uncovered. Both the size and the weight of the thing surprised her. It was nearly the size of her fist and as heavy as metal. How could this be a seed? But it had to be. The charts could not have been right about everything but this.

And though she believed it, she did not believe it at the same time. No one had seen such things since the time of the One Tribe, and many had questioned whether they existed at all. But most unbelievable was that she stood alongside the very person for whom the seed was meant. As Eau themself ordained it to be.

When she stood up, bag in hand, and said something to Ajeau, Syais thought only of her impending place atop the world.

Then, the wind from a passing arrow disturbed her.

*** 

THE SCREAM RIPPED THROUGH the forest. It sent birds flying into the air and mice into their burrows. It seemed to break the branches from trees and roll dislodged brush along the ground. Even after she stopped, the echo sent her tones into the blue sky.

Ajeau struggled against Syais's grip instinctively. She had seen the dagger pulled from its sheath and knew then what would happen. But then the words Syais had spoken came to her in fragments. "Trust me...going to fight...save us both...this is going to hurt."

Syais had been right; it hurt. But Ajeau didn't understand anything else the woman had said. If she was to fight and save them, why would Syais injure her? In Ajeau's condition, she could not save anyone.

Ajeau glanced down only to see a river of blood pouring from her, the dagger only now being removed from her wound. The pain seemed to slow time, but that was only a small taste of what was to come.

Syais held onto Ajeau's arm with one hand and fumbled with a bag with her other. Then, Syais opened the seed, took a piece of innards, and rubbed it into Ajeau's open wound. Ajeau felt a sharp pulse of pain and howled once again, but then stopped.

Ajeau's eyes narrowed in confusion. She felt no pain and everything around her calmed. There was no noise, no movement. A great stillness had set in; even Syais seemed to be affected.

She could not understand what had happened. A moment ago Syais had rubbed pieces of a seed into her arm. She was an image of furious movement, but now was motionless. Frozen. Her eyes were wide, but her pupils did not move. Her hand did not move. Ajeau wasn't even sure Syais's chest heaved with breath.

But Ajeau could still move, she made sure of that. She wiggled her fingers, curled her toes, and rotated her head from side to side. It changed her point of view, but nothing within it changed. Even the blood that gushed out of her wound still flowed at the same rate. Her body had not been affected in the least.

Neither had her mind, and she wondered if she was hallucinating, or worse, dead. Maybe it was some fate even worse than that.

In a fit of frightened rage, Ajeau thrashed with abandon. It was not directed against anyone or anything, except perhaps a growing dread within her. But in her writhing, she discovered something which tempered her growing fear. She still affected the world, and it still reacted to her. Even if the results were odd.

When Ajeau threw her arm around wildly, it connected with Syais's shoulder. And when it did, she saw the reaction it made. Syais's shirt and shoulder, expectedly, recessed. What was curious was that the indent was clearly visible to Ajeau even after her hand moved. The shirt and shoulder underneath remained indented for a long while until eventually bouncing back into place.

It was as though the world outside her was made of clay. It was set and inert unless she touched it. Then it reacted to her touch, only to set and become inert once again. But even that, Ajeau would soon discover, was not precisely correct.

For the moment, however, Ajeau's trepidation had been replaced by a sense of wonder. Not with what was happening, but at what she could do. If the world was clay, to mold as she saw fit, then she could achieve anything. She could find Vaten, even if she had to search the entire world. She would get her vengeance before the Zevacese even knew she existed.

But first she had to free herself from Syais's grip.

It was a surprisingly arduous task. Ajeau assumed that because Syais was malleable, she would also be weak. That was not the case. The woman's grasp on Ajeau's arm was still as forceful as ever.

After a moment of concentrated effort on one of Syais's fingers, Ajeau finally made a breakthrough. Syais's first finger popped off Ajeau's arm. Unlike Syais's shoulder, the skin of Ajeau's arm reformed immediately, covered in blood though it was.

Then, as Ajeau worked on the next finger, she suddenly felt Syais's grip relax. Her arm was free of their grasp but not their touch like a vice that had reversed its pressure by the slightest margin. It only further confounded her.

She stared at the fingers near her arm and saw them move. Even though it was nearly imperceptible to her, they moved on their own. She could feel each finger lose touch with her skin.

The world was not clay after all. It did not wait for Ajeau to change it. Then, there was only one explanation she could offer: the world was slow. Or she was fast. Faster than an arrow's flight, faster than the flicker of a flame, faster even than the wind.

She understood now. And somehow Syais had known it would happen; Ajeau would be imbued with this...power. When she heard Syais's words play back in her mind one more time, *You are going to fight. You are going to save us both.* She knew they were true.

Then, in an instant, the quiet world Ajeau had lived in for the last few moments disappeared. The calm, the silence, the stillness were all gone. She was once again flooded with pain and the commotion of the world. It was jarring and overwhelming, as if someone smashed two rocks next to her ear while moving frantically inches from her face.

"What are you doing? You must hurry before they reach us!" Syais shouted.

Ajeau heard the woman yelling at her, but it only made things worse. She closed her eyes to gain some peace from the surrounding chaos, but there was no serenity to be had. Ajeau heard the footsteps and voices of the attackers coming closer. Then an arrow struck the tree next to her.

Syais grabbed Ajeau and shook her. "There is not much time left. There is not much seed left. Next time, fight. Hear me? Stand and fight!"

Ajeau's eyes sprung open in time to see Syais grab another piece of seed. This time, Syais did not bother holding Ajeau's arm as she ground the seed into Ajeau's open wound.

A moment later, the pain again subsided, and a furious energy took its place. Ajeau was back in a world without chaos. But this time, she knew what she had to do.

Ajeau took a dagger from Syais, stood up, and ran to where she had last heard the attackers. It did not take her long to spot them; they were not hiding from the two cornered women. They were advancing on an outnumbered enemy.

The soldiers were wrong. They just didn't know it yet. And until the moment Ajeau stood in front of a man with a yellow hood, took the arrow off his bowstring, and plunged Syais's dagger into his chest and then his neck, they thought they were the aggressors.

Ajeau stepped to the side, stared at the second yellow-hooded man, and once again, thrust the dagger into his stomach. Then stopped and stared. Blood had not yet dampened the cloth he wore. The expression on the man's face had not changed. His pupils grew, the first sign that his body knew its defenses had been breached, but the muscles in his face remained unchanged.

While Ajeau rushed through the throng of attackers, a small smile crept across her lips. The possibilities of her power thrilled her. Not only did she have the strength to fend off any enemy, but she could also bend the world to her will. Whatever she desired, she could make happen, as Syais had said.

Dreams of vengeance raced through her head. Not vengeance against the yellow-clad soldiers she currently eliminated, but against the blue monsters who had taken so much from her. Each attacker was the person who killed Seule or the large man who took Vaten from her in the woods. If only she could have rescued Vaten from their vermin clutches. Still, she stabbed them all.

All twelve men and women died before the first one fell to his knees, before the ground even felt his blood. It was not a fight; it was a massacre.

Never once did Ajeau think about what her power would cost or why it was given to her by a woman who cultivated power for herself. Instead, she returned to Syais's side, pleased. When she arrived next to the woman, she found her mouth still open as if Ajeau had never left.

Ajeau rested and waited for the world to come crashing back upon her. It took some time; she did not know how long and whether time was the same concept it had been earlier that day, but when she came back to the world it was as jarring and overwhelming as the first time. No matter her preparation, when the world returned, it engulfed her.

*** 

When Syais glanced at Ajeau, she worried the girl had lost her spirit again and left them open to attack. But Syais soon realized the sounds coming from around them were not voices or footfalls, they were groans and whimpers, the sounds of the dying. She breathed deeply in relief; Ajeau had done her duty.

"You did well, Hijeuse," Syais said softly while placing her hand on Ajeau's head.

"Th...th...they..." Ajeau shook and then went limp and lost consciousness.

"That's all right," Syais said with her hand still on Ajeau's head. "You can rest now. You need it. You will need all your strength soon enough. This is only the beginning. Do you hear me? There is so much more for you to do before your time is up."

Syais looked to the trees and grinned.

# CHAPTER 41

VATEN STOOD NEXT TO Levitien and grasped the railing running the length of the deck as the ship lurched and pitched in the waves. Each swell that came their way sprayed them with water. The seas were rough, not from storms but from the wind charging unchecked across the blue expanse. And though it hastened their travel, it unnerved the sightless man.

It had not yet been a week since the two men awoke and though Vaten remained without his vision, Levitien had improved markedly. He moved around the boat with a dexterity that contradicted the seriousness of his condition only days ago. In his interactions with Vaten and the rest of his shipmates, he even appeared cheerful. It was as though the soil under the earth stripped him of his cynicism and instilled optimism in its place.

The change in heart was one not far from Vaten's own. The promise of returning to Bas bolstered his spirits, even if his sight never returned. He could still feel the wind and smell the salt air and taste his food and hear the voices of those who spoke to him. He had much, even if it was not all.

Of course, sight would have made it easier for Vaten to move about the ship. The ship's rocking often surprised him. Once he nearly fell overboard when a large wave struck the hull of the ship, and it listed strongly to one side. Luckily, someone grabbed him as he tumbled and helped keep him upright.

Levitien helped where he could—it was part of his newfound zest—though it did not extend much beyond helping Vaten from one point to another. Indeed, though they had much to speak about, the two men exchanged few words of consequence since Vaten first saw an ill Levitien on a cabin floor.

Without his sight, Vaten never knew who was around him or could listen in on a conversation without his knowledge. It made him feel watched, whether or not that was the case, and he shut himself up because of it.

But Levitien was also far too busy helping the Zevacese—Zejela and Aloc included—with the ship work to make time for Vaten. He called out movements for the sails, directed repairs, and kept watch if needed. It shocked Vaten.

The man who once casually plotted her death, now cooperated with Zejela to ensure their ship sailed true; the man who once raged at Vaten for assimilating into the Sentries, now sang songs with their leader; the man who once tried desperately to escape the Zevacese now labored for their success at all costs.

It did not seem like something the man Vaten knew would do. And there, standing next to Levitien, grasping the rails of the ship, he realized there was much about the man he did not know. And he sought to change that.

"Why was a man from Rigolade in V'eauvian territory?" Vaten yelled over the sound of crashing waves.

"What?" Levitien said, leaning his head toward Vaten. "What did you say, kid?"

"When we first met, you told me you were from Rigolade and I asked you that same question: why a man from Rigolade was in the North. You never told me. I remember you never told me."

"Ha!" It was a sardonic chuckle. "You have a good memory, kid. I don't even recall telling you where I was from. Maybe I lost some memories under the earth." Levitien knocked his head. Then shook it, remembering Vaten could not see him.

"So what is it?" Vaten said. "Why were you there? Tell me. Tell me something."

"It doesn't matter why I was there." Levitien had an ocean full of deflections. "Let's say I was running skin or wheat. Fruits for the Lord or iron for the guard. What of it?"

"Maybe nothing. I don't know." Vaten shook his head and threw up his hands momentarily. Then quickly returned them to the side of the ship. "I know about your family, that you were stewards, that you ate wild exotic fruits. But in all of it, nothing of you. I don't know an Eau damned thing about you. So, answer me. The first question I ever asked you. What were you doing in V'eauvian territory?"

"I'll tell you what I told you then. I was looking for something." He grimaced, realizing the sentence betrayed an earlier lie.

Vaten missed it, but stomped in frustration regardless. "What were you looking for? The same thing as the Zevacese?" He nodded at the man, accusing him with his head. "Were you all playing some game in my home, a game with rules I was never told? Or was I only a bug crushed by something bigger? What was it?" Sea water sprayed his face, masking tears.

"Why don't you ask them? Ask Zejela." Levitien pointed at the woman again, forgetting Vaten could not see him. "Ask her what they were looking for. Why it started a coup on their perfect island? Let's see what she says, huh?"

"If you know, tell me!" Vaten's muscles tensed. If he had not been clutching the ship, he might have swung at Levitien. "Everyone knows why my life was upended except me. You—"

"It's not me you should be mad at, but them. The Zevacese."

Vaten breathed deeply, steading his emotions. "I am. I am angry at them. But I understand them. I know what they were fighting for. What Zejela and Aloc are still fighting for. But you. I don't even know—"

"Kid, what has gotten into you? I'm a prisoner here, just like you, remember? I didn't ask for any of this. None of it! You hear me?" Not even Levitien knew if the outrage was an act. "You think you lost something on Bas? You have no idea. My whole life changed on a whim, not even my own. You want to know what I was looking for—"

A shout came from Aloc and stole Vaten's words.

Levitien glanced in Aloc's direction and saw the man waving at them. "Aloc is calling for us," he said.

"No." Vaten shook his head. "No, I'm not letting you slither away again. Answer me! What were you looking for?"

Vaten would get no answer. Only the feeling of a large hand on his shoulder and the words from Aloc, "Silly! Don't go over side here. Come! We speak."

The large man then grabbed Vaten by the arm, nearly ripping it out of its socket, and pulled him towards Zejela's quarters at the far end of the boat.

Levitien breathed and shook his head. He had been reckless, dumb, and if not for Aloc, he would have been trapped. He did not know whether he would have given away his secret, but he chastised himself for getting close. And with Bas so near, he couldn't let the façade crumble now.

He glanced at the waves. *Isn't that what you trained me for, dad? To be like sea water to a thirsty man; only a deception. Everything but nothing.* Then he turned and followed Aloc.

***

375

THE ELDER'S CABIN WAS dark and cramped and every so often a hint of Levitien's sick could be smelt as though it were a mouse hiding in the woodwork poking its head out to surveil the room, then retreating upon seeing the threatening creatures nearby. Despite this, the cabin was one of the few places on the ship one could get out of the sea's spray and find a modicum of peace.

Zejela stood when the three men entered her quarters and welcomed them. "Thank you for coming."

Aloc nodded, but no one said a word. There was no choice to be made, at least not for Vaten and Levitien.

"First, let me say, our trip is progressing well," Zejela said. "And some of that thanks goes to you, Levitien. Without you catching the fault in the rudder, we would have lost even more precious time."

Levitien smirked and began to say something, then stopped himself. He let the smile fall from his face and said earnestly, "It was easy to miss and I'm glad I could help."

"Yes, well." Zejela pursed her lips as though his genuine response was unexpected. "That is not all. The winds have been strong and true. We've been under full sail for days now. Of course, that means Wehlat and Ryiera are as well. And they no doubt run with a much larger crew."

Aloc shook his head. "Large crew slow ship if not careful."

"Maybe." She waved her hand dismissively. "Regardless, let us hope fortune continues to be on our side. But that is not why I had Aloc fetch you. No, that concerns something far more serious than this voyage. Our arrival."

***

MOMENTS BEFORE ALOC GRABBED Vaten and walked him below deck, Aloc and Zejela spoke about their plans for when they arrived on Bas. There was still much to be determined. First among them was what to do when they landed. The Zevacese were not ones to announce their existence on Bas.

But the urgency, and the small crew with which they sailed, meant they were in no position to cover their tracks. The ship they sailed on would have to be brought to shore.

"If that happens," Zejela said, "all our years of concealment will have been for naught."

"So be it. This is a new Zevaco." Aloc stretched his arms as though he presented the new land to Zejela.

"No." Zejela sighed. "That is exactly what we're trying to stop. That is what we left behind."

"We left behind traitors who only acted to benefit themselves. To empower themselves. To enrich themselves. We act to save a land—a people!"

She ran both hands through her hair. "This is for the good of Zevaco, then?"

"Always!" Aloc said with conviction. "Secrets are how we arrived here in the first place, and that has not worked well for us. Or our people."

Zejela nodded slowly, still considering Aloc's argument. "Then who should we tell? All of Bas? Who gets to know our secrets?"

"What do you think the Bassians on our ship will do when they return home? You expect them to remain silent? To say nothing of us to anyone? One speaks more than the wind blows these days."

Zejela chuckled. "I agree and that is why I have withheld our plans for them, too."

Aloc sighed, slapped his leg with an open hand, and shook his head. "That is also a problem! More secrets! You would tell no one anything, not even the crew that works tirelessly to sail us to safety."

Zejela said nothing. They both knew she had not told the crew anything.

He pointed a finger at her. "If we told them, they would know why they worked. It would make them work harder to hasten our voyage."

"No." Zejela shook her head. "To tell them now is to risk our lives on their word. What if they were to disagree? Or stop working? What then? We would be adrift, waiting for the traitors to find us and end us. There would be no escape this time."

Aloc put his hand on Zejela's shoulder and stared into her eyes. He spoke sincerely. "These people come with us because they believe in us. They trust us. And so we must trust them, too. Without trust, without revealing ourselves, Zevaco will fall to insurgents again and again."

"That is foolish. Sentiment over thought. These are not your Sentries—"

"Two are!" Aloc laughed.

Zejela let a small chuckle escape through her nose. She had forgotten about Vaten and Levitien's initiation. Though the notion that they were the only other Sentries on board, perhaps anywhere, was absurd.

"Let us tell them," Aloc said. "See their reaction and whether they abandon us."

"They are not the same as the others. They are—"

"Careful, you know what those words sound like."

Zejela did. She was about to call Vaten and Levitien the same thing some of the Zevacese had called her when she first arrived there. Some called her it to this day. An outsider. She would not be so cruel.

"Alright," Zejela said, finally relenting to Aloc. "We will start with them. Bring them here."

Moments later, Aloc escorted the two Bassians into the cabin to Zejela's welcome.

***

RYIERA SAT IN A small, dank room next to Wehlat and a man she did not know. There were no windows and the only door, a sturdy thick sheet of wood with a crank lock, was sealed shut. A lantern set upon the wall cast a warm orange glow over the occupants' faces and masked the bloodstains on the floor. Some were wet and fresh, though plenty were dry.

"Another failure," Ryiera said, as she removed the knife from the unknown man's wound. A red stream ran from a large gash on his arm, flowed down the length of his limb to a cuff of rope, then dripped to the floor. "I am losing hope."

Wehlat shook his head. "Do not be impatient. We will get this right if it takes a thousand attempts. You know great accomplishments take time."

"But we are making no progress. Yes, we have time and the materials. But how long until we run out of both? We wagered much on this working and so far—"

"Do you believe it does not work? Do you believe our purpose here is based on lies?"

"No, I believe. I only..." Ryiera swung an arm toward the man next to her. "I want to know why. What are we doing wrong?"

Wehlat shrugged. "There are no instructions here. Nothing to follow." His voice grew confident. "We are the discoverers. Like our ancestors who found this place, we will discover something new, wholly unlike what was before."

"But someone knows. Or knew. They knew what to do with these." Ryiera gestured to a box covered with a cloth under the table. "Even Zejela knew something—knew more than us."

"Who knows what that outsider knew!" Wehlat slammed the arm of his chair with his fist. "She came to her knowledge through personal experience. We do not have such a luxury here."

The unknown man stirred and drew the two Elders' attention. They stared at him briefly, not in disbelief—they knew the man was alive—but curious whether he was waking. There was no telling when one would awake from their sleep.

Not that it mattered; the subjects never remembered anything. They had no dreams nor heard any sounds. It was as though no time passed for them, like someone had cut a section of rope and tied the two separate parts together. They woke up thinking they were in a time before.

But this man was not waking. It was only a convulsion. Not an uncommon reaction, but not a common one either. And since the man was still unconscious, Wehlat and Ryiera were free to return to their conversation.

"And you are sure Zejela mentioned nothing to you about the ritual?" Ryiera said, not for the first time. "Never said what to do with these parts? Nothing?"

"I told you, she would not reveal anything to me." Wehlat waved his hand as if trying to swat a fly. "All I know comes from our scholars, same as you. There is something here we are missing, I agree, but I do not know what."

"Then what are we to do? Are we to continue the same process, simply hoping for different results?"

"You speak as if that is a bad idea. What would you rather do? Give up?" Wehlat scoffed.

Ryiera hung her head and sighed. "No, never that. You know I am with you. But there is one person we know who can give us answers. And she rides on a ship staffed by only a few hands."

"You want to leave for Bas without unlocking the tree?"

"If we move quickly, we would not need to land on Bas. We could intercept them before they arrived. We could get our—"

Suddenly, the unknown man convulsed wildly. Tied to the chair, he did not move, but blood flew from his wounds, spraying against the walls. This time, the Elders looked on with great surprise. The others had settled down after their spasms. But this man had not stopped, his tremors only increased.

Ryiera glanced at Wehlat, who remained fixated on the man. She thought she saw a small smile creep across his face. If it was a smile, she understood why. This was something new; they had gained some piece of knowledge, even if they did not know yet what it was.

The man shook violently now, rattling the chair against the dirt floor, nearly toppling over as the chair lifted off the ground. Ryiera wondered how long the chair would last against such torture. Or their bindings. She picked up the knife in case the man came free.

His eyes burst apart to reveal pupils as small as pinheads. They danced wildly, faster than his convulsions. It was like he was in between two worlds. His body moved in concert with the other world, ripping him apart in Ryiera's.

She continued to stare at him. And for the shortest of moments, his eyes locked with hers. They imparted a look of knowledge and power and fear and regret. She thought it like a man who touched flames, thinking he could control fire with his hands.

Then, all at once, his convulsions stopped.

"Too much...too much...the speed. It..." The man slumped in his chair. His head hung with his chin to his chest, his eyes open wide, but they no longer moved.

"Is he...dead?" Wehlat said as he leaned cautiously towards the man. He made a careful point to stay out of arm's reach.

"I...I think so?" Ryiera's heart raced. It was not an answer, but a piece of the puzzle had been revealed to them.

The man died. Before that, he shook. Before that, they cut him. Before that, he was like all the others. No, he wasn't. There was a vital difference; his kin were not of Zevaco. He had the blood of a Bassian. It was why they chose him.

They were outsiders, after all.

"What was that? All that shaking! My Eau!" Wehlat exclaimed.

"I don't know." Ryiera poked the man with the knife. It broke the skin, but the man remained motionless. "But he was different."

Wehlat nodded and smiled. "So, let's go ask another one who is different. Another one who invaded our land from Bas. Another outsider."

"You mean—"

"Yes, let us gather the remaining soldiers and our best sailors. All who wish adventure against the traitors of our land." He walked to the door and began unlocking it. "We are after Zejela at sunup."

# Chapter 42

"There it is!" Vrai said, pointing into the distance.

Savique followed Vrai's outstretched arm to a small patch of gray on the horizon. It could have been a cluster of desiccated trees, a fallen village or city, a pile of animal bones, or any number of gray features that had scattered the landscape as the two men rode. But this smudge was not any of those other things. It was a Noye camp, pressed against the desert; the home of the Ose.

As he rode closer, Savique marveled at the size of the village. It was a speck compared to Nevant and no larger than half, maybe even a quarter, of a field on Crevir's Estate. It seemed more fit for a band of passing traders than a home for Noye.

As the two men broke the perimeter of the settlement, they were met with cheers and joyful shouts. Young boys and girls rushed to meet them, throwing their hands in the air as their keepers trailed behind. Workers stopped working, stood up to take in the sight. The remaining guards in the camp thrust their spears into the air as though stabbing at the clouds floating overhead.

When Savique realized why the Ose greeted them in such a way, it caused his stomach to rise in his throat and his chest to tighten. Not a single Noye had made it back to the place following their battle against the V'eauvians. And as hard as it was to experience the loss of the Noye at Nouv'eau, now he would have to tell an entire camp what happened.

The welcome was wholly unearned, and tears welled in Savique's eyes.

Vrai brought his horse to a stop in the center of the camp. "Savique," he said, nodding his head at an older woman walking towards them with a slight limp.

Before Savique could wipe the tears from his eyes, Eyvo-Ille's horse whinnied loudly at the woman. If not for the horse's joy, Savique may not have recognized Navo-Ille's appearance, though he found it easy to recognize her presence. And her smile. When it crossed her face, he realized it had not changed since the first time he met her; the first time he met a Noye at all.

"Vrai! Savique! Welcome," Navo-Ille said with her arms stretched wide. "It is a wondrous day to receive two dear friends such as yourselves."

"I'm sorry, Navo." Vrai dismounted his horse and embraced her. "We do not bring joyous news."

Navo-Ille nodded. "Let us talk, as friends do, away from all these inquisitive eyes."

And with a wave of her arm, she sent the camp back to work, play, or whatever they were doing before the riders appeared. Though they met the gesture with furrowed brows and disappointed eyes, the camp followed Navo-Ille's orders.

\*\*\*

THE TWO MEN WALKED with Navo-Ille back to her hut and sat on the ground opposite her. She did not bring them water, food, or ask about their comfort. There was only one thing on her mind.

"Does she live?" Navo-Ille asked, staring past both men.

Vrai glanced at Savique, then to Navo-Ille said, "No. She returned to the earth in Nouv'eau. She nurtures the soil now."

Navo-Ille exhaled deeply, but her reaction was otherwise muted. Her head stayed upright and her hands remained folded over her lap.

"And what of the rest of them?" Navo-Ille said. "Those who rode with her?"

Vrai shook his head. "I don't know. Only a few survivors returned to their camp, but I was not involved in the raid."

Savique stared at the ground and said nothing.

"And what of you? How did you escape?" Navo-Ille eyed Savique, as though she was confused how he could be present without Eyvo-Ille.

"I..." Savique paused, choosing his words carefully. "escaped, with Vrai. Eyvo had already returned. It is what he told me."

Vrai nodded to confirm what Savique said. "The Lord was there. The guard..."

"The Lord?" Navo-Ille's eyes bulged. Then, with a sigh, she closed them and rested her head in her hands. "It would appear all is lost, then. Those dead faster than us in the race by only a step."

"What do you mean?" Vrai asked.

Navo-Ille told them about the visitor who passed through speaking of Lord Balay's ride and the V'eauvians' revenge on the Noye. "I didn't know if it was true. But now, with your report of the losses, it is probable. Our only hope was the mark. And it, too, is gone."

Savique grinned like a man with a secret. "I know where it is," he said proudly.

Vrai turned his head slowly to face Savique, disbelief washing over him. Navo-Ille's eyes grew wide. Her mouth opened and lips peeled back. A smile of excitement, surprise, and appreciation.

"What?" Vrai said. "How? Why didn't—"

"Never mind that." Navo-Ille waved Vrai's words away with her hand. "Where is the mark? Can we retrieve it?"

"Yes." Savique nodded, a wide grin still branded on his face. "Eyvo hid it. She described the place to me before we entered Nouv'eau. She knew as long as one of us lived, we would have the mark."

"Clever. Like her," Navo-Ille said. "So where is it?"

"Outside the Tentir. Near Nevant," he said. "She told me how to find it, where exactly it is buried. She told me to dig for some time when I arrived there."

"Nevant? It will take more than a fortnight to reach Nevant!" Vrai threw up his arms in frustration. "You didn't think to mention this when we were near Crevir's Estate? When we were riding from Nouv'eau? When we were but an arm's length from the place?"

"Calm yourself Vrai," Navo-Ille said. "We will ride there immediately and retrieve the mark. Preparations will begin now. And even a delayed trip will still leave us time before the Lord arrives, if he arrives at all." Navo-Ille stood and walked towards the door of her hut.

Savique did not move. He remained sitting, staring at the spot Navo-Ille had once occupied, the smile slowly disappearing from his face. It was another journey, another step away from what he wanted. He wondered if the Noye's tangled roots would ensnare him forever.

"No," Savique said quietly to the empty space in front of him. Then finally, he stood, turned to face Navo-Ille, and continued. "There is something I need first. An assurance that the debt to me is repaid. Navo, you are the only one alive who knows. You were there—"

If Vrai had been annoyed before, he was angry now. "Enough of this!" he shouted. "Tell us where the mark is or you will receive nothing from us. You will—"

"Vrai!" Navo-Ille broke the man's spirit in a word. Then, to Savique, she said, "Yes, Savique, I remember what Eyvo said on that day. But you are not done riding with us." She smiled.

Savique did not match it. "I have raided, fought, killed, nearly been killed myself." He punctuated each act with his hands. "I have met and enjoyed the company of your people from far and wide. I helped you—can still help you now—but it is time for you to make good. The only thing left in this world for me is the sliver of hope that my son still roams it. All I want is to find him. To know him."

"Yes. It is admirable. But like you care for your family, I care for mine. Everyone here," Navo-Ille gestured out towards the camp, nearly hitting Vrai with her outstretched hand, "every one of the Noye is my family. The mark is the only way I can protect them. That is why you were brought to us. Do you remember the Ascetics? Can you argue with them now? Would you abandon us in our time of greatest need?"

"I am not abandoning you," Savique said. "I have done all I can. Premonitions are wrong; prophecies are wrong. You should know that. And now, I merely no longer care for the mysteries and puzzles of your world. I want what is owed to me."

"The mysteries..." Navo-Ille smiled softly. "They are what make life worth living. Like lightning in a storm. Without it, it's only dull rain. But with it, there is energy, excitement. There is purpose."

"Savique," Vrai said, his voice cool, measured. "You need us as much as we need you now."

"Vrai—" Navo-Ille tried to interrupt him, but his fellow Noye did not stop.

"You have no other friends, no one to help you find your son," Vrai said. "Or help you withstand the drought. Without us, you would have no horse. Do you want to walk the world alone until you die without food or drink? It would not be long. If what you say is true, you want your son, then you will tell us—lead us to where the mark is and we can help you. That is your only chance to gain what you seek."

It was a truth that Savique knew but refused to embrace. Even if the Ascetics were right and he was destined to lead the Noye and save them, he still needed his son. "You are right, Vrai. I need your help, and you need mine. So, what assurances do I have that you will help?"

"We have always been forthright with you," Navo-Ille said as she gave an appreciative nod to Vrai. "From the beginning, we said we would help you after your time with us is done. That deal remains. We will help you find your son, but we need the mark. We need you to lead us or we will perish."

"The mark! What a bother. A burden! Nothing has been right since you took that Eau damned stone..." Savique stood up and turned away from the two men. "Why me?" He said to the ground. "Why is it my duty to save you?"

*Because only you can.* It was the answer the Ascetics gave to the same question all those years ago. Somehow, it made even less sense to him now.

"Savique," Navo-Ille said, trying to get the man's attention back.

He did not hear Navo-Ille call his name and continued speaking to the ground. "...I know nothing! I am as ignorant to its purpose and its use as when we met. How will it save us? How will it save anything? I will not risk—"

"Savique!" Navo-Ille said.

"What?"

"I learned one thing more from our visitor," she said. "We always knew that the mark would lead us to something. To use it as a map or a chart. And now, I know the answer. What will be there when we arrive. The Tree. The City."

"What tree? What city?" Vrai asked, unimpressed.

"Not a city. *The* city."

"You do not mean to say?" Savique said, stunned.

"Yes. The stone will lead us to the great city of the Balafre, the city that holds the Tree of Fate. It leads to the City of Z'eau."

***

SAVIQUE'S HANDS ACHED. THEY were stiff, cracked, and bled. Some of his fingernails broke off, while others bent back and filled with dirt. But he kept digging. *Dig for some time.* The words stuck in Savique's mind, like a tick on a sheep.

As he worked, he said nothing to the man next to him. There was plenty he could have asked Vrai about; why he carved symbols into the trees, what to do about their dwindling supplies, where their return trip would take them, how they would alert the other Noye tribes to join the Ose, and of course, anything about Vaten. But all was silent except for the scraping of dirt.

It had been that way since they left the Ose camp. The mutual respect and trust that had burgeoned in the aftermath of the raid on Nouv'eau evaporated as though it was dew on morning grass. They needed each other, but they did not have to like it.

In the legends following that day, both men would be given credit for finding the mark buried in the ground. As it would be told, both men's hands grabbed the dirt, making a hole in the earth until, in a serendipitous moment, each landed a hand on the box containing the stone. Cheers, smiles, and cries of joy followed.

Reality was not far from the myth. Each man dug until one saw the box and pointed and the other felt it. At that moment, they looked up from the hole they had dug into each other's eyes and smiled. They were not wide smiles of joy, as much as subtle smiles of relief. But they had found the box, the mark it held, and their journey had been a success. At least that is what they thought.

When Savique opened the box and laid eyes on the stone once again, he reacted with the same confusion he had when he first saw it beside Eyvo-Ille. How was *this* supposed to save them from anything?

The stone itself was still shaped into the form of some unknown seed, round with spines and angles like a bean with thorns. Though even the points were abnormal. Two thorns larger than the rest, and one larger than the other, were positioned on either side of the bean.

He passed the mark to Vrai, who scrutinized it. He sighed, shrugged, and as he was about to close the box, something strange happened. The stone moved, vibrated as though shaken by a hummingbird's wing. Then it stopped.

Vrai's eyebrows furrowed. He frowned with confusion. He glanced at Savique, then back at the mark like he was awaiting an answer. None came. He took a step, and the stone moved again. This time, it was not a vibration; the position of the stone had changed. It had shifted and reoriented itself as Vrai moved. Its largest thorn now pointed squarely at Savique.

No matter how Vrai moved the box, no matter the position he took, no matter how far or close he moved to Savique, the largest thorn remained pointed at the man. No, not only at the man, but at a small pouch Savique had carried with him since Nouv'eau.

"What's in the bag?" Vrai asked, his hand moving to the handle of his dagger.

"This." Savique removed a vial of blood from the bag. When he moved it in his hand, the stone's thorn followed as if it was the eye of a predator tracking its prey.

Vrai, no less suspicious, asked, "And whose blood is that? Yours?"

"No. I..." Savique shook his head quickly from side to side. He breathed in short, rapid bursts. "I took it from Nouv'eau. From the workshop where they performed the ritual—the...whatever you call it. That is all I know of it."

Vrai leaned in and squinted his eyes to read the word marked on the vial. He pronounced the word slowly, as though it was foreign. "Hijeuse."

"Do you know what it means?" Savique asked.

Vrai shook his head and said, "We must return to Navo at once. Perhaps she will know what any of this means and know what...or who this Hijeuse is."

Vrai put the mark in his bag while Savique did the same with his vial. Then, the two men mounted their horses and began the long trek back to the Ose. All the while, Savique wondered where he had seen a rock move before.

# CHAPTER 43

AJEAU RACED THROUGH THE forest as quickly as her legs would take her. She darted in between trees, over roots and fallen logs. She ran through bushes, thorns tearing at her shins. She nearly slipped on a rock covered in moss, but grabbed the bark of a tree beside her to keep her balance. As she glanced upwards, she saw the tree stretch endlessly into the sky. There was no time to linger on it, though. She regained her footing and took off once more.

Deeper and deeper into the forest, she sped, never once thinking to glimpse the beast behind her. What it was, she didn't know, but it screeched like a thousand hawks diving towards their prey at once. And if she stopped, even for a moment, she knew it would unleash unspeakable terrors on her.

But no matter how fast she fled, it was never enough. And when she made her way into a grove of trees with unnatural blue flowers and bizarre yellow fruits dangling from their branches, the noise grew deafening and it encircled her. The unholy creature that made it had trapped her.

But then the trees fell away and disappeared. There were no blue petals, no yellow fruits, no leaves, no branches. And the earth beneath her was no longer cool and damp. It was hot and dry. Even the noise seemed to calm in this new place.

Her head spun from side to side, fear still pulsing in every heartbeat as she scanned the terrain. She saw only a bronzed earth that extended until it met a blue sky.

From nowhere, a spirit appeared in front of her. She recognized it as the same one that had visited her before and pleaded with her to remember. Finally, the noise ceased entirely.

Ajeau took a step back and heard a rock crash against land as though it tumbled from some great height. Surprised, she turned and saw a gorge appear behind her. It had not been there a moment ago; she was sure of it.

Ajeau whipped her head around, faced the approaching spirit, and said, "What are you?"

The words echoed, but elicited no response from the phantom.

She glanced once more at the gorge and the blue line that punctuated its ravine, then turned back to the spirit, now a few paces away from her.

"What are you?" Ajeau said.

"Not what. But who," the spirit replied.

Ajeau breathed as if there was something in her lungs. She tried to speak the words 'then who are you?' but only water fell from her lips.

The spirit came to a stop only an arm's length from Ajeau. Its head wavered in front of her as though it were examining her. After a moment, its head returned to an upright position, and it said, "Do not fear it. Embrace it. Always remember to fight. *Fight to control your destiny.*"

Ajeau remembered the words instantly. They were the same ones she had as she watched a girl—older than her then, but still a young girl—fight against some small oppressor so she could live. So they could all live. She saw a dagger shimmer in her hand.

The spirit reached out and grasped Ajeau's shoulder with its shadowy appendage and the dagger disappeared. As the touch lingered, a wave of nausea cascaded through her and then exited. All was calm. Ajeau breathed deeply and fell backwards.

Her eyes opened wide, her jaw dropped, her arms swung upwards over her head as she descended into the gorge. It did not shock or upset her. No, Ajeau felt as though she was right where she was supposed to be.

She splashed into the river at the bottom of the gorge and smiled. It had been so long since she felt water surround her like this. It was beautiful. Then she awoke.

\*\*\*

SYAIS TRIED TO POUR water down Ajeau's throat. It did not work. She barely got any in the girl's mouth and what she did came right back out. But she had to do something to rouse Ajeau. The girl was unwell, hot to the touch and flushed as red as the seeds of a pomegranate. So, lacking a better idea, and despite the pain it caused her to waste water, Syais threw a bowl of water on Ajeau's face.

As soon as she felt the cool liquid hit her face, Ajeau's eyes burst open, and she inhaled deeply. Her skin slowly lost its red hue, and she no longer burned Syais's hand when the woman touched her. It was not clear who was more relieved, Ajeau or Syais.

"Hijeuse, you are awake?" Syais said.

"Yes," Ajeau said quietly, then tried to sit up.

"Easy." Syais grabbed Ajeau's arm to support her. "You were ill for quite a time there. But you appear to be recovering."

"What happened?" Ajeau blinked as though she had just learned the skill.

"That depends. What do you remember?"

"I was—you..." Ajeau looked down at her arm and saw a wound dressed with a poultice of some herb and a bandage. "You cut me."

"I did, but it was necessary. Do you remember that?" Syais pointed at several yellow-clad warriors beginning to rot in the sun.

Ajeau looked on in disbelief. For a moment, she wondered whether the entire episode was the hallucination of an ill, dying mind. Even trying to remember it now, it was hazy, like a light so far away it was impossible to tell whether it was a light at all.

But there was no uncertainty now. Despite the fog over her memories, the dead were proof of her actions. And her speed. She was the lightning to the tree, the bee on the flower, the wind through the grass; swift against the still.

"Do you know who they are?" Ajeau asked.

"No," Syais said. "Not as people. But I know where they come from. The yellow they wear, the arrows they fling. They worship Sol. And that means they can only have come from Rigolade."

Ajeau shook her head. "Sol..." The word was familiar. But she sighed and shook her head, unable to place it. "I've not heard of a place called Rigolade before. Why are they here? The same reason as us?"

"I do not know the answer to that," Syais said. "But I do not think it a coincidence. If the Rigoladers know of this place, then it means we must move with haste."

Ajeau smiled and let a small laugh escape her lips. "That I can do. But how—I mean, what did you do to me?"

"I gave you the power of the High Elders. A power only you, only a Hijeuse, can wield. I told you I could give you anything—friends, a place in the world, vengeance—and now you see." Syais announced the words as if she had conquered the world already.

"Why? Why me?"

"It is a hard question to answer. One I am not even sure of the details. But, in short, a long time ago, a man made a mistake. A woman too. They conspired against the Chief of the One Tribe and their treachery produced a daughter. Who went on to have sons and daughters, grandchildren and great grandchildren, through the ages."

"And I am—?"

"Yes."

"And you are not—?"

"No."

"But it doesn't make any sense. I have always had the blood of some elder within me. Why could I never do that before?"

"Because..." Syais laughed. "You cannot do that by blood alone. You need these." Syais held out the remaining fragments of seeds that she had gathered from beneath the structure in the center of the camp.

"Those are what you rubbed into my wound," Ajeau said it as a question as much as a statement. "And then everything that happened after was because of them?"

"Yes. The seeds of the Faine. The Istori also called it the Tree of Fate or the Alacri Tree."

Ajeau stared at Syais, but she finally understood. Her blood and the seeds of this tree together gave her a power unlike anything she had thought to be possible.

And now, she had her place in the world. At its top. She would no longer have to listen to others, do what they said, think what they thought; she had fought and now controlled her destiny. No, everyone's destiny.

Syais eyed her. "Now is not the time to become complacent," Syais said. "There is still much we need to do before we can reclaim what is ours."

"What do you mean? What must we do?"

"Look." Syais nodded to the seeds in her hand. "I hold but dry husks now; there is barely even a morsel of seed remaining. Perhaps it would be enough to enliven you again, perhaps not. But that is beside the point. The seeds are but a taste. We are after the tree's fruit. That is when—"

"So we will grow more trees. Gather more seeds. Grow more fruits," Ajeau interrupted Syais, a dash of arrogance on her tongue.

"That is not how it works," Syais said harshly. "Do you not think everyone would gather the seeds and grow the tree? Do you not think the world would know of their power? Do you not think there is a reason we came to this place and found them buried in an ancient altar?"

"I...I didn't realize. I thought—"

"You did not think, you assumed. Assumptions are not knowledge," Syais said to Ajeau as though she were an impetuous child. But then she sighed and softened. "There is much about this we do not know. Even me. The records simply do not exist. But what I know is that we must make it to Z'eau. There are answers in the city, answers to all our questions. But this," Syais glanced at the seed husks again, "is not our destination."

Another journey to another place, Ajeau thought; it did not matter. They would go where they needed to, find what they sought—seeds, fruits, cones, spores, whatever it may be—and then she could have the world. And then she could find Vaten. The power was still hers, after all.

***

WARDEN PASSIL PACED IN Syais's chambers. It had been weeks since he last saw the Vizier and had been ordered to raise an army for the long journey to the City of Z'eau. Passil had done that easily; he had raised an army in less time than it took most to raise a drink. People wanted to leave the city, and he promised water and food rations for the trip. It was better than what they had in Nouv'eau.

Sure, it meant most of the soldiers had never even held a blade outside of a harvest. But he could train them. And yes, he had emptied the jails, and thieves, vandals, and brutes of all types were among the forces. But they could be controlled. More people with more blades were always preferable. Especially when they were up against the unknown.

So it was not nerves about the army or a fear he had failed in his duties that made Passil pace. Quite the opposite. It was out of concern Syais had failed and lay injured, or worse, on some isolated path in the middle of the Tentir. It was a feral place these days.

And what began as a nascent thought, easily dismissed at any moment, became a fully realized terror; a single piece of thread tied into a knot that, much like his stomach, could not be unraveled. She was lost, in need of help. Something had gone horribly wrong.

He pulled at his beard as he walked, wondering whether he should send the Lord's Guard after her. Or maybe it would be better to search for her himself. No, he should wait, trust her abilities, and wait for her return. That was her order; to wait. He squeezed his head; what good was such an order if she failed to return? He was a wreck with indecision.

More days passed. As his fears mixed with indecision, Passil deteriorated. He had not left Syais's cottage in days, even refusing to see those who he put in charge of the soldiers. "Insignificant," he had barked at those who dared show their face to him. "All that matters is the Vizier! Where is she?"

Anxiety gave way to suspicion, which gave way to paranoia and delusion. In the darkness of night when no light found Passil, when the cries of the hungry and thirsty echoed through Nouv'eau, the voices invaded.

"The Vizier is alive," voices said to him from dark, empty corners. "She is well, but do not let it ease your mind. She seeks only to oust you. We have warned you of this!" The voices laughed.

He bit his lip until it bled, trying to make them stop.

"Do you still pretend to be blind? You are no different from Puy." The voices laughed again. "Yes, yes! You walk unknowingly into the trap that will end you. Ignorant and useless."

"No," he shouted, flecks of blood fell from his mouth. "I am worthy. I am loyal. I am the Warden. And you...you will be gone in the light of day."

The voices laughed, loudly. "Light of day? No. We do not care for it. Yes, *Warden*," the word spoken as a slight, "Tell us. What follows day?"

"No, there is always—"

"Tell us, tell us!"

Passil closed his eyes and shook his head wildly from side to side. He grabbed his hair and pulled. He screamed unintelligible words at the floor.

"Passil...No, no. Puy." The voices mocked him and laughed. "Yes, Puy. Tell us Puy. Tell us."

"No..." he groaned quietly. He grabbed at his arms and torso, rocking as though he stood on a boat. "No..."

"Yes, you see it now, don't you?" the voices said. "You will never be rid of us."

"No," he said, the words barely audible. "Morning will come. She will return. All will be right, and we will…"

The voices' laughter drowned his words. "You will what? *You* are no longer needed. You are the useless chaff and she is the wheat. How did you think it would end? There is no other way."

Passil's rocking stopped. His arms and legs lost tension, and he fell into the wall, then slid to the floor. He sat there against the brick, hanging his head in defeat.

"You only existed for her to find someone better, stronger," the voices said. "Yes, yes, someone with actual power. That is what she needed. You gave her the hammer to shatter your stone." They laughed. "Worthless."

"Yes," Passil whispered into his chest.

The voices, free of mockery and abuse, said, "Good. With your eyes open now, you see what must be done."

He said nothing in response.

"We will not give up on you so easily."

He sat in the same position until the light of dawn pierced the darkness. He heard the calls; riders on the horizon, two of them, from the direction of the Tentir. He didn't need to be told; he knew they were coming back. They were coming for him.

He stood and exited the cottage. As he walked towards the gate, he found the voices only grew louder, the sun no longer keeping them at bay. But he no longer wished them gone. Instead, he listened to their every word and smiled. "Yes. That will do."

# CHAPTER 44

"WHAT ABOUT OUR ARRIVAL?" Vaten asked.

They were the first words he spoke since Aloc led him to Zejela's quarters and he said them full of exasperation. First, Aloc had disrupted his conversation with Levitien, preventing any resolution and allowing the man to escape without providing any information. Now, Zejela had called their arrival 'dire.'

Vaten continued, "We are still going to Bas, right? You haven't turned us around or sailed us into some—"

"Stop. Listen." Aloc's voice, like his grip, was firm.

"Yes, we travel to Bas," Zejela said. "But I must speak about our plans for when we arrive."

"Our plans?" Levitien articulated each sound to show his displeasure. "We," again he stretched out the word, "have no plans. I will be returning to Rigolade. To my family."

"No. Your family us now. No other." Aloc's voice was soft, as though Levitien's words genuinely hurt him.

Zejela waved her hand to urge Aloc to settle, then said, "You are, I suppose, a free man, Levitien. Like on Zevaco, you can choose your path. But are you not interested in what I have to say? Do you wish to know where we are going? And what we may find there?"

Levitien's eyes narrowed. And though he said nothing in response, he did not leave either.

Zejela smirked. "Well, you may leave if you wish. If you stay, I will assume you are, at the very least, interested."

"Enough of this." Vaten slammed the floor of the cabin with his hand. "What of the plans? What of Bas? Speak on that."

"Yes," Zejela said, then inhaled deeply. "There is much you do not know about the Zevacese and their relationship to the world. To Bas. That is not your fault, nor is it ours. It is a simple fact, one you must fully appreciate before you can understand our plan."

Though he could see no one else's expression, Vaten's brow fell over his eyes.

"The Zevacese have always attempted to remain hidden from those outside their borders. You likely never heard our name before our paths crossed. If you had, it may have been in stories or someone may have sworn they saw something, but we work tirelessly to remove any evidence that confirms our existence. We are not perfect, but we have been successful."

Vaten shook his head. He could not stop shaking it. His voice cracked as he said, "Then why—why did you take me? I did nothing, I..."

"You saw us," Zejela said flatly. "You were a record of our presence. One that we could not allow to remain on Bas. We had no choice. You see? This is what I mean. We remain unknown by any means. When you saw us, we captured you and, because we did not seek your death, we allowed you to remain on Zevaco."

"But could you not have left me? I did not know you were from Zevaco!" Vaten shouted. "I did not know a thing! You ruined my life so I would not tell something I did not even know!"

"Vaten, you were there." Zejela raised her shoulders incredulously. "At the same place we were. You play innocent, but you were looking for—"

"Looking for what? I was simply travelling! I had no part in this game, or hunt." Vaten patted his chest. "I am innocent."

"Vaten!" Aloc's voice boomed through the small cabin. All sound, even that of the sea, seemed to cease. "It not make difference now. You are Sentry, like me. Remember the rain."

Vaten glared at Aloc and opened his mouth, ready to yell. But before he did, he recalled that day, standing amidst the deluge of rain and wind with Aloc's voice a constant buzz in his ear. He had never relented, always practiced. And instead of saying anything, he closed his mouth and nodded once at Aloc in acceptance of his rebuke.

The silence lingered until Zejela thought the situation defused. Then she continued speaking as though nothing had happened. "With our trip, secrecy will be impossible. The crew is small and untrained for such excursions. I may be able to pass, I know the language and customs well enough, but the others will not. And of course, you two may choose to leave. Regardless, it is the end of our concealment. Bas will come to know of the people of Zevaco."

Levitien sighed. He was growing impatient. "And why does any of this matter to me?"

"Well, it may not. I do not know your desires. Perhaps you do not care about the people of your land. Perhaps you do not realize what follows us across the sea. Did you not think there was a reason we would keep ourselves secret? Did you think it for our benefit?" Zejela chuckled.

"I...I..." Levitien stammered and provided no answers.

"Those who hunt us will wreak havoc all across Bas and Rigolade," Zejela said. "They have the—"

"I don't understand." Vaten's eyes narrowed. "What do the people who come after us care about Bas? Are they not only after you? Or us? Don't they only want Zevaco?"

Zejela sighed. "Yes. They are after me, you, and everyone aboard this ship. They already have Zevaco. And there is no doubt they are coming for Bas. They have...what we retrieved from Bas during our previous journey. It is only—"

"And what is that?" Levitien raised his eyebrows and tilted his head towards Zejela as though she was about to whisper a secret to him.

Zejela, despite her quick tongue, said nothing.

"Speak plain, Zejela. Truth." Aloc placed a hand on her shoulder. "They deserve it."

Zejela glanced at Aloc, then said, "The seeds, leaves, flowers, roots... of the Faine. The Tree of Fate."

"The what?" Vaten asked.

If he had been able to see, he would have caught Levitien smiling. That fiendish grin he had once hidden away now danced across his lips in full view of all.

"It is a rare tree," Zejela said. "One whose fruit provides an unimaginable power at an unimaginable cost. In the wrong hands, it can doom a world. It has done so once already."

Still confused, Vaten shook his head and asked, "What power?"

"The texts describe it as an infinite strength. The ability to move with the shades, disappear and reappear as you like, to affect this world without existing in it. Entire armies crumble at the feet of ones who possess it. Indeed, entire worlds."

"And this exists?" Vaten leaned forward. "Truly?"

Zejela nodded. "Yes."

"But still, what does this tree, or its power, have to do with us? So, the traitors on Zevaco have this...tree. Or its parts. And they have its power? What does that have to do with your secrecy? Our plans on Bas?" Vaten finally understood something. But in doing so, realized how ignorant he was of so much more.

"It is all connected," Zejela said. "We conceal ourselves to prevent the Bassians from knowing our mission. And that is to neutralize the Faine, to prevent its use. If anyone found out about us, about our work, it would mean the end for the peoples of Bas. And ourselves, of course."

"You should've destroyed it, burned the tree down. Why did you return any of it to Zevaco if you wanted to 'neutralize it?'" Levitien attempted a poor impersonation of Zejela.

"In some ways, we did destroy it." Zejela glanced at Aloc then continued, "We stopped its ability to make the fruit. But burning it would not stop it. Its roots grow deep throughout the world and once it was burnt, it would only have found another place to sprout.

"As to why we brought it back, that was hubris. We brought back pieces to study; all the samples from history are gone. We wanted—I wanted to know more, to understand it. I hoped to control it and stop it for good. I never envisioned such an outcome."

Levitien scoffed. "You should have. If you truly understood people, then you would have known—"

"Not all are like you," Zejela said with contempt.

Vaten folded his arms in front of his chest. "But you broke the tree, right? It no longer has power?"

"Yes and no," Zejela replied. "As with our past quests, we were successful. But what Wehlat and Ryiera have in their possession is enough to do great harm once they learn how to use it. They executed the coup knowing what they would have if they were successful."

"And they are after us," Vaten said. "You're saying they are going to kill us and destroy Bas unless we get there first? But won't they find us on Bas and end us there?"

"Yes." Zejela clapped her hands to stress her point. "Making it to Bas first is an essential part of our plans, but it is not the only part. If we arrive only to be found by Wehlat and Ryiera, our fate would be the same as if they were here now."

"Then what?" Vaten shrugged. "Are you able to find that tree again? Is that the plan?"

"No. The tree we found will be long dead," Zejela said.

Vaten hung his head. Then raised it up with enthusiasm. "What about other trees? I know Ortolan, at least I did. It has some of the richest soil on Bas. Maybe I could help find—"

"I appreciate that offer, Vaten," she said. "But it is not a common sycamore. Besides, we will not be using the Faine. It alone does not give one the power, and the cost is too high. It is our duty to prevent its use."

Vaten shook his head. "But how will we..."

Zejela smiled. "Don't worry. We are going to secure the aid of friends, or at least acquaintances."

"I thought no one knew of Zevaco," Levitien said. He had listened to the conversation like someone who was charged with committing the entire thing to memory.

"You are right. No one knows of the Zevacese, Levitien. Not even the friends I speak of. But some know me. This one...well, I met with her once. She stole something important of ours. A mark that..." Zejela waved her hands. "That is a different story. But I imagine she has not forgotten our meeting, nor me. And vitally, she is a Noye Elder. And I know where they will be."

When Zejela spoke the words, a ringing erupted in Vaten's ears. The Noye. He closed his eyes as if that would help dampen the noise or, at least, reduce the suffering from it. It did not. The sound did not stop, it did not fluctuate, it was a constant drone blocking out the rest of the world. Now he could not hear as much as he could not see.

He had not heard the word Noye spoken in what seemed like a lifetime. In some ways, it had been. And in that time, he had doused the fire of vengeance and let the smoke disperse into the world.

But embers remained. They simmered away, waiting for kindling to come and reignite them. Zejela's words were all it took. With the inferno ignited and the fury restored, the ringing finally stopped. Vaten smiled as relief washed over him. He was returning to the home of the Noye, no longer the weak child he was when he left, and Zejela would escort him directly to them. Vengeance would be his after all this time.

\*\*\*

RYIERA PACED THE DECK of her ship. Her fleet surrounded her, extending endlessly in every direction. Not every person on the island had volunteered to help bring justice to the traitors, but the force was substantial. And far larger than even she had anticipated.

But Ryiera was not thinking about their ships, nor those aboard them, as she strode from port to starboard and from bow to stern, ignoring calls from the sailors and bracing herself against fierce winds. Instead, she thought only of the open sea. The enormity of it. The distance from land. The strange creatures moving in bizarre ways below her. The unknown. Pacing was the only way she contained her panic.

"It is a wondrous day to sail," Wehlat said with a grin on his face and his arms wide open. "The sky is clear and the wind whipping. The sails are fully spread. I am not sure we could move with more speed."

"Yes," Ryiera said. "We run before the wind, but that means they do too."

"With their thin crew? They won't even work a single sail." Wehlat snickered, then grew serious. "We will catch them and have our answers soon enough. Do not worry."

"I am not worried, not about catching them." She sighed and gripped the handrail tightly. "I hope you are correct. I fear we will see the large continent before we see their vessel."

"And if we do, so be it. With this force, we could lay waste to the Bassians once and for all."

"Without understanding the seeds and the tree? That would be quite rash. We must wait until we know more before we become conquerors."

"Perhaps." he shrugged nonchalantly. "Perhaps not. I think you have too much confidence in the Bassians. They are fractured. We are united!"

"True. But you know as well as I, that what awaits us there is a mystery. And the only two who know the answer sail ahead of us. Our maps may not even be current."

Wehlat's eyes narrowed. "Do you wish to end our voyage? Turn our fleet? Remember, it was you who called for us to go."

"Yes, No—I..." Ryiera sighed. "The sea riles my spirit, that is all. We must continue and we will be successful no matter the conditions."

"I know." Wehlat smiled. "Now follow me. I have a surprise for you."

Ryiera followed Wehlat into his cabin, where she found a woman waiting for them. The woman's clothes were not fancy, nor were they in tatters. They were plain, appropriate for a tradesworker. To Ryiera, she looked like any of the others, one of hundreds on the ship, unremarkable.

Confused, Ryiera turned to Wehlat and shook her head.

Wehlat held up a hand and said, "Wait, listen to the story she tells. It is quite remarkable."

"Then speak," Ryiera said to the woman.

"Ah, yes, Elder Ryiera. Thank you." The woman bowed her head in respect. "Before this trip, I ran fermented drinks in the Outer Ridge. For the Sentries. I gave a drink to the newcomer Leriti—"

"Levitien?" Ryiera asked, pronouncing the strange name slowly.

"Levitien. Yes." The woman nodded her head vigorously. "I am sorry. I did not know I gave to an evil man." Again, the woman bowed her head in respect.

"Yes, fine. You could not have known. Now, continue your story."

"I gave drinks to this man. Lots of them. He liked to drink but always became very drunk—maybe he wasn't used to how strong I make them," she said with a smile. Then, losing the smile, continued, "One night when I did this, he mistook me for his mother. I do not know why. He was drinking many drinks that night and called me 'mother, mother!' He grabbed me. I didn't know what to do."

Ryiera looked at Wehlat as though he were playing a joke on her. She wondered if this was some attempt to take her mind off the sea. If it was, it wasn't working; it was only making her annoyed.

Wehlat noticed this and whispered, "Keep listening."

The woman continued, "He was saying strange things. That he was dying here. That he would never see home again. That he was sorry he disappointed father. That he would make it right. He was very upset, nearly crying. But then, and this is why I wanted to tell you," she pointed at Wehlat, "because he said Zejela had the answers! If only he got the answers from her, he could make it right. I didn't know what it meant, and I didn't care; I only wanted to escape. But now..."

"So Levitien told you that Zejela had the answers?" Ryiera pursed her lips and glanced at Wehlat from the sides of her eyes, irritated.

"Yes. But that is not all, is it Olleuse?" Wehlat said to the woman.

"No, Elders." Olleuse bowed her head again. "He said more. He stopped crying and became very angry. Then started saying that he would kill them all. All the Zevacese too! Kill Zejela, kill the Sentries, kill Vato—the other newcomer."

"Vaten?" Ryiera said.

"Yes! He would kill Vaten. Kill all of them and restore Reelog—"

"Rigolade?" Ryiera corrected Olleuse again.

"Yes, sorry, they are strange words," Olleuse said. "He wanted to restore Rigolade to power over the rest of the world."

Ryiera leaned close to Olleuse and said, "And no one else heard this?"

"No, it was only me and him." Olleuse shook her head. "It was very strange. After he said this part, he let go of me and fell asleep. But even in his sleep, he would mumble, 'I'll make it right, restore Rigolade. Once I have the answers. Once I have the power. I promise to make it right.'"

# CHAPTER 45

IT WAS AN EXTRAORDINARY scene. So unbelievable, Savique wondered if Vrai had ridden him to some new place or tribe. But the sparse grasses, endless dust, and unforgiving sun had not changed since they left. It was the land of the Ose. There was no mistaking it. Now, though, instead of a small camp, they rode into a bustling settlement stretching outward for what seemed like miles.

The number of people stunned Savique. Thousands of Noye walked and rode and ate and worked and cared for their horses, all of them heeding Vrai's call to escape the V'eauvians and join the Ose in the desert's shadow. And though Savique had once seen their camps individually, here, together, they seemed truly a people.

They were an empire sat upon a needle point.

Savique followed Vrai past the innumerable tents as shouts from happy and angry onlookers alike filled the air. They reached the heart of the village where the Ose and Navo-Ille waited for them like expectant parents.

"Did you—"

"Yes, Navo! We have it!" Vrai, unable to restrain his excitement, jumped off his horse and removed the bag holding the mark from around his chest. He held it high in the air, triumphant.

Navo-Ille smiled, creasing the sides of her eyes, then turned and began walking towards her hut. She waved her hand, telling the two men to follow her. They did, and a moment later, the three of them entered the hut and sat on the ground as they had nearly a month ago.

"Navo," Vrai said as soon as he sat. "There is something strange about the stone. It moves towards something. Points to it."

Navo-Ille shook her head. "It moves and points? To what? A direction?"

"No, not a direction but something—"

"To this." Savique reached into his bag and produced the small container of blood.

"What is that?" Navo-Ille asked.

"A vial of blood from Nouv'eau," he said. "I took it from a workshop where the ritual had been conducted. At least that is what the men there said."

"Interesting." Navo-Ille stared at Savique. "And why did you take it?"

"As an assurance. But that doesn't matter now. All that matters—It's a good thing I took it, and kept it, because..." Savique glanced at Vrai, who had already begun removing the stone from his bag. "Watch."

Savique demonstrated the same effects the two men saw in the forest. As Savique moved the vial back and forth, up and down, the stone appeared to follow it with its thorn.

"See," Savique said.

Navo-Ille said nothing, as her eyes, bulging from their sockets, darted between the vial and the stone.

Upon seeing Navo-Ille's reaction, Vrai thrust the mark into the woman's hands. She received it gently, like it was a fragile pot, then opened her mouth to speak. Before saying a word, her lips shut, and she glanced at the two men, waiting for them to explain what they had found. But neither said a word.

Vrai finally broke the silence. "Do you know why it moves?"

Navo-Ille shook her head.

"Then what about this?" Vrai pointed to the name written on the vial. "Do you know what a Hijeuse is?"

"I—I have heard that word before," Navo-Ille said. "Give me a moment."

With her top lip tucked under her bottom one, chin stuck out with her thumb pressed into it, Navo-Ille thought. She closed her eyes and sighed, but only shook her head in disappointment. Finally, she stood, placed the stone back in Vrai's hands, and walked towards the doorway of her hut. She stared out at the camp.

There she spied a horse and frowned. The beast pawed at the ground, tossed its head back and forth, opened its mouth, and roared. It was clear the beast was agitated, but only when it reared on its hind legs and the blood dripped from its wound did Navo-Ille understand why. And in the same thought, she recalled the meaning of the word Hijeuse.

She spun to face Vrai and Savique. "I remember! Hijeuse. It is a Balafre word. It means someone who has...royal blood?" She asked the question to herself, then answered it immediately. "No...not royal, but divine blood!"

"What does that mean?" Vrai stood up, matching Navo-Ille's excitement.

"That the stone points to divine blood! The blood of the High Elders perhaps!" Navo-Ille shouted with enthusiasm.

"Right...And?" Vrai stood ready to receive Navo-Ille's brilliant discovery.

But all Navo-Ille could do is return Vrai's gaze. There was no revelation coming. No help. And the excitement they had felt a moment ago disappeared, leaving only emptiness in its wake.

"I—I don't know," Navo-Ille said. "But it must mean something."

"Wait," Savique said.

He did not care about the meaning of the word Hijeuse nor about the High Elders. He knew nothing about them. But he knew about stones, had worked with them since he was a boy. And through all his years, he never remembered one quite like this.

But stones were strange. Strike the right two together and you'd get a spark. Strike a different set and you might hear echoes inside of them. Still others would crumble to dust. Most of them sink, but some float. Then there was that time—

"Wait," Savique said it again. "I know what—"

A horse outside the hut roared loudly once more. But this time, it was not out of pain or agitation; it was a warning. The three of them turned and gazed out at the camp and saw a rider approaching them at full speed. A moment later, it stopped not more than a stride from Navo-Ille's doorway.

The rider leapt off, hurried towards them, and began shouting, through panicked heavy breaths, "Navo! Navo! The Lord is here. Just miles from the outskirts. He is here!"

"What?" Navo-Ille's eyes grew wide. "No! What did you see?"

"His army," the rider said. "There are...so many of them. White clad and riding swiftly in this direction."

Navo-Ille's jaw clenched. She glared at the rider but chastised herself. She had been too slow and too obvious, their encampment as well hidden as a tree among the grasses.

She shook her head to clear her thoughts and decided. "There will be no battle here. We retreat. We survive."

The rider nodded but stood still, waiting for an order.

"Ride to the outermost settlements," Navo-Ille ordered, pointing north. "If it is not too late, tell them to ride towards the southern edge, the desert. Abandon everything else."

Navo-Ille stepped forward into the camp and shouted for all to hear, "The Lord is here! He aims to exterminate us. If you wish to live, we ride for the desert without delay. Leave everything but food and water."

The camp exploded into an uproar. Men and women ran in all directions, some to their huts to collect goods or rations, some to their horses to ready them to ride, some to their children and loved ones. But nearly all ran somewhere. Navo-Ille's words were the clouds that preceded the storm.

After she made her pronouncement, Navo-Ille turned back to her own hut and the two men still waiting there.

And though Savique's face should have worn the same expression of shock and dread as Navo-Ille's, he appeared calm. Yes, they would have to escape the Lord quickly to keep their lives. And yes, it would throw him even farther from finding his son. But he knew something about the stone. In that moment, he wondered if the Ascetics were right.

"Navo!" Savique tried to gain the Elder's attention amidst the commotion.

"What?" she said. "We must hurry and ready ourselves to—"

"Yes, but I know!" Savique held out his hands as though he were offering a present. "I know why the rock moves."

Navo-Ille stopped and eyed Savique. "Well, explain then. Hurry!"

Speaking quickly, Savique told them of the time when he was a boy and found a rock which, when broken into pieces, oriented themselves to the other.

"And what does that mean?" Vrai said. "Our stone does not point to some other—"

"No, this stone," Savique pointed towards the box in Vrai's hand, "isn't attracted to itself, it's attracted to the blood. The blood of the High Elders, right?"

"Yes. Yes!" Navo-Ille felt a shiver of excitement run through her. A connection began to form in her mind. It was not yet complete, but it had started snaking its way and that was enough for her to fill with anticipation.

"We already knew that!" Vrai said.

"And that the stone would lead us to the city of the High Elders, to Z'eau?" Savique continued, ignoring Vrai.

"Yes!" Navo-Ille exclaimed, the connection nearly complete now.

Hoofbeats shook the world around them. On the wind, screams could be heard.

"Then what if..." Savique said. He turned and walked back into the hut. He stood above the fire and raised his arm above it, the vial in his hand.

Vrai looked at him, concerned. "What are you doing? Be careful with that!"

"Don't worry," Savique said. "We do not need it. It only holds us back."

The vial fell from his hand and broke open in the fire. The blood inside simmered, then evaporated, forever gone from the world.

Vrai grabbed Savique's arm, which now no longer held the vial, and spun the man around to face him. Upon seeing the enthusiasm on Savique's face, rage consumed Vrai.

"Savior? Leader?" Vrai spit on the ground. "You are nothing but a fraud. Do you delay for the Lord's benefit? Do you work in tandem with our enemies?" He grit his teeth as his muscles tensed. "You are not even one of us. You are nothing. No...worse than that. You are salt in the soil, poison in the blood. A blight on us all."

Vrai turned and calmly set the mark down, then lunged at Savique's throat with both his hands. The move sent them toppling over each other and nearly landed them both in the fire. Savique grunted as he attempted to speak before hands were once again thrown at his face and throat.

They wrestled a moment more until Vrai prevailed. Sitting on top of Savique, Vrai cocked his arm as if to strike Savique until he heard Navo-Ille's voice.

"Stop! Vrai, enough!" Navo-Ille barked. "Check the mark!"

"What?" Vrai said, his arm still hanging above Savique.

"The stone!" Navo-Ille said. "Where does it point now?"

The screams outside the hut were getting louder.

Vrai scrambled off Savique and picked up the box with the stone in it. He opened it and studied it for a moment.

"Nowhere. The stone points there." Vrai gestured south, towards the desert.

"Move the box," Savique said through deep breaths. "Turn it. Does the stone turn?"

When Vrai moved the box, the stone did not follow. It remained pointing in the same direction.

"No...no! The stone still points there. See." Vrai held the box so Navo-Ille could see.

"That is because..." Savique caught his breath and stood. "It points to Z'eau. To the City. To the Tree."

Navo-Ille finally understood. Like a raindrop eventually hitting the earth after it forms, once the connection materialized in Navo-Ille's mind, she needed only to wait until it reached its destination.

"What?" Vrai shook his head.

"Amazing," Navo-Ille said, taking the box from Vrai and inspecting it. "It was not the blood, it was something *in* the blood. Something of the High Elders drew the stone's thorn. And it points toward Z'eau because it is attracted to that same thing there."

"Exactly," Savique said. "And the blood simply distracted the stone. It was a stronger reaction because of how close it was. If we follow—"

Screams drowned Savique's words. There was no more time. The Lord was in the camp.

The three of them ran from the hut in time to see a group of Ose scatter in front of a soldier riding past the Noye huts. More V'eauvians followed, swinging and stabbing their spears at all beneath them.

Navo-Ille walked towards her horse and weapons, then turned to face Savique and Vrai. "I will gather who I can and come to the desert. But do not wait for me! Savique, take the mark and find the city. Lead our people there. As swift as the wind."

"Will they follow?" Savique yelled back.

"They will follow, because you will lead. And only you can." Navo-Ille smiled as she mounted her horse, then rode off.

On the wind, Savique thought he heard a joyous shout. "The Ascetics were right!"

*** 

THERE WAS NO BATTLE, no war. There was only bloodshed and death. All that remained of the Noye camped with the Ose were tools and strings and logs and bowls strewn across the land and a trail of horses disappearing into the desert.

A rider arrived beside Lord Balay and stared at the line on the horizon. She exhaled loudly, angrily, then said, "Vile heretics." She grabbed the sickle from her belt, held it firm beside her leg, and leaned forward ready to ride. "My Lord, allow me to purge this world of their sin. Give me your word and I will follow them. None will survive."

The Lord turned to the woman with a smile on his face. He knew the words were genuine and she would make them into reality. But he shook his head. "No, Eyes." he said, pleased with himself. "Do not dirty your garb for them. Though it may not be their final day, they will not last long. The desert is not a hospitable place. Let them live out their lives gasping for drink and food in a place with nothing but sand."

The Eyes' head snapped to the Lord. "You let them live. They will breed like roaches and destroy our crop. We can finish them now. I have seen Noye—"

"I have decided," he said. "You will remain here. Do not concern yourself with it."

"Yes, Lord," she said and dropped her gaze. But as she clipped her weapon back to her belt, she glanced once more at the horizon. The Noye had already vanished. Her jaw clenched.

"We will make camp here tonight," he said. "To ensure no one reemerges. In the morning, we begin our ride back to Nouv'eau, as destroyers of the Noye."

And though she nodded and followed his orders, the Eyes saw only weakness in the man. The failure to finish his work, to see a job through to its rightful end; it was pitiful. That he would congratulate himself like a hero only enraged her.

But she repressed her fury under thoughts of returning to Nouv'eau and the new path the V'eauvians would walk. Never again would she allow the Lord's failings to impede her.

She had her eyes set on far more ambitious ends.

\*\*\*

SAVIQUE SAT ATOP A horse, emaciated and haggard. He melted under the scorching heat. And though his body ached and exhaustion overwhelmed him, his eyesight never wavered and the mark in his right hand never fell.

It had been weeks, perhaps months—Savique had no idea how long—since the Lord chased them into the desert and he, Vrai, and the rest of the Noye struggled to continue. They survived on brittle roots and meager sips from the stores of cacti and yucca plants, their sharp leaves and spines drawing blood from the wanderers' hands each time. They fed their horses what they could spare and collected dew that would form overnight on their cloth for them to drink.

But there was never enough food or water or shade or safety. And the wind would race, sending sand into their eyes and mouths and sores. The place eroded them like rocks on a beach and many died.

At first, it was the old and the sick. They were mourned appropriately and blessed in their return to the earth. Even in that barren place.

But then, as days passed, the healthy and young fell. And the living no longer stopped to mourn or bless them. They had to keep moving; stopping was death. So they rode on as their numbers dwindled.

That was not the end. Well after the people faded, the horses started to go mad. Some rejected their riders, others stopped and refused to move, and still others rode off frantically into the wilds.

Each day, Savique wondered if it would be his, or his horse's, last. But as long as he was alive, he resolved to look at the stone and the direction it pointed and keep moving towards it.

Until one day, his head lightened, and the world swirled as though it was being turned by a curious child. By the middle of the day, spots like stars flashed in front of his face. He closed his eyes and rested his head and torso on the horse's back. The only thing that kept him from falling were legs that seemed permanently molded to fit around the horse's trunk.

Though he did not sleep, he was not conscious either. He existed between the two states for a moment. And it was there someone spoke to him.

"I can't believe it worked," a voice he had not heard in some time whispered. "You understand that now, right?"

He did not open his eyes. He did not move his mouth, but he spoke the words, "Understand what?"

A different voice, old and wise, said, "It will not be the last time we are called upon to be brave. Even you..."

"Me?" he said.

A hand dangled from a tree. "I was wrong to question you. You did well...It would not have been a success without you."

"Was it?" he asked as a cloud of pink burst into his consciousness.

"Save them all...find the lost...see him again."

The words were like cool water on his neck. Savique's eyes burst apart, and his body flinched on the horse's back. He knew now, the words he had run from for so long were true. He finally believed them. He would save them all.

As he recited the premonition over and over in his mind, the world around him darkened and the air cooled. Above him, thousands of bats rushed as though unleashed from some great slumber. The sun was powerless in their presence.

For a moment, Savique wondered where they were going. But when he glanced at the stone, then back at the horde above, he realized they were travelling in the same direction as he.

*In your darkest hour, there will be light.*

And Savique saw it. On the horizon, where a line of black slowly receded to a point, he noticed a spot of color—of light—where none had been before. For days, weeks, months, there had only been pale yellow. But now, there was something else.

He rode towards it with abandon. The spot of blue and green grew larger and larger as he got closer.

Trees. Water. He did not think such things were possible. Amid a barren, desolate, forsaken world, there was life. They lived! If his body would have allowed it, he would have cried at the sight. He had found it. They had found it.

Savique turned to those still with him, those that made up the final tribe of the Noye and shouted through a burnt throat, "Behold, the city of Z'eau! Ours!"

Cheers, fit for a god, followed.

# CHAPTER 46

AJEAU AWOKE IN SYAIS'S cottage, refreshed. It had taken weeks after their return to Nouv'eau for her headaches, fatigue, and pain to dissipate. But now she was revived and ready to travel again. The quicker they left, the quicker she could find the tree and get to Vaten.

Still, there was a question that nagged at her. And only the Vizier could answer it.

Ajeau found Syais sitting in her study poring over texts as she had done nearly continuously since their return. She approached the Vizier quietly, but before Ajeau could speak, Syais, without looking up from her work, said, "Yes? What is it?"

"Is our trip ready to begin?" Ajeau said.

"Soon." Syais shuffled the scrolls in front of her and continued reading them, paying no attention to Ajeau. "We wait on the very last of our preparations. I told you, I will let you know when we are ready to leave."

Silence followed. Ajeau stared at the floor and, though her question had been answered, she showed no sign of leaving.

Syais glanced at her and sighed. She folded her arms and reclined in her chair. "But you knew that, didn't you? So why have you come? Speak your true intention."

Ajeau fidgeted with her hands. She opened her mouth to speak but found no words came out. She closed her mouth and swallowed loudly.

"Timid? After all we have been through." Syais chuckled. "Come on, out with it."

"What is—I mean—what, no, why..." Ajeau stammered then stopped, out of breath. She inhaled deeply to steady her nerves, then said, "Why are you doing this?"

"Doing what?"

413

"This. With me. Why are you helping me become...what I am? Why are you taking me to Z'eau?"

"Because you will be the great leader of our people. It is my honor to assist you." Syais stood and extended her arm towards Ajeau. "You are the Hijeuse."

"But..." Ajeau looked at her hands. "What does that make you?"

Syais smiled. "I am the Vizier. Make no mistake, Hijeuse, I lead now only because the Lord so unexpectedly returned to the earth. When you are ready, you will lead, and I will work tirelessly for you as I did for the man before. Do you wish a different arrangement?"

"I don't know." Ajeau shook her head. "I only want to see Vaten again and get my revenge on those who took him and Seule. I did not think about leading."

Syais stood and walked to Ajeau. She placed a hand on her shoulder. "Those things will come. We will find your friend and drive the blasphemers—all of them—from our land. But you must think beyond the immediate future. You are here to lead. And I am here to help you do so."

"And what if I cannot?" Ajeau said. "Even with this power, I—I am only a worker. I am not a leader, not a Lord or a Vizier. Not even high born. You are the leader."

Syais smiled with closed lips and bowed her head. "And you are the Hijeuse, do not forget that. We can sort out leading when the time comes. For now, remember the power you hold and wield for your people. You belong with them. Once the land is ours, we will worry about other matters." The grin never once left Syais's face.

Ajeau glanced at the floor and scratched her head, sure she accomplished something, but not at all what she needed to accomplish. It was as though she built a shed while intending to sow the fields. She was proud—Syais's words had reassured her—but confused.

Then the door behind her swung open as Passil burst into the room shouting for the Vizier.

"Yes, Warden," Syais said. "What is it?"

"We have a problem," he said. "The army has started sacking the city."

"What?" Syais lips pulled back and exposed her teeth. "Why have you—"

"I know." Passil held up his hands to deflect blame from himself. "They are looking for drink and have heard rumor there may be more in the city's reserves."

"Get them under control!" Syais fumed.

"Yes, Vizier. I have tried, but they are crazed and no longer listen to reason. Or commands."

"Then use the Lord's Guard and make them listen!"

"Or perhaps," he nodded at Ajeau suggestively, "we could use—"

"No." Syais said sternly. "If you cannot handle the soldiers, I will do so myself." She grabbed her dagger from the table. "Come with me Warden. But let this be our final delay. We will leave tomorrow at sundown. Make sure all preparations are completed by then."

Syais strode toward the door of her chambers. Upon reaching it, she turned back and said, "And you." She glared at Ajeau. "Rest now. Our journey will be long and arduous. You will need your strength."

Passil nodded once at Ajeau and flashed her an uneven smile that curled only the left corner of his mouth. "Yes, the trip will be arduous indeed." He followed Syais from the room, closing the door on Ajeau behind him.

***

THE TRAVEL WAS HARD, though Ajeau never once complained about it. Grueling schedules, endless riding, loneliness, chafed legs, and an unrelenting sun, stubbornly resistant to hiding itself even for a moment, tested her resolve. But she would have withstood far worse for a chance to find Vaten. And to realize her destiny.

Far worse was what the soldiers endured. Though Ajeau never once felt the sting of hunger or the craving of thirst, many did. Despite well-planned lines of supplies and all the provisions they could carry, hunger and thirst were a fact of life each day for the soldiers. And, as their rations declined over the course of the trip, many deserted. Some died.

And then they arrived at a place that threatened to break them. Sand and dust as far as the eye could see. There was hardly a shrub or plant in sight. It was a land devoid of life, and with an abrasive wind that raked at Ajeau's skin like a pumice stone.

Here, on the edge of the great desert, the Vizier called for the army to halt, make camp, and rest and recover for the rest of the day before embarking on the last leg of their trek. "It would be the most difficult," she said. "But the most rewarding."

As Syais spoke to members of the caravan, Ajeau saw unusual flashes of indecision and concern in her demeanor. The woman would stop mid-sentence, she would call for scrolls from Passil, she would pace with her arms folded in front of her, troubled.

When Syais walked past her, Ajeau stuck out an arm and said, "Wait."

Syais stopped and stared at her, annoyed. "What is it? There is much to be done before we can continue."

"Are we where we are meant to be? You appear uneasy and you wish to walk us into that." Ajeau gestured to the sands in the distance.

"Yes, this is where the charts lead. I assure you, our route has been meticulously planned. You have nothing to worry about."

"But there is nothing there. You said we seek a tree. How does a tree grow there?" Again, Ajeau pointed towards the lifeless expanse.

"I did not say our journey was complete, did I?" Her voice full of malice. "The City of Z'eau is a lush place, full of dense and rich vegetation. Trees grow there as," she kicked at the ground, "dust grows here. When we arrive there, you will know it."

"And you are confident it lies somewhere beyond this desolate place."

Syais eyed her. "Completely."

"And if you a wrong."

"Hijeuse, you have trusted me to lead you to this point. Why now would I turn you astray? We are on the verge of greatness. I assure you."

Ajeau sighed. "We will survive?"

"Yes," Syais said without hesitation. "We rest now because the sun is high and strong. All will benefit from it. Then, in the presence of the moons, we will resume our journey. Now," she waved at Passil, who pretended not to see her and kept walking. "I must continue with my work. Enjoy your time off-horse."

Ajeau nodded as Syais turned and walked from her. But when the woman was gone, Ajeau stared once more at the bronzed world ahead of her and saw nothing. On the wind, she thought she heard the words *embrace it*, no louder than the rustling of leaves.

***

PASSIL HAD LOST HIS nerve. He had been timid, skittish, and riddled with doubt as the caravan moved through the world. The voices provoked him, called him names, and did not let him forget his fate should he fail, but none of it was enough for him to act.

Of course, Ajeau did him no favors; she seemed always under Syais's protective eyes. It was where he should have ridden. He raged, but still did nothing.

"This will be your last chance," the voices said as Passil listened to Syais called for the army to rest. "If you do not act now, you may as well walk into the desert alone. You will not return either way."

"Shh!" he shouted. Seeing questioning glances from those around him, he glanced to the ground and whispered, "I know the stakes. They are mine to face. But there is no opportunity, no—"

"You lose the opportunity like the moon loses the sun," the voices said. "If you wished to—"

"What would you have me do?"

"Think, you fool." The voices laughed. "Yes, a fool, a fool."

"Quiet!" Again, his shouts brought on suspicious glances. He scurried to his tent and stared at his hands. "I cannot—"

The voices laughed. "Syais cannot watch the girl at every moment. Not when the army is in such disrepair."

"What do you mean? The soldiers are in good order, strained, but a rest will—"

"You must tell her of these developments," the voices said. "Yes, yes. The Vizier must know of the problems within her ranks. Her keen eye will be needed during this time. Only she can set them right."

A wicked grin crossed Passil's face. "I see the ruse now. If the Vizier must watch her soldiers, then the Hijeuse will require eyes from another. A trusted source of care and protection."

"Yes, Passil. There is only one who would be suitable for such a role."

He laughed in short bursts, then licked his lips and exited his tent.

\*\*\*

"WHERE IS SHE?" SYAIS'S voice erupted at her Warden the moment he was brought to her.

"Who? Vizier," Passil said as though he had rehearsed the words.

"The Hijeuse, Passil. Ajeau. Where is she?"

"I do not know, Vizier. She has gone missing? Have you checked—"

"Yes, she has gone missing! She was to remain here, in your care!" Syais grabbed him by his shirt. "Now, where is she?"

Passil shook his head and feigned ignorance. "I-I left her to see the camp. I thought her trustworthy and able. She is among—"

"Fool. You left her with these beasts? They would carve up their own kin for an extra portion of water. What do you think they will do with her?"

"My apologies, Vizier. I will find her at once."

Syais let go of Passil's shirt and pushed him away from her. "Yes, you will, Warden. And if she is hurt, you will suffer far greater injury than her."

Passil nodded and ran towards the center of the camp, barely able to contain his grin.

Syais stared at him as he ran. She did not believe a word he had said. Not even a fool would have left the Hijeuse to wander the encampment alone. It was a lie and a bad one.

But it was not his first. He had become unreliable long before they left Nouv'eau. And because he strained her trust, she had not let him go anywhere unsupervised. Even after she charged him with protecting the Hijeuse.

"Eyes must blink," Syais had once been told, "and when they do, other senses must take over." So, she relied on what she heard.

Syais summoned the man she tasked with observing Passil and asked for his report.

"Warden Passil escorted the woman from the camp," the man said. "At first, she seemed to resist him, though it was weak and ineffective. Ultimately, she fell, perhaps due to exhaustion, and that was when he dragged her from the camp."

"She was weak? Exhausted?" Syais folder her arms and furrowed her brow. "From what?"

"I do not know, but poisoning seems likely. Perhaps datori or liouc or—"

"Poison? Did you see him administer anything?" Syais's eyes opened wide. Her heart beat quickened. "Did you see him cut her?"

"No." The man shook his head. "No blood. Poison, ingested or inhaled, is my best guess."

Syais exhaled. "Good. Did you see where he took her?"

"Yes." The man pointed into the desert. "That way. He was not gone long—"

"Into the barrens?" She threw her arms up in disbelief. "Why did you not lead with that? Half-wit! She will not last long. Find her immediately!"

"Yes, Vizier," the man smiled. "I too am careful. I had one of mine follow them. She should be back with the girl soon."

"She had better. Now, as for you, find me the Warden and bring him—No. On second thought, I will find him myself." Syais paused for a moment to consider her options. Then, having arrived at one, continued. "The girl is to be returned to my tent and protected at all costs. No one but you and yours are to come near. If she is injured, tend to her as though your life depends on her survival. Signal me when you have her."

The man nodded, and Syais strode from her tent, surveying the camp as she walked. She mounted her horse and rode. It did not matter where Passil had gone. There was nowhere for him to hide, nowhere she wouldn't find him.

\*\*\*

PASSIL WALKED THROUGH THE camp, pleased with himself. The plan was working perfectly; he thought. All he had to do was keep delaying and eventually everything would work itself out. No one could withstand the datori weed for long.

The voices were pleased with him too—he much preferred their adoration to their abuse—and they told him stories of his place next to Syais. The two great V'eauvians would find Z'eau together and after that, they would take back what belonged to them.

So enticing were these thoughts that Passil did not take care to make himself discreet. He walked through men's pitiful rations, drawing their ire and nearly a few blades as well. He kicked dirt at the skittish horses and slapped them on their hindquarters, trying to send them off in a panic.

It was all in fun, of course, but a man of more sound mind may have realized he had accomplished nothing yet. And all he was doing, aside from entertaining himself, was making himself an easy target for anyone who might look for him.

A yell tore Passil from his reveries. And the moment he heard it, he knew his plan had failed. He knew he had been found out. His heart fell through his stomach. He lost his breath. He stood as rigid as a tree. The slightest breeze would have knocked him over.

"Passil," Syais yelled. "What have you done?"

"N-N-Nothing, Vizier." Passil's legs shook. "W-What do you mean?"

"You took the Hijeuse to the desert?" Syais pointed a dagger at him. "Your life or an explanation."

"I-I don't know. She must have wandered—"

"Liar. You took her. I know you did. Last chance."

Syais approached her Warden as he remained fixed to the ground, trembling. He knew it would not be a fight, even if he drew his blade. The woman would cut him to shreds before he took a step.

"No." He shook his head. "I-I promise. She wandered there. I tried to stop her."

Syais stood just out of arm's reach from Passil and waved her dagger through the air. She opened her mouth as if to speak, but before she could, she heard a loud horn. They had found and returned the Hijeuse to safety. She smiled. "I saw you," she said. "But I wanted to keep you, distractions and all. You were worthwhile once. Now..."

"No. I was never—I always served..."

"More lies," she said, staring into his eyes. "You dare insult me like this. I am no chicken following seed. I am the fox. I am the hunter. I am the Eyes. I see you!" She stepped forward and grabbed him.

"No, wait. Please. We don't need her."

"Your commitment to this act is your forfeit. It is your choice."

"Z'eau can be ours together! That is all we need." He tried to shake her grasp but could not. "We don't need her! Do not replace me!"

Syais ignored the ramblings of the dead man. She pulled him towards her and whispered in his ear. "I'll always remember our chambers." She licked his cheek and then, in the next instant, she plunged her blade into his stomach. She twisted the dagger, removed it, then stabbed him once more.

As Passil doubled over himself, he grunted, "She is...not...one of us."

"Of course she is not." Syais spit on his writhing body. "She is the Hijeuse."

Passil fell to the ground, his breathing ragged, his heart fading, his eyes open. He stared at a tent where, in the distance, unbeknownst to him, Ajeau lay in nearly the same position, fighting her own battle against the poison ravaging her body.

\*\*\*

Ajeau wandered the sandy dunes, dragging her legs up and down infinite piles of pale yellow grains. No matter where she stepped, her footprints filled in the moment she moved. There was no record of her coming and going. She was always where she was. And there was never anything there. There was only her. Why was she here?

"To walk. Your journey is nearly done." A familiar voice rumbled as though it came from the dunes themselves.

"Is it you?" Ajeau asked the dune. "The one who chased me before?"

"No. I keep your pursuer at bay. Now keep walking. You are very nearly there now."

Ajeau did as the voice asked and walked. On and on she went, directionless, until she crested a dune and looked at the sky above her. The sun, as it always had been, was directly overhead.

She tried to take another step, but found her feet weighed down as though someone pulled on them. Unable to keep her balance, she fell over backwards. Sand flew in the air. When she landed at the bottom of the dune, she was no longer in the desert. She sat on solid ground.

Dirt and clay, loam, surrounded her. She reached out to touch it with her hands, to make sure it was really there. Soft and moist like the kind that would birth endless yields. She smiled as she took a handful, pressed it into oblong chunks, and threw it at the lush world around her.

Trees, tall and healthy, dotted the landscape. Shrubs and grasses, greener than she could recall ever seeing, grew endlessly in every direction. In front of her, a small lake of clear water, as blue as the sky, sat undisturbed. It was a paradise, the complete opposite of where she had been.

Not even a shadow could unsettle such a place.

A black specter shimmered against the blue water, somehow completely erasing its color, blocking it out like a storm cloud in front of the sun. "Welcome," the spirit said in the same familiar voice that had beckoned Ajeau from the dunes moments ago.

"What is this place?" Ajeau asked.

"This is our home. Or it was once long before you and your kin. It had no name then. But now they call it Z'eau."

"You mean this is...I am here?"

"You are here and not here. The correct location at the wrong time. This is how it looked to me. It will be different when you arrive."

"But...Then...How will I get there? Through the sands?"

The spirit chuckled and shook its head. "No. I told you, you will walk. This exists only for us. I have brought you to this place."

"Why?"

"So many questions," the spirit said. "There will be answers soon, but first let us partake in the great abundance of this land. Look!"

The shadow pointed to trees with large amber fruit hanging from beneath their leaves. Ajeau did not know what they were, but watched curiously as it floated to the treetops, removed the fruit, and brought it to her.

It was then she realized it was not a single fruit but many, perhaps a hundred or more, small oval fruits the shadow had taken from the trees. Ajeau had seen them once before in a cache meant for Foreman Crevir. It took her a moment, but she finally remembered their names, dates.

The shadow handed them to her and said, "Eat!"

Ajeau took a fruit and placed it in her mouth. She bit down and her teeth sunk into a soft, chewy, and exceptionally sweet delight. The taste was more intense than her senses could take after so long with bread, nuts, and seeds. She savored it as long as she could until only the hard pit remained in her mouth.

She spit out the pit and said, "Delicious!"

"Yes, have as many as you like. Here they nurture us, as we will someday nurture them."

After eating a few more of the treats, Ajeau asked, "Are you not eating any?"

"Unfortunately, my days of eating anything are long past. But I miss dates. They were a favorite among our people."

"And who would that be? Who are you?"

"It may be difficult to explain. I am a freeman of the blood, a distant ancestor perhaps, in the way these date trees are ancestors to the ones you will see upon your arrival."

"You mean you were the first Hijeuse? The first with the power."

"I am unfamiliar with such a term, but no, I was not the first. They all had it before me. I was simply the first that was born here, the first that fixed the divide."

"So then...What am I doing here? Why did you bring me here?"

The shadow sighed and said, "Because, Ajeau, there is much you do not know about your people, your blood, your power. I brought you here as my last attempt to convince you to stop."

"Stop me from doing what?" The sweet taste of dates had left Ajeau's mouth, and she felt resentful of the shadow and its riddles.

"From becoming who you think you are. From achieving what you think you want. From using your power."

"Who are you, shadow, to stop me from finding my friend, from gaining my vengeance?" Ajeau became defensive in her confusion. "What veiled threats do you cast at me from your side?"

"There are no threats here, only truths. Look." The shadow gestured towards the trees once more. There were no more dates hanging from the leaves, no more leaves at all. They were dying, perhaps already dead, and next to them was darkness. Like the color of the world had been sucked dry and left only a black void in the shape of a tree.

"What of it?" Ajeau said.

"The tree you seek, it steals from all and desires only death. Do you wonder why it arises during droughts? Only then does it have enough substance to grow and bear fruit. When life thrives, it fades into the earth like a memory."

"So?" Ajeau rose to her feet. "What does that have to do with me? I am not responsible for the drought! I am not responsible for all—"

"Yes. You are. And, should you choose to use your power, know this: whatever the Faine gives you, it takes in kind. Even us, who are bestowed its haste, are affected."

Ajeau laughed. "Then so be it. I will find Vaten and have my vengeance, no matter the cost. No specter from another time will—"

"I am not finished!" The shadow's words echoed across the world, silencing Ajeau. "The time it gives is the time it takes. Doubled. Tripled. A hundred times more. Not even we can resist its effects endlessly."

"Liar," Ajeau said. "Charlatan. The power was given to me to save those in need. To cast out those unworthy. Perhaps that is you! Perhaps you are an outsider trying to save yourself."

As Ajeau spoke, she grew, physically towering over the land and trees that had once dominated her. Even the shadow became nothing more than a spec of black sand.

"Yes," the black tree behind her said. "Do not fear it. Embrace it. Embrace your power!"

Taller and taller, Ajeau grew, feeding off the words as she had fed off the dates.

"Petulant child, think!" the shadow said, craning its head to shout upwards at the giant Ajeau. "This is what it wants. Death. A world of blood upon which it flourishes. Do not allow it dominion!"

"I have dominion. The power is mine, not yours." She grabbed the black tree and picked it up as though it were a small flower. She did not hesitate; the spirit's words were already a forgotten memory. She took the tiny black tree and threw it into her mouth. The world burst apart like a cracked stone.

"Embrace your power!" echoed endlessly across a black space.

***

AJEAU AWOKE PANTING, DRENCHED in her own sweat. She blinked away the dream. It was only her body excreting poison. It meant nothing. No, it meant everything. The power was hers. Unencumbered.

"Hijeuse, you're awake. Thank Eau," Syais said. "Passil tried to—never mind. He is no longer a concern. How do you feel?"

Ajeau smiled at Syais as though stretching tight muscles. "I-I feel well. The dreams," she hesitated and shook her head, "I vanquished it. And in doing so, I was restored. I have been revived. No, better. Born anew."

"That is good to hear because, look," Syais pointed at a patch of green and brown in the distance. Unable to contain herself, the excitement erupted from Syais. "We have made it! Z'eau is in front of us!"

"We made it?" Ajeau let the words sink in. "I—That is—Yes. Yes. I am ready."

"I am too Hijeuse," Syais said with none of the excitement of a moment ago. "But there is a problem."

"What? What problem could there be?"

"Someone is already here. Someone who will not take kindly to our presence. The Noye."

# CHAPTER 47

VATEN DID NOT KNOW who said it first, but it did not matter. Someone shouted, "Land ahead," and for a moment, Vaten's heart caught in his throat. He could not believe it was real, but the bursts of roars and whistles coming from the crew corroborated it. He had finally returned home.

"You must be excited." Zejela said, resting a hand on his shoulder.

"I...I..." Vaten stuttered, unsure how he felt. Part of him was eager to return to the land where he knew the language, the foods, and the customs. And a chance to deliver justice to the Noye excited him.

But concern found cracks in his excitement and worked to destroy it. He had been away so long that everything would be different. He was different too. Even if he could speak the language, he was still a stranger. Worse, he imagined returning to a land of ghosts; a place where everything he came back for—his friend, his father—was gone.

"I don't know if I'm excited," Vaten said to Zejela. "But I am terrified."

The ship slowed along a rocky coast and came to a halt as close as it could to land. The crew unloaded what they could, as quickly as they could, and came ashore. As they did, they left the ship anchored, floating on the waves to be destroyed by the sea or those that followed them.

And Ryiera and Wehlat were not far behind. Zejela spotted a small boat—"a scout, likely," she said—while they unloaded supplies on the beach. The vessel waited for a moment, then turned and rowed back out to sea. "To report what it has seen."

They did not wait for an explanation. There were no discussions, no questioning of plans. There was no time for any of it. Zejela, Vaten, Aloc, Levitien, and the rest of the crew took what they could carry, ran to their horses, and rode into the grasslands beyond. They did not stop until the sun set for the second time since their landing.

\*\*\*

"It's amazing, isn't it kid?" Levitien said to Vaten as they sat around a small fire, sparks jumping into the night sky, then disappearing.

"What is?" Vaten said, startled. They were the first words he had exchanged with Levitien since they arrived. It may have been the first words Levitien exchanged with anyone. Gone was the determined man who strode around the ship, ordering the crew to work the rigging, inspect the sails, and fix any broken part. In his place was a floundering soul who walked as though each step conflicted him.

"The land here..." Levitien glanced all around him. "I guess you can't tell. It's like the rains never came back. We've been gone ages and the land here was dying all that time."

"There's nothing?" Vaten said. "It's all dead?"

"Kid, there isn't a green thing in sight."

Vaten's head dropped, and he reached a hand to the ground. He picked up a handful of soil, letting the dust fall through his fingers. Though he could not see it, he could feel it—dry and sandy—and picture it in his mind.

"How is anyone to survive this?" Vaten said softly. "There won't be a seed of food to fight over. They'll all starve. If they haven't already."

Levitien nodded. "That's right. The lot of them will starve but...someone will survive. People always do. And those that make it will rebuild the world their way. That's why..."

"What?"

"No," Levitien said, shaking his head and sending his eyes to the ground. His voice grew quiet. "We can do nothing about it now. It's not my fault no one saw this coming."

"Saw what coming? What do you mean?"

Levitien drew his head back up and stared at Vaten. He exhaled deeply and said with all his usual confidence, "Kid, the world is changed. It has happened. Only those willing to do what is necessary will live. Remember that if you want to survive."

"What is nec—"

"That's what the Zevacese have done," Levitien continued, ignoring Vaten. "They saw the great change that would come and they acted. They did what they needed to ensure their people would survive. Zejela's attempts are a lost cause. Blowing out the candle after the house has burned. It's a wasted effort."

"But she aims to save our land, your lands, too. Why is that a lost cause? Is that not worth everything to you?"

"The land is dead. Many people probably are too. There is nothing here worth saving. Instead..." Levitien hesitated, as though each word was a tile in a mosaic. "Instead, we must endure by any means."

"Endure?" Vaten shook his head and sighed. "And how do you plan to do that? How do you suppose you endure the Zevacese with their immense power?"

"By..." Levitien shut his mouth.

"By what? By leaving? By ceding your land to those who will conquer it? Do you intend to sacrifice all for yourself?"

"No." Levitien glared at Vaten, who stared blankly into the dark night. A crooked smile formed on his face, one he had hid countless times before. But here, in front of a sightless man, he let it free. "You mistake me even after all this time. I am here for my people above all else. I will never leave them, never sacrifice them. I will survive—we will survive. It's the others who should be concerned."

Vaten heard Levitien stand up, ending their conversation. He cursed his blindness; if only he could see, he would have been able to discern the man's intention. But then he remembered, he had seen so much of Levitien and still knew so little of him.

***

ZEVACESE SCOUTS STOPPED A man on horseback far from his destination. Not that this upset the man any; he was looking for the scouts and had little idea of where the camp he intended to reach was. If he couldn't get to the camp, getting captured by the scouts was the next best thing. Either way, he would end up where he wanted.

Levitien had intended to escape back to Rigolade, but a poor sense of location got him lost. And once he caught sight of the scouts' movements, he decided on capitulation. There was no other safe option; both escaping and returning to the others risked imprisonment, or worse.

And he refused to lose all he had worked for, so close now to success.

Though he had trouble communicating with them—they did not seem to understand who he was and what he wanted—he eventually got their attention. Levitien knew the names of their Elders and that was enough to earn him a trip to their camp. Exactly as he desired.

As they entered the settlement, Levitien heard shouts that roused the Zevacese from their slumber. From the center tent, a man and a woman emerged and began striding toward them with wide grins on their faces. He had not seen them in some time, but he remembered their faces.

Ryiera and Wehlat stopped before they reached Levitien and spoke with the scouts. He didn't understand a word, but from the scouts' expressions, he could tell they were all in high spirits. He wondered if he got them a commendation for his capture. It would be worth it for them. For him too, he thought to himself, and smiled.

The group talked more, followed by some pointing in the direction where they had come from. But then he saw Ryiera frown. As she did, Wehlat shook his head and glared at Levitien. "Isn't that right?" he said in Bassian.

Levitien bowed his head in deference. But as the man continued to watch him, he shrugged. Neither appeared satisfied by the act and each took a step forward, leaving the scouts behind.

"Why did you allow yourself to be captured thusly?" Ryiera said.

"Your scouts—I hope they relayed my message. I am Levitien. I ride with Zejela, Aloc, other Ze—"

"Drop the act. We know who you are and you know who we are." Ryiera folded her arms and stood tall in front of him. "Answer the question. Why did you surrender to us without provocation?"

"I come with terms."

She gestured for him to continue. "Speak your offer."

"I will give you the location of those you seek."

Ryiera stuck out her chin and glanced at Wehlat. "You mean Zejela and the rest of the traitors?"

"Yes." Levitien nodded. "I have come from their camp and can provide an approximate—"

"What do you want in return?"

"For you to let me go," Levitien said. "I ride off to my home without injury or incident. And you do not chase after."

Ryiera nodded her head slowly, as if thinking through each step of the deal. Then she turned to Wehlat and shrugged. She said something in Zevacese. Wehlat scratched his head, then bit his lip as he stared at Levitien.

"Let us say this deal is legitimate," Wehlat said, pacing in front of him. "You are not always authentic. You plan. Scheme. But if true, how can we be sure of your intentions?"

"My word is not enough?" Levitien smirked as though he knew it was not.

"No." Wehlat shook his head. "It is not."

"Then how about I remain here, bound until you find and secure Zejela and the rest. Then you let me go free. If you do not find them..." He chuckled. "You will find them."

Levitien knew there was no way they could pass up such a deal. Even to him, it seemed almost too good to be true. They would get everything they wanted, without cost. If his words were a trap or a scheme, they would be at the cost of his life. Even for a liar, it was a strong assurance.

"You would trust us to make good on this deal once we have captured Zejela and the rest," Ryiera said.

"I would. I take you at your word." Levitien bowed his head.

"You have a deal," Ryiera said. "If you are lying, we will make sure you stay buried this time. Now tell us the location of your camp."

Levitien did not know if they would let him go, but he knew they did not want him either. Larvae were only useful as feed to sustain a chicken; the bugs were no meal on their own. And he was happy to be the maggot, leading the Zevacese to a bigger feast. Once they had their fill, he would be inconsequential. They could release him with no doubts, to dig into the ground and disappear.

\*\*\*

ZEJELA AWOKE TO SCREAMS. It was not the first time there had been shouting among the crew, but even before she heard their words, she knew something was amiss. There was anger and fear in the voices not present before.

A hand grabbed her arm and pulled her to her feet. When she glanced at the man, she saw an unfamiliar face and her heart sank. They had been discovered.

"Aloc, we need defenses!"

"Traitor," the man restraining her said and spit in her face.

She closed her eyes and felt the moist fluid drip down her face. Rage quickly replaced the despair and Zejela lunged at the man with her other arm. The swing was wild and off balance and ultimately futile. The man dodged the blow, then trapped her arm against him with a section of rope.

He called for help, but before they could arrive, Zejela stomped on the man's foot with her heel. He screamed and grit his teeth, but he didn't let go of her arms. She stomped again, hoping to bring the man to his knee where she could strike his face with her leg.

But before her foot landed for the third time, she felt something connect with the back of her head, sending shockwaves of pain and numbness through her body. Her vision blurred and her legs buckled and she would have collapsed had the man holding her arms simply let her go.

"Careful," a woman's voice behind her said. "You remember the orders, subdue only. We are not here to return her to the earth."

"I think she broke my foot!" the first man said. "I had to stop her."

There was silence as Zejela saw another unfamiliar face pass in front of hers. She blinked her eyes to help her focus, but the blurriness remained. The face did not remain in front of her for long. Once it was gone, she closed her eyes, hung her head, and let her body hang lifelessly.

"She's alive," the woman said. "Dazed, but her eyes still track. You are lucky there isn't more damage. Now stand and ready yourself to return to camp."

The man winced audibly, but said, "Yes, I am ready." He shook the bound Zejela by her arms to get her attention, but she remained limp. "You too. We'll be marching soon."

"If I go...you'll...have to...carry me."

A sharp point in her back got her attention. "I cannot kill you," the man said. "But I can ensure you feel pain every moment until we spy our camp. The Elders do not know what force was needed here. And until they see you..." He dragged the blade along her back, opening a minor wound and sending a trickle of blood to the ground.

Zejela stiffened and bit her lip. She did not say a word, did not move to look at the man, but she moved forward as slowly as she could.

"Enough, Lienve," the woman said. "Bring her along, already." Then she turned and walked away from him. "How are the others?"

"Took nearly all of us to bring down the big guy, but they're bound," an unknown voice responded. "This one here can't see. Should we leave him?"

"No one is left behind," she said. Then she swung around and raised her voice. "Line them up and let's get them back to the camp."

Zejela walked through the forest staring at the ground and the feet in front of her. Every few steps, she would pick up her head to see if her entire crew had made it. She did not have long. Each time she looked up, the blunt end of a spear shoved her forward, but in separate quick bursts, she saw Aloc and Vaten and so many familiar faces.

It both raised and dropped her spirits to see her comrades with her. They were alive, but she had failed them. It was her decisions that had gotten them captured. And though they weren't dead yet, they would likely not last long in Ryiera and Wehlat's presence. She resolved to not let that happen. She would save them no matter what, even the Bassians.

As she stepped, she frowned. Then, quickly, she darted her head up and spun. This time she let it linger as long as she could until the familiar thrust lurched her forward. Still, she could not see Levitien.

It was curious. She could understand not seeing the man, she could not see the entire line, but she did not hear him either. And she could not remember a time, other than his trip underground, when he remained silent.

There were plenty of explanations—they gagged him or broke his jaw or even returned him to the earth upon finding them—but none of them felt right. And she could not say why.

But when she walked into the Zevacese camp, an even stranger sight struck her. Levitien was already there. Still bound, but not scared or angry. Indeed, he appeared untroubled by his ordeal, a familiar smirk plastered on his face.

She glared at him until soldiers carried her off to be tied to a stake in the ground in front of the two other Elders. On her knees, she could barely move the arms behind her back. Ryiera and Wehlat circled her as though they were wolves surrounding their prey.

"Zejela!" Wehlat said. "Traitor to Zevaco! Murderer of our Elders. Did you think that escaping to Bas would free you from the judgment of your people?"

Men and women around the camp cheered. They taunted Zejela. Some threw stones, dirt, and sand at her. Wehlat put his hand in the air to stop the commotion, but could not hide the joy from his face.

"Liar!" Zejela said, the sight of the man's grin enraging her. "The only traitors here are you. The only murderers are you two."

"Nonsense." Wehlat chuckled. "We did not run from Zevaco. We did not cavort with the outsiders. We had nothing to gain from our friends' death." He composed himself, as if thinking about the murders of Diros and Uluard was too much to bear.

"You," he continued, "tried to destroy everything you knew, all for some story. You thought you could get away with it too, but the people of Zevaco will not allow you to escape justice."

Wehlat pointed his dagger in Zejela's direction to raucous cheers.

Ryiera stepped forward and grabbed Zejela by the neck. But instead of squeezing hard, instead of screaming at her for the delight of her comrades, Ryiera whispered so that only Zejela could hear. "There is a way for you to survive. Tell us. Tell us what you know of the tree."

"That is what you want." Zejela smirked, then chuckled and nodded her head. "You have failed and need me to clean your messes. I am no servant. I labor not for free. Such things are objectionable on Zevaco."

Ryiera squeezed tighter. "Do not speak to me of our nation. Speak of the tree or find your predicament deteriorates quickly."

"You will get nothing from me. I would rather die then—"

"Silence!" Ryiera yelled. Then her voice grew quiet again. "I expected resistance. But what about the lives of your companions? Would you rather watch as they perished?"

"They will sacrifice what they must to protect this world."

"You mean protect you. Protect your world." Ryiera stared into her eyes. "Are you sure they are willing to die for it?"

"I am." She spoke the words confidently, without knowing their certainty.

Ryiera was not done, however. She let go of Zejela's throat and waved to one of her soldiers. He nodded and began dragging one of their prisoners towards her.

Before he reached Ryiera, she leaned in close to Zejela and said, "What about that poor Bassian you abducted, brought to our land, and used for your schemes? You would condemn him to the earth? All to protect your secrets?"

Zejela struggled furiously in her binds when she saw the soldier dragging Vaten towards them. "No. He has not—"

"But you can save him, Zejela. You can right the wrong you committed all that time ago. You can leave him here, in his home, where he belongs." She shrugged coolly. "Or you can ensure the last thing he knows is your condemnation."

Zejela stopped struggling. Her heart pounded and stomach churned as though she was going to be ill. It was exactly as Ryiera said; Vaten was only here because of her and the decisions she made for him. If she cared for him at all, she could not let him die. If the tree was worth Vaten, it was not a price she would pay. There would be another way to stop the two usurpers yet.

"Stop," she whispered to Ryiera. "Don't."

"What is that, Elder?"

"I said, stop!" Her voice cracked. "I will give you what you want. I will tell you all if you spare their lives."

"Good. That was not so difficult, was it?" Ryiera smiled and thrust her arms in the air to celebrate. The crowd roared back. "Now, tell me, how do the seeds work?"

"The seeds are..." She coughed. "Are unstable. They are not what you want. You want the fruit. And the only way to get it now is to journey to Z'eau."

"Z'eau? The tree grows there? Is that why..." Ryiera looked to the sky.

"Yes," Zejela said. "That is why I created the mark. The answers have always been in Z'eau. And I will tell you how to get there, so long as everyone stays alive."

"You are in no position to make demands."

"Neither are you. You need my information. I am the only one who can find Z'eau without our mark. And this is the only way you will get it."

"Fine," Ryiera said. "Lead us to Z'eau. If you fail, you will die. But you will watch the execution of everyone who journeyed with you go first. Starting with him." She pointed at Vaten.

Zejela nodded, but said nothing. No matter how unsure she was of her decision, she would not let any emotion show. At least until she heard Ryiera's next words.

As Ryiera walked from Zejela, she pointed to Levitien and said to the man next to him, "Unbind him and let him go. He made good on his word."

Zejela watched on in disbelief as the soldier untied Levitien and led him to his horse.

Levitien mounted his horse and breathed deeply and finally disposed of all his pretenses. He glanced at Vaten, who stared blankly at the horizon, not a clue what had transpired. He turned to Zejela. They locked eyes for several moments, but neither person said a word. Then he rode off.

Zejela screamed and nearly ripped the stake that bound her out of the ground.

***

"WAKE UP, VATEN." ZEJELA'S voice was soft, calming. She tried to wake him without alarm. "We are here."

Vaten opened his eyes and saw. For the first time since Zevaco, his eyes showed him a picture of the world instead of blackness. It was blurry at first; the colors washed out. But as he blinked, he saw clearer and clearer. He spun his head side to side, soaking in everything he missed.

Zejela grabbed his head in her hands and said, "Look." She pointed into the distance, at the horizon.

It was wondrous. Not only because he could see it, but also because he had assumed the world would be brown, consumed by drought. Yet, here was a place greener than he could imagine. A thriving, verdant landscape stretching in every direction.

He squinted and gestured towards Z'eau. "Are those...people there?"

"Yes." Zejela said with a smile. "We are late."

# PART V

Book 22: The Echo of the First Split
Iffreux, The Thirteenth Branch

*You must understand, I only know little of this tale. There is much that died with them. Instructions, ideas, plans—knowledge. I know but a single straw of grass in an infinite field of it. But I will tell you what I know, what has been told to me. I must, or else this will all happen again.*

*In the beginning, there was much. Plenty. The land gave us all, more than we ever needed. No one went without; all were nurtured. And it allowed us time to create and invent, which produced more and greater harvests. Even the animals were well fed. They grew large and provided more for us.*

*What began as simple comforts for us soon became an excess. We created houses to store our supplies. Dug into the ground to ensure that our reserves would not rot before they could be eaten. Our population grew—doubled, tripled. We took in neighboring tribes and shared with them in return for their labors. Even that was not enough to deplete our surpluses.*

*Life in the* Fre *was good, peaceful, and the Balafre were happy.*

*But all things change. The weather grew hotter, and the rains fell less often, then not at all. The soil, once moist, grew dry and chalky, then turned to dust. The crops became disturbed, produced less and less, then almost nothing at all. Not long after, they failed entirely.*

*Our people were resilient in the face of this disastrous threat. We began to scavenge and hunt as we once did. Even those new to our land worked to ensure our survival. But there was simply not enough food for all.*

*Thus, we created order from chaos. All food collected and hunted went into a supply for all. Food would be distributed to those who needed it based on how much was needed and how much remained in the supply. It was a simple structure in theory but grew to become so complex as to require a team of people to manage it.*

*Those in charge could no longer assist in scavenging or hunting and had to devote their time to administering rations. Most understood this. But those who were forced to work longer, harder, and under more dangerous conditions, all to appease those who had once been no different from themselves, resented the change.*

*"What is the difference between us and them?" they would ask.*

*"Nothing," others would answer.*

*It was only meant to be a temporary arrangement. Once the soil bore crops again, once fields were sustainable, once the animals returned, life would be comfortable again.*

*But the sun remained unblocked. The rains remained a memory. The soil grew dustier, more inhospitable each day. And resentment was the only thing flourishing.*

*Accusations of theft and misuse ran rampant. It spread faster than fire, seeped into souls quicker than water into soil. And deeper. There was no stopping it at that point; the Balafre fell apart.*

*Words turned to violence. Friends fought friends. Small fights grew to large battles. Stones, some sharpened, some not, became weapons. Once a land more peaceful than a dream turned into a savage nightmare.*

*And this was only the beginning. These skirmishes were a wash. There were no clear winners or losers. The battles would start at a moment's notice and finish just as quickly.*

*Though the workers had the numbers, they were also disorganized and ill-equipped. The Masters of Supply were fewer but strategic and well-armed. And, of course, they had the rations.*

*But it is not an easy thing to win a war against one's own people. Even the victories weaken you.*

*Battles came and went over days, weeks, and months. Some were injured, a few died, but no one gained ground. And no one was working for the common good. No one worked at all. And it meant no yields were added to the supplies.*

*With no incoming food, the remaining supplies dwindled quickly. There had been lean times before, but this was a famine now. Many starved.*

*Yet still, the combatants fought. Perhaps with more intensity, with time slipping away. Every failure to advance brought with it the prospect more would go hungry. There could be no truce. There would have to be a victor, and soon.*

*And there would be. But the cost was inconceivable.*

*There were learned people in Z'eau. Those who knew the writings of our people, the stories of the past. They looked for solutions and found what would save them. They were right...and wrong.*

*Aligned with the Masters of Supply, they sought a tree that could grow during shortages of rain. It was difficult to find, so alike it was to others, but eventually they made their discovery. What more, they had found the tree produced fruit! A single fruit with a single large seed.*

*It would not save them from starvation, but that was not the purpose of their quest, not the purpose of the fruit. Instead, it was meant to put an end to the fighting. To restore peace to Z'eau. In some ways, it did exactly that.*

*I do not know the specifics of their rituals, nor its effects; I was not involved in such blasphemy. But afterwards there was no more war. Many people died, and the rest—save the Masters of Supply—all left Z'eau.*

*The scavengers, some of the fiercest remaining warriors, rode their horses and promised never to settle in any one land again. Always wander. That was the only way to survive.*

*The workers who lived headed towards the sea. It was rumored that they built a ship larger than a city and sailed for a new home out of reach of their previous masters.*

*Those who stayed no longer called themselves Balafre. No, the Balafre were no more. To call themselves that was an injustice to Eau, to that which was responsible for their victory. They renamed themselves in Eau's spirit. They called themselves the V'eauvians.*

*In the wake of one, now were many.*

*But soon after their triumph, several V'eauvians died. Not from starvation, as best as I could tell, but they died as if it were fated to occur. Some died in the middle of taking counts or resting in the shade. One moment alive, the next dead. And for no obvious reason.*

*There were rumors they were the ones who had found the fruit and their deaths were retribution for their impiety. There were other rumors that spirits from another realm came to ravage their bodies. Still others said the blood of Eau protected those who performed the sacrilege and it was the naysayers who perished. I do not know if any of these stories are true.*

*Regardless, after the deaths, I found the tree. It had grown another fruit, as though it fed on the rotting corpses. After some deliberation, I removed it. I did not want it snatched by some beast and used to bring more destruction to our people.*

*And then I left, followers in tow, as many before me did. But I did not seek the sea nor wish to ride forever. I found a place where trees were tall and endless. In their shadow, my followers and I laid the first bricks of a new wall, for a new city. And there the rain fell once more.*

*The fruit is long destroyed; the journey saw to that. The only remnants of it, its seed, I buried safely underground where it will be unable to sprout. Only I know the markings that lead to the Silvan Altar. And I will be dead soon.*

*I am Iffreux.*

# CHAPTER 48

THE CITY OF Z'EAU was a respite from the outside world. Light to its darkness. It provided shelter, safety, and, most importantly, reliable sources of food and water. It was a paradise, created from surreal shades of green, blue, and yellow. And though it was everything to the Noye, it was not, despite its name, a city.

There was a grove of trees and a field of grasses full of wild crops. A shining blue lake of water sat in its center and rocky cliffs that climbed up the dunes. No huts or buildings were present, nothing that would indicate people had ever been there before. They had been, of course, but the land erased them.

The whole thing was about the size of Crevir's Estate. And that may have presented a problem to the Noye if their entire nation arrived. But Savique saw no more than a hundred who had survived the trip and earned their place in such a haven.

In the beginning, Savique, Vrai, and the rest of the Noye did little. They ate, drank, and revived themselves as best as they could. When their energy allowed them to, they nursed others or told stories of those they lost with all the appropriate flair.

Eventually, Savique and the others recovered enough to begin creating their world anew. They built shelters, created tools to work the land, and weaved cloth. It felt like a return to normalcy, to the familiar. But nothing else in Z'eau was normal. And Savique's life there was far from familiar.

Everywhere he went, the Noye showered Savique with their admiration and respect. They called him Elder and respected his words above all. It had been some time since the disparate tribes of the Noye followed a single leader, but they did again now. And their leader was Savique.

What he thought of it all was inconsequential. He had done something great, found something the Noye thought to be a myth, and in doing so, he gave credence to every story they ever told, every performance they ever gave. It was more

441

than being correct; his discovery validated them. "See what you made possible," they said to him with every glance.

This, as much as anything, made Savique happy. He thought of Eyvo-Ille; he thought of the men and women he spoke with outside of Nouv'eau; he thought of the families he met riding from tribe to tribe and smiled. Yes, they were gone now, but their people would live on with a renewed sense of possibility and wonder. And he would too.

Especially after he saw the Tree.

Initially, when Vaten and Vrai wandered Z'eau to look for the legendary Faine, they were confused. All the trees appeared similar. Brown trunks, green leaves at the top. Some were larger, some were fuller, some bore fruit, and some were brittle, but nothing distinguished any of them as unique. Savique chuckled, wondering if the trees thought the same thing about people.

The two men tried using the mark, but found it unreliable. Whenever they took more than a few steps in the direction it pointed, they found the stone would turn and point in a new direction. A few steps in that direction and the stone would turn again. It led them in circles.

"Perhaps it is broken," Vrai said once.

"Or perhaps the Tree was not real. The stone points only to something in the lake or the earth under this place," Savique countered.

"Z'eau is real. This," Vrai picked up wet moist dirt, "is real. If one of them is true, then surely the other can be as well."

Savique shrugged and smiled. "Then we should continue looking. We have all the time we need."

They did as Savique said and examined the trees, searching for any sign of their target. But they saw nothing. Plenty of fruit, plenty of leaves, plenty of branches, but nothing distinctive. The trees all looked like trees.

Until one day, while out searching, Savique stepped on something hard and spiked. It lodged in his sandal so deeply that it poked through the sole and punctured the bottom of his foot. He hopped on one foot, then glanced down at it. Upon seeing the strange object, he bent over and pulled it out. He knew immediately where he had seen it before. It was the same shape as the mark that led them to Z'eau, round with angular spikes, one of which was longer than the rest.

It had to be more than mere coincidence. And the seed was not typical of the other trees in the area. The figs had small seeds and dates had larger pits. But no fruit tree had produced such a round and spiked seed.

And when he looked up, there was no doubt. There was a single black fruit, about the size of a fist, hanging from between the leaves.

This was the Faine, the Tree of Fate. These were the seeds. That was the fruit. Savique was sure of it. And in that moment, fantasy became reality once again. It was all real. And the line between story and truth further blurred.

There was jubilation among the Noye, even if no one in the camp—Savique himself—truly understood what he found. It was enough for the others that it was a thing only spoken about, something miraculous. He was far from cursed; he was blessed.

Until he spotted something on the horizon. It took him a moment, but once he saw it, he knew it was people. He could not yet tell who it was, or how many. Part of him hoped it was lost Noye who had finally found their way. Perhaps Navo-Ille rode with those she had rescued from the camp. Or other friendly travelers from all over Bas.

He knew these were dreams, lies he created to soothe himself, because the reality was far more troubling. Someone else knew where Z'eau was. And whoever they were, they would not be pleased to find the Noye occupying the land, eating the crops, straining the resources.

As the mass of people grew closer, Savique found himself torn between options. The concerned glances of the Noye who had celebrated him weighed heavily on him. He could not lose more, so soon after they thought they had found salvation.

But then, without warning, the group on the horizon stopped. Savique did not know why, but he also did not care. All that mattered was they had some time to plan a defense or escape. Some scheme that would keep him, and the people who now relied on him, alive.

There were no good options. They did not have the numbers to mount an attack, they could not escape back through the desert, and defense within Z'eau risked the elimination of the oasis, and the Noye.

Savique consulted with Vrai and others and decided. "We will convene with the people in our shadow," he announced to the Noye. "We will invite them into Z'eau and speak with them. Understand who they are and what they want. If necessary, we will forge an alliance to allow us all to share this land peacefully. It is the land of all our Elders, after all."

The Noye did not make a sound. It was as quiet as Savique ever heard it in Z'eau. But it did not matter, the decision was final. And if the group proved hostile, at least Savique would know it and face no surprises. In the end, it could be the difference between existence and extinction.

Savique summoned a woman in a green cloak to his side. "When you arrive, state your purpose. Invite them. Then ride away. Do not wait for them to acknowledge you or for their leader to approach. You do not need a response. Whoever is in charge will get the message. And you will survive. Do you understand? You must survive."

The woman nodded her head, mounted her horse, and rode. Fearlessly, she raced into the unknown.

***

"AND YOU BELIEVE THEM to be authentic?" Ajeau said to Syais about the message heaved into their camp earlier that day. "Not using the Noye name to create fear?"

Syais stared toward Z'eau and the little flecks moving about. "No, it was a Noye. She wore a green cloak and made no attempt to disguise herself. They wanted us to know."

"Know what?"

"That they had beaten us here. They have Z'eau and perhaps..." Syais inhaled sharply. "The Tree."

Ajeau drew back in surprise. "You mean, they can use the power, the same as me?"

"We do not know that. All we know is that the Noye occupy Z'eau. They may have the Tree or they may not. There may be other schemes afoot." She scowled and ran her hand through her hair. "But why else would they send an invitation to meet?" The question was as much to herself as to Ajeau.

"Because..." Ajeau thought for a moment, then her eyes grew wide with insight. "They don't have the Tree. Or at least the power to wield it. They are weak and scared. If they could, would they not seek our destruction?"

"Yes, you may be correct," Syais said. "Or they may wish to bring us close to ensure our demise. They are conniving rodents. Regardless of their plans, I must meet with them."

"What? You said they may try to bring about our end. And if they are weak, we could crush them. I could—"

"Patience." Syais held up a hand. "If they are weak, then I will see their weakness. Exploit it. But we will not reveal our strength now. Not until we know."

"Then I will accompany you. Once we know their position, I can rid Z'eau of those savages and we can search for Vaten."

"No, I will not risk your death, even accidental, on this. You are too—"

"I did not ask." Ajeau glared at Syais, full of insolence. Her heart pounded in her chest. "I am the Hijeuse, am I not? The power is mine."

Syais stared at her and said nothing.

"And so is that city," Ajeau continued. "The sooner we have it, the sooner I can find my friend. And then deliver justice to the deserving."

"Fine," Syais conceded with an indifferent wave. "Ready yourself immediately. We ride before the sun crests."

As soon as Ajeau turned her back to Syais, she beamed. She kept her back straight as she walked, but her legs wobbled and she thought she might fall. She could not believe a worker like her had persuaded a Vizier. But she had, and in doing so, she understood the true power of her gift. Control.

It may not have been more than a speck, but it was more than she ever had before. She had only known following others, not commanding them. Here, now, finally, she held sway.

Later that day, Ajeau met Syais at the front of the camp. The Vizier wore an outfit that covered her in white. Shirt, pants, cloak, gloves, shawl, even a hood that fell in front of her face were pristine, not a spot of color on it. She shimmered in the sun, almost too bright to look at.

Ajeau wondered why the Vizier had changed clothes, then realized it was a message. A response. If the Noye rider had told them they possessed Z'eau, Syais would tell them the V'eauvians were there to take it.

"Are you ready?" Syais asked.

Ajeau nodded.

"Then let us ride."

And they did so until the sand ended and the soil began. They dismounted and entered paradise on foot beside their horses, as if riding the beasts violated the land they sought to honor. Whether it was out of deference for the land or to not be seen as a threat, they walked into Z'eau slowly and calmly.

A handful of Noye soldiers eventually met and escorted the two V'eauvians, who thought their attendants were too young and unconfident in their gaits. If this was the strongest the Noye offered, they were weaker than Ajeau had imagined. She smiled, wishing she could tell Vaten his hated enemies were powerless. She knew it would make him happy wherever he was.

They followed the soldiers to a small tent next to the lake sitting in the center of the oasis. The water glistened in the sun, a perfect reflection of the blue sky. Ajeau thought she could have drank it all if they offered. But they did not. Instead, the Noye prodded her forward into the shelter where a man sat alone inside.

He rose, extended his hands, and said, "Welcome to Z'eau."

*** 

WEHLAT'S PLAN WAS SIMPLE, if not rash. "Let us destroy them now. Take them by surprise and wipe them from the earth. They look like such a haggard bunch and we are as well-supplied as we will be. It would be no harder than a day's work in Zernais."

Ryiera showed more thought and restraint. "No. I agree they may look exhausted, but the Tree still resides there. Is that right?" She turned to the woman standing next to her.

Zejela nodded. She had told the truth thus far—if ever asked, she would say it was all part of a plan, and that was true too, she would exclude the fact that her plans kept changing—and she would not stop now. They had followed the path she had once traveled, then found the bats flying overhead, and now sat on the edge of Z'eau. If the two usurpers knew the Faine was there as well, then so be it. They still knew nothing of how to unlock its power.

Ryiera continued, "So they possess the Tree and, possibly, the power it offers. Perhaps they know how to use it. If they do, they would be far stronger than we realize and unafraid of our advances. We should not be hasty."

"If they knew how to use the power," Wehlat mumbled quietly. "We'd all be dead already."

It was not clear whether anyone heard him, but no one responded. After a silent moment, Wehlat said, "Well then, what is your plan?"

"For now, we wait," Ryiera said. "Send the scouts in under the cover of darkness and find out what we can about the people there. Then we can act, but not before."

Wehlat kicked sand into the air and pointed at it. "You would have us wait in this? It is suicide!"

"Patience has served us well so far." Ryiera placed a hand on Wehlat's shoulder. "Remember what we worked for. We do not need to jeopardize it by rushing blindly into the unknown."

"She is right," Zejela said, out of turn. Another ploy for time.

"Silence!" Ryiera stared contemptuously at Zejela. "We are nearly done with—"

"But they are enemies." Zejela pointed towards Z'eau.

Ryiera and Wehlat glanced at each other and then at Zejela with furrowed brows. They were interested. Her gamble was successful.

"They are Noye and V'eauvian." Zejela continued to gesture at Z'eau. "You can tell by the colors they bear. Long enemies from the time of the Great Separation. They may not last long—"

"Those are Noye and V'eauvians." Wehlat stroked his beard. "That is...interesting, if true."

"I have been forthright with you—"

"Yes, yes." Wehlat waved at Zejela dismissively. "You have been honest. And, assuming that has continued, then I agree with you, Ryiera. We should wait. Let us see what these enemies do in their shared space. And perhaps our scouts can stoke their animosities, so that we may have them destroy each other."

Ryiera smiled and nodded.

And with that, Zejela was dismissed. Guards escorted her back to the cart she shared with her crew, Vaten included, and bound as a prisoner.

***

For Vaten, the road to Z'eau had been empty. Not only the world itself, but his heart, too. Zejela had explained Levitien's betrayal, in all its depressing detail.

And for what? Vaten spent much time on the trip thinking back through their interactions, picturing Levitien's behaviors and trying to understand his motivations. But none of it explained why he had delivered Vaten, and the rest, to Ryiera and Wehlat.

For periods it gnawed at him, but ultimately, he gave up wondering and simply lamented that his once-friend had condemned him so brutally.

But by the time they arrived on the outskirts of Z'eau, and with his eyesight returned, Vaten had let the winds of the desert carry the past from his mind. Instead, he turned to the future. What awaited him in Z'eau? Zejela had been confident, the Noye—the very people who stole his father—would be there waiting.

It renewed and energized him even though he remained imprisoned. He was supposed to be here; he knew it. His destiny was so close. He only needed a free arm to reach out and grab it.

So, when Zejela arrived back amongst the prisoners following her discussion with Ryiera and Wehlat, Vaten asked with a sincere interest, "What did they say?"

"We wait," Zejela said. "They are going to make camp here and—"

"What about we?" Aloc gestured at the surrounding prisoners. "Is where we death?"

"No, not if I can help it. I..." Zejela cleared her throat. "I have a plan."

Aloc translated for the Zevacese. As he did, Vaten leaned towards Zejela and whispered, "Should we make our own escape?"

"No. Remember," Zejela said and nodded to make her point.

Vaten gazed at the ground and remembered. He had tried to escape from the Zevacese once before and it had not ended well. No, escape was not an option.

There was some discussion among the prisoners until Zejela quieted them.

"They still need me because of who is here," Zejela said. "And as long as they need me, you are safe. I will do everything I can to remain essential. For now, like them, we wait. Someone will come."

"What do you—" Vaten began, then stopped, his attention drawn to a strange buzzing sound like one made by cicadas on a warm night. There were no bugs here though, and the sound rose and fell, unlike the constant hum of the flying pests.

It was loud enough to catch the guards' attention, too. They glanced around, confused, trying to track the sound's location. For a moment, they suspected the prisoners. But seeing the perplexed look on the faces of their captives, they moved on.

One prisoner did not look confused. She looked assured and pleased. Zejela leaned to Vaten and said, "They are early. But that is not unwelcome. I told you someone would come soon. I only wonder who it is."

# CHAPTER 49

SAVIQUE STARED AT THE two V'eauvians entering Z'eau. The white garb of the one on the left gave them away. Those colors had been seared into his mind in Nouv'eau and the moment he saw them, he knew they were V'eauvian. And it sent a shiver down his spine.

For a moment, he could not control his panic. He envisioned himself back in the dark of the Cave and or tied to a chair awaiting torture. He saw the death of so many Noye, Eyvo-Ille and Navo-Ille included. The great enemy of the people he now led—his people, he supposed—had shown up to finish the job.

But he calmed himself and remembered his position; he had control of Z'eau and the Tree. The V'eauvians, even though they likely abhorred the idea, came to speak with him. With the Noye. That gave him hope. Perhaps it was an opportunity for peace.

Still, he was not naïve. He would not forgo preparations over a flight of idealism.

"Vrai," Savique whispered to the man next to him to get his attention. "Quickly. Find cover nearby and watch over the meeting. If any trouble arises, take the rest out of the city. And do what you must so that today is not the last one for the Noye."

"But..." Vrai pointed at the incoming V'eauvians. "You see—"

"Yes, I know. Now go."

Vrai stared a moment, then nodded. He ran off and found shelter out of view of the tent, but still well within earshot. And depending on where the V'eauvians stood, he might even catch sight of them. But when they arrived, Vrai found he could only make out their feet. Still, he was sure there was something familiar about the gait of the person in white.

450

Savique had the same thought. Even as he welcomed the V'eauvians and waited for them to sit, his mind raced, working to figure out where he had seen this person before.

It was hanging there like the branch of a tree he was climbing, just out of reach. He kept trying to grab it and ascend higher but couldn't. Until finally—as a smile cracked his lips—he grabbed the branch. He knew the wickedness standing in front of him.

He wondered if Syais recognized him—it had been many years since she had him restrained in her room, and even longer since he drove a dagger into her back to save Eyvo-Ille—but the look on her face gave nothing away. If she remembered him, it was not obvious to Savique. And if she did not remember him, he did not want to offer that knowledge freely. The two stared at each other in silence, pretending to be strangers.

But the quiet extended too long, and the awkwardness became palpable. If only to ensure his understanding of her remained a secret, he began speaking. "Welcome to Z'eau," he said.

"Thank you for your welcome. We are honored to be here in this place," Syais said. Ajeau and Syais bowed their heads in respect, then sat on a bench of stones across from Savique. "But since when do vermin overrun Z'eau?"

"Since sometime after the V'eauvians tried to wipe a peaceful people from the earth," Savique responded.

Unseen by anyone, Syais smiled under her hood. "So you were there? At that battle."

"What battle? It was a slaughter." He slammed the arm of his chair, then stood. "Yes, I was there to see families, children no higher than one's knees butchered by soldiers. A battle..." He scoffed.

Syais' smile only grew. "It was a fate they brought on themselves," she said, as if it were some widely known fact. "Or were you unaware of the atrocities your people committed in Nouv'eau?"

Savique shook a finger at Syais. "Those are not comparable. One was fighting between soldiers and combatants. The other, a campaign to eradicate a people."

"So you admit to being the aggressor?"

"I said no such thing. I saw both encounters and—"

"You were there?" Syais faked surprise and outrage. "At Nouv'eau? Monster!"

"Me? A monster? Laughable. I was there, but I killed no innocent man, woman, or child. Can you say the same? I know you cannot." The façade crumbled. And the moment that it did, Savique destroyed it all together. "I have seen you before," he said. "And you have seen me. I am the reason—"

"I know who you are!" Syais yelled back at him.

As she rose from the bench, Savique swept his robes behind him and revealed the dagger hanging from his hip. The move surprised Syais; she finished standing but tensed her muscles, never once moving to her weapon.

Instead, she lowered her hood and stared into his eyes. Savique stared back with eyes full of rage. But as they held each other's gaze, he realized it was over. The rage disappeared, replaced by acceptance and resignation. The conflicts of the past ensured no peace in the present could ever be found.

*** 

Ajeau could barely stand to listen to the bickering any longer. It was all about battles and slights and old scores; the ancient disputes of a world ended. She cared so little for it. The only reason they were there at all was so Ajeau could access the Tree. She did not need them to be friends; she needed them to...

She saw her path forward, a way to bring the Noye and V'eauvians together. They would never settle their grudges if they thought of each other as their enemy. So she would give them a new enemy, someone else to hate. Strong, mysterious, and vile; the Zevacese would work perfectly.

"Sit down, the both of you," Ajeau said, like a mother to her children.

Syais and Savique both glanced at her with nearly identical questioning glances. They did not sit, but in their surprise, they dropped their guard. That was enough for Ajeau. All they had to do was attend to her. She would do the rest.

"I do not know who you are and I do not care," Ajeau continued. "And I am not here to speak about past conflicts or slaughters. They are gone. No more. I am the future. I am the Hijeuse. And I am here to save us all from something far worse than the people in front of you."

Savique scratched his chin and narrowed his eyes as he glanced at the mark hidden behind his seat. It was her blood he had taken from Nouv'eau and her connection to Z'eau that allowed them to make it there.

"Have you heard of the Zevacese?" she asked.

"I have not. Who, or what, is that?"

"They are a people," Syais said.

"Yes." Ajeau nodded. "They are a formidable foe who move across Bas like spirits. They exist and then they do not as though they were never there. The only proof of their presence is what they destroy. What they take. And they are coming for us."

Savique glanced from side to side. "I see no others. It is a spectacular story, though; powerful unseen people that seek my ruin." He moved his hand to his dagger and his voice grew serious. "But I need no tales or inventions. I know of real people that seek such things." He stared at Syais.

"Then you know such acts are possible. They *can* happen." Ajeau gestured at the world around her. "And they are happening. Indeed, I would not be here if they had not."

"Let me ask you, then," Savique said. "If such people are real, how have you come to know about them?"

"I have seen their brutality, their existence through their actions. They took one friend—who I fear has returned to the earth—and murdered another for no reason at all except that it is in their vile nature to commit such unspeakable acts."

Savique's head tilted slightly to the left and stared at Ajeau with eyes full of compassion. "I can see the loss on your face. But that does not mean these people are real. You understand I cannot simply take your word."

"You may have no choice," Ajeau said.

"There is always a choice," he replied.

Ajeau sighed. The man was testing her patience. "Yes, and what will yours be? If the Zevacese arrive here, with your defenses...There would be nothing left. Z'eau, maybe the entirety of Bas would be destroyed."

Savique returned to his chair and rested his chin on his hand, his face pointed to the ground. Ajeau thought the man on the verge of submission. She had outmaneuvered him and left him no choice but acceptance. Surrender.

But when his eyes met hers again, they were full of pride. "Let us say that these...Zevacese are real," Savique said. "And that they venture here. What do you offer us? And what do you want in exchange?"

"We offer protection," Ajeau said. "At the cost of the City and the Tree."

Savique laughed. "You would have us give up Z'eau on a tale. You would have me hand over this land, the Tree, to our enemy," Savique gestured at Syais, "so that we could save ourselves." He shook his head. "No, such an action would not save us. It would remove the dagger from our chest only so that it could be stuck in our back."

"Do you not see?" Ajeau said. "You live in a world no longer here. The rivals of the past are gone. I told you, I am not here about your history. I am here about the future. Those who died have returned to the earth. Do not sacrifice those who survive because of it."

Syais chuckled cynically. "Remember what Alopsis said, 'Peace is not made with those you are not at war with.'"

"That may be true, and Alopsis wise," Savique said as he peered at Syais through thin slits. "But I do not think I need to offer anything for your protection."

Ajeau furrowed her brow and drew back. "We will not help you without recompense. We are not providing alms."

"Yes," Savique stood and began pacing. "But if these Zevacese are real and if they come here bent on destruction, then either they do so to eliminate all, in which case you will be forced to defend yourself. Or they do so to capture Z'eau and the Tree, and you will be forced to fight them for your desires. Either way, you must fight them."

Ajeau's muscles tensed. She scowled and clenched her jaw, annoyed. The man was wholly resistant. She exhaled. "You may be right. We will have to fight. But you die. In either scenario, the Noye are extinguished. You would seek such an end?"

"Of course not, I..." Savique's voice trailed off.

Though Ajeau knew he had argued himself into a corner, she did not grin or gloat. She allowed Savique to think about his choice—give over Z'eau or risk the Noye's extinction—and imagine their outcomes.

But she was also impatient. After a spell of silence, and after seeing Syais nod at her, she continued, "We are offering assistance. Yes, it comes at a price. But it will save your people. Perhaps save all of us."

Savique blinked at her and rubbed his hands together. Then he scratched the top of his head. "I can see your words are heartfelt. Whether they are true is another matter. But I will consider them. Wait here while I confer with my advisors." He gestured towards the guards. "They will ensure you remain comfortable."

Ajeau returned to the bench and watched Savique exit through the back of the tent as the guards drew the weapons and stood tall. It was a show of force—a weak one—but it did not bother her. She was confident, proud of her tact.

But she did not know Savique went in search of another who knew the treachery of the V'eauvians and their leader. He sought counsel from a man who had experienced the worst of what the V'eauvians could do and who believed in the good of the Noye above all. *Come quickly, Vrai,* he thought.

***

THE DECISION WEIGHED ON Savique like the first stone he carried on Crevir's Estate. He had wanted to show his strength and tenacity then, and it left him hunched at the waist, limping for a week. Now, as then, his back felt tight, his legs unsure. He wondered what agony would this choice leave him with.

But as he paced and considered every outcome, Vrai appeared beside him as though he heard Savique's silent call. "You recognized the woman. Who is she?" Vrai asked immediately, as though the question had been at the forefront of his mind for some time.

"I do not know her name," Savique said. "The woman wears white, always has. She was with the Lord in—"

Vrai nodded. "She goes by many names. But I know her best as Syais. She was once the Warden of the Lord's Guard, then Vizier, but it would seem those days are over. I wonder who she is now."

"And the younger one with her? Do you know her?"

"I don't know, I couldn't see."

"Interesting. Perhaps a new Lord?" Savique glanced upwards, then waved as if dismissing the thoughts. "But that doesn't matter now. The longer we wait, the more confident they will become in their position. They may even remove the offer entirely."

"You do not mean to deal with these fiends?"

Savique shrugged his shoulders. "What other choice would you make? Risk our—"

"I would not hand to our enemies the very thing they seek for our destruction."

"And what of the Zevacese?"

Vrai threw his head back in disbelief. "A story invented to frighten children. They are not real, they are not threats. They are simple fantasies."

"Would we not have said the same of Z'eau, not long ago?" Savique glanced at the ground. Soil in the desert seemed unreal too. "I believe the young woman. I saw the pain on her face."

"Manufactured! For this very purpose. To make you feel you had no choice but to hand over Z'eau."

"And what if we reject them? Do we fight? Do we return to animosities that resulted in the deaths of so many?"

Vrai nodded. "If that is what much be done, I would rather die fighting than giving up."

"But I fear..."

Vrai put his hand on Savique's shoulder. "You cannot let fear decide for you. It makes a coward of us all."

Savique met Vrai's gaze, despondent. "Are you not worried that even in this paradise, we will find only our ends? That leading the Noye here was nothing more than a delay in the inevitable. That we will be a fire put out by the sand."

"No." Vrai smiled and shook his head. "We are a fire, wild and untamed, that will rage and consume all in its path. We will bring light to this place. We cannot concern ourselves with the dark." He shook Savique as if to emphasize his point. "We must choose to fight. All else is left to fate."

A bird perched on a rock behind Savique crowed and startled him. He spun around to see a small spotted wren staring at him. He stared back, the alarm fading, as he watched the small animal hop twice, then fly away.

But in his wake, Savique noticed something in the distance. A small child ran on the far side of the lake, their caretaker chasing after them. The scene filled him with a mix of sorrow and hope. He wondered whether the child would know peace and prosperity in their life. Or, like his son, would they know only pain, death, and diaspora?

Savique turned back to Vrai and nodded. "I have decided."

He strode back into the tent, waving the guards away. He stood facing the two V'eauvians and said, "I will agree to your deal. We will give you access to Z'eau and the Tree in return for protection. But there is one more condition I must demand."

Ajeau smiled and hurriedly asked, "What is it?"

"From this day forth, the people of this land are one. No more V'eauvians, no more Noye. One Tribe, as it was before. The Z'eau. If you are truly interested in a future without hostilities, then that is what I offer. That is what this place can be."

"Nonsense!" Syais exclaimed. "We will not allow our people to share space with these defilers. Ajeau, we do not need such insidious stipulations. We will take the land by force."

Ajeau listened to Syais's words, but she never considered them. She had gotten what she wanted, perhaps more. A place and a people and, with them, the power to find Vaten and have her vengeance. She couldn't agree to Vrai's plan quickly enough.

"I accept your terms." Ajeau stepped forward and bowed. "From this day forward, one people—the Z'eau—will reside on this land. You will forfeit the Tree and any fruits and seeds to us."

"What are you doing?" Syais whispered, keeping her eyes focused on Savique. "We do not need—"

"We have the Tree and the fruit. All else is irrelevant." Ajeau smiled at Syais, eyes glittering even in the shade. "We can do as we please."

"Careful girl. It is a dangerous game you play."

Savique leaned towards the two V'eauvians with an inquiring glance. "Are we still in agreement?"

"Of course," Ajeau said with a bow.

Syais said nothing, though when Savique's glance found her eyes, she gave a single nod.

Ajeau continued speaking. "I will bring word of our arrangement to the V'eauvians and we will return with those who would seek the new beginning we offer. The rest will be free to roam the desert."

"Agree. But allow me a final question." Savique examined Ajeau closely. "How do you intend to protect us?"

Ajeau smirked. "That is for when I return. Until then, tend to the Tree so that I may show you what it means to be Hijeuse."

Ajeau and Syais rose and walked from the tent.

*\*\*\**

SYAIS FUMED. SHE WANTED to yell and throw the insolent, brash, stubborn girl to the ground. The Hijeuse needed a reminder of who was in charge. Syais wrote the rules to the game they played, not Ajeau. It did not matter if her gamble was a ploy, Ajeau knew too much of her power. It was inevitable, she supposed, though she wished it would have come after they captured Z'eau and drove the Noye from the world.

As she strode to her horse, Syais realized she needed a new plan. If Ajeau could not be relied upon, then she would have to destroy her. It was better to have no Hijeuse than to serve under one who resigned their world to the impure.

But she could not rid herself of the girl immediately. She was a valuable weapon. Though the Noye appeared weakened, they held the Tree, its fruit, and, most importantly, the city. Her soldiers' rations would not last forever. But the Noye had water and food and shelter as long as they needed it.

They could not lay siege to the place, it would only exhaust her soldiers. They could not invade the place. The Noye would retreat and strike from the shadows. And that was if they had not unlocked the power of the Tree.

She sighed. As much as it pained her, she needed Ajeau. At least for now. Once they settled in Z'eau, there would be no ridding the place of the V'eauvians.

She smiled as she galloped over the dunes, and the plan coalesced in her mind. Yes, she could have Z'eau, the Tree, the fruit, all of it, and destroy Ajeau, too. And every Noye, and that Eau damned Savique, would watch it all from under the sand.

*\*\*\**

VRAI, JUST OUTSIDE THE tent, listened to Savique's decision with shock and anger. Not only had he relinquished the Tree and the city to infidels, but he had ended the Noye so unceremoniously. It was as if they had been wiped clean by the Lord years ago.

But then he heard a strange name. One he knew without a second thought because, despite its uniqueness, he had heard it so many times during his days on the estate. When Vaten was younger, Vrai remembered, he talked about a girl named Ajeau nonstop. She was a child then, a little troublemaker, but she had captured Vaten's eye all the same.

For a moment, Vrai did not believe it. It was not possible the girl standing there now, barking orders at Syais and controlling the V'eauvian army, was the same one Vaten knew on the estate. But the name clawed at him.

His eyes grew wide as he realized she was the one who had left with Vaten. She would not have suffered the fall of the estate. If they had survived their wanderings, if they had kept away from the thieves and raiders, then...

Once the meeting had concluded and the two V'eauvians left, Vrai approached Savique. "There is something I must tell you!" Vrai's words were rushed with excitement.

"Yes, yes. I know." Savique waved off the criticism he assumed was coming. "You do not trust the V'eauvians. But my decision is—"

"No, that is not it!"

"Then, what?"

"The girl, the Hijeuse," Vrai said with a grin on his face. "I think I know who she is!"

"The one that sits beside the woman in white? The young woman with whom I made the deal? Ajeau, I believe, is what Syais called her."

"Yes! Yes!" Vrai's excitement broke free from its restraints. "She was on the estate, with Vaten and I, before its end. Your son knew her well then."

Savique's eyes narrowed, and he turned his head to the side ever so slightly, as though he was looking at something he could not quite identify. "You are sure of this?"

"I believe so, yes. And there is more—"

"But how? How does an estate girl end up as the leader of the V'eauvians, and now the Z'eau? Who is she?"

"That, I do not know." Vrai shook his head, then clapped and pointed at Savique. "But there was a time when it would have been equally absurd to suggest you would be a Noye Elder. Yet here you are."

"Yes, but..." Savique was still confused.

"You distract me," Vrai said. "Not only was she on the estate, she is the one who Vaten departed with! She may know..."

Vrai kept talking for a bit, but Savique heard nothing. He lost himself in possibility and hope of what Vrai's words could mean. If he was correct about Ajeau, then she might know if Vaten was alive and where he was and how to reach him. She was the bridge between them, and he had every intention of crossing it. Tears welled in his eyes.

"Savique. Savique!" Vrai's voice and gentle shaking broke the man's reveries. "Did you hear what I said?"

Savique nodded, but even as he did, he fell back into fantasy. The three of them, Ajeau, Vaten, and himself, sitting in Z'eau as the words he had heard so long ago became reality. *You will save them all, you will find the lost, and that is when you will see him again.*

\*\*\*

THE NEWLY PROMOTED WARDEN Lienve approached Ajeau and Syais as soon as they arrived back in the V'eauvian camp. "What of the meeting? A success? Or are we to ride to battle?" he asked.

"Yes," Ajeau nodded. "A success. No battles are necessary. We are welcome in Z'eau peacefully. Ready the soldiers to move."

The Warden looked at Syais. "Vizier?"

Syais nodded as well. "As the Hijeuse says. Ready the camp."

The man frowned but nodded and then walked away, shouting orders.

Syais wanted nothing more than to tell the man to dispose of the Hijeuse then, but it would've been premature. There was much left to be done. And she could still tempt Ajeau with her friend and vengeance.

Yes, they were simple goals; Ajeau could have had the world and instead, she chose a single blade of grass. It was disappointing. But she was the Hijeuse and if Syais wanted her own lofty goals fulfilled, she would do so herself.

# CHAPTER 50

AJEAU ENTERED Z'EAU AT the head of the V'eauvian army. She had not made a point of leading them, nor had she told Syais to fall behind her, but the Vizier did and Ajeau had no qualms about continuing her pace. There would be no slowing now, not so close to the Tree and everything that came after. She could nearly taste the fruit on her tongue.

Unlike her entrance earlier, a horde of Noye met her where sand met soil. She held an open hand high in the air and reined her horse. It was a show as much for the V'eauvians as the Noye. She—they—rode for peace, not blood, no matter how many V'eauvians scowled and pointed their blades at those that greeted them. They may have been incensed, but not one advanced past Ajeau.

A woman dressed in green, no different from the others around her, stepped forward out of the crowd and approached Ajeau. She did not bow or avert her eyes, but her hands remained open and away from her weapons. It was all the respect Ajeau would receive from the woman.

"The Elder has requested an audience with you," the woman said. She glanced at Syais, then back to Ajeau. "Only you."

Ajeau dismounted her horse and walked to the woman. "Why? For what purpose? Does he think me foolish enough to walk into a trap now? Deliver him—"

"Your people are welcome here. They may set camp north of the lake," she said, each word like a dagger in her back. "There are no deceptions now. But there are matters that can only be discussed privately. Beyond watching eyes."

"Meet with the man," Syais called to Ajeau, chuckling. "Make your arrangements. It is no bother to me. I will take the soldiers to the camp and ensure each one knows their responsibility in this new place."

Ajeau nodded at Syais, then turned to the woman wearing green. "I will trust your words. Should I find them deceits, if my people come to harm, it will be your end."

The woman shrugged. "Follow me."

Ajeau followed the woman to the same tent in which she had met with Savique earlier. She entered and found Savique sitting in his chair, lost in thought. When he noticed her, he smiled gently and gestured for her to sit across from him.

"I do not believe we exchanged names at our previous meeting. Mine is Savique. And yours?"

Ajeau's eyes narrowed. She had heard that name somewhere before. But like a breeze that disappears as soon as it is felt, the feeling of familiarity vanished as soon as she examined it. "I am Ajeau."

"Yes, I heard the woman by your side refer to you as such. But I did not want to presume. You see..." Savique paused and glanced at the man standing outside the tent. "I have a son, or had a son—"

Ajeau followed Savique's gaze to the side of the tent, where she saw a man enter. He had aged so much since she last saw him, but his eyes had not changed. And when she stared into them, she found the same hatred coursing through her body as had back then. That hate, those eyes, were unforgettable.

She turned back to the man in front of her, who was still talking.

"—that you may have known from your time on an estate," Savique said with a grin on his face. He could see it in the girl. Vrai had been telling the truth. "I was also there a time ago. As was this man. You may know him as—"

"Vrai," Ajeau said with a mix of uncertainty and contempt.

Savique nodded. "So you do know him."

Ajeau glanced at Vrai, then back to Savique. "Yes. But he was no friend of mine." Her voice grew defensive. "What is he doing here? Why is he with you and the Noye?"

"I could ask you the same question," Vrai said. "How does an orphan girl from an estate end up the leader of the V'eauvians? How does she talk over a Vizier?"

"It is my destiny to be here," Ajeau said. "And you?"

Savique spoke before Vrai could answer. "He is not who you think he is. Vrai tricked me once upon a time as well. Vrai is Noye, and he worked on the estate to ensure we would one day be able to find this land."

Ajeau glanced at Vrai, questioning him with her eyes. "That may be so, but it does not excuse his actions." She turned back to Savique. "He assisted Crevir in all kinds of punishments and wickedness. His guards tormented and ruined many friends. Noye or not, he did those things."

"You are right," Savique said, as he looked at the brands Vrai had given him, still visible after all these years. "I have no doubt you suffered from his actions. I share that same fate." Savique held up his hands for Ajeau to see. "But I also know he had to do those things. To serve—no, to save his people. Surely you can understand that."

Ajeau folded her arms and stared at Savique. "I do not know the man's ideals or his values. Perhaps he committed his acts with great pain. But saving his people at the cost of my friends is not one I can forget. I can't let that go—"

There was something about those words that elicited a great joy in her heart, like the smell of burnt sage always made her think of food. And before she realized it, her mind already found the memory of them. And she heard every word Vaten spoke before they left the estate. *He's different from the guards. He's fair and thoughtful...He looks after me.*

Perhaps there was kindness in the man's heart.

Ajeau unfolded her arms, rose from her seat, and faced Vrai. "As a show of goodwill, I will allow you to remain in Z'eau. The past is gone. But should you cross me again in the future, you will find me far less merciful."

Vrai chuckled. "I am unafraid of—"

"There is nothing more to be said." Ajeau faced Savique and stuck out her hand. "Produce the fruit of the Tree or I will take it."

Savique nodded and then turned to Vrai. "Leave us," he said to his fellow Noye.

Vrai lingered a moment, then bowed his head to his Elder. After he rose, he gave a last glance to Ajeau, then exited the tent.

With Vrai gone, Savique rose from his seat and approached Ajeau. Looking deep into her eyes, he said, "Now, let us speak directly."

Ajeau stared back and was struck by a strange sense of familiarity. The light gleaning off his eyes, the shape of his mouth, his long nose; she had seen them before. No, not exactly them, but a shadow of them. Of Vaten. And finally, she remembered where she had heard the name Savique.

Savique smiled as though he sensed Ajeau's realization. "I believe you knew my son, Vaten."

Ajeau choked on her breath. A small cough forced its way from her mouth to ensure she remained breathing. With the last of her exhalation, she asked, "Is he here?"

"No." Savique shook his head. "I have not seen him in some time. Since his birth, truly. I was hoping you might tell me where he is and if he is alive."

"I do not know." Ajeau spoke the words as if a boulder lay on her chest. "I'm sorry, but we separated some time ago. I have been looking for him ever since."

"Then perhaps you can tell me something of his life. Of your time with him."

Ajeau smiled at Savique, savoring every moment she could remember of Vaten. "That I can do. I can tell you many stories."

And for some time after that, she did. She told Savique everything she could think of, from meeting Vaten at the estate when she was a young girl, to their escape and their wanderings. She relished all of them, not only because it was a chance to relive old times but also because Savique was so like his son. If not for the wrinkled face, the two could've been the same.

Savique too delighted in the stories, even the sad ones. They warmed him more than sitting by a fire, consoled him more than a mother's embrace, invigorated him more than the music of his people. They were everything to him. And he wished they would never end.

But in the middle of a story, Ajeau stopped talking, stood, and stared at the horizon. A chill ran through her body as something whispered in her ear, "Embrace it..."

"What is it?" Savique asked. "Is something the matter?"

"Yes," Ajeau said. "Something is coming. I feel it in the pulse of my heart."

She fell to a knee. Savique quickly attended to her, but she waved him off and said, "Get me the fruit from the Tree. It is time I showed you how I will protect us."

\*\*\*

SYAIS WAITED PATIENTLY FOR Ajeau to return from her meeting with Savique. True to her word, she had spoken to the soldiers about her plans. It was easy to convince them. Most were as angry as her at having to share space with such pests. And no one had to know anything about the Hijeuse.

But as the sun set, Syais's patience waned. No matter what Ajeau and Savique spoke about, their meeting was taking too long, and it filled her head with questions and suspicions. They became flies buzzing around her head. Despite her best attempts to swat them away, they came back again and again.

She walked down the path towards the lake to see if she could find a spot to observe the two talking. Perhaps a glance would provide the reassurance she needed. Even if it didn't, she had to know what they were doing.

Fortunately, she found an ideal spot atop some boulders laying not far off the trail. It provided her some cover if they were to look in her direction, but it also gave her a vantage point to see into the tent. From atop the rock, she saw the two in deep conversation. Then, after a few moments, it appeared they stopped and stared off into the distance.

She turned and peered in the same direction as them, but saw nothing. When she glanced back at Ajeau and Savique, Ajeau had fallen to a knee. Syais's heart raced, and she spun once more, following their gaze.

Now, something had appeared. A speck, no bigger than a mite, shook against the horizon. Then more and more appeared, moving closer, becoming slightly larger. Syais grit her teeth and wondered who was there. She did not like the first answer that came to mind.

Her eyes darted back to Ajeau and Savique. She watched him walk off, then return, holding a small, nondescript bag that made her nervous. It was the type of bag used to throw attention from onlookers, the type of bag someone would forget existed if they weren't looking at it. She knew this type of bag; she used them all the time.

And when she saw Savique open the bag and pull out a fist-sized object, Syais's breathing stopped. Even with the distance between them making the object difficult to discern, Syais knew immediately what it was. The fruit of the Faine.

Syais did not take another breath until after Ajeau had taken the fruit from Savique, put it to her lips, and bit into it. Of course, nothing happened. The power was not so easily unlocked. But it did not reassure her in the least. Ajeau was willing to use the power, and Syais did not know against who.

But then an idea formed in her mind. An opportunity to be had, even if it was not her original plan. Ajeau did not know where Syais stood at the moment. And though Syais didn't know everything about the fruit or Ajeau's power, she knew its effects wore off, eventually.

So hide, she told herself, wait out the power. And when its effects wore off, Ajeau would be weak, as she had been in the forest. Then she would be helpless to whatever attacks came her way.

And the only person who stood in her way was the man who sat in Z'eau like its Lord. Yes, she would have to start with him. He would, no doubt, come to her aid and shelter her from harm while she recuperated. Yes, Savique first—she owed him that anyway—then she would be free to dispose of Ajeau. Then Z'eau, and the world beyond, would be hers.

Syais jumped from the rocks and rushed to the nearest brush to hide in. She had barely settled when she heard a frantic scream from the direction of the tent where Ajeau and Savique remained. The Hijeuse had finally remembered.

And though she would never admit it, panic gripped Syais unlike any she had ever known. She clenched her eyes shut to prevent herself from seeing her demise.

An instant later, Syais realized she was not the target. Or if she was, Ajeau had failed. Either way, by then, Ajeau would have appeared somewhere, her powers used and herself weak. Even if the fruit extended the time Ajeau could move in the shadows, it would feel like only a blink of an eye to Syais. She was safe.

Syais stood and looked around her. Everything seemed as it was a moment before. That was for the best, even if it puzzled her. She wondered where the Hijeuse had gone. If she had looked towards the horizon, she would have seen the dots there had nearly vanished.

Instead, she walked towards Savique, knowing he was alone. Her lips spread and peeled to reveal a depraved grin. He should have finished her when he had a chance. It was a careless mistake. She would not be so rash.

\*\*\*

AJEAU KNEW IT THE moment the pain in her arm stopped. The fruit had worked. She could see the dust caught in the desert wind, suspended in front of her.

With Savique's dagger in hand, Ajeau began her march towards the approaching force. Thankfully, the distance between her and the Zevacese was not as far as she expected. And, in her state, she seemed less affected by the heat and the scorching sun, which was frozen above her. It was like her body remained beneath the tent in Z'eau, in the cool shade, rather than walking through the open desert.

As she walked, Ajeau imagined the blood and carnage she would unleash on the Zevacese. She wished they could see her and hear her as she screamed the names of those they took from her. It was too good a death for them, she thought, to be plucked from the living without even knowing why.

But there was nothing she could do about it. This was her chance, and she would not let it pass her by, waiting for a better one. Besides, there was no telling what weapons the Zevacese brought with them. Perhaps powers that would match—or exceed—hers.

The thought did not stop her. No matter what they had brought with them, whether they would fall like the soldiers in the forest or capture her with ease, she had her mind set on facing them. *Always fight to control your destiny.*

No, fight for Vaten and Seule. For the young girl who planned their escape from the merchant. For everyone cruelly taken by those in power. Now she had it and she would use it.

She rushed forward, sprinting over the sand until she was upon the Zevacese camp. She darted through bodies and slashed at men and women who had no look of surprise or pain on their face, only the tired look of those crossing a desert.

Zevaco had no power to stop her. She was supreme, again. She smiled, turned her head to the sky, and yelled. No one but her heard it.

She continued her dash through the waves of Zevacese, turning the sand beneath them a chalky red. She did not stop until a sight stopped her, until she reached the back lines of the mass of people and recognized a familiar face.

Her heart stopped. Her breath would not come. Her eyes widened. She no longer felt her hands or feet. Everything was blank, numb.

And for a moment, she wondered if it was all some hallucination. Or perhaps she was asleep, and this was simply a dream. A very pleasant one, she thought.

But unlike a dream, her experience was vivid and clear, not at all surreal. As she reached out and touched Vaten's shoulder, she could not hold back tears. It was him. Alive. She had found him at last. And she embraced him.

If only she could speak to him, too, but she was not of his world then. She could have screamed as loud and as long as her lungs would have allowed. It would not have mattered. Vaten would remain on the cart with that blank stare on his face, oblivious.

Ajeau stared at him for some time—at least in her world—and resigned herself to waiting there, with him, until whatever came next for her.

But then a hand grabbed her arm.

\*\*\*

THE MOMENT SHE FELT the touch of another, Ajeau collapsed into oblivion. One moment, she was staring at Vaten with tears in her eyes. The next moment, darkness surrounded her. An endless mob of black spirits encircled her, drifting as though made of smoke.

"You were warned. But you did not listen," one voice, made of thousands, said to Ajeau.

"Do not stand in my way!" Ajeau tried to shove the spirits away from her, but her hand moved through them as though they were air. "I am too close. My vengeance and Vaten are here. All within my grasp. If you seek to stop me, I will banish you as I did before."

Laughter arose from the group like the wind through the trees.

"Do not laugh. I am the Hijeuse!" Ajeau shouted.

"And who do you think we are?" the spirits replied.

"What? You are nothing. Weak shadows from another time! I am unafraid of you."

All at once, the laughter stopped. "She is unafraid? Of course. Well, that is...Good? Yes?" The spirits seemed to speak amongst themselves. Then, to her, they said, "You may be unafraid of us, but that is only because you do not understand."

"Do not understand what?" Ajeau said.

"What we are. What you have done. Your fate. Allow us to enlighten."

Ajeau tried to yell back at the spirits, decline their offer, but found she no longer had a voice.

"The Istori first brought the Tree here as a test to ensure their gift would survive in the harsh lands of Z'eau. And it did. It prospered for the people who lived here. The Balafre. But it came with a man—an Istori man—who knew of its true power. The power you have.

"This man tried to show the power to some of the Balafre. It had no effect on some, but others died gruesomely. No one experienced the power. And so, for the

468

good of the people, he stopped trying. He lived a normal life, fathered sons and daughters, and returned to the earth.

"It was by chance that someone, many centuries later, discovered such power again. But it came too late for him. His actions put him under the blade of the very people he sought to help. A shame! But it would not have mattered; the cycle had ended. Hunted, he wrote what he discovered and entrusted only his daughter with his knowledge.

"That knowledge was a single drop of water in a lake. But she carried it with her always. Passed it along to her children. Her children passed it along to their children. On through the generations, it went until it found a home in the hands of an illegitimate queen.

"Eventually, the weather turned sour and Z'eau no longer provided for all its people. Strife and discord ran rampant. War broke out.

"The power was used to end that war. And it did so easily; yet, at a terrible cost. One the Balafre did not know about. All they knew was of the power. That was all that had been told to them. They did not see their ends. A cycle begins!

"Even out of these ruins, sprung one who kept the Tree alive. He wrote he destroyed its lineages, but it was a lie. One to obfuscate the truth; he wanted to know all there was to know about this power.

"And he learned all he could—indeed, much—about the Tree and its power. He traced bloodlines for who could use it, who died immediately, and who remained unaffected. He devised tests to determine whose blood worked and whose didn't. He created maps and charts about where and when the Tree grew and about its home in Z'eau. His work vanished in his death. A cycle ends.

"You see, even he could not resist temptation. And still, what he and none of the others knew, what none of them could know, was that all those who had suffered the same fate as him, ended up here. We are the Faine. We are the power. And you, Ajeau—call yourself whatever you'd like—will end up here, like us. Forever."

Ajeau trembled. She was stuck in this place? Forever? No, it could not be true.

Her voice returned. "You lie! I used the seeds before and returned to my world."

"The seeds?" The spirits laughed as one. "They bestow nothing. They are thunder, not lightning. Even still, you lose years, now even more. There is no escape."

"No! Let me return. The Zevacese, Vaten, they are so close. Let me return!" The words were as much a plea as they were an order.

"It is not our decision. All who use the fruit are bound here. You will suffer the same fate as us. You will nurture the Faine for all time. Cycles turn. They give and take. This time it has taken you."

The mass of dark spirits advanced on her. There was nowhere to flee. There was nothing to strike against.

"No!" Ajeau yelled at them. But as they reached her, her final thoughts were of Vaten. "I must let him know. Savique is in Z'eau. Vaten, Savique is in Z'eau!"

She screamed the words like none she had ever cried before. If the veil between worlds could be punctured, such a scream would have done so. But there was so much she did not know.

The words echoed around her. Darkness consumed her vision. And Ajeau faded away into darkness. One with the spirits.

***

VATEN SAW ONLY CHAOS in the Zevacese camp. People exploded in bursts of blood and gore all at once. It was as though someone had thrown pebbles into a pond and they hit the water at the same time. Except it was people, not a pond, and blood, not water.

For a moment, Vaten did not believe his eyes. They had betrayed him before, sold him lies about what was real, but this was no fantasy. It couldn't have been. It so completely defied his understanding of the world he knew, even in his wildest imagination, he could not have dreamed it.

One moment, they moved to set up camp. And the next moment, almost all the Zevacese, friend and foe, lay bleeding—if not dead already—on the ground.

But Vaten was not the only one who had seen what happened. The others who witnessed the carnage, and remained alive, stood still and held their breath as if it would save them from exploding in a horrific red burst like the others.

Then panic gripped the Zevacese. They ran in every direction, scattering into the desert like flies trying to avoid a hand. It was madness. They knew they were far more likely to die in the open desert than in a well-supplied camp, but they didn't care. They acted solely on fear. Even if it led to their demise, they would not stay where they were.

Fear gripped Vaten too. The shrieking and the fleeing of the Zevacese did nothing to ease his mind—worse, their fear seemed to exacerbate his—and he struggled against the restraints binding him to the cart.

But slowly, a strange warmth grew in his heart, as though an old friend had told him a joke. One that made him feel like he had never left home at all. He could not be sure, but he thought he felt a hand on his arm.

The deep voice of Aloc startled Vaten. Though he did not understand what the man said—the words were Zevacese—he was overjoyed Aloc had survived too. And when he turned and looked at Aloc, he was free of his ropes and pointing at Zejela.

"That was her," she said to Aloc with a nod of her head toward a young woman who lay collapsed a few steps from the cart. Then she held up her hands, showing Aloc she was still bound. "Vaten too," she said.

Aloc stared at the girl on the ground for a moment and shook his head. Then he picked up a dagger from one of the deceased guards and used it to cut Zejela and Vaten free. "You welcome," he said with a smile.

Vaten exhaled, relieved, and, for the first time, saw the girl. As he eyed her, he immediately knew she was not Zevacese. If anything, the dark hair and skinny frame looked more like Zejela. "How is that possible?" he said.

Zejela walked to the girl, then stood over her. "That is the power of the Faine."

"You mean... They are already using it?" Vaten asked, though he did not know who the 'they' were.

"Someone is, yes. But I believe we are safe." Zejela bent down and touched the young woman. "It seems she has...expired. As all do."

"Returned?" Aloc asked.

Zejela shrugged and shook her head. "No, but...no longer here. If she is of the blood, then...It is difficult to explain. But as I said before, there is a cost to this power and she is paying it now."

Vaten finally realized why Zejela worked to ensure this power would not be used. Whoever had it could cause unending suffering, death, and destruction. Even with its cost, it was far too much power for one person to wield.

A horrific idea materialized in his mind. Perhaps it was not a single person wielding it, but a people. One who Zejela had confidently proclaimed was in

Z'eau. Yes, the Noye were vicious enough to take the power and use it to wipe out their enemies, as they had done with his father.

All this time spent fortifying himself for vengeance, for justice, and he was once more powerless to stop them. He was *still* useless.

"Vaten." Zejela's voice pulled him from his thoughts. "Come here. Help us with this." She gestured to the woman on the ground.

Vaten nodded and walked in their direction.

Before he had taken three steps, he saw the features of her face. And as soon as he did, he knew who it was. Somehow, it was her. Lying in a bed of sand and dust, older, emaciated but also strong and confident, it was Ajeau.

Vaten ran the final few steps and nearly dove to embrace her.

"This is Ajeau!" He shouted, as if the words would mean something to Zejela and Aloc, who looked on quietly bewildered.

He squeezed her again and then stared into her eyes. "Ajeau!" he said, delighted. When she did not move, he shook her. "Ajeau!" This time his voice was not joyous but frantic. He turned to Zejela and Aloc. "What is wrong? Why won't she wake up?"

"I told you, she must pay the price." Zejela replied.

"What does that mean?" Vaten moved from worried to angry in a breath. "No more games. This is my friend!"

Zejela shook her head. "She is alive but incapacitated. Most die quickly. It is good she has not. She may yet return to this world. Or..."

Vaten gripped Ajeau tightly and whispered, "Wake up, Ajeau, it is me. Vaten." Tears rolled down his face. He realized the last time he saw Ajeau, he had cried then, too. Zejela and Aloc were there as well. But everything else was different.

If only she would wake up, they could tell each other the tales of the lives they lived while apart. Oh, the stories he had. She would not believe them. He did not care; he would be adamant. And what of her? How did she end up here? "Wake up Ajeau, please. Wake up and tell me."

"Savique is in Z'eau," leaked from unparted lips.

"What?" Vaten asked, stunned. "Did you hear that?" He turned to Zejela and Aloc, who shook their heads at him. "She said something!" Vaten inspected Ajeau's face for any signs of life. "She did, I promise. I heard her say something."

Vaten shook Ajeau, but she did not respond. "Ajeau, wake up! What did you say? What did you say?"

The words were like a scream from a panicked child. "Vaten, Savique is in Z'eau!"

# CHAPTER 51

"WHAT DOES IT MEAN?" Zejela asked Vaten.

Vaten paused. He knew what it meant; only, it was unbelievable. Even more unbelievable was that Ajeau had somehow discovered it. She only knew the tales he had told her of his father. There weren't many.

"It..." Vaten shook his head. "It means my father is alive and in Z'eau. But that is not possible."

"Why?" Zejela said. "If the Noye took him, it would seem likely he would be in Z'eau with them."

"Because he was a prisoner," Vaten said, staring at Zejela as if the answer was obvious. "Why would they keep a prisoner alive all this time? Why would they bring a prisoner to Z'eau with them? And how would he meet Ajeau? And why was she given this power? And will she wake up?" The questions fell out of him all at once as he kicked at the sand in frustration.

Zejela rested her hand on his shoulder. "I don't know. But there is a place where we will find out."

"You want to go to Z'eau, like this? We have no army. No weapons. Nothing!" Vaten yelled. "The people in Z'eau will kill us—we may never even see it coming—and you want to walk right up to them?"

Zejela nodded. "I do." She smiled softly and gazed into his eyes. "We must finish our journey, Vaten, together. Z'eau is where the Tree is and it is where you will find your answers. We were always headed there, even if we did not always know it."

"And if they kill us?" Vaten asked.

"That is a risk we take. But as you said, we may never see it coming."

"I have girl," Aloc said and hoisted Ajeau onto his broad shoulders.

Every few steps, as he walked behind Zejela and Aloc, Vaten would glance to each side, expecting someone to appear next to him and stab him. Things in this new world were strange and unfamiliar. And he had no idea what awaited him in Z'eau.

But the last thought he had before he stepped into the oasis was of what he wanted. The dream he had carried with him since he was a child. His father.

\*\*\*

As the unrelenting desert sun fell below the horizon, the three travelers—four including the unconscious Ajeau in Aloc's arm—arrived at the outskirts of the city of Z'eau. It was indeed as lush as had been foretold, as awe-inspiring as would befit a fabled city. But it was not a quiet one.

Though the travelers expected to arrive at a serene place, they found nothing but mayhem and commotion inside. Arguing, yelling, wood and rocks striking into other wood and rocks could be heard throughout. Clouds of dirt and dust would rise into the air sporadically. If Ajeau had been awake, she would have barely recognized it as the same place she had left hours before.

The disturbances presented an opportunity for the travelers, however. There were no guards preventing them access to the city or from foraging for food and water. They entered, ate, and drank without being seen. Then they found refuge under trees within the brush growing near the edge of the city and waited for the morning.

Though they were meant to rest, the night brought more chaos. In the dark, each sound, no matter how distant, took on sinister tones. They huddled for warmth—a fire was too risky—and protection and hoped to see morning.

But eventually, the sun's soft rays crawled back over the dunes and illuminated Z'eau once more. By then, the three travelers had been awake for some time and were restless.

"We should not waste any more time here," Vaten said. "I need to know whether my father is here. And if there is anything we can do to help Ajeau."

"You're right." Zejela nodded. "And I need to find the Faine and who has harvested it."

"What you plan?" Aloc asked Zejela.

"It seems to me," Vaten responded before Zejela could speak. "Those tents would be a good place to find our answers."

He pointed to a small set of tents that decorated the far side of the lake. They were far from regal, but they were positioned in a way that would provide them a view of nearly the entire oasis. The set up reminded Vaten of the Forgotten Rest at the Outer Ridge. It was not the decoration of the building that mattered; it was the location. By seeing all, the Elder knew all. And knowing was far more important than any adornment.

Zejela nodded. "I agree, but how do you plan to get there?"

"The route between the lake and those trees, where those men yell and throw rocks," Vaten said, pointing to a burgeoning argument in the distance. "That will be our path."

Zejela chuckled. "You want to walk into their quarrels?"

"Something I learned from you," Vaten said, staring at her. "Disguise yourself by becoming who you seek to trick."

"What?" Zejela looked at him, confused.

"We'll pretend to join in their argument," Vaten said, as though it was obvious. "We'll look like anyone else who should be here and by becoming like them, we can sneak by them."

Aloc shook his head. "That not work so well last time. What about long trip?" Aloc pointed around the outside of Z'eau.

Vaten shook his head. "There is no way to enter near the tents. And anyway, I don't need to uncover a coup. I only need to walk past some guards."

"But you—"

Zejela interrupted Aloc with her hand and said, "It is fine. An acceptable plan. Even if we are captured, I'll meet the Noye in charge."

"We will not get captured," Vaten said, annoyed, then turned to Aloc. "You have to stay here." He smiled meekly. It was the first time Vaten ever told the man to do anything, and he felt like a child ordering their parent. "We need someone to stay with Ajeau, and your size would give us away when we try to go unnoticed."

Aloc shook his head. "No. I stranger. If girl wake, she fear!"

"Tell her..." Vaten paused, thinking of something that would let Ajeau know she was in safe hands, that the large Zevacese man with her was a friend, or at least as close as one could be in these times. "Tell her you are like Keriala, our old neighbor. And I have gone to get her clay pot fixed again. If she wants to see it, she has to entertain our guest."

Aloc responded only with a questioning glance.

"Do not worry." Vaten smiled. "She will know what it means."

Zejela nodded in agreement.

Aloc sighed and turned back to look at the girl. He hoped more than anything that she would stay asleep. He would never be able to remember the words Vaten spoke.

***

VATEN AND ZEJELA STARTED down the path towards the growing dispute he had pointed to earlier. What had seemed like a minor spat moments ago drew more people. It was perfect, Vaten thought. He was only another of the aggrieved parties come to join the fray.

But that thought vanished in the next moment when he recognized someone on their route. Vaten could not place him initially, but as the man ran towards the skirmish, the way he moved and held his dagger, and, ultimately, his voice jogged Vaten's memory.

"Vrai?" Vaten said, barely loud enough for Zejela to hear him.

"What?" she whispered back to Vaten.

He said nothing, but continued to stare at Vrai.

Zejela gave him a light shove. "Keep moving. This distraction will not last forever."

"But I—I know that man."

"Is it your father?"

"No." Vaten shook his head, but never once averted his eyes from Vrai. "I grew up with him on the estate. He was the Captain of the Guard there and oversaw my training when I was a novice."

"A strange coincidence," Zejela said, unimpressed. "Even so, we must move."

"It is not a coincidence," he said as the images of a drunken conversation replayed in his mind. "He knew my father. But what is he doing—why is he here?"

In the blink of an eye, Vaten thought of a million answers to that question. But they were all guesses, all led to more questions. He couldn't shake the feeling that none of this was happenstance. Something was transpiring. Only, he didn't know what.

"Vaten, come on," Zejela whispered urgently, then slowly moved her way down the path.

Vaten did not move with her. He stood and walked towards the fighting as if he had no control over where he went. Any sound mind would have thought it was a mistake, a foolish one at that, but Vaten did not care.

A few hundred paces from his old captain, Vaten stopped and called to him, "Vrai!"

Vrai spun around and glanced in Vaten's direction. He waved the dust away from his face and leaned forward slightly to peer through the crowd.

"Vrai! It is Vaten!" he yelled again, this time waving his arms.

A moment later, Vrai stood in front of Vaten, eyes wide, as if he stared at a ghost.

"Vaten?" Vrai held him at arm's length, looking him over. "You are alive? You are here?" He shook his head in disbelief. "How?"

"I could ask you the same question."

Vrai smiled and embraced Vaten, who stood dumbfounded, but accepted the hug.

Zejela stopped moving towards the tent and, upon seeing the two men together, scowled, but then reversed course. She hurried back to Vaten, but Vrai heard her approach. And before Zejela got close enough to say anything, he turned and drew his dagger.

"Who advances on the Chief of the Noye?" Vrai said.

Zejela stopped and reached for her own blade when she realized what the man said. "Noye?" A smile broke across her lips. It was exactly where she needed to be. She put up her hands. "My apologies. I meant no disrespect. I have traveled here to speak with Navo-Ille on important matters."

Vrai's eyes narrowed. "And who are you?"

"I am Zejela, Elder of Zevaco," Zejela said, conceding that the time for obfuscation had passed.

Vrai sighed, sheathed his dagger, and said, "I know not who you are, nor where you are from. But I have not seen Navo-Ille since before our journey to Z'eau. She likely returned to the earth during a raid from those we now must share this glorious bounty with."

"Dead?" It was a deep blow to Zejela, not only because Navo-Ille was the only Noye who would recognize her, but also because she was the one who had Zejela's compass. The implications were dire. There was no way to erase the Faine from the world while the mark remained out of her possession.

But she kept her composure and said, "I am sorry for the loss of your Elder."

***

VATEN STOOD AND WATCHED the brief exchange between Vrai and Zejela. He had every intention of joining the conversation, at least to introduce the two to each other. But when he heard the first words from Vrai's mouth to Zejela, he kept his mouth shut and seethed. The man was a Noye.

At one time, not so long ago, Vaten would have thought the idea ridiculous. A Noye working on Crevir's Estate was akin to rain ascending from the ground to the sky; it was not how things worked. Now, however, Vaten was unsure whether he knew much about anything. In this place, the impossible appeared commonplace.

And that was when he gave up. He no longer cared about the puzzles, about the mysteries of the Tree, or even about why his past sprouted in this place like grass in a field. It didn't matter anymore. There was only one thing that mattered. Revenge.

And it stood right in front of him. A Noye, perhaps the very one that took his father all those years ago, was within arm's reach. And he could finally reach out and take retribution for everything that had been stolen from him. His father, Ajeau, himself.

Vaten screamed, then rushed at Vrai.

As he crashed into Vrai, Vaten knocked the man's dagger out of his hand and brought him to the ground. Aloc, had he seen it, would have recognized the technique, and thought it a worthy attempt, though far from perfect.

The two men wrestled on the ground for a moment until Vaten, still with the advantage surprise had lent him, pinned Vrai to the ground. Atop the man, Vaten took his free fist and pummeled Vrai while yelling, "You Noye bastard! You took my father! You ruined my life!"

Vrai tried to speak, but only mumbled words fell out of his beaten mouth. Vaten could hear nothing, much less any complete words.

After several punches, Zejela caught Vaten's arm as he reached it above his head. "Enough," she said. "You have made your point."

Vrai rolled to the side and covered himself in anticipation of more blows. None came.

The crowd that had once focused on a quarrel between V'eauvians and Noye now turned their attention to Vaten and Vrai.

Zejela helped Vaten to his feet and said, "We should leave quickly, head back to Aloc, and cover ourselves. Many will come looking for those who assaulted a chief. We will find another way to—"

"W-Wait." Vrai forced the words from broken lungs, past broken lips. He picked his head up and said, "Vaten—wait. Your dad—I did not. He is, here, our Elder."

Vaten stared at him. Another impossibility. But why would the man lie? Why would Ajeau lie? And this time, he did not give up. He did what was asked of him; to believe in the unbelievable.

"Where is he?" Vaten said, still panting from their fight.

"Help me up and—and I will show you."

Savique and Zejela helped the man to his feet and stabilized him. Vrai brushed at his clothes, now covered in dirt and dust. Then he drew his arm and pointed toward the tents at the top of the rocks. "There," he said, straining to keep his arm elevated.

Vaten followed Vrai's hand with his eyes and gazed at the location of his father. It was the same direction he had been traveling a few moments before—and all the time before that, he supposed.

But before turning his gaze from the tents, and back to Vrai and Zejela, he swore he glimpsed something. For a moment, it looked like someone running past the tent. Someone dressed entirely in white. He blinked and it was gone.

\*\*\*

SYAIS'S PLAN HAD WORKED perfectly. The V'eauvians she ordered to create strife throughout the city had done exactly that. Without Ajeau in Z'eau, there was no tie between the V'eauvians and Noye. No reason for the two rivals to stay peaceful with one another. And with Syais's help, the city erupted in chaos.

The turmoil drew Savique's guards from his tent. Even Vrai left his side to soothe the tempers raging among their people. And when he did, it left Savique isolated.

That, too, was part of her plan. Because once Savique was alone, no one, not even a suspicious Ajeau—should she return—could say why the man died or who had done it. No one could condemn Syais without proof. Hidden in the shadows, unseen by anyone, she grinned.

A chill ran up her spine. Not one of fear, but of excitement. Finally, she could finish her plan. Finally, she could execute the man who stymied her so long ago. Finally, she would have Z'eau.

Yes, it was fate. There was no other way to explain it. It would have been simpler if it was someone else standing in her way. But it would not have been right. No, the only way to the power she deserved—that was rightfully hers—was through him. So, she went through him.

Syais moved quietly, quickly, and without being seen up to the tent. And when she arrived there, she threw back her hood, uncovering her face, and walked confidently towards Savique, as though it was her throne room.

"What are you doing here?" he said, annoyed but lacking fear or suspicion.

Syais grinned and said nothing.

"If you have nothing to say, you can leave. I am not in the mood for visitors. The city is in an uproar."

She continued to smile, held it for too long, revealing its inauthenticity. "Yes, I know."

"What do you know about it? Have you set your people against us? How foolish are you? You ruin paradise for feud."

"What does it matter? This place will not be your responsibility much longer." She continued to approach him.

Savique rose from his seat, pointed at her, and said, "You dare threaten me? The people here will forever be my duty. No matter who sits beneath this cover. For sure, it will not be you."

Syais laughed. "The Hijeuse will fall after you. And then..."

"I do not imagine she will be pleased to hear of your insolence."

"And who will tell her?" She glanced from side to side. "I do not see her here. Do you?"

With those words, Savique drew his dagger. But Syais was unbothered. She continued to advance slowly on him.

"Vrai! Guards!" he shouted, but no one responded or entered. And, as though the words were only a distraction, he rushed at Syais as soon as they escaped his lips.

The move surprised Syais, but she drew her blade in plenty of time to deflect Savique's strike. The clang of the clashing metals seemed to reverberate through the city. No one but the combatants heard a thing.

Savique pressed his advantage and tried to unsteady Syais with a kick to her leg. But she expected such a move and shifted her legs, causing Savique to sweep his foot past her without making contact. Instead of Syais losing her balance, it was Savique who wobbled.

Syais pounced before Savique could straighten himself. She swept out his planted leg, sending him tumbling to the ground. He made a loud thud and groaned as he did.

But he did not lie there helplessly and before Syais could pin him, he quickly rolled to the side and sprang back to his feet. He readied himself to strike again.

Syais admired his movements. They were smooth, graceful, and quick. He always kept himself balanced, centered, which made it difficult for her to keep any advantage. It was a deftness she had not seen from many on Bas, as though Savique had trained somewhere foreign.

She did not linger on it, instead she scanned the man's stance for a weakness and prepared to unleash herself. Before she found any, she heard a terrible sound from outside the tent. The sound of footsteps coming closer.

The encounter had already taken too long and now she was in danger of being found out. She had to hurry and finish it. Finish him. Though as much as she wanted to watch the life drain from his face, she knew she did not need to kill him now. No, she only needed a cut. The rest would fall into place without her.

She bolted at him quickly, her dagger held at her midsection as if to strike his torso. Savique produced an appropriate defense. But, in a move that surprised him, Syais slid to the ground and drew her dagger against his leg.

For a moment, Savique did not even feel the cut. But when he looked down, he saw she had drawn blood. He glanced back at Syais and shrugged. The cut was not deep, nor did it affect his ability to stand. And now, he knew not to allow such a move to catch him unprepared again.

But there was to be no more fighting. Syais, after cutting Savique's leg, rose to her feet and absconded from the tent. Over the rocks she went, in the opposite direction of the footfalls. She continued racing until she arrived on the far side of the lake, near the fields. There she found cover.

Savique thought it odd Syais would flee their battle so soon. She had accomplished little, other than outing herself as a traitor. Whatever the reason for her escape, he would find her and exile her from the land.

Her punishment would have to come after he tended to his wound though. It throbbed mercilessly, hurt as though she nicked the bone. How could such a small gash cause such pain? He stared at it, not liking the black outline beginning to appear on its borders.

# CHAPTER 52

"Savique, what's wrong?" Vrai hobbled to his Elder, leaving the two others he brought to the tent behind. It was not the entrance he desired, but when he saw Savique lying nearly motionless on the ground, he rushed to the man's side as quickly as he could.

"Syais. She..." Savique coughed. "She must've poisoned her blade."

"Syais was here? I told you that woman was not to be trusted."

"You were right." Savique coughed again and then laid his head against the ground as if speaking took all the energy from his body.

"Is there nothing we can do?" Vrai looked at the guard standing next to Savique.

The guard's eyes widened, and she shook her head in a declaration of ignorance, more than of certainty in an answer.

"Damn those V'eauvians. Those treacherous scum. They would do anything—" A tug on his arm stopped him. When he glanced down, he saw Savique pointing at the two visitors who had remained outside the tent. One viewed the scene with concern, the other with curiosity. But neither were familiar to Savique.

"Who are they?" Savique asked to Vrai.

"That—" Vrai turned and pointed at Vaten and Zejela.

In that moment, Vrai wrestled with what to do. Savique was unwell and seeing his son would no doubt stress his body further. Vaten was unstable. He had gone from embracing Vrai to thrashing him in what seemed like a heartbeat. And the woman, well, Vrai wasn't sure whether she was friend or enemy.

No, it was not a simple decision, but he waved them over all the same. He could not stand in their way. Something was happening in Z'eau and Vrai knew what it was. *Retrouvaille.* Reconnection.

"—that is your son." Vrai finished his sentence as Vaten appeared before Savique.

"My son?" Savique's eyes grew large. A thin film slowly covered them. "Vaten?"

*Only then will you see him again.* The words of the Istori Ascetics, so long ago, had become truth. If only he had believed them earlier. No, it would have made no difference at all.

Vaten stared at the man he had dreamed of meeting for so long. Even if his father was essentially a stranger to him—more alike to a legend than real—Vaten could not resist the feelings that overtook him. Joy but also relief and excitement and fear, all mixed in an overwhelming storm that flooded him.

"Yes, father. It is me."

Tears rolled down Savique's face as he spoke. "I have waited for this a long time, son. Everything I have done was to get back—to see you again." He choked on the words. "I know you will never understand what that means, but it is true. Everything was for you."

Savique coughed violently as the poison made its way to his lungs.

"Me too. I've traveled so long, so far and now, here, with you..." Vaten lost the words he wanted to say.

Vaten wrapped his arms around his ailing father and embraced him. Savique squeezed him back with the last of his strength.

When the two men separated, Vaten noticed a stain on his shirt where his father's head had just rested. He glanced at his father's face and noticed black bile running down his father's chin.

Then Savique's eyes rolled upwards into his head, and he slumped to the ground.

"Father? Are you—Wake up." Vaten shook his limp father and though Savique's eyes fluttered momentarily, they never opened.

"What is happening?" Vaten asked to anyone that could hear him.

"He was poisoned," Vrai said. "By the blade of a wicked V'eauvian."

"No!" Vaten slapped the ground in anger. "I just found him. After all this time." Then, an idea flashed through his mind. Hope. "Zejela, you know plants and herbs well. What can save him?"

She placed her hand on his shoulder and shook her head. "I don't know. I don't know the poison. And it appears to have reached his heart and lungs. He may be too far—"

"There must be something!" Vaten said through tears, his hope fading. "You knew enough to have me brought back to life after being buried alive. Surely, you can find the cure for whatever is doing this."

"I'm sorry. If there was anything I could do, I would do it. But…"

Vaten looked up and screamed. After so long, he had finally found his father, finally spoke to him, and the man left him again before Vaten could finish a conversation with him. It was cruel, worse than never finding his father at all.

And now he would know only his father's death. That would be his memory of the man. Not some joyous reunion, though it had been that for the smallest sliver of time, but his return to the earth. Premature as it was.

And though he wanted to rage and exact vengeance on the person responsible, Vaten found those flames no longer burned. Vengeance had consumed him for too long, and it led him to attack the one man who had helped him at every opportunity. If Ajeau never awoke, Vrai was the closest thing he had to a friend. To someone who knew him.

Amidst the torrents of emotions, Vaten endured—as he had done once in the Outer Ridge. Except here he laid down and shared one final thing with his father. The land.

And that is when something clawed at Vaten's wrist. He looked down and saw his father's hand weakly clutching him.

"Father!" Vaten said.

"The girl…" Savique whispered with great effort. "Ajeau. She…has…the power. Syais will…will end her. Find the girl… help her…she is…the one. Our Elder now." His words finished, he collapsed back onto the floor, black bile continuing to flow from this mouth.

"What?" Vaten asked his father hurriedly. Then, seeing his father unconscious once more, he turned to Vrai. "What does he mean about Ajeau? And who is this, Syais?"

Vrai quickly detailed the situation in Z'eau and who Syais was, but added, "Neither have been seen since the army that approached our city arrived."

Vaten sat up and shook his head, overwhelmed. His father, Vrai, the Noye and the V'eauvians, and Ajeau, all tied in some complex knot. Pulling on one thread made the whole thing tighter, even more twisted. He did not know what to do and wished he could lie down again and wait for the land to claim him.

But he could not. He knew one thread, and it was the only one that mattered now. Ajeau was in trouble.

Zejela walked towards Vrai. "We have the woman, Ajeau. She is hiding in the city with another of our group."

"What? Hiding?" Vrai said. "Bring her here. She can help us—"

Vaten stood, tears still drying on his face. "No." He spoke the words as if giving an order. "Ajeau will not be of help to anyone. She is injured, or asleep. But if she is in trouble..." He strode towards the exit of the tent.

Vrai glanced at Zejela and then at Vaten. "Where are you going?"

Vaten did not turn, did not stop walking. He said nothing and departed.

Vrai tried the question again to Zejela, who said, "He is going to help his friend."

"Vaten!" Vrai called to him. "Syais is not to be trifled with. She is formidable, even for one as skilled as your father. If you meet her, you will not be victorious. But—"

Free of the shelter, Vaten broke into a sprint towards Aloc and Ajeau's hiding spot. Vrai's final words, carried on the wind, reached him. "...if you will not heed my warnings, know this. She wears white and moves with a slight limp."

But he did not care what the woman looked like. He would protect Ajeau against all, as she had done for him.

***

AFTER SYAIS ESCAPED THE tent, she walked calmly down the path towards the V'eauvian camp. She had no reason to hurry; she was not foolish enough to flee in haste like a criminal. No, she was only another person moving through the place, observing the widespread chaos.

Occasionally, she would stop and turn around as if to orient herself—she was simply having trouble navigating her new surroundings, as were many others—but it allowed her to ensure no one was following her. No one was.

No one had seen anything. Even if the footsteps she heard in the tent were from an oncoming guard, she would have been gone before they could see her. But perhaps it wasn't a guard at all. Perhaps she fled too soon.

No, she did not regret that. Not while her plans were incomplete and Ajeau was still missing.

Syais found a small rock to sit on near the lake and wiped her weapons. No one would find a trace of blood on her, nor a drop of poison. As she cleaned them, she watched the city further devolve into unrest. Fights broke out everywhere now, screams became as common as the buzzing of flies.

But to Syais, there was no sweeter sound. It was a celebration. She was a step closer, inches from everything she had planned all those years ago.

And that was when she glimpsed a large man shaking the branches of a tree. He greedily collected the fruits that fell and walked several paces back into the brush. It was a curious scene, if only because the man's blades were painted a stunning blue.

Syais clenched her jaw. The Zevacese were here. Not only that, but they were hiding, waiting to spring some trap. Perhaps they could even see her now, sitting on the rock enjoying herself. Well—she unclenched her jaw and smiled—let them watch. She would destroy them either way. Starting with that giant of a man.

He was an odd choice for a spy, Syais thought as she snuck around the perimeter of the lake. But he was no doubt strong and perhaps swift as well. Syais never forgot the word Ajeau used to describe them all those years ago, *lithe*. It didn't matter how quick he was; he could not outrun a dagger in his back.

She would have laughed at the thought if she was not trying to remain hidden. Instead, she continued crouching among the plants and trees until she found the large man's hideout. And when she did, she couldn't believe her luck.

There, lying next to the large man, was the only person Syais wanted to see. Ajeau. And not only that, but she was unconscious, still recovering from the effects of the Faine's fruit. There was no more welcoming sight. She could deliver a warning to the Zevacese and destroy Ajeau all at once.

But, by the looks of it, the man was defending Ajeau. Or at the very least, trying to keep her hidden. Perhaps the Zevacese wanted Ajeau for themselves. Perhaps they had learned how to resist the power of the Tree. No matter, if she could dispose of him, then she could finish Ajeau. Then she would have Z'eau and an army to defend it. Come what may.

It was slow, tedious work to sneak up on the man. His attention was indivertible. But Syais, in her white clad outfit, moved like a specter in the bright light.

The shimmering of the sun covered her approach better than darkness. And once she reached him, she knew how to eliminate him.

She unsheathed her dagger and walked towards him, reflecting the sun's light off into his eyes. He looked up, then closed them reflexively. He planted himself, roared like a beast, and swiped his arms as though swatting at bees.

Every time he opened his eyes, Syais blinded him with the sun. And even as he hunched over, covered his forehead with his arm, stared at the ground, and tried to march forward, she knew she beat him. Before he could lay a hand on her, Syais drove her blade into his chest.

And that was it, she thought, Ajeau was hers, and the plan was complete. Nothing could stop her now. Then why did she have this feeling, like the damp breath of someone about to whisper in her ear.

When she whipped her head around, she realized why. A strange man ran in her direction, a dagger not so subtly concealed in his hands.

\*\*\*

AJEAU'S EYELIDS BURST APART, revealing a cavern as damp and dark as the soil deep under the surface. Despite the absence of light, she could sense everything around her as if she saw it. The spirits were there, as were several rocks and a series of strange, translucent channels that ran along the walls of the cave. They throbbed erratically.

"Ah yes, she finally awakens," the spirits said, their hostility gone. No longer did they chastise something different. Now, they addressed one of their own. "Are you rested?"

Ajeau nodded. She was no longer tired, nor angry, nor did she seek vengeance. It was as though her desires from before were a dream. Now that she had awoken, all was serene.

All except for the strange pulsing sounds echoing throughout the place, as if someone was beating a drum in a perfect rhythm. Each beat seemed to flow through her body, a sharp pang arriving with it.

"What is that?" Ajeau asked.

"That is life!" they shouted triumphantly. "It is the movement of all. What you worked so hard to bring into existence."

"I do not...understand," she said.

"Of course, you are still new," a distinct voice said. "That pounding is the work of the Faine. It is the sound of nutrients being passed from bodies to our station to the realms above. It is why we are—"

"Silence!" another distinct voice, this one low and deep, said. "Something in the world beyond is afoot. A leaf falls."

The spirits mumbled in response to the new information.

"What is happening? What does it mean?" Ajeau asked.

"Silence!" the low voice said again. "The seed may become dormant!"

More murmurs from the spirits. A feeling of alarm pierced Ajeau without her understanding why. All she knew was it spoke of something worrying.

"I don't understand. What is happening?" she offered again.

A whisper came in response. "The readers have foretold the end of the cycle. The Faine will ensure its own birth with the blood of a leaf. Soon, another will leave. We will move. The mountains—"

"Silence!" the low voice interrupted. "We will be visited again."

"Another visitor? Who? Who calls on us again?" a spirit asked.

Glances fell in Ajeau's direction as though she were responsible for the newcomer's visit.

"The Dura."

Stillness followed, the spirits' attention directed at Ajeau.

***

AT FIRST, ZEJELA DID not try to follow Vaten. Yes, Ajeau had the power, but Zejela knew the girl was unlikely to awaken in this world ever again. And for Zejela, the man who might know how the Faine was harvested, and where her mark was, stood in front of her. Vrai was the more important man at that moment.

But she could not ignore her concern for Vaten. And Aloc too. He was perhaps the only living countryman; certainly the only who did not view her as a traitor. And they were both in danger from a woman who had killed a Noye Elder while he sat on his throne in this sanctified land. She was not only formidable, as Vrai had said. She was malicious.

So when Vrai nodded at her and said, "Go with Vaten, he will need you. I must stay with my Elder," she did not hesitate. She ran out of the tent and followed Vaten.

But before she did, she picked up a small bag that lay on the floor, a bag most would have forgotten even existed. Zejela knew better.

When she arrived at their hiding spot, she saw chaos. Ajeau covered in dirt and sand, Aloc on the ground with a dagger in his chest, and Vaten fighting the woman who must have been Syais.

It was a generous use of the word fighting; Vaten was no match for the woman. Despite her old age, she moved quickly, easily dodging Vaten's rushed attacks. Each time she did, she stabbed him superficially in his legs, arms, and once even his cheek. The cuts were not deep—blood dripped from them, not poured—though they served their intended purpose. To remind Vaten he would die slowly and painfully.

Vaten would not yield, though. After each strike, he would regain his footing and attempt another attack. But, as the fight wore on, his attempts became less controlled, more easily deflected, and tired him further. He would not be able to carry on in such a fashion for much longer.

Zejela had hoped it would not come to this. For a few moments, she let herself believe Vaten could be victorious. Recall, he had trained well with the Sentries. He could be quick and precise with his movements, too. But Syais was too strong. And Vaten cried out in pain as another cut fell upon his legs.

Zejela sighed and glanced at the bag she had picked from the floor of the tent. She reminded herself of what she knew, of the oaths she had taken long before this moment. But she could not stand idly by and watch Vaten be tortured. Nor could she watch a V'eauvian such as Syais come to power in Z'eau.

She opened the bag and said aloud to herself, "Only one for the Faine. Not of the blood. That is all I offer."

She took out the fruit, cut a small piece of it, and returned the rest to the bag, securing it to her chest. Gently, she sliced the back of her right hand to draw a trickle of blood. Then, she placed the fruit on her cut and was gone.

***

VATEN SAW SYAIS CUT to pieces in less than a moment. She fell to her knees in front of him with a look of shock and horror on her face as blood poured from deep wounds all over her body. Her once pristine white uniform turned a pinkish hue. Insult and injury.

Syais gasped out a last word, "Hijeuse." Then she collapsed to earth.

And though Vaten could not be sure, he thought Syais looked as though she understood how she was cut down so brutally. As though she had expected it to happen, only not at that moment.

After the shock subsided, Vaten's heart leapt. Ajeau must have awoken and used the power to save him. After all, she had been the one who dispatched the Zevacese earlier. But when he glanced in her direction, he saw her still lying on the ground, covered with dirt and sand.

And that is when he looked down and saw Zejela unconscious on the ground behind Syais, as if she had always been there. But she had not. No, it was not Ajeau who had saved him; it was Zejela. She had used the power, even though it was her duty not to.

He walked over to her, kneeled by her side, and put his hand on her back. "Thank you," he said, his head resting on her still body. "For saving me. Again." He wondered if she heard him.

He stood and glanced at Aloc and Ajeau. She rested as she always had, but Aloc appeared in terrible shape. His chest still heaved, though he appeared too weak to move.

Vaten closed his eyes and drew a deep breath. Then, despite his injuries, he hurried to Vrai, hoping to find a healer. He would accept no more losses on this day. There was nearly no one left, anyway.

*** 

ZEJELA AWOKE IN A sea of black spirits chanting the words, "Dura! Dura! Dura!" She knew the chant, knew the name, but never wanted to hear it again. Then she glimpsed one not chanting. She looked at the spirit and recognized her. She had seen the young woman in the Zevacese camp. They had carried her to Z'eau. She was Vaten's friend. Appropriate, Zejela thought.

"Hello niece. It is good to finally meet you. Even here," Zejela said to Ajeau.

\*\*\*

Digging a hole in Z'eau was slow work. The dirt was loose and easy to move, but when the winds blew, they would fill in some of what had been dug. Though it was tedious, it didn't bother Vaten much. He would have dedicated an entire year to it if he needed to. Because the hole he dug was one for his father to rest in.

Vrai was there too, to help Vaten dig and to pay his respects to the man he clashed with, but respected enough to follow. Despite the disagreements, and even outright hostility, Vrai understood Savique and grew to trust him. He was glad he did, because it meant surviving long enough to see Z'eau and inhabiting the city of his elders with his fellow Noye.

They were there on that day, too. What was left of the great nation came to pay their respects to a man who delivered them from certain death. Though they did not help dig, they watched with solemn faces as their Elder returned to the earth. In their tradition, they slapped the ground in reverence of the man, as if to feel his energy once more.

After they completed their work, Vaten leaned on Vrai and stared at the spot where his father lay. He wondered about who his father was and who the man had become. Though Vaten did not know him, he missed him. The idea of his father as much as the reality. And Vaten cried.

In the coming days and weeks, Vaten would come to learn much about his father. The Noye would tell stories of Savique, how the outsider had joined them, rode with their chiefs and elders, rescued them for mortal peril, and ultimately produced Z'eau for them. He made the legendary real.

As they often did, the Noye told fantastical stories, ones that made Vaten question whether they were real or exaggerated. But it no longer mattered to him.

He had seen many fantastical things lately, things he would have never believed real if he had not experienced them. So even if the stories were implausible and unrealistic, they may have been real. And if not, they were important to these people. Perhaps that was all that mattered.

Absent from any of the ceremonies was Aloc. He recuperated on his own, but never strayed too far from Zejela. Ajeau was there too, and Aloc watched over the young woman as well, but only out of duty and proximity. Zejela and Ajeau were in the same place, in the same state.

Neither had improved since they fell unconscious. That did not mean they had deteriorated either. No, they were stable, as if they were frozen. But Aloc watched over them, hoping that one day his friend would awaken and explain to him what happened.

Vaten visited them often as well. And though his concerns were always on the well-being of Ajeau and Zejela, he spent a great deal of time speaking with Aloc on countless topics. From the Faine and Z'eau to his father and Zevaco, they spoke about whatever interested them on any day and let the conversation take them where it would.

But they usually came back to Ajeau and Zejela. Aloc and Vaten missed their friends too much to leave them. It did not help that the two unconscious women held the knowledge Vaten and Aloc so desperately wanted. Where were they? And would they ever return?

If only they would wake up and tell the two caretakers. But they did not.

Following the deaths of Savique and Syais, and Ajeau's incapacitation, it was Vrai who took control of Z'eau. This was out of necessity; the city could not function without a leader. There needed to be someone who could regain control of the city, douse its various fires, and restore peace and order to the land. Vrai was the only one in a position to do that.

And though the V'eauvians were dismayed, they were also disorganized. Without Syais they could not provide any unified resistance and so, eventually, fell in line with Vrai and the Noye. It was tenuous, but peace found Z'eau. The people and the city.

And while Ajeau was not there to enjoy her vision of the two tribes uniting as they had been eons before, it would have pleased her to see them living in peace. Her people, her place, the belonging she so desired, had been realized.

# EPILOGUE

## Part I

HE WAS FREE. FINALLY, after what felt like ages in captivity, Levitien was free. And he had unearthed all the knowledge he intended to when he set forth on his journey, when his father had told him the plan.

Yes, he had to secure his release by betraying the only friend—indeed, Vaten was a friend—he had made in quite some time. And he had to collaborate with those who had kept him in captivity and wanted him dead. Nevertheless, he had succeeded.

He did not want it to happen that way, but it was the only safe path he could find. And now, it was no longer his problem. His home awaited him. Nothing sent his heart soaring like the thought of returning to Rigolade and his family.

Levitien rode west, then down the coast, the sea air a familiar taste on his tongue, until he could go no farther south and reached the shores he knew so well. There, he found a boat hidden in the caves along the beach. It could have been the very one he rowed all the years before, or it could have been one of his fellow Rigoladers' vessels. It didn't matter.

As he boarded the boat and began the slow row back to Rigolade, he wished for calm seas, a steady current, and durable oars. Fortune provided him with the calm water and oars but not the current. It would take him nearly a day to cross the strait.

But when he did, collapsing on the beach of his homeland, he could not have been more overjoyed. Freedom, now home. They had long been thoughts, ideas, and memories, nothing more. Now, they were real. Now, he was back.

It did not take him long to find someone who recognized his name and provided him help. Such was the fortune of the Heir. And he didn't need to go far, just over the cliffs and hills, to the fortress that lay inland, to the house he grew up in, to his family which waited inside.

Levitien entered the house like a returning hero but was met with anger and mockery from his family.

"Where have you been?" his sister said. "Your duty should've ended months ago. Have you been wandering Bas looking for more cheap thrills? Have you been dancing with the blowseed?"

Levitien said nothing but stood in the hall confused and hurt. He had returned from a mission that was rife with peril and had survived. No, not only survived, but succeeded. They should not have met him with such resentment; he did not deserve to suffer such insults.

Following behind his sister, his cousin entered and said with a chuckle, "No, look, he is haggard. Perhaps he got lost in the Annonay for months, living on sand bars and surviving on decayed fish and illean leaves."

Levitien would take no more derision. "I bring news that will save our family and our people. My journey has been a success. Not that you would know anything of it." He hoped his words cut as deep as he meant them to. "Where is father?"

His sister scoffed and said, "In his chambers but I would not enter, he does not wish to—"

Levitien ignored the words and proceeded up the stairs to his father's chambers. He rapped on the door. Hearing no response, he cracked the door open and said lightly, "Father, I have returned. I bring news of the Tree."

"Who is that?" His father said without glancing up from his work.

The man sat at a desk scribbling away on some scroll with one hand while another pulled at his long, black beard. He shook his head as though something was amiss, then said, "Sol damn it!"

"Father?"

The man rose and turned to see Levitien poking his body into the room through a small slit in the doorway. "Levitien!" He sang out with joy. "My boy! You have returned."

The reception from his father surprised him as much as the one he received from his sister and cousin earlier, but for the opposite reason. He didn't know why, but at that moment Levitien felt as if he had been gone a lifetime.

"Yes, father," he said. "Everything went to plan. I have much to tell you."

"Come in, come in! Tell me everything. You are well?"

"Yes, and happy to be on familiar land." He smiled, then relayed his tale from his intended trip to Bas, to every word Zejela spoke on the Tree, to his harrowing escape.

"And what about the other suitors?" his father said. "Were you able to eliminate them? Tell me no one else who knows remains alive."

"I tried. I was—"

"Tried?" His father scowled at him and then burst into a rage. "Yes or no, my boy! Answer the question!"

"No, father. I was not able to purge all of them. I was lucky to escape—"

"Not able? Not able?" His father slapped his hands together in anger. "Or not willing? What did I spend all this time training you for?" He sighed and began to pace. "I was wrong to trust your abilities."

"You weren't." He said as if he was a repentant child. "I was successful. I know where the Tree is."

The words brought Levitien's father to a stop. He stared at his desk a long while, then said, "Interesting. Perhaps I was hasty in my judgment. What do you know?"

"It is in Z'eau. A city that holds some prominence for the Northerners. I don't know—"

"Ah yes, I am familiar with Z'eau. Not the place exactly, but what it represents for their people. They say it is where their gods lived and forged the world. I never believed it to be real." A satisfied smile crossed his lips as though he solved a nagging problem. "A fascinating wrinkle."

"Yes, it is real. And one of the Zevacese knew how to find it, too."

The old man's bushy eyebrows rose up his forehead, and his eyes opened wide. "And you know this too?"

"Yes, father, I believe I know where it is."

"Well done, my boy. Well done. We will finally take back Bas from those infernal Balafre and their descendants. We will have our land again." The old man smiled as he looked into his son's eyes. "But that is for another day. For now, you can rest."

***

# Part II

"I RECOGNIZE YOU. YOU were there with Vaten. Who—who are you?" Ajeau asked.

Lightning flashed, a crack of thunder echoed, and rain poured from above. But Ajeau never felt a drop. She remained as dry as the desert sand where her body lay in the other world. In this one, she stood next to a spirit she somehow knew to be Zejela, even if she didn't know who the woman was or how she recognized her.

"It is a shame you do not know. You should have been told—they should have taught you long ago. I am your blood. Your aunt. Your mother's sister. Here, the Dura."

The chants of "Dura! Dura! Dura!" reverberated in the background, steadily growing louder, faster, rising to a crescendo. Zejela raised her hand. The chanting stopped. It would have been silent if not for a pulsing, unrelenting beat.

"I—I do not understand. I never knew my mother or father. Certainly not an aunt. How do you know about me?"

Zejela laughed, as though the answer was obvious. "Because you are here. All is made clear in the Tree."

Ajeau stared at her, confused. She shook her head. "Where? Where is here?"

"In the heart, of course. Can you not hear its beat?"

She nodded. It was impossible not to hear—not to feel—the sound. She only now realized it beat in time with her pulse.

Zejela smiled. "Good. Now, have you been given a name?"

"My name is Ajeau."

Zejela brought a hand to her chest and laughed without a sound. "No, my dear. That is what they may have called you on Bas. But that is not your *name*."

"You mean, Hijeuse then?" Ajeau said. "That is what—"

"No." Zejela grew serious. "Such a word is perverse here. The V'eauvians may have called you that and, had you known better, you would have been insulted. You are a branch of the Tree, not some common émigré."

"Those are—I don't know any other names."

Zejela sighed. "That too is a shame. I would provide you with one, but it is not my place. We can ask Lysant to do so."

Ajeau shook her head. She did not know if she was supposed to know who Lysant was or not. And Zejela gave her no sign as to the meaning of the name.

Her aunt continued, "For familiarity's sake, I will use your Bassian name. But it is not one that should remain."

Though confused, Ajeau did not protest. "Fine," she said. "But tell me, why were you with Vaten? How do you know him?"

"Ah yes, your friend. I came across him in the woods and he joined us on our journey. But his time will come later. We needn't worry about him now."

Ajeau shook her head. "No, but I want to know about him. What has his life been like since we separated? What has he done, who has—"

"I know, I know," Zejela said with genuine sincerity, as though she knew what it was like to be without one's kith for so long. "He is alive and well. But that is all I can tell you for now. There are other, more pressing matters at hand."

"What do you mean?"

"I mean, we must make plans to leave this place."

"Leave? We are stuck here, aren't we? That's what they told me." Ajeau gestured at the spirits.

Zejela chuckled. "They may be stuck here, the poor souls. But that is their fate, not yours. Nor is it mine. We are Istori, after all."

Though she did not understand the revelation, she felt the hope it brought. If there was a way out of this place, she could go home, she could see Vaten again, and maybe she could discover more of what this woman spoke. Her family, her name, and everything else about her.

"You aren't lying? We can go?" Ajeau said.

"I am not saying we will be successful. It is not an easy place to leave, and we will need help. But if we are able, we will return to the world of our friends. Indeed, it will be our friends who we will need help from most of all."

Ajeau nodded and beamed at the possibility of leaving. And this time, she thought, the woman beside her was trustworthy.

"Now come, let us hurry. There is no time to waste. The Tap awaits," Zejela said and stuck out her hand for Ajeau to grab.

Ajeau did so.

# ACKNOWLEDGEMENTS

This book is the product of many years' efforts and the help, support, and keen eyes of so many people. Without their work, encouragement, delicious food, or other assistance, this book would still just be a dream.

First, thank you to my wife, Mikaela, who read early drafts of this book and found a way to both cheer me on and get me to think critically about what I was writing. She is chiefly responsible for me improving the book in so many ways and being confident enough to publish it.

To my children, thank you for making me finish the book. Watching you grow motivated me to complete it. I could not waste another day tinkering with it. I know you are too young for it now, but I hope you read it one day.

To my parents, thank you for instilling me with a love of reading and books from a young age. Seeing you read all the books you did made me want to write one. It took some time, but here I am.

I could not have finished this book without my beta readers. Thank you so much for putting up with my mistakes and typos and for your wonderful feedback. You made this book much better and made me a better writer. I am forever thankful for the work you put in to improve this book and for all your support and kind words.

To the writing community on Mastodon, Bluesky, and Absolute Write, thank you endlessly for your knowledge and insights into all aspects of writing and publishing. This book would have been far worse without you. Your support on the days when writing was hard kept me going. It is good to know I am not alone.

To Particular, my cover designer, and Lilly Lockwood, my map illustrator, thank you for taking my complete lack of vision and turning it into the beautiful cover and maps. I am so happy that the readers will experience the world through your wonderful illustrations.

Lastly, to you, the reader. Thank you so much for taking a chance on this book. I hope you enjoyed it! And stay tuned, we are nowhere near done yet.

# ABOUT THE AUTHOR

Will Elm is an independent author who loves all things fantasy and science fiction. He lives in Maryland with his wife and two children who keep him endlessly busy. There, in a small basement office, he creates worlds full of stories and writes them down. When not writing or parenting he plays board games, hikes, rides his bike, and endeavors to find a perfect cup of tea.

For more information on Will's books and other writing, visit his website https://www.willelmauthor.com/

Or follow him on social media.
Mastodon: @willelm@indieauthors.social
Bluesky: @willelm

Reviews are vital for independent authors. If you enjoyed *Shadow of the Elders*, please consider rating and reviewing it on your platform of choice to help introduce it to fans of fantasy worldwide. Thank you.

**The story continues in 2027...**

www.ingramcontent.com/pod-product-compliance
Lightning Source LLC
Chambersburg PA
CBHW030538020726
47494CB00005B/1424